CASTLE IN THE MIST

MIYUKI MIYABE

ICO

CASTLE IN THE MIST

MIYUKI MIYABE

TRANSLATED BY
ALEXANDER O. SMITH

SAN FRANCISCO

ICO: Castle in the Mist
ICO - KIRI NO SHIRO by MIYABE Miyuki
Copyright © 2008 MIYABE Miyuki
All rights reserved.
Originally published in Japan by KODANSHA LTD., Tokyo.
English translation rights arranged with OSAWA OFFICE, Japan,
through THE SAKAI AGENCY.

English translation © 2011 VIZ Media, LLC

HAIKASORU
Published by
VIZ Media, LLC
1355 Market Street, Suite 200
San Francisco, CA 94103

www.haikasoru.com

Library of Congress Cataloging-in-Publication Data

Miyabe, Miyuki, 1960-
 [Iko, kiri no shiro. English]
 Ico, castle in the mist / Miyuki Miyabe ; translated by Alexander O. Smith.
    p. cm. -- (Haikasoru)
 ISBN 978-1-4215-4063-4
 I. Smith, Alexander O. II. Title.
 PL856.I856I4613 2011
 895.6'35--dc23

                                                      2011022616

Printed in the U.S.A.
First printing, August 2011
Fifth printing, August 2023

CONTENTS

PREFACE

THE BOOK YOU hold in your hands is a novelization of the story found in the PlayStation 2 game *ICO*.

Sort of.

My heartfelt thanks to the producers and creators of the game for so willingly giving me permission to write this, my first attempt at novelization. They gave me free rein with the story and world found in the game so that I might find my own path through the tale, for which I am also eternally grateful.

If you picked up this book hoping for a walkthrough of the game, look elsewhere. The order of events, solutions to puzzles, and even the layout of the castle have changed. While it is certainly not "spoiler-free," someone who reads this book and goes on to play the game will find much there that is not here.

For those of you who have played the game and love it as much as I do, I hope you will enjoy this variation on the world of *ICO* as much as I have enjoyed revisiting the Castle in the Mist.

Miyuki Miyabe
June 2004

A story of an unknown place,
Told in an unknown age.

CHAPTER 1
AS THE PRIEST SAYS

[1]

THE LOOM HAD fallen silent. The old man had noticed the absence of its rhythmic *clack-clack-clack* some time before, and now he waited patiently for it to resume. He sat at an old desk, its surface worn to a golden amber from years of use, on top of which he had laid open several ancient tomes. A faint breeze coming in through the lattice window ruffled the edges of the yellowed paper and made the tips of the old man's long white whiskers tremble.

The man cocked his head, straining to hear any sound—*weeping, perhaps.*

They had completed the weaving room several days earlier. All the necessary purifications had been made. The room stood waiting for her whenever she was ready to begin—*no,* he thought, *she must begin right away.* Yet Oneh had wept and shouted and cursed and would not go near it. "It's too cruel," she had said, clinging to the old man's robes. "Please stop this. Do not ask this of me."

He had no choice but to let her cry until her tears ran dry. Then he spoke to her, explaining patiently, as one talks to a child. "You knew this would come. You knew it on the day he was born."

He had pleaded with her from sunset of the day before until well into the night. Finally, around dawn, Oneh had allowed him to lead her into the weaving room. From his study, he had heard the heavy sound of the loom's shuttle. It was an unfamiliar sound, which made its absence even more noticeable.

The old man looked out the window at the leaves shaking in the grove. Birds were singing. The light of the sun was bright, and it warmed the room where its rays struck. Yet there were no sounds of children playing, and when the villagers shuffled out to work the fields, they did so in silence. Disconsolate sighs rose in place of the forceful thudding of hoes that echoed down the furrows. Even the hunters, the old man imagined, stopped in their chase along the tracks that ran through the mountains and exhaled long laments as they looked down upon the village in the distance.

It was the Time of the Sacrifice.

The old man was the elder of Toksa Village. He had turned seventy this year, thirteen years after inheriting the position from his father. He had only just stepped into his post, filled with ideas of how he would do the things his father had not been able to do, and the things his father had never tried to do, when the boy had been born. That unlucky child, doomed to be the Sacrifice.

At that time, the elder's father had been deeply ill, his body and spirit greatly weakened. Even still, the night when he heard that a boy had been born to Muraj and Suzu—a boy with horns growing from his head—he had leapt from his sickbed, his face filled with a furious grief. He had rushed to the birthing place in the village and cradled the newborn child in his own arms, brushing his fingers across its soft head until he felt the horns.

Upon returning home, he summoned his son. He shut the doors and windows and shortened the wick on the lamp until the room was dim, and when he spoke, his voice was a whisper, no louder than the night breeze.

"I did not pass the mantle of elder to you readily," he had said. "Even while I saw how the other men and women of the village regarded you with pride and trust, I held you back. I'm sure you wondered why this was at times. You were unhappy, I know, and I do not blame you for it."

The new elder sat, unspeaking, his head hanging low. He lacked the courage to meet his father's eyes. That night had transformed the tired, sick old man who was his father into something altogether strange and frightening.

"But know this—I did not cling to my role as elder out of a reluctance to let go. I merely wanted to spare you the burden of the Sacrifice. I was too cowardly, and put off that which I knew must come to pass sooner or later. What a fool I was. The one who rules in the Castle in the Mist sees through all our flimsy schemes. How else can we explain that just now, on the very day that my illness compels me to pass you the title of elder, a boy with horns is born to our village?"

His father's voice trembled as though he were on the verge of tears.

In Toksa Village, it was a fact of life that every few decades, a child with horns was born. The horns were small at birth—soft, round bumps, barely noticeable beneath the infant's fine hair.

The horned child grew up stronger and more quickly than ordinary children. His limbs grew long, his body hale. He would dash through the fields like a fawn, leap like a hare, climb like a squirrel, and swim like a fish.

While the child grew, his horns would remain much as they were at birth, sleeping beneath his hair. It was impossible to tell the horned child apart from regular children at a glance. Only his boundless energy, a voice that could be heard for miles through the forest, and eyes that glimmered with precocious wisdom set him apart.

And yet, the horns were an undeniable sign that this child was to be the Sacrifice; that one day he would have to fulfill that task dictated by the customs of the village; that he would have to go to the Castle in the Mist.

The horns were the mark of the castle's cursed claim upon him and everyone he knew.

When the boy reached the age of thirteen, the horns would reveal their true form. Overnight they would grow, one on either side of his head, like a small ox's, parting the hair where they jutted out and upward.

This marked the Time of the Sacrifice.

The Castle in the Mist was calling. Time was up. The child must be offered.

"The last Sacrifice was born when I was but a child," the elder's father told him. "The old books say that sometimes as much as one hundred years might pass after a Sacrifice is born and sent to the castle." He winced and shook his head. "I hoped our fortune would be as good. How I prayed that your generation might come and go without seeing a Sacrifice—only to have one appear now, so early! I'm afraid that the previous Sacrifice was not potent enough."

That was why, his father explained, the Castle in the Mist hungered again so soon.

"Still," he continued, "time yet remains before the child born tonight reaches his thirteenth year. I can teach you all you will need to know about offering the Sacrifice. You'll have to consult the old books our family keeps. When the boy is of age, and the Time of the Sacrifice arrives, an entourage from the temple in the capital will come and arrange everything. You merely need do as the priest says."

Then the elder's father grabbed his wrist with astonishing strength. "Whatever happens, you must not let the Sacrifice escape. You must not allow him to leave the village. And you must impress him with the weight of his destiny, train him in every particular until he truly accepts it and will never choose flight. You must not be lenient or frail of heart. The castle has chosen him as the Sacrifice, and about that there can be no mistake."

The elder quailed, thinking of the newborn child. How adorable, how helpless and priceless he had seemed. Even if he bore the horns of the Sacrifice, he was still just an innocent babe. How could the elder be stern with something so small? What words could he use to tell the child that his life would one day be offered up to the Castle in the Mist?

He could not protest his duty to his father. Instead, in a weak voice he asked, "What happens if I succeed in keeping the child from escaping, only to watch him fall ill? What if he is injured? What if he does not live to the proper age?"

"The Sacrifice cannot fall ill," his father said with grim confidence. "Nor can he be easily injured. He will be exceptionally healthy, in fact. You need only raise him to become as solitary as the hawk, as pliable as the dove, and deeply committed to his fate."

"*Raise* him?"

"Yes. As elder, you must raise the child born this night as though he were your own."

"But what about the parents?"

"Once his birth mother is able to walk, the parents must be cast out from the village."

"What? Why?" the elder asked, even though he knew what the answer would be.

"That is the custom," his father replied. "The couple who has given birth to the horned child must leave Toksa Village."

Then, for the first time, the hard lines of his father's face softened, and tears shone in the corners of his eyes.

"I know it sounds harsh. But it is in fact a mercy. Imagine the anguish of parents forced to raise a child they know must leave them before he is fully grown. If separation is preordained, the better it be quick. Muraj and Suzu will live a good life in the capital. They are free to have another child, or three, or five—as many as they wish. Greedy though the castle may be, it will not take more than one child from a single family."

The steel in his father's voice left the elder speechless for a time, until at last he managed to utter a name. "Oneh…"

His wife. What would Oneh think? She knew the village custom as well as he did. How would she take the news that they were soon to become direct participants?

"How will I tell Oneh?"

He already had six children with his wife. Four had been claimed by accident or disease before reaching adulthood, leaving them one son and one daughter. They had grown well. Their son had already taken a wife.

"Are Oneh and I even qualified to raise a child at our age?"

"Of course. He will be like a grandson to you." The new elder's father smiled a thin smile, showing dark gaps where his teeth had fallen out. "Think of it this way. Because the horned child was born tonight, your own grandchild, who cannot be far off now, will be spared his fate. You should consider yourself fortunate."

The elder shivered. His father was right. Because the Sacrifice had been born tonight, the village would live in peace for many years, maybe decades. *My grandchildren will be spared.* Still, he could not tell whether the chill that ran down his spine was one of relief or of horror that his father would say such a terrible thing.

His father clasped his hands once more, shaking them with each word. "Know this," he said. "The elder must never fear. The elder must never doubt. No one will blame our village for this, nor will they blame you. We are merely following custom. Do everything the priest tells you to do. Accomplish your task, and the Castle in the Mist will be sated."

Do as the priest says. It is the priest's doing—no one will blame the village—or the village elder—the elder—

"Elder!"

The voice brought him back over thirteen years of time in an instant. Back to his seventy-year-old self; back to long whiskers growing from his chin; back to thin, bony shoulders.

"Sorry, Elder, didn't mean to intrude."

In his doorway, several men of the village stood shoulder-to-shoulder, still dressed for field work.

"It is no intrusion, I was merely doing some reading."

The men exchanged glances until one of them spoke.

"Mistress Oneh's weeping in the weaving room."

"She became violent," said another man, "like a madness took her, and she tried to break the loom. We held her back, Elder, but she's wild yet."

That explained why the loom was still silent.

"I will go myself," the elder said, placing both hands upon his desk for support as he rose from his chair.

Oneh, sweet Oneh. There have been enough tears.

How long would it take for her to understand that no amount of tears or rage could change what had happened? That no matter how high she raised her fist to the heavens or how hard she beat the ground in lamentation, it was all for naught.

Their cries would not reach that ancient castle perched upon the cliff at the end of the world, far to the west where the sun sank after its daily journey. The only thing that could lessen the rage of the master in the castle, that could stave off the castle's curse for even a short time, was the chosen Sacrifice.

[2]

SMALL PEBBLES FELL down from above the boy's head, plinking on the sandy floor. First one, then another.

The boy sat up, looking up at the small window set at the highest point of the cave. The window had been hewn out of the rock, and long years of wind and rain had smoothed its edges.

A face appeared.

"Psst! Hey!" a voice called down. "I know you're in there!"

"Toto!" the boy replied with a smile, wondering how his friend had managed to climb up to the window like that.

"What," Toto said, "don't tell me you were still sleeping."

The boy had been lying on his side—there wasn't much else to do.

"You'll get in trouble if they catch you."

Toto grinned. "I'm an old hand at this. No one saw me."

"You sure?"

"Hey, you should be thanking me. I brought you something—"

Toto threw down a white cloth bag into the cave. The boy

snatched it up and looked inside. There was a fruit and a wrapped bundle of baked sweets.

"Thanks!"

Toto grinned. "Don't let them catch you eating those," he advised. "That old fogey they got by the door will take 'em away."

"He wouldn't do that."

The boy's guards weren't particularly friendly, but neither were they cruel. When they brought him his three meals a day or came to set a blaze in his fireplace on cold nights, they would look down at the floor or off to the side—fearfully, apologetically—and leave the moment their business was done.

"Psst, Ico." Toto lowered his voice to a whisper. "Don't you ever think of running away?"

Ico—for that was the boy's name—turned away from the window at the top of the cave, letting his eyes travel across the gray walls. This cave was on the northern edge of the village. It had originally been a small, rocky hill until the men of the village hollowed it out by hand, specifically to house the Sacrifice. Ico would remain here until the priest arrived to lead him away. The years that had passed since the cave's construction had smoothed the marks left on the walls by the stonecutters' chisels and axes. Ico could run his hand over it and feel nothing but featureless rock.

That was how long ago the custom had started and the sacrifices had begun.

It would take many words to describe how he felt at that moment, and they all jostled for attention in Ico's head. Yet he lacked the confidence to choose just the right ones and line them up in just the right order. He was thirteen.

"I can't run away," he finally answered.

Toto gripped the edge of the window with both hands and stuck his head farther in. "Of course you can! I'll help you!"

"It won't happen."

"Says who? I can break you out tonight, and then it's a quick run to the woods. I'll swipe the keys and you're free!"

"Where would I go? Where would I live? I can't go to another village. When they see the horns they'll know I'm the Sacrifice, and they'll drag me back."

"So don't go to a village. You could live in the mountains, hunt game, eat nuts and berries—you could even clear a field for a garden. You never get sick, and you're strong as a bull, Ico. If anyone can do it, you can." Toto frowned. "Of course, I'd be going with you. Let's do it! Let's go live in the wild! It's better than…this."

Toto was a full year younger than Ico. As good a friend as he was, he was also fiercely loyal to his family, especially his younger brother and sister. Ico couldn't imagine him leaving them behind. And yet, there was a sincerity in Toto's voice that made Ico think he really meant what he said. That sincerity hurt. *Toto's willing to throw everything away…because of me.*

"Thank you, Toto," Ico said, trying to sound somber. His voice cracked.

"Don't thank me. Say you'll come!"

"I can't."

Toto shook his head. "You're a lot of things, Ico, but I never figured you for a coward."

"Think of what will happen to the village if I run. Without a Sacrifice, the Castle in the Mist would grow angry."

Not just the village. The capital too would be destroyed, all in the space of a night. No, he thought, *there probably wouldn't even be time to blink.*

"So what if the castle gets angry?" Toto asked, growing angry himself. "What's so scary about the castle anyway? My parents won't ever talk to me about it—Mom practically covers her ears and runs when I ask questions."

It wasn't that Toto's parents didn't want to talk about it—they were forbidden to talk about it. It was part of their custom, because they knew that the Castle in the Mist was always wary. Not even a curse could be whispered under the breath. And the castle suffered no one to challenge its authority. No one.

"When you turn fifteen, they'll hold the ceremony for you," Ico told him. "You'll learn what it means then. The elder will tell you everything."

"That's great," Toto said, a bit too loud, "but I want to know now! How do they expect me to just sit here and accept it until they think I'm ready? Once they take you off to the castle, you know you're not coming back, right? Well, that doesn't work for me. I'm not going to just stand around and let that happen."

"But, Toto, I *am* the Sacrifice."

"Because you got horns growing out of your head? Why does that make you anything? Who thought all this crap up anyway?"

It's just the way it is, Ico wanted to say, but he held himself back.

"You know something, don't you?" Toto's voice suddenly grew much quieter. "Tell me, Ico. I have to know."

Ico slumped. Hadn't the elder told him—in a tone that left no room for interpretation—not to speak of what he knew, of what he had seen?

It was already several days ago that Ico's horns had grown suddenly in the space of a night and the elder had taken him over the Forbidden Mountains. They had ridden on horseback for three days to the north, going where not even the hunters dared tread. They saw no one on the road, no birds flying overhead, no rabbits in the underbrush, no tracks of foxes in the soft mud left by rains the day before.

Why were the mountains forbidden? Why did no one come this way? Why were there no birds or animals to be seen? All of Ico's questions melted like a springtime snow when they reached the top of the pass and he saw what lay on the other side.

"I brought you here to show you the horror the Castle in the Mist has wrought, the depth of its rage—and the true meaning of your sacrifice," the elder told him. "Only the Sacrifice can quell the castle's wrath and prevent this tragedy from happening again. Look well upon it. Carve the sight deep within your heart. Then fulfill your duty and do not think of flight."

The elder's words still rang in his ears.

Ico had known he was to be the Sacrifice since he was a child. He had been raised for this purpose and none other.

Ico's daily life had been no different from that of any other child in the village. When he was bad, he was scolded; when he was good, he was praised. He tended the fields and the animals. He learned how to read and write, he swam in the rivers and climbed in the trees. The days went by quickly, and he slept soundly at night. Before his horns poked out from beneath his hair, even Ico often forgot they were there at all.

And yet, he knew that he was the Sacrifice, that he was different from the other children. The elder told him that often, almost every day. What he had seen across the Forbidden Mountains, however, had a greater impact on Ico than any words. It made him painfully aware, beyond a doubt, of the weight of his burden. Ico reached up, absentmindedly brushing the tip of one of his horns with a finger. Here was the proof that he was the one chosen to prevent calamity, to save his people.

How could I run from that?

On the trip home from the mountains, Ico's resolve had become as hard as steel. Whereas his duty as the Sacrifice had only been something vague before, a role in a distant play, now it took a clear and definite shape. He never noticed the tears the elder shed as he hurried his horse ahead of him on the path. When they returned to the village, Ico had moved into the cave without being asked.

"I got it!" Toto shouted from the window, jarring Ico from his reverie.

"What? What is it?"

"I'm coming with you, Ico. I'm going to the castle!"

Ico jumped up, standing against the wall directly beneath the window. "You're not going anywhere! If the priest found out, they'd lock you up. Probably the rest of your family too. You really want that to happen?"

Toto gulped. "Why would they do that? Who says I can't see the castle? If only the Sacrifice is allowed to go, what about the priest? Does he have to throw *himself* in jail?"

"Now you're just being ridiculous."

"Why do I even bother?" Toto grumbled. "*You're* not even on your own side."

Ico shook his head. He looked up at his friend's face, beet red with anger, and suddenly he felt the tension leave his shoulders, and he laughed out loud.

Toto's a good person. A good friend. And I'll never be able to see him again once I leave.

That thought made him feel lonelier than any other.

A good friend...Which is exactly why I must go to the castle.

"Toto," he said after a moment of silence, "I know what will happen if the castle gets angry. But I can't tell you. I can't go against custom. It's just like when they say we're not supposed to swim in the deep water on days when the west wind blows or ride into the mountains without trimming our horse's hooves. It just is, and you'll have to wait for your ceremony to know why." Ico's voice was calm and even. "It's true, though, that when the Sacrifice goes to the castle, the danger is gone. And you know I won't die, right?"

"Sure, but you'll never come back. What's the difference?"

"It makes a big difference to me!" Ico said with a grin. "The elder told me that after the Sacrifice goes to the Castle in the Mist, they become a part of the castle—they live forever."

Ico wasn't lying. The elder really had told him that. It had surprised him at first when he learned that being the Sacrifice didn't actually mean going to your death.

"So you're going to live forever?" Toto lifted an eyebrow. "You're just going to live at the castle? That's it?"

"Pretty much."

The conversation was quickly entering an area where Ico felt less sure he was right. In fact, he didn't know what he would be doing once he arrived at the castle. He suspected the elder didn't know either.

As it was, from the moment he had heard he wasn't going to die, his curiosity about the Castle in the Mist had grown. What would happen there? What did it mean to "become a part of the castle"?

Toto wasn't buying any of it. "How does the elder know what's going to happen to you? It's not like *he* was ever the Sacrifice."

"The priests told him."

"So the priests know what's going to happen to you?"

"Of course. They're big scholars in the capital, you know," Ico explained, trying to sound more confident than he felt. "But, Toto, you have to promise me that when the priest comes to the village you won't go asking him all kinds of questions. I wasn't just trying to scare you—they really will lock you up. And I don't want that happening because of me. If you try to do something when they come for me, they might punish the whole village."

"Fine," Toto said at last, but his expression made it clear he wasn't happy with the arrangement.

"Good," Ico said. "I'm glad." And he meant it. He breathed a sigh of relief.

"Well, don't think you've seen the last of me yet," Toto called out. "And I haven't given up, either!" He disappeared from the small window.

"What do you mean?" Ico shouted after him.

"That's for me to know!" came his friend's distant reply.

"This isn't a game! It's really serious! Seriously serious! You hear me, Toto?"

"I hear you just fine. Don't get all worked up over it, okay? See ya."

And with that, Toto was gone.

For a while, Ico stood there, looking up at the empty square of night where his friend's face had been.

[3]

ONEH THOUGHT IT was her tears that made it hard for her to see the thread upon the loom, but she soon realized her error. *The sun is setting.* Darkness pooled in the corners of the weaving room, and when she looked up, she could not see the rafters above her head.

Oneh slid from her weaving bench, walked around to the other side of the loom, and examined the fabric. In half a day, she had only produced a finger's length. The pattern was so muddled she had trouble making it out.

No light was allowed in the weaving room on account of the danger of a fire; she would not be able to continue work today. She pressed her fingers to her temples and felt her head ache. She was not fatigued, really. *Perhaps it was all my weeping.* Oneh sighed. *I don't want to be doing this work. I didn't raise him for this—*

That is where you are wrong, her husband, the elder, had scolded. *The elder's wife cannot be seen flouting custom. You may pity Ico, but the boy is ready. It's your inability to let go, your tearful clinging that makes him suffer.*

She wondered how Ico was doing. Already, ten days had passed since he entered the cave. All women, even her, were forbidden to approach that place. Not once had she seen his face or heard his voice. *Is he eating properly? The cave must be so dark and chilly. If he's caught cold...*

It would be the first cold he'd ever caught in his life. Oneh had witnessed proof of Ico's fortitude enough times to know he would be fine. He could fall from the very top of the tree onto his back and be up on his feet a moment later to open his hands and show her the chick he had plucked from its nest. His strength and skill had even gotten him in trouble—like the time when, just after his age ceremony, he had gotten into a fight with some young fishermen over Ico's uncanny ability to swim deeper and hold his breath longer than any of them. He took on six other boys that day and came home with only a few scratches. They were fond memories. Proud memories.

The others in the village thought Oneh's feelings for Ico came from some deep sympathy for him and her chagrin at being the one who had to raise him though he was not her own. Even the elder thought this. But they were wrong. Ico was the light of her heart. She loved him as much as any mother could love her own child. Raising him had been a delight.

The children understood her—they were always more aware of these things than the adults. Her own grandchildren by blood often pouted and asked her why she favored the horned boy over them.

"Because Ico knows his place and does not talk back, and is not always wanting things or teasing other children," she wanted to tell them, but she would refrain and say instead that she was kind to him because he was to be the Sacrifice. Then her grandchildren would smile and wink at each other, glad that they had been born normal, without horns.

Only one other adult had seen through her admittedly thin façade—her brother, dead now for five years.

"The boy has you enchanted, hasn't he?" he had told her once. "Don't forget, Oneh, why he is so pure and kind and without fault. He is not human. His soul is empty, and evil cannot cling to a void as it does to our tangled hearts. Emptiness absorbs only love and light, and reflects it back. No wonder it's so easy for the one who must raise the horned child to love him—they see their own love reflected in his eyes."

He reminded Oneh that to go to the Castle in the Mist was no tragedy for the boy. "The boy's soul has resided in the castle since the very day he was born. He returns to the castle to reclaim it and be whole for the first time in his life."

Oneh had been born to a merchant house in the capital. She was well educated, and her childhood had been easy. Her brother, six years her elder, had attended seminary in the capital and received the qualifications to become an ordained priest by the age of twenty-two, yet just before the ceremony he had withdrawn his application and left city life for the countryside. His teachers and parents both were violently opposed, but her brother hadn't listened. He rented a small house in a small town, where he earned his keep by teaching the local children how to read and write, never took a wife, spent his evenings steeped in ancient books, and lived a life of austerity. He never once returned home, not even for a visit. Their parents' opinion of him had softened over the years, and several times they sent a messenger to attempt reconciliation, but he had always refused them, gently, but firmly.

It was a year after her brother had left that Oneh went to be married in Toksa Village. She was seventeen years old. She had other siblings, but she had always been closest to her gentle, studious brother. That was why, near to the time of her wedding, she snuck out of the house and together with a maidservant visited her brother's village. Marriage meant she would be leaving their family, and she wanted to tell him goodbye.

Her brother was overjoyed to see her. She found her brother's home startlingly poor, yet the brightness in his face warmed her heart. He made her a simple meal that night. There was only water to drink, but it was cool and refreshing.

"Off to Toksa, eh?" her brother asked.

"I know it's far," she told him. "Farther from the capital than I've ever been. But the land is fertile, the water clean, and it is close to both the sea and the mountains, where there is food for the taking. The people in Toksa want for little."

"So I've heard," her brother nodded, looking at her with eyes like still pools of water. "Tell me, how did this marriage come about?"

Oneh didn't know the details. As her parents' daughter, it was her duty to do as they bade.

"I'm guessing," her brother said, "that our father suggested the union. You mentioned that the man who will become your husband is the son of the village elder?"

"He is. Which means that, one day, I will be the elder's wife."

Though the thought of traveling to an unknown place to wed a complete stranger made her nervous, she felt some pride in knowing that she was to be a person of standing in her new home.

"Tell me," her brother said then, "have you heard of the role that the elder of Toksa must play in their local custom—a custom not observed anywhere else?"

Oneh shook her head. Her brother turned his gaze away from her to the rough, mud-plastered walls of his home.

"Brother?" Oneh said after he had been silent for some time.

When he spoke again, his voice was as calm as before, but it seemed to her that a shadow had come over his eyes. His eyes had always betrayed his emotions. That had been true since they were children.

"You know I would never object to your being married. Toksa is a peaceful, prosperous place, as you say. You needn't be worried about a thing."

"But—"

"You are strong, Oneh. Stronger than your parents think. And you have wisdom far beyond your years. You will make a good wife."

She knew her brother meant what he said, but to hear such sudden praise made Oneh all the more uneasy. "What is this custom you speak of?" she asked.

"I was wrong to say anything," her brother replied, his smile weak. "I did not mean to concern my lovely sister with trifling matters so soon before she is to be married. There is no cause for alarm. All villages have their customs. That is all I meant."

Her brother's smile did not fade, but the darkness in his eyes grew deeper. Oneh knew that he had something else to say, as she also knew it was better not to ask so many questions at times like these. Her brother was an honest man. If there were something she needed to know, he would tell her when the time was right.

"Toksa is a beautiful, bountiful place," her brother said, speaking slowly. "That is its reward, you might say."

Oneh didn't understand. She was about to ask him after all, when he smiled broadly and turned to face her. "You must write," he said.

"I'd like that."

"I know you couldn't have from home, not with everyone watching over your shoulder. But in your new home, no one will think twice about a sister corresponding with her distant brother."

Oneh nodded, smiling.

"And if your lord husband should become jealous, just tell him you write to your peculiar brother in the capital. Tell him all I do is read books, that the dust from between their pages collects in my hair, and I delight in nothing more than walking between library shelves, my long sleeves dragging upon the floor behind me."

Oneh laughed. "I will tell him that you are a renowned scholar. That the seminary begged you to become a priest—no, the high priest."

"Ahh," her brother exclaimed, "that is why you are my favorite sister." He laughed out loud then, but even that merry sound did not drive the sadness from his eyes.

Their correspondence began soon after. They did not write often —all together, her brother's letters fit easily inside a single parchment box. He wrote mostly concerning Oneh's living arrangements, the weather, and how the crops were faring that year.

Once Oneh became a mother, he wanted to know everything about her children. Oneh sent detailed reports, and in return, her brother would tell her about the children he taught in his village and the fascinating books he had read. Sometimes he would talk about his studies or write humorously of the latest fashions in the capital. But not once did they correspond regarding the custom of Toksa Village he had alluded to that night.

Not until that day, thirteen years ago, when Ico was born and Oneh's husband told her everything. Overcome with emotion when she rubbed her hand across the baby's head and felt those round protrusions that would one day be horns, she wrote another letter to her brother that very night.

At last do I understand what you were talking about that day I visited you before going to be married.

Her brother's response, when it came, was the longest he had ever written.

> *Because you are my sister, you know well that the great Sun God, Sol Raveh, to whom we pray in our temples, gives birth to all, mends all, and governs all with love's power.*

It seemed to her that her brother's voice on the page sounded different than it had before. Even the letters were written in a careful, elegant style.

> *Yet even the God of Light had to walk a path beset by hardship before bringing peace to our land. He waged wars and fought many battles. Toksa was the site of one, particularly fierce.*

He went on to tell her that Sol Raveh had fought a powerful adversary near Toksa. The enemy had been defeated and successfully imprisoned, yet victory had not come without a sacrifice: Toksa's unusual custom, and the first child born with horns upon its head.

> *The Sacrifice is born a captive, even as he is a warrior of the Light and a keystone in the wall that imprisons the enemy. Though the horned child may appear human, that is not his true nature. The child is a pawn of a greater power. You who must raise him must never forget that the child carries a part of that divinity within him.*

Oneh quickly wrote a response. She asked whether the enemy that Toksa Village had feared for many long years was the master of the Castle in the Mist. She asked how it was that the Sacrifice eased the master's anger. He replied:

*In Toksa, this is known only to the Sacrifice. Only
a horned one, or the highest of priests, may seek to
learn this.*

Parts of her brother's letter made sense, while others did not.
Though each ended as it began, with words in praise of God, as
she read reply after reply Oneh started to wonder whether he truly
believed the words he wrote.

Once, she asked him straight if there was a connection between
why her brother had given up on becoming a priest and the custom
of Toksa. She was, in effect, asking whether he had questioned his
faith in his youth. Oneh knew that if she showed the letter to
anyone else, they would have taken it from her and thrown it away.
*The God of Light is great. Through his benevolence is our land blessed
with peace.* To cast doubt on the divine was to sin deeply.

No reply came. Instead, she received word that her brother had
passed away.

The Sacrifice is born a captive, even as he is a warrior of the Light—
Oneh closed her eyes and talked to the familiar ghost of her
brother that lived on in her mind.

Brother, she said, *to me, Ico is nothing but a child, a dear child.
How can I send him to the castle with a still heart?*

"Mistress Oneh?"

She heard a small voice from the window. Oneh looked up. "Is
that you, Toto?" *He must be standing on tiptoe to see in like that,* she
imagined. "Have they sent you to summon me?"

The sun had set some time ago, and the weaving room was
already completely dark. Oneh fumbled with her hands to retrieve
the copied pages from an old book she had propped up next to the
loom and rolled them together like a scroll. Without a light, she
couldn't even see her own feet between the times when the sun set
and when it rose again in the morning. This was one of the reasons
they gave her an escort to and from the weaving room.

"No," the boy whispered quickly. "I came on my own. It's

secret." He looked from side to side, belatedly checking that no one had seen him.

"Why are you here then?"

"I figured you'd know where that priest from the capital is by now."

The capital was distant. A rider had come ten days before to announce the priest's departure. It had been two days since they received word that the entourage had finally arrived at the lodgings nearest to Toksa on the high road, but that was still two mountain passes and a river ford away.

"Whatever do you want to know that for?"

Toto's eyes glimmered in the dusk. "The priest from the capital is real important, right?" The boy's voice was filled with hope. "If the priest says I could do something, then even the elder couldn't tell me not to do it—right?"

Oneh smiled cautiously and took a step toward the window. "Toto, are you planning to do something the elder doesn't want you to do?"

"No, 'course not!" He shook his head vigorously. "I just wanted to know how close the priest is."

"I'm sorry, I don't know," Oneh lied.

"But I was just talking to Ico, and he seemed to know a lot about the priest, so I thought—"

Oneh walked up to the window. "Toto! You were talking to Ico?"

"Huh?" Toto blinked. "Er, I guess, yeah," he stammered.

"You went to the cave? How did you talk to him without the guard seeing you?"

"I climbed a tree and went from branch to branch. Then I jumped down onto that little rocky hill and crawled across the rock until I reached the window on top."

Oneh shook her head. This was not the first time she had heard of Toto's acrobatics. He and Ico were the talk of the other children in the village for their daring antics.

"Was he well?"

"I guess. Pretty bored, though, locked up there all by himself."

Oneh nodded, turning her head from the window to hide the tears welling in her eyes.

"You angry, Mistress Oneh?" Toto asked timidly.

"How could I be mad at Ico's best friend going to pay him a visit? I'm sure he needed the company. Thank you."

Toto's smile returned to his face. "You know, I was trying to get him to run away," he admitted. "But Ico said he wouldn't. He said the whole village would be in trouble if he did. That's why I'm going to the castle with him."

"What?" Oneh said. "Toto, you can't go to the Castle in the Mist!"

"Yeah, that's what Ico said. He says if the priest found out there'd be 'trouble,' whatever that means." Toto frowned. "Since when did Ico become such a field mouse? And how am I supposed to wait until my age ceremony before I get to know what any of this is all about? What kind of friend keeps secrets like that?"

Oneh understood how the boy felt all too well. She too had felt abandoned when her husband had taken Ico over the Forbidden Mountains and returned with a secret that only the two of them shared. The elder had never been a talkative man, but now it was as if he had sealed his lips with wax. *And Ico is in the cave...lost to me.*

"I would tell you," she said, "but the truth is, I don't know much myself. The elder says all we need to know is that protecting our village's custom is a sacred and very, very important task. We mustn't go against the elder's word. That includes you, Toto."

Toto snorted, puffing out his cheeks. "Yeah, but the priest outranks the elder, doesn't he? So what he says goes. That's why I was thinking I could ask him to take me to the castle."

It took a moment for Oneh to find her voice. "So that's why you wanted to know where he was," she said.

"Uh-huh."

"Did Ico not mention the trouble there would be if the priest knew what you intended?"

Toto shrugged. "Well, sure, if I tried to sneak after him. But if I got his permission..."

Oneh shook her head. How could she expect a mere child to understand when it was so hard for her?

"I really don't think the priest will let you go, Toto."

"Never know unless you ask."

Oneh tried a different tack. "Perhaps—but it shouldn't be you who goes."

"Huh?"

"I will go with Ico to the Castle in the Mist. I'll ask the priest to let me join him."

"You don't wanna go all that way, Mistress Oneh. You'd probably break somethin' just getting to that old castle."

"Even so," Oneh insisted, "it's no place for a child. I'm sure the priest would agree."

"Then I'm sneaking after you," Toto said.

"You must not!" Oneh reached out through the window and placed a hand on Toto's head. "You cannot."

"I can too."

"I'll tell your father."

"No fair—" Toto began. Then he shrank away. "Someone's coming!"

Oneh stuck her head out the window and saw a torch approaching through the darkness. Someone from the village was coming for her.

"Run, Toto. Quick!"

"I'll do better than that!" Toto grabbed the window frame and scampered up the side of the hut onto the thatched roof. "They won't find me up here."

Toto's words were just trailing off when Oneh saw the torch swing in a small half circle, and a voice called out, "Mistress Oneh, that you there?"

"Yes," she replied, shutting the window and turning to open the door.

"Sorry I was so late in getting out here," the man from the village said once she had made her way outside. He was a muscular man dressed in hunter's garb, with a short sword at his waist and a bow and quiver slung across his broad back. Oneh recognized him as the head of the hunters in the village. His skill with a bow was such that he could pierce an apple hanging from a tree on the far side of the river with his first arrow.

The weaving room had been hastily constructed in a patch of cleared forest outside of the village. *There may be animals around when night falls, so I'll be sending a hunter,* her husband had told her. But Oneh knew the truth. The armed men were sent to make sure she didn't try to escape.

The sole purpose of the weaving room was for her to make the Mark that would be worn by the Sacrifice.

The Mark was little more than a simple tunic that went on over Ico's clothes, but it was woven with a special pattern detailed in the pages of that old book Oneh had received from her husband. It was not difficult to make if she followed the instructions.

"Will you be returning directly home?"

"At once, yes." Oneh held the roll of paper to her chest and closed the door to the small hut behind her. The torch sputtered and a bright spark drifted through the air, crossing her path.

The man walked ahead of her slowly. "I was late in coming because one of the hunters was hurt in the mountains today."

"My! I hope he was not hurt too badly?"

"He fell from a ledge, broke both his legs," the hunter replied, his voice even. "Even if he mends, he will not hunt again. It's not certain he'll even walk."

The hunter's name was familiar. He was a boy who had just undergone the age ceremony this past spring. Oneh shook her head. "Such misfortune..."

"He was inexperienced," the hunter said. "When you're climbing, you must never look toward the mountains in the north—even if the view is clear. I told him this myself many times, but he did not listen."

Oneh tensed. "The Forbidden Mountains?"

"Indeed," the hunter said.

"What does one see…up there?"

"Nothing, most times. But every child knows you're not supposed to look. There's always the chance that you might see something."

"So what did he see?"

The man replied that he did not know.

"But how—"

He shrugged. "The boy's been muttering all kinds of nonsense. I'm afraid he hit his head too."

For a moment, Oneh closed her eyes.

"Besides, even if he did see something and managed to keep his wits, he's not supposed to talk about what he saw. That's how I was raised, and that's what I would do in his place. Did you know that my father was lead huntsman in his day? He told me about a man who went up into the mountains looking for a bird to shoot for his supper. Said he looked too long toward the mountains in the north." The man paused. "His body made the trip back, but his mind never returned."

"A frightening tale."

"It's just a story," the hunter went on, "but they say it happened right around the Time of the Sacrifice." The hunter stopped and turned. Sparks from his torch drifted toward her. In the torchlight, the hunter's face looked hard and pale. "Mistress Oneh…" he began. "The castle knows when it's time. If the Sacrifice isn't quick about his business, the castle gets impatient. And it's not like when you or I get impatient, Mistress Oneh. The castle's black mood rides on the wind—that's what the boy saw today."

Oneh looked the hunter in the eyes. He stared back at her, unblinking.

"The castle may be far beyond those mountains, but its anger reaches as far as the sky over their peaks."

"What are you trying to say?" Oneh managed to ask at last.

"I know you don't like the weaving," the hunter said, his voice iron, "and I know it's hard for you to let go of your boy. I'm a father too. But Ico is the boy of no man or woman. He's the Sacrifice. And there's no good that'll come from staying his time."

It occurred to Oneh that the hunter had probably been late in coming to summon her because he'd been conferring with her husband, deciding what he should say.

"I do not stall for time."

"Then that's fine," the hunter said curtly, turning and beginning to walk away, his pace quicker than before. "I'll come for you tomorrow before dawn. If we don't get that Mark made soon, the priest will arrive before you're finished."

Oneh followed behind him, her head hanging low.

Toto crouched on top of the roof, his ears pricked, and he heard everything.

Someone was hurt. That was the kind of trouble even Toto understood. But he was far more interested in the other thing the hunter had to say—now he knew where the castle was.

Then it struck him, an idea so great he wanted to jump up and dance for joy on the spot. Oneh told him he couldn't ask the priest's permission to follow Ico, but she hadn't said anything about going *ahead* of them, before the entourage even left the village. He could wait for them on the way to the mountains, and once they passed, he'd trail them the rest of the way. That would get him to the Castle in the Mist for sure.

Once the priest leaves them, Toto thought, *I'll jump out and announce I'm joining Ico on his adventure!* Toto was sure that Oneh would rest easier knowing that he would accompany Ico. Together, there was nothing Ico and Toto couldn't do.

Then Toto had an even better thought, and this time he actually did jump up, standing atop the roof. *I bet the two of us could find that master in the castle and take him on! We might even win!*

"Yaaaahoo!"

Toto's exhilarated shout echoed through the trees as he jumped down off the roof to land softly by the edge of the forest.

[4]

DEPENDING ON WHICH way it blew, the wind would sometimes carry the sound of the loom to Ico's cave. Because no one else in the village was allowed to use a loom in the days after he entered the cave and the moment he left for the castle, whenever he heard the noise, he knew it was his foster mother weaving the Mark for him. It was hard to judge the passage of time, sitting alone in the dimly lit cave. Thick, leafy branches shadowed the narrow window through which Toto had spoken with him the other day, letting in barely enough light to tell whether it was the sun or the moon that shone. But Ico knew that when he heard the loom start up it was the beginning of another day, and when it ended, it was evening. Thus Ico had counted three days, and on the morning of the fourth day, the guard who brought him his morning meal said something entirely unexpected.

"Toto's gone missing."

Toto's father was a hunter. He awoke very early at this time of year to prepare for the hunt, yet when he had risen from bed this morning, Toto's cot had lain empty. When one of Toto's sisters admitted seeing him sneaking out of the house in the middle of the night, it caused a stir in the village.

"Toto told his sister he was leaving and that she'd better keep it a secret."

"He didn't say where he was going?"

"Not a word. Not that his little sister would have remembered. She was too sleep-addled to even think to raise a fuss."

Worse, one of the two village messenger horses had been taken from the stables in the night. The horses were kept ready at all times in case there was a need to carry an urgent message from Toksa to another town. They—a white horse named Silverstar and a chestnut called Arrow Wind—were smart and swift.

"It must have been Toto…"

Ico's friend had been a caretaker at the stables, and the horses knew him well.

"Most likely," the guard agreed, his face dark. "He took a change of clothes and a little dry food with him too. Who knows where that troublemaker's gotten to? We have people out looking for him, but if he left on horseback in the middle of the night, without knowing which way he's headed, they'll never find him. That is, unless you have any idea?"

His conversation from a few days before came back to him, and Ico swallowed. Could Toto be headed toward the castle? *But Toto doesn't know where the castle lies*—only the elder and Ico knew that. He couldn't have gone by himself.

Still…

Even if it seemed to others that Ico couldn't compose himself, it was only because his mind never stopped moving. He made himself replay the conversation in his head and remembered specifically telling Toto he couldn't go to the castle—but Toto had never agreed. Maybe he had guessed that the castle lay in the same direction as the Forbidden Mountains and gone ahead to lie in wait for Ico and the entourage from the capital.

Of course, in order to actually reach the Castle in the Mist, you had to do more than just cross the Forbidden Mountains. From there, the elder had told him, you would take a trail west through a deep forest and over rocky highlands, along a steep and treacherous path that went on for days. Only the priest from the capital knew the way. It would take more than a miracle for Toto to reach the castle himself.

But he would be able to reach the mountains.

"Which horse did he take?" Ico asked.

"Arrow Wind."

Arrow Wind was good on rocks and steep trails. Like his name suggested, he flew like an arrow through the narrowest ravines and across the highest cliff tops without fear or falter.

"He's gone to the Forbidden Moutains," Ico whispered.

The guard turned pale. "How do you know that?"

"No one from the village has gone north looking for him, have they?"

"Of course not, it's forbidden. No one will go close."

"No one except Toto. If he left in the middle of the night, he's already there by now." *And when he sees what lies on the other side—*

"I want you to ask the elder something for me," Ico said suddenly. "He must lend me Silverstar. I'll catch Toto and bring him back."

The guard took a step backward. "What are you talking about? We can't let you out of this cave. You know that."

"But except for the elder, only I can enter the Forbidden Mountains, and he's too old to ride Silverstar so far."

The guard took another step back until he was flat against the door. "You mean you've been to the mountains?"

"Yes. The elder took me there when the Time of the Sacrifice came."

"Why'd he do a thing like that?"

So that I would play my role without question, Ico thought, but he said, "We don't have time to talk about these things—I have to go after Toto!"

The guard turned and dashed from the cave, locking the door behind him. Ico's heart pounded. He paced in circles. He could not hear the sound of the loom today. The entire village must be in disarray. He wondered how his foster mother was taking the news.

What seemed like only a few moments later, the elder entered. The guard opened the door for him then quickly fled, leaving Ico and the elder alone inside.

"Elder, I—"

The elder's open hand hit Ico's cheek with such force that he lost his words and gaped. "Elder?"

"What nonsense did you put in that boy's head?"

The elder's face was severe, his mouth strangely twisted. Ico

had never seen him this way before, not even on the day that he
had taken him into the north.

"I haven't told him anything—"

"I know Toto came here the other day. I looked the other
way because I know he's your friend. And now I see I have
made a terrible mistake. What did you put him up to? What
are you planning?"

Ico's mind reeled. *Planning? Me? Why would I want to involve
Toto in any of this? He's my best friend. Why is the elder accusing me of
things I haven't done?* So great was Ico's shock that he didn't even
notice how his face stung.

"I'll admit, I didn't imagine children were capable of such
scheming," the elder said, his hands clenching into fists at his
sides, as if he were holding them back from striking Ico again.
"Toto disappears, and you leave the village on the pretense of
finding him. With you two on Silverstar and Arrow Wind, no
hunter in the village would be able to catch you. Tell me plainly—
where is Toto waiting to meet you? Where were you going to go
once you were together? I shouldn't have to mention that there is
no safe haven for the boy with horns."

"We weren't planning anything! I swear!"

"You lie to me, even now?" the elder said.

"It's not a lie! Why don't you believe me?"

Ico went to hug the elder despite himself, but the elder brushed
his hands away and turned his back to the boy. "It gave me much
pride that day you accepted your fate as the Sacrifice so readily.
Even as it filled me with sorrow that you must bear this burden, I
felt great gratitude. And now, you have betrayed us all."

Ico stood there, staring at the elder's withered back, unable to
think of anything to say. That back was cold and hard, a barrier
that none of his explanations or pleas could hope to pass.

When Ico had been younger, he had often gone for rides upon
that back. And he had known since the time when his horns had
been nothing more than bumps, that before the day came when

he could give the frail, weakened elder a ride upon his own back, he would have to leave the village.

"The Mark will be ready for you by the end of the day," the elder said, still facing the wall. "Once it is complete, a signal fire in the watchtower will inform the priest's entourage in their lodgings across the river that the time has come. They will be in Toksa within a day, and you will leave with them without delay."

"I won't go anywhere until Toto is back in the village," Ico managed to say, forcing out the words.

"I thought you might say that." The elder snickered; it was a cold, derisive sound. "Buying yourself more time, no doubt."

"I'm not, I swear it!"

"Whatever the case, Silverstar has already left. A messenger has gone to tell the priest what has happened. We will wait for word from him before deciding what to do about the boy. Until then, we can only keep searching for Toto in hopes that he was struck with a sudden urge to go hunting and will return of his own accord. I will send no one toward the mountains in the north, let alone you. Your plan has failed."

Ico felt something cold on his cheek and lifted his hand to touch it. For the first time, he realized he was crying.

"I never thought to run from my responsibility."

The elder was silent.

"Especially not since we went to the Forbidden Mountains, and I saw what lay beyond. My heart hasn't wavered, not even for a moment. I couldn't let something like that happen to Toksa, or to any place. If I can help stop that—if that's my fate—then I accept it."

The elder stood as silent and still as an ancient tree. The only motion in the cave was Ico's trembling lips and the teardrops that fell from his eyes.

"It's not a lie," Ico said. "I haven't lied to you. I could never send Toto into danger, even if I wanted to escape. I couldn't."

The elder hung his head and spoke in a low, rough voice. "The old books tell us we must never trust our hearts to the Sacrifice. How I wish I had understood the meaning of those words before now."

With his long robes dragging across the dirt behind him, the elder walked unsteadily from the cave. Ico didn't try to stop him. He sat there in silence, quietly sobbing.

In the distance, the sound of the loom began.

Mother—I want to see her. She'd understand how I feel. Like she always does. "I know, Ico," she'd say. "Don't cry."

Or maybe that, too, was only a dream. Maybe she would never be like that again. Maybe to accept his role as Sacrifice was to accept that the elder, and Oneh, and everyone else he knew would change forever.

For the first time, the cruelty of it all sank inside his heart. Ico covered his face with both hands and wept out loud.

Yeah, you're a good horse, real good.

Arrow Wind's hooves skipped lightly over the stones, never flagging. The horse's body was sleek and supple beneath Toto's legs, his neck thick and strong, and his eyes alight with a black luster. Arrow Wind galloped onward, his chestnut mane whipping in the wind.

Toto had never felt so *alive* in his life. He had always wanted to ride like this. He was having so much fun that he had almost forgotten where he was going and why he had snuck out of the village late in the night.

By the time the dawn star shone in the sky, he had already reached the foothills of the mountains in the north. There, he stopped to give Arrow Wind a rest, watering him and rubbing him down as he whispered words of praise in his ears. They had ridden hard across the grasslands separating the village from the mountains without stopping. Toto ate some baked crackers, drank some water, and waited for the first light of dawn before beginning the climb up the Forbidden Mountains.

It was his first time coming here—he had never even heard

of someone making the trip until the other day. Even still, in the morning light, the mountains seemed almost disappointingly peaceful and green. There was no path up them, but the slope was easy, with only short, mossy grass growing beneath the swaying branches of the willow trees. Arrow Wind kept his pace well. Toto gave him an occasional rub on the neck to keep him from going too fast. Other than that, he leaned forward and listened to the pleasing sound the horse's hooves made on the grass below.

By the time the sun was shining on him directly, he was nearly halfway up the mountains. He looked back down at the grassland over which they had come. It spread out flat as far as he could see. It was beautiful.

These mountains aren't scary at all, he thought. *What's so forbidden about this?*

Toto's chest swelled. A light of hope lit his face from the inside. His heart danced, running ahead of him toward the Castle in the Mist. He would go there together with Ico, defeat the master in the castle, and save the village. There was nothing to be scared of after all. Everyone had let themselves be frightened into cowardice by rumors and stories. If only they had ever dared to face it head on, they would have realized that they were stronger.

Arrow Wind's footfalls mirrored Toto's heart, growing lighter with every step as the little warrior and his gallant horse made their way up toward the pass.

If Toto had been just a little older, and his eyes a little more like those of the wary hunter, he would have noticed something very strange. Other than himself and the horse beneath him, there was no sign of life on these hills. No birds sang, no insects buzzed. Only the leaves of the trees swayed in the cool forest air. This was why the hunters never strayed here, why it was taboo to venture under these boughs.

But Toto noticed nothing. Nor was Arrow Wind frightened. Together, they reached the pass. Here the forest and sky opened around them, and they could see for miles in every direction. Toto dismounted and walked through the pass, coming to a stop at the other side.

He saw something that staggered his imagination.

A city, surrounded by high, gray walls. It was giant, enormous, the largest city he'd ever seen. It was dozens of times larger than Toksa, at least. The houses were monumental stone edifices, standing close together. Brick-lined streets crisscrossed between them. He spotted something that must have been a church, with a tall spire that reached for the sky and a large hall with a flag flying above it.

And there were people. A great throng, filling the streets.

Toto's eyes went wide, and his mouth gaped. Then, for the first time, he felt uneasy.

Why was the entire city so gray, from corner to corner? And the people too—why were they gray?

Why isn't anyone moving?

Everyone stood in the streets, perfectly still. When he squinted his eyes and looked, he noticed the flag wasn't moving either. Perhaps the breeze that blew against Toto's cheek up here in the pass did not reach down so far.

[5]

THE MEN OF the village returned empty-handed from the day's search. They watered their horses and rested aching limbs before quickly conferring and heading back out. The looks of determination in their eyes were undermined by a growing certainty that Toto had gone north, toward the mountains—though none dared say it.

Sometime after noon, the elder met with a messenger from the lodge across the river, come to tell them that the priest from the capital was growing tired of waiting.

In the weaving room, Oneh worked the loom tirelessly. She

had only paused once that day, to glare at the elder when he came to make sure she wasn't worrying about Toto instead of her task.

The elder had sent word back with the messenger, asking with utmost politeness for another three days. The messenger returned bearing both a message and an air of grandeur, and he cast a disparaging eye at the hunters hurrying to and from the village.

"If the situation here is beyond your ability to handle," the messenger told the elder, "it would be a simple matter for us to send our guards to *assist* you." There was a haughty ring to the man's words.

The elder bowed deeply. "Please tell them it is nothing so serious. We are merely doing all that we can to carry out our instructions in accordance with the priest's wishes. We remain, as always, entirely loyal."

After the messenger left, the elder stood clenching his fists. He told himself that he was furious at Ico's betrayal, at Toto's recklessness, and Oneh's stubbornness—but the more he tried to summon his wrath, the more his true feelings interfered. *If that self-important, self-serving priest wants the Sacrifice so badly, why doesn't he come dirty his own hands?* Whatever excuses he might make, he knew the priest didn't stay in Toksa because he didn't want to hear the village's laments at having to hand over the Sacrifice—to feel the accusatory stares of the villagers. The priest could lock Ico up in a cave, make Oneh weave the Mark, and silence the villagers' questions himself...*if he wasn't such a coward.* It left a bitter taste in the elder's mouth to realize that no small part of his anger was directed at himself for striking Ico and speaking to him as he had.

A woman from the village arrived, breathless, calling for him. The hunter who had taken a fall several days before had just passed away. The elder's heart sank even deeper, and the lines in his face hardened so that he looked more like a statue carved from stone than a man of living flesh. How easy it would be if only his heart would turn to stone as well. *To stone. All to stone...*

Toto sat astride Arrow Wind, gaping down at the scene below him. *That's why nothing moves.*

Even the flag flying from the hall had been frozen in mid-flutter.

Toto urged Arrow Wind down the mountainside and rode directly through the city gates. The horse walked smoothly with Toto gripping the reins, but Toto no longer rode gallantly. He crouched low against the horse's back, clinging to its living warmth for encouragement.

The world around him was petrified and gray.

The people in the streets around him had been frozen in time. Some pointed toward the sky, others ran, holding their heads in their hands, while still others held their mouths open in soundless screams. Toto wondered how many years they had stood there like this. When he reached out hesitantly to touch one, it crumbled into dust beneath his fingertips.

Arrow Wind whinnied and Toto steadied his grip on the reins.

No matter which turn he took on the winding streets, people turned to stone awaited him. At first, he tried to believe that these had all been created. Perhaps someone important from the capital had crafted a sculpture of an entire city here for some purpose beyond Toto's comprehension. They had made countless statues—entire houses—and encircled the grim tableau within a wall when they were done.

But why would they do that? Was the city a decoy of some kind? Toto nodded, pleased with his theory. *It has to be that.* When the enemy saw a city full of people unprepared, men without helmets, with bundles on their backs, leading children by the hand, people carrying baskets and fetching water, they would be tempted to attack. *And then—*

Toto's imagination failed to produce the second phase of the strategy. It also struck him as odd that the statues would be crying and shouting and obviously fearful if they were intended to appear an easy target. And nothing explained why so many of them were pointing upward, toward the western sky.

Toto was not the brightest boy, but he had a keen eye for detail, and everything he saw undermined his attempts to remain calm. The looks of abject fear on the faces of the stone people. Hands raised as though to ward off the fast approach of...something. Lips shaped around cries of despair when there was no longer time to escape.

He reached the entrance to a street where a pile of barrels sat, one stacked upon the other. Toto stopped. Dismounting, he reached out to touch one of the barrels, and its surface crumbled like a castle of sand. Craning his neck, he saw a figure behind the barrels—a boy about the same height as he, cowering. Fragments of the crumbled barrel dusted his stone hair.

The boy was smiling.

Toto understood instantly. *He wasn't hiding from whatever it was everyone else had been looking at—he was playing hide-and-seek.* Whatever happened to the people in this city had happened so quickly, he hadn't even had time to realize that he was about to die.

Reluctantly, Toto admitted what he had known for some time already. This city was no grand work of sculpture. This was the reason why the mountains in the north were forbidden. This was the curse of the Castle in the Mist.

The master in the castle was capable of dooming an entire walled city in the space of a breath.

This was what Ico had seen. This was what he meant by "trouble," why he was so determined to sacrifice himself for the village.

Arrow Wind gave a light whinny and rubbed his nose on Toto's shoulder. Toto stood, rubbing the horse's neck, unable to take his eyes off the stone boy. At the end of the street, he saw a stable. The horses were still inside, their manes a uniform ashen gray. Toto was acutely aware of Arrow Wind's warmth beneath his hand, the softness of his mane, and the musty smell of him. He pictured

Arrow Wind turning to stone, a cold gray like the other horses.

Arrow Wind whinnied louder, his front hooves lifting off the ground. Toto pulled on the reins and looked up at him, when he spotted something in the western sky—something that shouldn't be. It was a thin black mist, or perhaps a distant swarm of insects. As the mist drifted closer, it began to coalesce into a shape. He saw a broad forehead, the straight bridge of the nose, and flowing black hair. Finally, he saw a pair of eyes.

It was a woman's face, covering the sky above him.

Toto heard a soundless voice.

Who are you?

Toto remembered playing once with Ico in a cave near the village. They had gone deeper than any of the other kids dared and discovered an underground pool. The water was as clear as crystal, and a faint light glowed at the bottom. Ico and Toto threw stones into the pool. The echoes of the splashes reverberated off the walls of the cave, followed by another splash and another echo. They kept tossing stones until the echoes overlapped one another, making a strange music that sounded almost like a vesper prayer. That was what this voice reminded him of—though the woman's face hung in the sky, her voice seemed to echo from the depths of the earth. Or maybe she was speaking directly into Toto's soul.

Who are you? Why are you here?

The woman's lips twisted like pennants in the wind.

Intruder.

Now Arrow Wind reared and shook his mane, and the reins slipped from Toto's hand. Before he could regain them, the horse galloped off madly.

"Arrow Wind!" Toto screamed after him.

The horse kicked his way through a crowd of stony faces. In the sky above, the woman turned her gaze to follow him. Lips of black mist pursed and she blew a gentle breath.

Toto felt an icy wind blow over his head. The breath swept down the street, catching Arrow Wind in an instant and wrapping around his beautiful chestnut coat. Toto watched as his bushy tail, his hind hooves, his legs, and finally his back and mane turned to gray.

Arrow Wind's scream ended abruptly; he was frozen in stone, front legs rearing up, hooves inches away from another of the stony city dwellers.

Toto's breath stopped. *Arrow Wind—*

"No!"

A scream ripped from Toto's throat and he started to run. *I have to escape. I have to get out of this place—away from her. I have to get out of here alive, back to my village.*

Toto ran in a daze. He did not dare look behind him, but he could feel that face floating there in the sky, giving chase, the same way he understood without looking that the face was *smiling*.

He pushed down a crowd of stone figures in his way, leapt over the fragments, and rounded a corner. A woman carrying a basket of ashen flowers crumbled into pieces at his feet when he slammed into her on the other side. Coughing from the dust, Toto ran even faster. If only he could reach the city wall, the gate where he had entered. *Which way was it? Right, left? Where am I?*

He felt a frigid breeze blow over his head, and a scream rose in his throat as he tripped and fell to the ground. Just ahead he saw the yawning door of a house, propped open by a stick. The inside was darker than the street, but still that same uniform gray. Everything within had been turned to stone as well.

Another breeze raced overhead, and Toto dashed into the house. As he darted through the door, something hit his leg and crumbled with a loud noise—a chair or a person, he wasn't sure. Daylight streamed in through the window. Toto crouched low, crawling through the rooms of the house. Out of the corner of his eye, he caught a glimpse of the dark swirling mass of the woman's face outside the window. It warped as it moved, swelling first, then thinning into a line, speeding after him like an angry swarm of wasps.

Toto shoved aside the rubble in the room with both hands, reaching a patch of wall beneath the window. He slumped, back to the wall. He was out of breath, and his heart felt like it might leap out of his throat.

The face made no noise when it moved. In that, it was different than a buzzing swarm of insects, and it made it difficult for him to get up after he had found what felt like safety against the wall. What if he risked a peek outside only to see that face filling the sky, those dark eyes staring straight at him? He wished he had some way of guessing where it might be.

A tear fell from his cheek—apparently he had been crying with fright, though he hadn't noticed until now. Toto forced himself to steady his breath, and rubbed his face with his hands.

He took a look around the room.

A table carved from what had once been wood stood by his feet. There was a round cushion on the floor and a chair lying on its back. Everything was the color of ash. A tapestry hung on the wall opposite the window, the sort that was a specialty of Toksa's weavers. He could still make out the design: an intricate depiction of the sun and the moon and the stars wheeling through the sky. Though it was drab now, Toto could imagine how it once looked, sparkling and bright—a masterpiece. The fabric would have been soft, yet weighty, the luxurious threads plush against the skin. Now it was more like a thin slice of dry, crusty bread stuck to the wall.

I wonder how long the city has been like this. How long has it been since the city was last alive? A perfectly shaped fruit sat next to him on the floor. Its skin was unblemished. He touched it gently with one finger, and the surface crumbled, leaving a round impression in the shape of his fingertip. He grabbed it and squeezed as hard as he could; the fruit disintegrated into a fine gray dust that ran between his fingers. *In time*, Toto thought, *that's all that will remain of this place. Dust.*

As Toto took another shuddering breath, he noticed something—a pair of eyes near the floor on the other side of the room. They were looking in his direction. Gradually, he made out the form of a slender person, with the long hair of a woman, lying on her side. She had fine features and lay with her right ear against the ground. Her shoulders were hunched and her legs were bent at the knees, as though she had been cowering in a chair. Even in stone, the supple lines of her shape, like the branches of a willow tree, were beautiful.

Her eyes were open wide in a stony stare. She almost seemed to be smiling at Toto. Perhaps she was someone's mother or sister. He wondered what her last words had been—what she had been thinking when she died.

"I'm sorry," Toto whispered, covering his face with his hands. He began to cry. *I never should have come here. I shouldn't have set foot in this place. What a fool I am.*

He sobbed out loud now, unable to restrain himself any longer, and his shoulders heaved. The motion must have disturbed the wall behind him, for he heard a loud noise and the sound of something crumbling. Toto jumped to his feet and looked to see that a pole holding the window shutters open from the outside had fallen and collapsed into dust.

On his knees now, Toto shuffled away from the window. He saw the face flying through the sky, drawn by the noise. Toto's stomach did a somersault.

She'll find me!

There was no escape outside. He considered moving into another room. He could see a doorway, but a large cupboard had fallen over in front of it, and he didn't think he'd be able to climb over in time. He looked around for any other exits.

Toto spotted an opening in another wall. He moved, quick as a woodland hare, dashing through the opening and then falling headfirst. As he began to tumble, he realized he was on a staircase leading into a cellar.

At the bottom, his head hit a wall, sending stars through his vision, and he heard an incredible crashing noise from above. A moment later, the light coming in through the doorway at the top of the stairs dimmed.

Toto sat up and looked around in the meager light. Where he had rolled through the cellar, things lay broken, just like the fruit upstairs.

I'm trapped...

Toto looked up at the thin ray of light shining through a hole in the rubble above. It looked like pieces of the house had fallen over the top third of the stairway. He wondered if he might be able to clear it out by hand.

But if I go up there, that monster will be waiting for me.

Toto turned back to the darkness of the cellar. The chilly air and dusty smell were the same as they had been above. It seemed large for an underground room. Maybe that meant another exit.

Toto began to crawl along the floor, searching. His hands met only the cold stone beneath him. He groped toward the right and found another wall. He pried at it with his fingers for a moment, then stopped.

Wait, that's not a wall. It's a piece of furniture. It's divided into sections—and there's something inside.

In the darkness, Toto's face took on a serious, grown-up expression—the kind he'd never shown to anyone before, not even Ico. He began probing the cavity intently with his fingers, feeling the shapes of the objects, tapping them lightly with his fingers. He wrapped the tips of his fingers around one.

It moved and fell into Toto's hand. He picked it up carefully and brought it into the light at the bottom of the stairs.

It was a book. He had found a bookshelf.

Of course the book was stone. He couldn't open it, and his fingers left small indentations in the cover. In the dim light it was hard to make out the words, but he could see enough to tell that they were written in unfamiliar letters.

Toto was reminded of the bookshelves in the elder's house. He and Ico had been scolded once when they snuck in to take a look. In that house, every part of the wall, save the door itself, was covered in books. The book of stone he held in his hands now looked a lot like those in the elder's study.

Maybe this place was a study too? He wondered if the master of this house had been an important person like the elder. A scholar of ancient wisdom. Toto tried to be careful, yet even steadying his grip on the book made it break and crumble. He laid it gently on the floor and resumed his search, sweeping across the ground with his hands. Toward the back of the room it was so dark he couldn't even see the tip of his own nose. Still, he was able to discover that three of the walls here were bookshelves, all filled to overflowing.

Somehow, it put him at ease. The elder was always saying they should read. *Study*, he told them often. *Knowledge makes a man strong*. Toto had never really listened. All a hunter needed was a keen eye and a steady hand. He could leave the studying to the slow of foot.

Even still, in this city of mysteries, hiding from something more frightful than the darkness around him, that tiny seed of respect for knowledge that had been planted inside him stirred and whispered to him in a tiny voice.

This place is safe.

This place is protected.

Or, Toto thought, *maybe I've gone crazy and I'm hearing things.*

He was standing in a fortress of books—a fortress with no other exit but those stairs.

There was nothing to do about it but find a way up and out. If he waited too long, the sun would go down and he would be left to cope in the pitch dark.

Wait—

Maybe it was better for him to remove the rubble and go upstairs *after* the sun had set. If the face couldn't see him, how could it find him? Once darkness fell on the city, there would be any number of places where Toto could hide.

I'm a hunter, Toto thought furiously, putting a fist to his chest.

He could run at night. He wouldn't lose his way. He merely needed to look up at the stars and judge the moon's height and he would be able to find his way out of the city and back home.

It'll be hard without Arrow Wind.

Toto gritted his teeth and held back the trepidation he could feel growing inside him. It would be too easy to drown in self-pity. *But that's no way to be,* he thought. *No more crying. I have to get home.*

Okay! Forgetting where he was for a moment, Toto stood tall. As he did, his left elbow smacked something so hard he gasped in pain. Whatever he had hit collapsed with a thud—a small piece of furniture he hadn't noticed, perhaps.

Toto felt something moving through the air, and he sprang back in the nick of time. Something much larger than whatever his elbow had just encountered *whooshed* by his ear to collapse on the floor with a reverberating crash.

Toto had to cover his mouth and nose against the dust. He guessed that whatever little thing he had disturbed had knocked against one of the bookshelves and brought the whole thing down.

After waiting for the dust to settle, he began to feel around with his hands, quickly finding a mountain of shattered books. Something shimmered amongst the fragments.

At first, he doubted his eyes. It couldn't be catching the light from upstairs; this part of the floor was pitch black, which meant something here was giving off *its own* light. It had a pale, beautiful gleam, like that of the Hunter's Star, visible even on cloudy nights.

Toto felt through the pile with both hands, quickly retrieving the glimmering object. It was another book, not of stone, but of paper. It felt old and weathered, and there was no mistaking the feel of it in his hands.

Toto quickly moved into the light and began to examine his finding. The book was thin, with a white cover. Even when held directly in the light coming from upstairs, the book clearly gave off its own light.

Gingerly, he wiped the dust from its cover. The book's glow brightened. Five words were written on the front in a script Toto had never learned, but he recognized it as the same script used in the old books back in the village.

The elder could read this.

More than its contents, Toto wondered how this book—one single book—had managed to avoid the dreadful curse that the Castle in the Mist had laid upon this city. And why did it glow with such a pure white light?

Whatever the book was, it must have been very strong indeed to have stood up to the castle's wrath. *Maybe,* Toto thought, *it can save me too.*

Toto examined the rubble covering the staircase, then set to work, picking up one piece at a time, moving as carefully as possible so as not to make a single sound. By the time he had removed enough to pass, the sun had already set. Still, Toto remained crouched at the bottom of the stairs, waiting patiently. *Come on, night,* he thought. *Moon, don't show yourself, please. Hang darkness like a curtain over my path and let me get out of here alive!*

He dozed while he waited, clutching the glimmering book to his chest with both hands, like a warrior holding his bow or his spear before battle, so close that it almost became a part of his body.

When all had fallen into the darkness of night, Toto climbed the steps. The curious book in his arms glowed, giving him courage and lighting the ground at his feet. He found he was able to make the glow stop simply by placing his hand over its cover. That would keep him safe from the watchful eyes of that face in the sky.

Toto began to run through the sleeping stones of the city. He didn't get lost. As frightened as he was, his hunter's instincts did not abandon him this time.

He came upon Arrow Wind, and for a moment, tears rose in his eyes, and he stopped. Toto stroked the horse's rigid mane with one hand and hugged his back. *I'm sorry. I never should have brought you here. And now I have to leave you all alone.*

"But I'll come back for you someday, I promise."

With that whispered oath, Toto made for the city gates.

He was out of the cursed city. Toto ran to the foot of the Forbidden Mountains without stopping. His breath was ragged, his chest ached, and his muscles screamed with exhaustion, but he did not rest. If he didn't run now, he would be too late.

In Toto's arms, the book glowed.

As he began to climb, the moon showed its face on the far side of the forest. It was as if it had waited for him to find the shelter of the trees.

Under the moonlight, the book glowed even brighter. It seemed to Toto then that, by some means beyond his comprehension, the moonlight and the book's light were smiling at each other.

It was only a little farther to the pass. Not even the best hunters in the village could run like this. But Toto ran and ran faster, as though his very feet were enchanted.

[6]

THE ELDER AWOKE feeling even more exhausted after a night of fitful sleep than he had when he lay down the evening before. His eyes opened at the first shout at his door.

"Elder! We found him! We found Toto!"

He sat up and bade the man come in. The face of one of the older hunters appeared in his doorway. "They're bringing him in now."

A search party who had gone out at dawn had discovered Toto lying in a field.

"How is he?"

"Too weak to talk. But his eyes are open, and he can hear us."

The elder quickly dressed and went outside to see a commotion at the village entrance. The search party had returned, carrying Toto between them on a wide wooden board. Oneh ran out from the back, but the elder waved her away. "To the weaving room, now."

"But—"

"You are to do *nothing* but weave the Mark. I demand it."

Oneh's thin shoulders drooped and she withdrew.

The elder hurried to Toto's house. Toto's father was a hunter and a craftsman besides, skilled at making the implements needed for the hunt. He was not a man to be easily alarmed, but his face was pale and rigid as he watched the others carry his son through the door. The elder guessed that the woman he could hear wailing from inside the cottage was Toto's mother.

"Have you called the physician?" he asked one of the men standing there.

"We sent a man on Silverstar to fetch him, Elder."

Inside, the men carrying Toto lifted him gently onto his bed. His father stroked Toto's hair and his mother hugged him, still weeping, while his little brother and sister pushed their way through the small crowd of men, crying and calling out Toto's name.

Toto's eyelids fluttered, and the elder saw his lips move, but there was no sound. Though he was covered with dust and scratches, he appeared to have been spared any serious injuries. His legs lay limp across the bed and his arms were clutched tightly across his chest.

The elder noticed that Toto was holding something. He took a breath, and in a loud, clear voice, announced, "Everyone, thank you for bringing Toto back to us safely. This is a time for all to rejoice. However, I must ask that, for a moment, you leave me alone with the boy. There's something very important I must discuss with him."

Most of the men hadn't even realized the elder was there among them until he spoke. Quickly, they stepped away so that he might reach the boy, but Toto's parents would not leave the boy's side.

"I'm sorry," the elder apologized to them, "but my duties require that I speak with Toto alone." The elder looked at each of their faces in turn. "The physician will be here shortly. I need only a moment's time before he arrives."

The fate of our village might very well depend upon it, he thought.

Finally, they seemed to understand. Toto's father gently touched his wife's shoulder and they stood. Tears streaming down her face, his mother rubbed Toto's head and cheek before she left.

Once everyone had gone, the elder gathered up his robes and hurried over to Toto's bedside where he knelt.

"Toto. Do you know who I am?"

Toto's head nodded slightly.

"Can you speak?"

The boy's dried, cracked lips parted. "E-Elder…"

The elder placed a hand on Toto's forehead. It was as damp and cold as clay never touched by the sun. He rubbed the boy's skin and his hand came away covered with a fine gray dust. The feeling of it between his fingers sent a shiver up the elder's spine, and he recalled what he had seen from the pass in the Forbidden Mountains.

The elder touched a hand to Toto's arm and then to his legs. Everywhere he touched felt cold, and everywhere was covered by the same ashen dust. His clothes were infused with the smell of the stone city.

"You went beyond the mountains."

Toto blinked and nodded.

"You went through the pass and down the other side. And then into the city."

Toto nodded again.

"You saw the people turned to stone?"

Toto's lips formed the words *I saw*.

"And you saw something else. What?"

In response, a single tear fell from the corner of Toto's eye, and his entire body began to tremble.

"You met someone, didn't you? Who? What did you see in that city of death?"

Toto's breath quickened as though he were struggling to wring the last strength from his tiny frame. "F-face."

"A face? What kind of face?"

"A woman...a woman's face. I was...afraid," he managed through tears.

Pity swelled in the elder's heart, but his fear was greater. His hands clenched into fists. "Did she chase you?"

Toto closed his eyes and nodded. The elder's blood went cold, and his heart began to beat raggedly in his chest.

"You have gone to a place where you should never have been and done something you should never have done."

Toto's small teeth chattered. "I-I'm sorry."

Toto tried to move his arms on his chest, but they seemed to be stuck together. Toto's slender muscles tensed and the layer of ashen dust covering his skin cracked and began to flake, like rust falling from iron.

"I found...this," Toto said, finally loosening his arms enough so the elder could see what they held.

It's a book—an ancient book.

"The book..."

The elder gently grabbed Toto's wrists, helping the boy loosen his grasp.

"The book protected me," Toto said in a hoarse whisper, and his eyes looked up at the elder. He was trying to give him the book.

Once the elder had helped Toto pry his arms far enough apart, the book slid easily out. Quickly, the elder caught it in his hand and lifted it up.

The cover was coated in gray dust, but the elder could tell that the cloth binding was a lighter white. The smell of dust filled his nostrils—the same smell the wind had carried when he stood looking down upon the city.

The elder carefully wiped the front cover and read the short series of letters running across it.

The Book of Light.

His eyes narrowed. *How could it be?*

"Toto," he said, eyes still fixed on the book, "where did you find this? Did you truly find this in the city?" He grabbed the boy's shoulder and shook him, his voice growing louder. But Toto's eyes had lost their focus, and his arms fell limply to his sides, their task complete.

"Answer me, boy!"

Toto's gaze drifted slowly, coming to rest for a moment on the elder's face. His mouth moved. "The…light."

"Light? What about the light?" The elder held his ear to Toto's mouth, straining to hear. "Tell me about the light, Toto!"

Then the elder thought he heard the boy whisper *I'm sorry*, but whatever he said next was lost in the elder's own scream.

As he lay there on the bed, Toto's body began to harden, starting at his fingertips. It was as though a gray wave washed over him, covering his entire body while the elder watched.

"Toto!" The elder reached out as if to snatch Toto away from that wave, but where he touched the boy's shoulder it was already cold and hard. A breath later, his chin, nose, and cheeks turned to stone.

Toto's eyes went wide, as though he saw something there, hanging above him—but before it could come into focus, his pupils shrank and turned to stone. The elder swiftly leaned over the boy as if he could catch in his eyes a reflection of what Toto had been looking at, but by then, even the boy's hair had turned gray and rigid.

Dizziness came over the elder, and he staggered, dropping the book from his hands and leaning upon the boy's bed for support. The book bounced on the bed with a soft sound, then landed flat on its back beside the boy's cheek.

The Book of Light.

The book came to rest, touching the side of the boy's face as though to give it one last stroke. Toto was still crying when the last patch of skin finally turned to stone.

Hands trembling, the elder picked up the book and clasped it in his own arms, much as the boy had done until a moment before.

It wasn't supposed to exist. He had thought it long gone, lost to a distant past.

It protected him.

The elder raised the book to eye level. It glowed with a steady light. Though it was covered with dust from the cursed stone of the city, the light itself was unblemished and pure. The book breathed in the elder's hands, pouring the strength it held within its covers into the old man.

The elder felt the shaking in his limbs quiet, and his breathing became easier as the light purified him to the very core of his being.

"God of Light," the elder whispered. "Ancient knowledge, guardian of eternal purity."

A single teardrop ran down his wrinkled cheek, tarrying a moment on his chin before falling like the first drop of spring rain upon budding crops down onto Toto's right cheek. He looked at the book. "You called Toto to do this."

You lay hidden deep, waiting year after year until the time was right for you to return to me in my confusion and fear.

The elder lowered his head to touch the cover of the book, and with all his body and spirit, he prayed. When at last he looked up, he gently rubbed his hand over Toto's head.

"You did it, brave Toto. You did it."

The elder stood.

There was no time for delay. The elder called all of the villagers together and quickly gave instructions.

"For the next three days, there is to be no hunting. Men must stand in the four corners of the village with fires lighted, keeping watch in shifts. The fires must stay lit both day and night. The women must purify all the village with water and salt, and work every loom we have. Children, while the sun still remains in the sky, you must sing festival songs. Those who can play instruments, bring them and play. Once the sun sets and the village gates are closed, all must remain inside, save those men who are on watch, and no one is to make a sound. Rest your bodies and sleep holding hands, that you may bar entrance to nightmares. When the dawn comes, we will do again tomorrow what we have done today. These next three days are the most important."

The people of the village looked at the elder in bewilderment. His instructions to work all the looms flew directly in the face of his earlier command that only the loom in the weaving room might be used during the Time of the Sacrifice. Some wondered if he had gone mad—but the elder permitted no discussion.

"I need you to follow these new orders, and follow them well. On the morning of the fourth day, we will set the signal fire and summon the priest from his lodgings. He will come that day and take Ico with him to the Castle in the Mist."

"But, Elder, why light watch fires around the village if we are not preparing for war? What's going on? Why do these things without reason?"

"There is a reason," the elder replied firmly. "And this *is* war."

When all instructions had been given, the elder left for the weaving room. Without a word, he took Oneh's hand from the spindle and tore the half-woven Mark from the loom, nearly startling her to death.

"What are you doing, husband?" she cried, her face flushed. "What is the meaning of this?"

The elder put both hands on Oneh's shoulders. "When the knowledge and courage once separated are again together bound, then the long-cursed mist will lift, and the light of the ancients will be reborn upon the land."

"What..."

The elder reached inside his robes and withdrew the book, opening its cover and showing it to her. "Look. See the design drawn here? See how it is like the picture of the Mark I gave to you?"

Oneh looked between her husband and the open book. He was right. The resemblance to the Mark was striking, though it was not a perfect match.

"*This* is the Mark you must weave for Ico. Throw away all you have done until now. You must make this new Mark as quickly as you can. We have no time. We must weave it together while the strength of the village still holds."

A light shone in her husband's eyes. It was that light, more than his words, that moved her.

"Will this new Mark save Ico?" she asked, grabbing her husband's sleeve.

The elder nodded. "I pray so, yes. And then Ico will save us all."

[7]

A THIN LIGHT drifted up from the bottom of the pool, washing over Ico like a fresh, chilly breeze.

"Think it's deep?"

"Probably."

"We could try swimming down. I bet it goes somewhere," Toto said, tossing in a small stone.

"It's cold here, but I like it."

"Yeah. Really cleans out the chest."

These are memories, Ico thought. *This isn't happening now. We were exploring the cave. We found a pool of water. I almost dropped my torch...*

Ico opened his eyes with a start.

A thin light trickled through the small window at the top of the cave. *Dawn, probably,* he thought. His body was frigid down to the bone, and everything ached. He hadn't been able to sleep well the night before due to the cold. *That explains my dream.*

It hadn't been easy descending into that cave with Toto. There had been a lot of scaling up and down sheer rock. But thanks to the cold he hadn't even broken a sweat. He remembered the sound of his chattering teeth echoing off the walls of the cave.

The dim phosphorescence at the bottom of the pool was beautiful, yet fleeting—a spectral gown worn by a dancing ghost. He could close his eyes and see it. There was Toto, standing next to him, eyes sparkling, enchanted by the light in the water.

Things had been busy in the village outside his cave these last three days. He heard drums and bells and children singing, starting with the first light of morning and carrying on until nightfall. *Maybe,* he thought, *this is how they welcome the priest.*

He wondered what Toto was doing. He couldn't picture him singing with the other kids.

"What nonsense did you put in that boy's head?"

Ico hadn't been able to eat or sleep for a day after the elder's visit. All he wanted to do was smash his head against the wall of the cave. But a day later, the guard had told him that Toto had returned. Weeping with relief, Ico begged the guard to tell him how they had found Toto. "Was he hurt? Why'd he leave? Can I see him, just for a little?"

The guard was silent.

"Do not worry about Toto," the elder had told him on a later visit. "All you need to worry about is fulfilling your role as the Sacrifice." His voice had sounded confident and serene, but bitterness stained his face.

"Be sure to eat. You'll be leaving soon."

Then the elder had left, and Ico was alone again in the cave. The only company he found was in his dreams.

Ico took up walking in circles around the cave, swinging his arms and stretching his legs to keep his body limber. He had just finished a round of these exercises when he noticed something unusual. Silence. There was no singing or music this morning. He couldn't hear the loom either.

Something had changed.

A silhouette appeared at the entrance to the cave. Ico rubbed his eyes. It was the elder. His long robes dragged on the ground, and his thin shoulders were thrown back as he stepped inside.

Oneh followed directly behind him.

"Mother!" Ico shouted. Oneh smiled at him, but no sooner had she done so than tears began to stream from her eyes.

She made to run to him, but the elder put out his hand, holding her back. He took the beautiful cloth she held in her arms and reverently hung it over one arm, nodding as he examined it.

"Ico!" Oneh called out, opening her arms wide. Ico glanced at the elder's face, but all he saw there was kindness. The next moment, Ico ran into Oneh's arms.

"Ico, my dear Ico, my sweet child." Oneh called his name over and over again, like a song, and she hugged him tight and stroked his hair. "How lonely you must've been—how sad," she repeated, crying. "Please forgive us. We forced this on you. If we'd only been stronger—"

"Mother..."

In Oneh's arms, Ico looked toward the elder. It had only been a few days since he had struck Ico on the cheek, but it seemed as though he had aged years. Still, the gentle look, filled with authority, that had fled his eyes when the Time of the Sacrifice had come, returned. This was the elder who had raised Ico. He had come back.

"It's time, Oneh," the elder said gently, and then he smiled. "It is difficult for me as well. But we must say our farewells. The Sacrifice waits for no man."

Oneh nodded, her eyes filled with tears. She gave Ico's head one last hug before letting him go and stepping back to stand beside the elder.

He spoke. "Last night, we lit the signal fire. The priest's entourage should arrive before midday. Once the ceremony is complete, you will leave for the Castle in the Mist."

Ico swallowed, quickly wiped a lingering tear from his cheek, and straightened his posture. "I understand."

He would have liked to sound a bit more determined, but his voice was choked with tears, and he couldn't say anything more than that. Still, he managed to meet the elder's gaze directly, to show his resolve was unfaltering. *I won't cry or yell again, no matter what. I won't sulk, I won't question.*

But a moment later, when the elder and Oneh knelt reverently before him, Ico couldn't help his mouth from dropping open.

"Elder?"

Ico was about to join them on the floor when a strong word from the elder stopped him. "Stand."

Oneh smiled at him then and intertwined her fingers in front of her, bowing her head in prayer.

On his knees, the elder's eyes were on a level with Ico's shoulder. Looking down at him, Ico was reminded of the dream he had just before waking. *His eyes have that same light as in the pool.*

"You are the light of our hope," the elder intoned.

Ico had heard the elder's resonant voice pray many times before. Prayers for the harvest, prayers for the hunt—a voice that echoed far and wide, calling out to that vaulted deity, the Creator of all life in this world.

Now that voice was directed at Ico.

"The knowledge and courage separated long ago come here together once more. You are our sword, our beacon-light."

A gentle smile from the elder stopped Ico's question before he could ask it.

"Come."

Ico took a half step forward. The elder spread out the beautiful cloth he held draped over his arm.

In the very center of the cloth was a hole just large enough for Ico to stick his head through, like a tunic. Its pattern was embroidered in three colors: white, deep indigo, and a very light crimson. The colors intertwined in a complex pattern. Ico thought he detected shapes in the pattern that looked more like ancient letters than random swirls.

"Put it on," the elder said, lifting the tunic in his hands. "This is your Mark."

Ico put on the Mark. It did not quite reach down to his waist, but it was exactly as wide as his shoulders and draped nicely across his chest and back.

Ico felt his chest grow warm, as though a hand were pressing down upon it, directly above his heart.

He heard a sound like a tiny flute playing in the distance. Ico spread his arms and looked down at himself. Every thread woven to make the Mark was shining with light. It was as though the light had begun to flow like blood through the veins of the design. A silver glow passed from end to end, from whorl to whorl.

And then the glow faded along with the warmth, but they were not gone. Rather, he felt as though the light and the warmth had passed from the Mark into him.

"There," the elder said, his eyes sparkling. "That's it. The Mark has recognized you."

Oneh was crying again, with her hands over her face.

"Elder, what is this?" Ico asked.

The elder stood and placed both his hands gently on Ico's shoulders before answering. "The Mark is worn by every Sacrifice. However, yours is different. No other child sent to the Castle in the Mist has worn one quite like this."

Ico ran his hand over the fabric. It was smooth to the touch, but now that the light had faded, it felt no different than any newly woven piece of fabric.

"These threads have been imbued with a prayer," the elder said, indicating the design. "In ancient times, the words of this prayer were our only source of hope that we might one day rise up and cast off the darkness governing us."

Was this some kind of myth? What did he mean by darkness? The master of the castle? But that's just the same as now, Ico thought. They still feared the Castle in the Mist. That was why they had to send the Sacrifice. Or had there been a time when the Castle in the Mist had ruled them even more fiercely than it did now?

"I did not mean to cause you confusion," the elder said. "There is little we can say about the past, for much of our knowledge was lost in ancient times. There is much that even I do not understand.

But, Ico, there is one thing I can say with certainty." The elder gave Ico's shoulders a gentle shake. "You bear our hopes upon your back as you go to the castle today. I'm sorry I do not know what awaits you there or what you must face. But I know that you will prevail. As I know that you will one day return from the castle and come home to our village."

Ico couldn't believe what he was hearing. *A Sacrifice...coming back home?*

"Go now to the castle and see what lies there with your eyes. Listen with your ears. You will be victorious." The elder's words echoed in Ico's heart. They dropped down deep into the pool within him, lifting back up again in glorious reverberating tones.

Still on her knees, Oneh leaned forward and gave Ico a hug. "We will be waiting for you," she said through her tears. "We will be waiting for you to come home. Never forget that."

A shiver ran through Ico's frame. He was no longer cold or frightened—it was something else, vibrating within him, filling him with courage.

"It was Toto who found the prayers woven into the Mark you wear."

Ico's eyes opened wide. He grabbed the elder's long sleeve. "Is Toto all right? He went into the mountains, didn't he?"

The elder's smile faded, and his face took on a grave look. "Yes. Toto went to the same mountains as we did and saw the same sight." *That horrible city.*

"And this prayer—did it come from the city?"

The elder nodded.

Ico's memory of the walled city of stone rose again in his mind. He wondered where Toto had gone in those ashen streets. Where had he walked, and how had he found the prayer?

"I am sorry to have doubted your intentions," the elder said, his voice hoarse.

Ico shook his head. He didn't care about that anymore. "Is Toto all right?"

"He's fine." The elder's quick reply brooked no further questioning.

Ico looked him in the eyes. "When I return from the Castle in the Mist, I'll be able to see him again, won't I?"

"Of course."

Ico bit his lip. *I'm not afraid.*

Oneh stood, wiping her tear-streaked face with a sleeve. Seeing the look of determination in Ico's face put her at ease. She smiled. "Now, Ico," she said, "you must return your Mark to me."

She said his name just as she had when he lived in their house. *Ico, you're covered in mud again. Change your clothes this instant. Dinner will be ready soon.*

"I can't wear it?"

A conspiratorial look came into the elder's eyes and he smiled at the boy. "Actually," he said, "it is the priest's duty to place the Mark upon the Sacrifice at your departure ceremony. We only brought it here to you because we wanted to see with our own eyes that the Mark was truly yours, that you were the chosen one, and that you were fit to wear it."

"That's why," Oneh continued, "when you speak with the priest, you must not mention that we met here this morning, and you must on no account tell him that your Mark is special, that it's not like the others."

Ico nodded, but a thought occurred to him. "Elder. Wouldn't the priest from the capital be pleased to know that my Mark is special, just as you and Mother are? Why do I have to hide it?"

"You are clever," the elder replied, dodging the question. "Your cleverness is knowledge. It falls to you to find the courage that long ago was kin to this knowledge and to give us the light once more."

[8]

THE THREE BLACK horses walked in a single line, treading the dry grass beneath their hooves.

The priest had arrived in Toksa Village, flanked by two temple guards. The fields sparkled beneath the bright sunshine, and a gentle breeze rustled the leaves of the trees.

Silence hung over the village. People had dressed carefully for the ceremony and swept out their doorways, where they knelt to greet the entourage. Everyone was exhausted—the children from having danced and sung until Oneh finished weaving the Mark, the adults from standing watch day and night. More than one child slept soundly on their mother's back.

For so long they had been patient, and now the end was near. Once the priest had come and gone, village life would return to normal.

It was strictly forbidden to speak aloud, let alone address anyone in the entourage. Nor was it permitted to look directly at them or their horses.

After the entourage had offered greetings to the elder and his wife before the elder's house, they began preparing for the departure ceremony. From this point onward, only the elder, his wife, and three specially chosen hunters would be allowed to take part in the proceedings. The rest of the villagers were obliged to remain indoors, in silence, their windows shuttered.

The priest removed his black travel cloak, revealing robes of pure white beneath. From a leather saddlebag, he withdrew a long surplice woven with an intricate pattern and a single phial of holy water. Chanting a prayer, the priest touched his fingertips once upon the surplice's shoulders, chest, and hem.

The departure ceremony was a beautiful, almost enchanting event—despite the unusual appearance of the priest, whose head was entirely shrouded in a cloth that trailed down to his shoulders, without holes for his eyes or even his nose. The cloth was made of a loose-woven material through which the priest could see out, but no one could see in.

The two temple guards followed a short distance behind him. They wore light traveling armor fashioned from chain rings and leather, with swords hung at their waists and sturdy woven leather boots on their feet. Their faces too were hidden by silver helmets—helmets with horns.

One had horns exactly like Ico's, while the other's were the same as Ico's in size and position, but with their tips turned down toward the shoulders instead of upward.

This was not typical garb for temple guards. Even the elder had only seen these helmets once before, in an illustration in one of his books. They were to be worn only at the Time of the Sacrifice.

Moving slowly, the priest withdrew the scepter at his waist and raised it to eye level. A round orb at its tip sparkled in the sunlight. He then walked in a circle just inside the village gates, using his scepter to draw a line in the dirt. He walked to the east, west, north, and south sides of the circle, stopping in each station to ask the help of the land-spirits who guarded the cardinal directions, and lightly tapping the ground with the tip of his scepter. With the cloth drawn over his head, it was impossible for the elder to make out the words.

The priest knelt in the center of the circle and began to pray. The temple guards withdrew even further back to where the elder knelt beside Oneh, who was trembling so violently she nearly collapsed.

The elder reached out and, with his fingertip, lightly touched the Mark that hung neatly folded over her arm. The gesture seemed to calm her somewhat.

"You may bring the Sacrifice here," said the priest, turning to face the elder. The elder looked around and raised his arm toward one of the hunters who stood waiting. The hunter immediately turned and sped down the path to the cave.

A few moments later, Ico appeared.

Three hunters walked with him, one in the front and two behind. All of them wore costumes typically reserved for the harvest festival. On their backs they bore bows that had never once been fired and arrows with tips that had never once tasted blood. They had no swords, but each carried a torch. The torches sputtered noisily and gave off an inky black smoke in the daylight.

Ico had already bathed and changed into simple clothes—a hempen red shirt and rough-woven white trousers. On his feet, he wore his own comfortable leather sandals, worn in through years of use. His lips formed a single straight line across his face. Ico stopped just before the circle in the dirt.

"Come here," the priest ordered. "Come and kneel before me."

Ico did as he was told. Behind them, the elder spotted a single teardrop from Oneh's downturned face.

The priest lightly tapped Ico on both shoulders with his scepter, then touched it lightly to the top of the boy's head, chanting prayers all the while.

"Stand."

Ico stood, and the priest touched both sides of his waist, then his left and right knee.

"Turn around."

Ico turned. The elder could feel the boy's gaze on him. Unable to speak, the elder whispered words of encouragement in his heart. Next to him, Oneh struggled to keep herself from looking up.

The priest tapped both of Ico's shoulders one last time, then touched the scepter to the small of his back.

"Turn back around and kneel."

The priest lifted the phial of holy water and shook it over Ico's horns.

Small damp spots formed on Ico's fresh clothes where the water splashed.

The priest handed the empty phial to one of the guards, then held the scepter in both hands, level with the ground. He brought it up to the height of his shoulders, lifting it over his head as he chanted the words to a new prayer.

Suddenly a brilliant light sparkled along the circle that the priest had drawn in the dirt—as if a ring of silver had floated up from the ground beneath them.

With a *whoosh*, the ring vanished.

Ico stood, eyes wide. The priest slowly lowered his arms and, holding the scepter vertically, brought it before his chest. The tip of the scepter sparkled.

"The ritual is complete. He is the true and rightful Sacrifice. Blood returns to blood, time marches on, and the Sun God indicates the path we men must walk."

The priest turned to face the elder, his expression hidden beneath the cloth.

"The Mark."

The elder shuffled forward on his knees, head bent low, and stretched out his arms as far as he could to offer the embroidered tunic to the priest.

The priest accepted it and held it out between his hands. Then he paused.

The elder could feel the blood rush to his head. His heart beat in his throat.

What if he notices that this *Mark is different? What if he realizes that it was made for Ico alone?*

"Step forward, Sacrifice," the priest said. He placed the Mark over Ico's head.

The Mark draped over Ico's chest and back, giving life to his otherwise simple clothes. The elder had to admit, it looked good on the boy. A breeze blew through the village, lifting the edges of the tunic, and when it settled back down, it seemed to almost have become a part of Ico's slender frame.

The boy's black eyes looked up unblinkingly at the priest's covered head.

"It is time to leave," the priest announced. "Bring the horses."

The elder and Oneh stood at the village gates, holding hands, watching until the priest's entourage was gone from sight.

"He'll come back, won't he?" Oneh whispered in her husband's ear, her voice full of tears.

"Yes," the elder replied simply. *The Mark will protect him. It has to.*

Once on horseback, the temple guards put Ico's wrists in irons. Ico rode with the priest seated behind him on the same horse. "You must not speak on the journey," the priest told him. "Even should you say something, we will not answer. You must follow our orders. It will take five days for us to reach the Castle in the Mist. We will ride with you the entire way, but know that if we see you attempt anything unusual, we will cut you down on the spot. You have been warned."

Ico replied that he had no intention of running, but the priest didn't even seem to be listening as he held the reins.

With the irons on his wrists and the chain keeping them close together, Ico couldn't get purchase on the horse's neck. Should the horse decide to break into a gallop, he might fall off. Yet there didn't seem to be any danger of speed. The guards kept the horses moving steadily but slowly. They did not speak a word between them, nor did they seem to be consulting any maps.

Guess they know the way, Ico thought.

They crossed over the grasslands, heading north along the same trail Ico had taken with the elder. Memories flooded Ico's mind. The mere thought of seeing the stone city beyond the Forbidden Mountains again left him cold.

I wonder how Toto's doing? I wish I'd gotten to see him before leaving.

They reached the foot of the mountains before evening, but the entourage veered away from the narrow path Ico and the elder had taken. They followed the foothills to the west a short while, stopping where the forest was thick.

"There is a spring nearby. Rest the horses," the priest ordered, dismounting behind him. One of the guards came and lifted Ico off the horse, keeping hold of the chain attached to Ico's irons while the other guard led the horses off to drink.

The priest looked up at the forest covering the mountainside, then he withdrew his scepter and began to pray. At one point, he thrust his arms directly overhead toward the sky, and the tip of the scepter gleamed brightly.

Ico gaped. Where before there had been nothing but thick forest, the tree branches parted with a great rustling sound, revealing a path up the mountain.

A spell ward. Ico had heard of these in stories. An enchantment had been laid over this path so that only the priest could find it.

The lifeless woods were silent, save for the *clip-clop* of the horses' hooves on the white stones of the path. Ico was wondering how far they had come when they reached a small clearing and he spotted the first star of the evening above them.

They camped there that night, on the side of the mountain, resting their feet around a small campfire as they made dinner. Ico ate first. They didn't take off his chains, so he had to lean over his bowl like a dog.

Oneh would give me a talking to if she saw me eating like this at home.

When Ico had finished, one of the guards approached and quickly slipped a sack over Ico's head. He felt chains wrapping around his feet.

"You should rest. We will ride again before dawn."

In the darkness inside the sack, Ico strained his ears. All he could hear was the wind.

Those guards must be going crazy, having to keep quiet like that.

Ico realized that they would probably have to take off their head coverings in order to eat—that was why they had covered his eyes. *I'm not supposed to see their faces.*

Ico fell asleep on the grass, listening to the occasional snuffle of the horses.

They crossed the Forbidden Mountains without ever seeing the path Ico had been on before or the stone city. Beyond, they found grasslands and gently rolling hills. On the third day, they forded a river. Once they were away from the mountains the sounds of life had returned.

However, there was a noticeable absence of people and villages. All Ico could see in every direction were grass and trees and the occasional bird.

To give himself some comfort on the journey, Ico had decided to befriend the horses. When they stopped to rest, he would steal up to them and gently pat their necks. All three of the horses were strong and sturdy and walked lightly without ever showing signs of tiring. These horses were far better behaved than the ones they used for farming in Toksa.

One of the guards—the one with upturned horns on his helmet—would let Ico touch and talk to the horses. But the other one, when he noticed, would immediately jump up and yank Ico away roughly. Once, he had shoved the boy so hard Ico had fallen to the ground.

The priest, for his part, barely acknowledged Ico's existence. Ico did not think the priest had even looked at him once. Between the cloth over his head, his long sleeves, and the high woven boots, Ico couldn't see the man's skin. At times, he wondered if there was really a person under those robes.

On the fourth day, Ico detected a curious scent in the air, entirely unknown to him, and different from that of the woods and grasslands through which they had passed. Ico sniffed the air, and the guard with the upturned horns, who happened to be riding alongside, whispered, "It's the smell of the sea."

Ico felt the priest tense, and there was a loud *crack*. The guard quickly pulled the reins and fell behind them. For a few paces, the hoofbeats were staggered, but they soon resumed their usual rhythm.

Close to the sea means close to the castle.

On the morning of the fifth day, they were making their way along a gentle path through a hardwood forest when Ico spotted white birds wheeling overhead. The smell of the sea was stronger in the air now.

Seabirds. I wish Toto was here to see them.

Soon, Ico heard the sound of the wind. At least, that was what he thought it was—but there was no stirring in the air through the forest around them. When he listened closely, he could hear it rushing in, then sliding away. *Those must be waves!*

The path turned uphill, quickly becoming very steep. The horses whinnied with exertion. At the top of the climb, the forest fell away on both sides.

They could see the sky now. Over the pounding of the surf, Ico heard one of the guards gasp.

CHAPTER 2
THE CASTLE IN THE MIST

[1]

THEY HAD REACHED the edge of the forest.

Birds chittered in the sunlight, and from somewhere high above came the keening screech of a falcon chasing its prey.

Two weathered stone columns stood under the dappled light that filtered through the leaves at the wood's edge. The track of lightly trodden ground they had been following ended here in a stone stair that led into the clearing

The guard in front urged his horse forward, and his mount's hooves made a loud *clack-clack* on the stone. The steps were weathered at the edges. Some of the stones were covered by moss, and others were missing altogether, but there was no doubt they had been placed there by human hands. ·

The horse bearing Ico and the priest followed, its bridle rattling, a sheen of sweat on its neck. The three horses stood side by side on the cracked stone terrace they found atop the stairs. Ico squinted in the bright sunlight, feeling a gentle breeze against his face. A sudden dizziness came over Ico as he realized that they stood at the very top of an incredibly high precipice overlooking the sea.

Far below, the water glinted in the sun. It was Ico's first time at the sea—but he had no eyes for the gentle flow of the current or the sparkle of the white waves that crashed along the cliff base. The water was a mere inlet, and all of Ico's attention was focused on what lay on the other side atop another cliff just like the one on which they stood.

A massive castle of giant rough-hewn stones, a dark silhouette against the crystal blue sky, dominating the view. The castle did not perch so much as grow from the cliff face as though it had been carved from the stone itself. It was almost as if some aberration of nature had caused the rock to erode into the shape of a castle that men might construct. It looked solid. The only curves in its construction were the elegantly sloping pillars that supported the outer wall, their bases planted firmly beneath the waves.

Ico couldn't imagine something looking more different than the Castle in the Mist he had seen in his daydreams and nightmares. Perhaps it was the clear blue sky above or the merry sound of the songbirds in the trees. Still, there was nothing dark, terrifying, or even vaguely ominous about the castle atop the cliffs. It was beautiful, elegant even—an ancient, noble edifice.

"So this is it..." the guard with the upturned horns on his helmet breathed.

The horse carrying the priest and Ico whinnied and raised its front legs, bringing Ico's attention back across the water. A strong sea wind blew, rippling the edges of the Mark where it hung over his chest and back. On the side of the castle facing them stood a massive stone gate, its doors open wide. But there was no way to reach it.

Ico realized that the stone platform upon which they now stood had once been part of a bridge leading to the castle. The bridge had been wide, large enough for three horses to pass abreast. But now, just a few paces ahead, the stone ended. He held a hand over his eyes to shade them from the sun and saw the other end of the bridge at the foot of the castle gate. It, too, ended abruptly where the cliff began. Between them, only sky.

You may not enter.

You may not leave.

The inlet between the two cliffs formed a moat more effective than any crafted by men.

For the first time since arriving, Ico detected an undeniable eeriness to the beautiful view. As his eyes adjusted to the light, he noticed that despite the blue sky overhead, a fine white mist hung over every part of the castle. *How had I not noticed that before?*

"Down the cliff," the priest said from the depths of his cowl. He pulled the reins, leading their horse toward the left-hand side of the terrace, where Ico spotted the top of a steep switchback winding down the cliff face. The three horses made their way in single file down the simple path of trodden earth. There was no railing, nor anything else to prevent a single misstep from sending them plummeting off the edge, but the priest kept an easy grip on the reins.

The entire way down, Ico craned his neck to look up at the castle. He could not take his eyes off of it. A flash of light caught his eye—sunlight reflecting from two large spheres that sat atop the columns to either side of the main gate.

Ico felt a stirring in his chest.

You've come to me.

Finally.

Soon the gate was high above them and the sea close below. White seabirds hopped from rock to rock, and eddies swirled in the inlet. A small stone structure stood at the cliff base, its roof supported by slender pillars. The air was cool in the shadow of the cliff, and the spray from the rocks left a lingering chill on the bare skin of Ico's arms.

The party dismounted. A short wooden pier with rotting pilings extended into the water in front of the structure. Beside it, a small rowboat had been pulled up onto the shore. While the two guards moved the boat to a small channel of water leading out into the inlet, the priest stood on an outcropping, facing the sea.

Ico strained his ears, thinking he might hear the words of the priest's prayer, but if he said anything, it was lost in the roar of the surf.

When the boat was ready, the guards waved for them to board. As Ico approached the stern, one of them extended his hand to help him in, but Ico leapt instead, landing directly in the middle of the boat so softly the tiny craft barely rocked in the water.

Ico imagined the guard was smiling inside his helmet—the same way Oneh would smile whenever she saw Ico jump or climb.

"Must be nice to be so light," she'd say.

But whatever expression the guard wore, it could not have lasted long. He turned away from Ico, a distinctly apologetic hunch to his back.

It was the other guard's duty to row the boat. The priest sat at the bow, perfectly still, save for the motion imparted by the water beneath them. A seabird with pure white feathers on its breast and a red beak glided across the waves toward their small craft, barely skimming over the priest's head. Even still, he did not flinch. Ico trailed his arms from the side of the boat, touching the water that streamed past. Through the clear waves he saw the shapes of fish swimming below.

They cut across the flow of the tide, slowly advancing toward the opposite shore. Ico looked back up toward the castle. The sky was split into smooth curves by the tall arches that rose between the stone pillars of the outer wall. The guard rowed toward the left-hand side of the castle, and soon the side wall came into view. Ico realized that the castle was not a single structure but rather a collection of several towers. Copper-colored pipes and narrow causeways of stone extended from the tower walls, spanning gaping ravines to link the towers together. The castle was so vast that Ico found it hard to take it all in at once.

The moment before the boat slipped beneath the castle's shadow, Ico saw the spheres by the gate glimmer one last time.

As they neared the far shore, the boat veered further left, heading toward the side of the castle. From here, it was impossible to tell where the sheer cliffs above them ended and the Castle in the Mist began. *Is the castle becoming part of the earth beneath it,* Ico wondered in a daydream, *or is the cliff slowly swallowing the castle whole?*

"Into the grotto," the priest called from the bow, raising his hand and pointing. Ahead, a cave opened in the rock face. The cave looked like it had formed naturally, but it was reinforced on either side with stone pillars. The guard swung the boat toward the entrance.

As they paddled in, darkness fell around them. The boat advanced gingerly, a child afraid of being scolded, and the sound of the surging sea fell away.

Ahead of them, a portcullis made of thick logs lashed together barred their path. The priest looked up at the rocks to the right and called to the guard with the downturned horns. "Now."

The guard jumped lightly from the boat onto the rocky ledge of the cave and disappeared into the darkness. The boat continued sliding forward, and just as its bow was about to hit the logs, the entire portcullis lifted out of the waves with a loud creaking noise, allowing them passage.

The guard reappeared along the side of the cave and jumped back in the boat with a loud thud.

A short while later, a small wooden pier very like the one they had left on the far shore drifted into view. It even resembled the other in the way that its wooden pilings had rotted, leaving the planks along the top slanting toward the water.

The priest was the first to disembark when they reached the pier. The guard behind Ico pushed him lightly on the back. Though they were still inside the cave, the ceiling here was much higher, and the cavern seemed to extend ahead for some distance. A sandy path led from the pier, splitting to the right and left.

"Get the sword," the priest said.

The guard with downturned horns nodded and walked off down the right path, disappearing down a stone passageway.

Ico stood examining his surroundings until the priest tapped him on the shoulder, indicating that he should proceed down the left-hand path. They began to walk, the wet sand making an incongruously humorous *slup-slup* sound under Ico's leather sandals.

A round hole opened in the cave wall. They passed through, and the floor beneath their feet was now smooth. They no longer walked on rocks and pebbles; the passageway here was carved from stone.

Ico looked around, his eyes wide.

He had never been in a place like this before. It resembled a grand hall, with sides that rose straight up like a chimney. The room itself was perfectly round, and it hurt his neck to look at the ceiling far above.

A winding staircase, and in some places ladders, lined the chamber's outer wall and would once have permitted someone to climb all the way to the top. But as Ico looked closer, he saw that the stairs had fallen away in places.

A thick, cylindrical pillar rose from the center of the chamber, reaching all the way up to the top—though, as Ico considered it, the structure was far too wide for a pillar. It must have been placed there for some purpose other than supporting the roof.

The smooth path extended into the middle of the chamber and ended at that central column, where Ico spotted two stone idols, roughly human-sized in height. The idols were rectangular, their sides meeting at sharp right angles, yet they had what looked like bodies and legs and even heads, complete with carven eyes.

Ico had never seen idols quite like these anywhere around Toksa. Their shape resembled the small idols that travelers prayed to for protection along the road.

The priest slowly approached the idols. The soldier with the upturned horns stayed back with Ico.

"Are you cold?" he asked in a voice so faint Ico could barely tell it from a breath.

Ico shook his head. The guard said nothing more, but he rubbed his own arms as if to say *Well, I am.* Or perhaps his gesture meant *I'm frightened.*

Heavy footsteps approached. The other guard had returned. Ico was startled to see him holding a giant sword. *No wonder his feet were dragging*. The sword was so long that if the guard placed its tip on the ground, the hilt might reach up to his shoulder. It was sheathed, though it looked double-edged by its shape, with a chain attached to the pommel. The grip was as thick as Ico's wrist, and its color was the dull silver of ancient metal.

The guard hesitated, looking toward the priest. The priest nodded and indicated with his hands that he should stand in front of the idols. The guard took a few steps forward. He glanced at the other guard, standing next to Ico. Both men's faces were hidden in the depths of their helmets, but Ico thought he could imagine their expressions: they were terrified.

"Draw the sword," the priest commanded. "There is nothing to be frightened of."

Holding the blade level to the floor, the guard gripped its hilt with his right hand. His arms shook with the weight of the blade. Though the sword appeared ancient, it slid from its scabbard without a sound, like the well-oiled blade of a soldier.

A light flared in the dimly lit chamber.

Ico closed his eyes and lifted his hands in front of his face. The light that bled through his eyelids was painfully bright.

He timidly opened his eyes to look and saw the soldier standing, feet apart, straining his shoulders to hold the blade level. A brilliant light emanating from the blade bathed the man's body. The light swelled, enveloping both guards, Ico, and the priest.

Ico realized that the light wasn't just coming from the blade— the idols were glowing too. Their glow echoed the brilliance of the sword, and both grew brighter until a light passed from one idol to the other and they split down the middle with a loud crack, sliding apart to reveal a passage beyond. The light faded.

"Sheathe the sword," the priest ordered. The guard looked down, bewildered. The blade's color had returned to a dull silver. After a moment's hesitation, he reverently returned the sword to its scabbard.

The priest led them between the two statues. Ico reached out to touch one as they passed. The stone was cold beneath his fingertips. *Where did that light come from?* he wondered. Ico spied a cavity in the statue's side with a tiny carving inside it. He looked closer and found that it was a depiction of a tiny demon. *It's like something from a fairy tale.*

The passage opened into the central column. In the very center a small dais like a copper knob protruded from the floor, with sheets of steel radiating out from it in bands.

The priest said something too low for Ico to hear to the guard without the sword. He walked over to the copper knob, pulled something like a lever next to it, and the entire device began to slowly spin. With a reverberating *clang*, the floor began to lift and Ico nearly lost his footing.

The room is rising!

Ico reached out and touched one of the walls, feeling it slide against his fingertips. A deep sound rumbled beneath them, and he could feel vibrations coming up through the floor. They continued to climb.

Of all the things Ico had expected to find in the Castle in the Mist, this was not one of them. "Amazing," he whispered.

The kind guard gave Ico a reassuring nod. The priest had his back to Ico, while the other guard held the sword with its tip against the floor, clutching its handle with both hands as though he feared it might walk away if he didn't keep a firm grip on it.

The clanging stopped.

They had arrived at the top of the column. Here stood another pair of stone idols. This time, the guard stepped forward and drew the sword with a mere nod from the priest. Again, a brilliant light ran across the idols and they parted.

As soon as the way was clear, the priest stepped through, the hem of his robes drifting above the floor.

There were no signs of life. The only sounds were their own footsteps and the metallic chatter of the guards' chain mail. The castle was abandoned.

At first, Ico thought they had emerged into a room with a low ceiling, but as he walked further on, he realized his mistake. The room had only seemed low because they had entered beneath a wide staircase climbing from the center of a vast chamber. Ico took a deep breath, trembling as he exhaled.

You could hold a festival with everybody in Toksa here and still not fill this place. The small stones covering the floor were as many in number as the stars he could see from the village watchtower, and Ico doubted that any of the hunters in the village were strong enough to loose an arrow that could reach the vaulted ceiling.

What is all this for?

Stone alcoves formed a grid along the walls, each cavity holding a strange coffinlike box with rounded corners. *No,* Ico realized. *Not just* like *coffins.* They were stone sarcophagi.

Ico followed the priest up the steps, recalling a story Oneh had told him.

Once upon a time, the story went, malicious spirits were born within the void that separated heaven and earth. Resentful that they lacked a realm of their own, they stole away human children and robbed them of their souls. But when they found that the stolen souls could not fill the emptiness inside their hearts, they seethed with anger till their rage became like tiny demons inside them.

Though they had brought the demons into being, the void-spirits were weaker than their own anger, and soon they were forced to do as the demons commanded. Distraught, the Creator hastily imbued the void-spirits with souls of their own, thinking this might placate them. But the demons within the spirits' hearts took those souls and devoured them, so that no matter how many souls the Creator gave to the spirits, they were never sated but grew even hungrier than before.

At a loss, the Creator gathered magi from across the land and requested that they fashion stone sarcophagi in which to imprison the void-spirits together with their demons. It was the humans who had suffered when the void-spirits stole their children, so it must be humans who imprisoned them, the Creator declared.

The sarcophagi they made looked like eggs grown long and were covered with carved incantations of purification and placation. The wizards chanted their spells, imbuing the carvings with power, and the sarcophagi began to glow. Like moths to a flame, the void-spirits were drawn to the light and thereby trapped for eternity.

Ico looked over the stone sarcophagi lining the walls. These, too, were carved with ancient letters and patterns. Ico's hand went to the Mark on his chest. The whorls of the patterns there were not entirely unlike those upon the stones. Ico could read neither, though he thought that the patterns on the sarcophagi looked a bit like the outlines of people.

What does it mean?

"This is your Mark," the elder had said when he placed the tunic over Ico's head. "The Mark has recognized you."

The elder had a hopeful light in his eyes when he gave Ico the Mark—*so why can I think of nothing but scary fairy tales when I look at these stones?* Ico pressed a hand to his chest, lightly squeezing the fabric against his skin.

While Ico stood in a daze, the priest made his way to the wall and looked up at one of the sarcophagi.

"There," he said, pointing to one that looked no different from the hundreds of others save one thing: it glowed with a pale blue light, pulsating like a beating heart.

As the priest intertwined his fingers and began chanting a prayer reserved for this occasion alone, the stone sarcophagus slid forward on its base, emerging from the wall with the heavy grating of stone upon stone. The guards took a half step back, the horns on their helmets colliding as they did, sending a ringing sound through the hall.

The lid of the sarcophagus slowly opened.

"Bring the Sacrifice," the priest ordered. The two guards stiffened and exchanged glances. Even without seeing their faces, it was clear neither of them dared to do their next task.

"You." The priest indicated the guard with upturned horns. "Bring him."

The chain-mailed shoulders of the other guard slumped with relief as his companion turned to walk toward Ico, dragging his feet as he went.

Ico considered his handlers as the guard approached. These men had been chosen to protect the Sacrifice, a deed of tremendous honor. They were sure to be commended upon their return to the capital. Even before they received this duty, temple guards enjoyed privileges as guardians of the faith. They were the sanctified warriors of the Sun God, the defenders of souls. They were also men of authority—regardless of whether that authority came not from them but from the priests behind them—who wielded power over other officials of the church and capital. They had undergone harsh training to earn their rank. Both their loyalty to the realm and their faith in the Creator who forged heaven and earth and bestowed souls on mankind were infallible.

And yet, as children of men and fathers in their own right, it was no easy task to offer up the healthy, innocent boy standing before them to an unknown fate.

The priest had lectured them before they left the capital. "The Castle in the Mist does not demand that we be heartless. The compassion you will feel toward the Sacrifice and the sadness you will feel upon leaving him are all necessary to the success of the ritual. The castle will not be satisfied with just the Sacrifice. We must also offer up the pain in our hearts for it to be sated."

It was all right to be sad. It was all right to lament. It was all right to feel anger.

But it was not all right to run away. The castle must have its due.

The priest walked over to the Sacrifice and laid a hand upon his shoulder. The horned boy looked up at him, though it was clear from his expression that the boy's mind was in another place.

The priest knew that the guard had a child of his own—a boy roughly the same age as the Sacrifice. He knew the pain that man had felt on their journey whenever he saw the irons on the Sacrifice's hands. How could he help but imagine, *What if it were my son?*

But if they did not offer the Sacrifice, the anger of the castle would not abate. And should the castle's fury be unleashed, there would be no future for the world of men.

Though our Creator is good, thought the priest, *our Creator is not omnipotent. The enemy of our Creator is the enemy of peace upon this world—in league with evil, maker of a pact with the underworld. So men must shed blood and suffer sacrifice, and be allies to god, that evil might be driven back. What else can we do?*

Forgive me, the priest whispered deep in his heart.

"Take my hand," the guard said at last, extending his arm toward Ico, thankful for the faceplate that hid his tears.

The guard lifted him lightly off the floor. With heavy steps, he carried him toward the stone sarcophagus that sat pulsing with light, growling…hungry.

[2]

"DO NOT BE angry with us. This is for the good of the village," the priest said as he closed the lid. It was the first thing he had said to Ico since their journey began, and it was also the last.

There was no apology in his words, no plea. The voice behind that veil of cloth was even and cold.

The good of the village…

For the first time, he felt angry. *This isn't just for Toksa,* Ico thought to himself, recalling the stone city he had seen from the mountain pass. It wasn't fair to blame the entire custom of the Sacrifice on the village. It wasn't their fault.

The interior of the sarcophagus was spacious. Seated, his head wouldn't even have touched the top, but his hands had been secured in a wooden pillory fastened to the back of the sarcophagus, forcing Ico to stand with his back to the front, bent over like a criminal placed in the village square as a warning to others.

But I haven't done anything wrong…have I?

There was a small window in the door of the sarcophagus, but in order to look out, Ico had to twist his neck around so far that it soon became painful and he had to give up. So he stood, listening to the footsteps of the priest and the guards fade behind him.

A short while later, he felt the reverberations of the moving floor. The priest and guards were leaving.

I'm alone.

Silence returned to the great hall—the silence of the Castle in the Mist. *The silence itself must be the master of the castle,* Ico thought, *so long has it ruled this place.* At least, that was how it seemed to him.

Ico could hear his heart beating—*thud thud.* He took an unsteady breath. For a long while he stood there, alone, just breathing.

Nothing happened.

Am I supposed to stay hunched over like this forever? Am I supposed to starve to death in this sarcophagus? Is that my duty as the Sacrifice?

The image of the elder's face loomed in Ico's mind. He could hear Oneh's voice in his ears. *We will be waiting for you to come home.*

So I'm supposed to go home…but how?

He felt a slight vibration, no more than the quivering of a feather in the wind. The sarcophagus was swaying.

At first, he thought he was imagining it. He hadn't eaten anything since the small meal that morning. *Maybe I'm already starting to tremble with hunger. Maybe I'm getting dizzy.*

But the rocking only grew stronger, and he was forced to admit it wasn't him—the stone sarcophagus around him was shaking.

The sarcophagus shook up, down, and to the sides with increasing violence. Hands bound to the wooden frame, Ico tensed his legs and swallowed against the fear. A low rumble accompanied the growing vibrations, filling his ears. It seemed as though the entire hall around him shook. Even the air keened with the tremors.

Soon, the rocking motion became more than the sarcophagus could withstand, and the wooden frame broke off the back. The mechanism the priest had used to slide Ico's sarcophagus into its cavity worked in reverse, spitting the sarcophagus out. It smashed onto the floor, cracking open the lid and sending Ico flying into the open air. His body rose, the world spun around him, and the next instant he crashed onto the cold stones of the floor. His right horn struck the floor, giving off a hollow *clink*, before everything faded to black.

Rain was falling outside, a downpour.

Ico was climbing a tower so high it made him dizzy. Looking up from the bottom, the top was lost in shadows.

A stone staircase wound around the inside wall of the tower, as ancient and decrepit as the tower itself. The staircase had a rail at about Ico's eye level, with spearlike spikes protruding all along its top.

Thunder rumbled, and Ico flinched. Night had fallen and a storm had blown in, though Ico couldn't be sure when.

Halfway up the tower, Ico ran out of breath. It was cold. A ragged curtain hung in the window ahead of him, flapping in the driving wind of the storm. The frigid air blowing in through the window and the cold stones of the wall chilled Ico to the marrow.

Lightning flashed, bright in Ico's eyes—but in that moment of illumination, he spotted something hanging far above him. One hand pressed cautiously against the wall for support, he peered into the darkness. *What is it?* The dark silhouette resembled a birdcage, but it would hold a bird far larger than any Ico had ever seen. It seemed to be suspended from the ceiling of the tower. Stepping quickly, Ico resumed his climb. In another two or three circles around the tower he would reach the cage.

The closer he came, the more unusual the cage seemed. Though fowl in Toksa were allowed to roam freely, nightingales, said to have the power to ward off evil spirits, and stormfeathers, who sang upon the altar at festival time and were said to augur the future, were often kept in intricately woven cages of long, delicate reeds and young willow branches. It was not uncommon for the beauty of the cage to rival that of the bird's song.

There was nothing elegant about this cage. It seemed to be made of black iron, and it looked immensely heavy. The chain upon which it hung was thicker than Ico's arm, and the spaces between its thick bars were scarcely a hand's breadth apart. Thorns of steel sprouted in a circle from its bottom edge, their function less to prevent whatever was inside from escaping than to discourage rescue.

The cage swayed slowly in the strong wind. Ico ran higher. He was only a few steps from being able to see what was inside when he noticed something dripping from the bottom of the cage. He stopped and pressed up against the railing to get a closer look. *Is that…water?* Drip, drip. Drip. The drops fell steadily to the floor of the tower, leaving dark circles on the stone. *No, not dark*, Ico realized. *Black.* Whatever it was that dripped from the cage, it was blacker than pitch, the color of melted shadow.

Something's in there!

The thick drops reminded Ico of the hunters as they returned to the village, prey lashed across their saddles, blood dripping past the horses' hooves. Something was alive inside the cage, and it was oozing black blood.

Thunder rumbled outside, as if to warn Ico from climbing higher. Still, he continued up. The bottom of the cage was at eye level now. He craned his neck to look inside…and saw nothing. It was empty.

Wait…

Something moved in a shadowed corner of the cage, though it was too dark to make out what.

Is someone in there?

Ico froze as a dark figure lifted its head and faced him. The figure was slender, graceful, like a shadow cast on the night of the full moon. The outlines were hard to make out in the darkness, but the figure was moving, silently. Ico could just discern the arch of a neckline and the curve of a shoulder.

Biting back the scream that rose in his throat, Ico retreated against the wall behind him, feeling the firm stone behind his shoulders and back. He was no longer sure that the figure was looking at him—he couldn't see any mouth or eyes. Yet Ico felt its gaze upon him.

Lightning flashed and thunder roared, limning the silhouette in the cage.

There's someone there. Looking right at me.

With his eyes fixed on the vision in front of him, Ico never noticed the black shadow spreading on the very wall against which he had sought shelter. The shadow formed near his left fingertip and spread quickly, until it was large enough to swallow him whole.

By the time he jerked away from the cold against his back, it was too late. The shadow had begun to emerge from the wall, engulfing Ico like living quicksand. Ico felt himself being pulled backward, sucked in—he flailed, grabbing for anything he might reach, but his hands closed on air. The black shape in the birdcage watched him. At the last moment, he realized that it was the black blood dripping from the cage that had seeped into the tower, climbed the wall, and engulfed him—yet there was nothing he could do about it now.

Ico opened his eyes.

It was a dream. I was only dreaming.

Ico was lying facedown, flat against the floor, arms and legs spread wide. For a while, he was content to lie there. He didn't want to move until he understood at least a little of what had happened to him, or where he was.

I'm still in the castle.

He sat up and looked around, checking himself for injuries and finding none. He stood and tried stretching his legs. He performed a little jump. Nothing hurt; he felt as healthy as he always did.

As he took in his surroundings, he spotted the stone sarcophagus lying like an overturned wheelbarrow a short distance from where he had awoken. Its lid and metal hinges were broken. Ico picked up a piece of the shattered stone. It was rough and cold.

The sarcophagus no longer glowed.

It's dead, Ico thought. The sarcophagus had opened its mouth and swallowed him whole—but Ico had been poison to it. It had spit him out, but not before suffering a lethal dose. What was poison to the sarcophagus might also be poison to the Castle in the Mist. The Mark rippled across his chest and back, though no discernible wind blew in the great hall. As the Mark was his, so too was he the Sacrifice—his horns were proof enough of that. Yet the sarcophagus had broken, failing to hold him.

What does it mean?

The countless stone sarcophagi set in their alcoves were as quiet as they had been when Ico first saw them. All were in their places, save the one that had held him.

Thin light spilled in through a small window. It didn't seem as though much time had passed since he had been knocked out; the rain and thunder had been an invention of his dream. Yet his memory of the black silhouette in the cage was as clear as though he had seen it with his eyes. *Was that the master of the castle? Did the master show himself to frighten me?*

Ico cupped his hands to his mouth. "Hey!" he called out.

The sound reverberated off the far wall of the hall, carrying his voice back to him.

He called out again, "Is anyone there?"

Echoes were his only reply. The priest and the two guards had left. He looked up again at the silent stone sarcophagi surrounding him—Ico thought of the Sacrifices within, turning to dust, becoming part of the Castle in the Mist.

Only Ico was free.

Free to leave. The elder and Oneh were waiting for him back in Toksa.

Closer examination of the walls in the great hall revealed that they were cracked with age. Ladders had been set beside the sarcophagi to provide access to the upper levels of the stone shelves that ringed the room, but these were old and rickety.

Ico ran in circles, hearing the sound of his footfalls on the stones, carried by curiosity, wondering if anyone was there or if someone in one of those sarcophagi might hear him and cry out for help. He even tried climbing some of the ladders. He found no one, but in his wandering he had spotted something at the top of the staircase—what looked like a wooden lever protruding from the wall.

Ico raced up the stairs. It was, indeed, a lever. It looked like it might move up and down. Standing on his tiptoes he could just reach it.

The lever was stiff. It probably hadn't been used for many years. Ico pulled with all his strength. His face turned red. Part of the wooden lever objected to this treatment by breaking off and falling in splinters on his face.

Finally, Ico's strength won out and the lever slid downward. A breath later, he heard a loud sound coming from another part of the hall nearby.

Ico looked down from the handrail of the staircase and found that the large doorway directly beneath had opened—it was a wooden door directly across from the one through which he had entered with the priest and guards. He had tried opening it before, but no amount of tugging and pushing could make it budge. The surface of the door was pitted and scarred, making him think that, if it came to it, he could break it down somehow—but finding a magical lever to open it was far preferable!

Grinning, Ico ran down the steps and through the door, finding himself in another room, narrower than the hall he had left, with several vertical rises in the floor. He wondered what the room was for.

A crackling sound made him stop. He looked up to see that the ceiling here was not quite as high as it had been in the great hall, and torches had been set along the walls. They burned with red flame.

The look of the flickering flames was somehow comforting— it reminded him of the fireplace back home—until a disturbing thought occurred to him.

Who lit *these torches?*

The priest might have lit them on his way out of the castle— but that didn't make any sense. Ico had heard the circular floor descending right after they put him in the sarcophagus. And if they had gone through the wooden door, who had lifted the lever to close it again? *Why light torches here at all?* If the master of the castle had lit them, was it to welcome the new, fresh Sacrifice?

The Castle in the Mist is alive.

Ico shook his head. There was no point in thinking about that; he would only frighten himself. Thankfully, the rise in elevation in the floor wasn't too high for him to climb up. He seemed to have recovered from his fall, and the movements of his hands and feet were quick and strong.

He reached the upper level and found himself at a dead end. Looking up, he saw another level high above him, but he would've had to be able to fly in order to reach it. Then he noticed a thick chain hanging from the ceiling. It looked as though something might once have hung from its end, but years of rust had caused the chain to drop its charge, leaving the links to hang without a purpose.

Ico remembered the iron birdcage in his dream and shivered. He jumped, catching the end of the chain, and began, hand over hand, to climb. He had always been good at climbing ropes, and the links in the chain made it even easier. Once he was close enough to the topmost level of the floor, he used his weight to swing, and when it began to sway, he reached the edge with his feet and landed. *I made it. I can do this.*

A row of square windows were cut into the wall in front of him. He jumped up to one, catching the edge with his hands and pulling himself up to find an even larger room on the other side. *That's more like it.* It was time to find a way out and leave this place for good.

[3]

ICO LEAPT FROM the edge of the window into the next room—and realized too late that the drop on the other side was much longer than he had imagined. Wind whistled in his ears.

Before he could regret his blunder, Ico's feet connected with the stone floor with a *fwoosh*. Years of dust rose around him like white smoke.

He shivered and looked up at the window overhead. He often jumped out of trees and off roofs back in Toksa, but never from so high. Yet he didn't hurt anywhere, and his legs and knees were steady. He knew he was tougher than other children his age—but had he grown even stronger since reaching the castle?

Could it be my Mark?

However strong he was, he was still hungry. And thirsty. *I wonder if there's water around here.* He pricked up his ears and listened, but all he could hear was the crackling of torches high up on the walls.

The room he had entered was very large. He guessed it was about half the size of the sarcophagus room. There were idols here too—not just a pair, but four of them, heads side by side, blocking his path. Light came from an opening just above the idols, indicating that a passage or some kind of room lay beyond them. But he wouldn't be able to move the idols without that strange sword. There seemed to be no other exits.

Directly in front of him was a smooth section of stone, a round dais rising slightly above the surrounding floor. Ico marveled at the incredible height of the walls and ceiling. Although the shape of the room at the floor was square, as the walls rose, they began to curve. As his eyes followed the walls upward, he spotted a spiral staircase winding around the inside wall, climbing toward the ceiling. *This is the place in my dream!* It was the same staircase, with the same spiked railing. And not just similar—identical in every respect.

Ico gasped and looked up again. If this really was the place from his dream, then there should be a cage—and there it was, right near the top, its base dully lit by light from the window.

Ico looked down at his feet and made a realization—the circular dais was a platform for receiving the cage.

A shiver ran down his spine, and goose bumps rose on his arms. The events of his dream ran through his mind. Carefully, he walked up to the edge of the dais. He stopped and looked up again, half expecting to see black blood dripping down from the ceiling. But there was nothing.

Nowhere to go but up.

There were ladders on either side of the room. Ico took the ladder leading to the lowest ring of the spiral staircase. Surprisingly, the rungs seemed to be in good repair, and they held Ico's weight without complaint. Ico scampered up one of the ladders and soon was climbing the stairs. The events of his dream were playing out again, only where once a storm had raged, now sunlight streamed through the windows. After he had gone quite a way up, he saw the same window above him, with the curtain flapping in the wind exactly as it had in his dream.

The farther he climbed, the clearer he could see the cage. Ico's heart began to leap in his chest. *Any moment now I'll see that strange black shape. Then the blood will drip, and it will look up at me, and...*

Ico stopped.

There *was* something in the cage. But it wasn't black; it was white. And not just any white, but a gentle, glowing white, like a firefly flitting along the water's edge at dusk.

It wasn't a shadow, but a person.

"Is somebody there?" Ico approached the handrail and called out toward the cage. "Who are you?"

Behind the bars, the white silhouette moved.

"What are you doing in there?" Ico asked, then hastily added, "Hold on. I'll get you down."

Ico resumed climbing the staircase, feeling his heart dancing in his chest. There was a prisoner in the Castle in the Mist! *Is that person a Sacrifice like me? Why are they in a cage instead of a sarcophagus? I have to get them out!*

As he ran, his mind whirling, he suddenly came to a place where the staircase had collapsed, leaving a large gap. On the far side, the stairs continued up. But even with a running start, he didn't think he could jump across.

Ico looked at the window in the wall to his right. It was higher than the staircase, yet if he jumped, he might be able to grab on to the edge. He couldn't be sure where it led, but he was running out of choices. Heaving himself up, he grasped the edge of the window and stuck his head outside. Ico gaped when he saw that it opened above a wide veranda. He could hear the distant roar of the sea and the faint cries of seabirds.

Out on the veranda, Ico squinted against the bright light. Clean, crisp air filled his lungs. He was up on one of the towers. The sky felt much closer here, as though he could reach up and grab one of the clouds. Nearby rose another of the castle's towers, with causeways connecting the intricate structures below. Everywhere there were windows, but no life stirred behind them. Cliffs towered in the distance, and far below, the sea crashed against the island. But nowhere could he look that was not shrouded in mist.

I'm really here.

A strong wind blew. Ico circled the veranda and climbed back in through a window a little farther around the circumference of the tower. Even inside, the wind whistled in his ears. But Ico was not afraid—to the contrary, the air encouraged him. Smelling the sea on the wind and seeing the bright sky above meant he was not stuck here, unable to move. The natural world around the castle was alive and thriving. If he could just find the way out, he would be back in that world.

A little farther up the staircase, he came to a true dead end. The railing blocked off two sides, and there was a wooden door on the right. The door was the same shape as the one Ico had gone through when he left the great hall, only slightly larger. Next to the door he saw a lever similar to the one he had found in the hall, only this one was set in the floor. It offered no resistance as he pulled it. He thought that it might open the door, but he was wrong. Instead, behind him, the cage moved.

With a loud squeal, the chain holding the cage began to play out from a winch against the ceiling, and the cage began to descend toward the base of the tower. Ico went up to the railing to look down after the cage. It descended farther and farther, until he was practically looking down at its top. Inside he could see the white figure lying on the floor of the cage.

He was just thinking he was right about the round dais being a platform for the cage to rest on, when the chains let out another squeal, and the cage stopped its downward motion. The sudden halt made the cage rock from side to side. It hadn't yet reached the platform—it had stopped midway.

Ico tried the lever again, but nothing happened. He thought that the cage might have caught on something along the way, but it was too far down for him to see clearly from where he stood. Ico darted down the stairs, wiping the sweat from his brow as he ran. His throat ached with thirst.

The cage had stopped with its base hanging roughly at the height of the heads of the four idols. Ico reached the bottom of the staircase, where he could look directly inside the cage. The white figure stood at its center. It was a woman.

Her body was slender, with an elegant curve to her neck, and she wore a strange white dress that came down to her knees. She was looking down at her feet, and though she must have noticed Ico by now, she did not look at him. Ico went to call out to her again, but stopped himself. He didn't know what to say. She hadn't answered him before. Perhaps she couldn't hear him at all.

He had a bigger problem, though. How could he lower the cage the rest of the way to the floor?

Ico caught his breath and pondered. He could feel the sweat drying on his skin. *If I could only get a closer look at that cage.* A narrow ledge ran around the edge of the room, and it looked like it might lead him just above the place where the light was peeking through over the heads of the idols. The ledge widened there, protruding almost like an awning. He would have a clear view of the cage.

Ico scrambled down the ladder and ran to its twin on the other side of the room. He climbed it and began running across the ledge, never taking his eyes from the girl inside the cage. She stood motionless. For a moment he wondered if that glowing white form wasn't human after all, but some kind of spirit given shape.

He recalled the forest sprites Oneh had told him about in stories. They were kind, gentle creatures who loved all life in the woods, and even protected those people who lived off the bounty of the forest. When they found a lost traveler or wounded hunter, they would appear in the form of a young girl to help them.

Ico paused when he reached the wall above the four idols. The woman inside the cage had her back to him, and she still wasn't moving. From here there could be no doubt that she would be able to hear him if he spoke. *Should I call out to her? Maybe she can force open the cage door.* Ico dismissed the thought as soon as it occurred to him. Her arms were even more slender than his. She could scarcely rattle the bars of that sturdy cage, let alone break them.

Now what?

Ico looked more closely at the chain holding the cage and saw to his surprise that though the links were thick, they were covered with rust. Some even seemed damaged. Maybe the cage wasn't as sturdy as he'd first thought.

Ico knew what he had to do. From the top of the cage, he and the girl might be able to work together, using their combined weight to free her. As long as he avoided the dangerous-looking spikes protruding from the top and bottom edges, it didn't look that difficult.

Ico jumped and landed easily on the roof of the cage, sending it lurching to one side. He had been half right about the chain—though it was damaged, it was far weaker than he had imagined. His added weight was enough to break one of the links, and the cage dropped to the platform below, landing off balance. The shock of the impact knocked Ico from the roof and sent the broken chain rebounding upward to slap against the wall, knocking down a single torch, which fell with a soft sound beside him. It was still burning. He gave it a quick glance before returning his attention to the cage. Still sprawled on the ground, he watched in wonder as the woman in white stepped through the cage's door.

The woman crossed over the threshold of the cage gingerly, like someone wading in the shallows of a stream. Ico's eyes fell on the gentle curve of her leg. She was barefoot, and a white light suffused her skin down to the very tips of her toes.

She looked back around at the cage that had held her, then at the stone walls of the room, and then finally down at Ico. She was definitely a woman, but much younger than he had guessed from a distance. She was more of a girl, really. Still, she stood taller than Ico and looked a bit older.

Her chestnut hair was cropped short, lightly falling across her cheeks. Her eyes were the same color as her hair, and they were fixed on Ico's face. *She must be a spirit,* Ico thought. *A spirit trapped here. No human girl could be this beautiful.*

Her lips moved, and she spoke—but even though the room was quiet, save for the crackling of torches, Ico could not make out her words. Whatever they might have been, he was sure that they were unlike any he had heard before.

She stepped across the floor soundlessly, walking closer, saying something. *She's talking to me.* But Ico couldn't understand.

"Are you…" he began, finally summoning the courage to speak, "are you a Sacrifice too?" Had someone trapped her inside this castle and put her inside that cage? Did they imprison spirits here too? Ico couldn't find the right words for his questions. Instead his mouth moved all by itself, telling her that he was a Sacrifice, that they brought him to the castle because he had horns.

The girl walked up to Ico and knelt gracefully. She extended her hand toward Ico's cheek.

Those pale white fingers. Eyes like jewels. All aglow with the same ethereal light he and Toto had seen rising from the bottom of the pool in the cave.

Ico's eyes went wide as he noticed a cloud of inky black smoke looming behind her.

[4]

WHERE THERE'S SMOKE, there's fire, Ico thought—but the only flames in the room were the flickering torches on the walls. *What's burning?*

The thought was banished a moment later when two thick arms emerged from the swirling smoke behind the girl and scooped her up. The dark form turned and began to move away toward the corner of the room, carrying her upon its shoulder. The girl gave a quick scream, but the smoke did not seem to notice.

It's walking, Ico realized, dumbfounded. Its shape was almost human, but it had no more substance than ink-black smoke, a dark mist. It even had a head, swollen and misshapen—topped with horns, just like Ico's.

That's no smoke—it's a creature, a monster.

The realization hit Ico like a slap in the face, catapulting him to his feet and after the creature.

It moved without sound, gliding quickly across the room like a cloud of mist. Even with its back turned, Ico could still see the glow of the creature's eyes. They were as large as Ico's fists, without pupils or eyelids, gleaming like shooting stars just before they wink out after cutting across the night sky.

The girl hung limp over its shoulder.

Ico noticed something he had not seen before on the stones in the corner of the room—a black disk, as dark as the shadow creature. For a moment, he mistook it for a pool of water, but then it began to move. He realized it, too, was made of the black, shadowy mist. The disk seethed and began to bubble as though it were boiling.

The creature approached the ring and knelt before it. It stuck one of its legs in and began to sink into the swirling pool. With the girl still on its shoulders, its entire body began to dissolve into the floor.

Within the space of a few breaths, the creature had sunk down to its waist, everything else disappearing beneath the ring of inky blackness. The girl reached out with both hands, trying to grab on to the edge of the pool. It was dragging her down, taking her under. The girl shook her head, shaking loose her fine chestnut hair, and clutched at the ground with all of the strength in her two slender arms. But the force of the pool was greater—she'd never be able to escape on her own.

Ico ran so fast he nearly fell forward, reaching out for the girl. In his shock and fear, he had no voice. He grabbed for the girl's wrist and pulled with all his might. The pool of darkness pulled back, until Ico feared he might wrench the girl's arm from its socket. His own shoulder made a cracking noise with the effort, and his sandals slipped on the stone floor. Ico tumbled to the ground.

The fall brought his other hand close enough for the girl to reach, and soon he had both hands on her wrists. Getting his feet back under him, Ico pulled with his legs to drag her from the swirling darkness.

At last, the tips of her bare feet left the edge of the darkness and she collapsed on the floor. Ico loosened the grip on her wrists, then fell to his knees on the stones, panting for breath.

The girl was breathing raggedly, as though she had been drowning. Behind her, the black pool was beginning to churn.

"What was that creature?" he asked, his mind racing. He had to get her away from the pool. They needed to run from this place. "Why are they after you?"

The girl lay on the floor, gasping for breath. Ico felt his own heart rise in his throat, choking him. He put a hand on his chest, touching the Mark. *I need to stay calm.* He took a deep breath, but before he could even exhale, the girl disappeared behind a swirling veil of darkness.

Ico gaped. It was another of the dark creatures dragging her off, this time toward the far corner of the room where he spotted another pool whirling. Waiting.

This time, Ico's anger rose quicker than his fear, and he ran at the creature swinging his fists wildly at its back—but all he touched was air. No matter how hard he swung, it was like trying to punch a cloud.

Staggering and occasionally falling to her knees, the girl was being dragged away. No matter how much Ico punched and kicked or threw himself at the creature, it didn't seem to feel a thing. The outline of the smoke would shift slightly wherever his limbs connected with it, but no more.

How can I get this thing?

Ico whirled around so fast it made his neck hurt. The girl was farther away now, closer to the dark pool. Worse, there was more than just the one black creature in the room. They were everywhere—pairs of eyes, glowing with a dull white light. Some lingered near Ico, others followed after the girl, joining the one that held her. When he tried to run after her, two of them came and blocked his path.

I can't hit them, I can't kick them—I need a weapon.

The crackling sound of the burning torches reached his ears, and he had the answer. *Fire. What better to drive back the darkness?*

The torch still lay next to the fallen cage, sputtering. Ico made a beeline for the torch, picking it up in both hands and turning to charge at the creatures.

With Ico's first swing, the tiny flame at the tip of the torch went out—his torch had become a club.

But his next swing cut across the waist of one of the creatures, and its outline lost its form, coiling through the air as loose smoke. The thick blackness vanished before him, leaving only two eerie eyes floating in space, surrounded by a small wisp of smoke.

Courage swelled in Ico's chest. He swung the club back and forth, making for the girl. Already she was being dragged into the swirling pool at the far side of the room, the black arms of one of the creatures coiled around her waist.

Swoosh, swoosh! Ico could feel the wind as he swung his club, breaking apart the smoky mist. Finally, he reached the girl. He swung his club at the neck of the creature holding her, and the smoke swirled. The creature's eyes moved, the right drifting from the left, and the line of its shoulders dissipated.

"Grab on!"

Ico thrust out his left hand, shouting to the girl. She had already sunk to her knees.

For the space of a breath, barely long enough to blink, she hesitated. Her eyes focused on Ico's, questioning, trying to peer into the bottom of his soul. Where her gaze fell on him, he felt cool, as though clear water washed over him. Ico gasped with the sensation.

She thrust out her arm and grabbed his hand.

Their fingers met, then their palms, and it felt like a current passed between their hands, pure and warm. It reminded Ico of the southerly wind prized by the hunters of Toksa Village that blew down from the mountains, guaranteeing a good hunt. It was a gentle wind, full of fond memories and happiness. Full of safety. It enveloped him in an instant, and the room shifted around him.

Ico was sitting on the same stone floor, looking up at the same stone walls, the same high ceiling. Torches flickered in sconces.

The thorny iron cage sat resting on the round dais. It wasn't broken, it wasn't leaning. It stood empty, and the door was shut.

Beside the cage stood an old man. He was leaning on a staff and wore heavy-looking robes woven of silvery thread. An intricately carved jewel adorned the top of his staff. Ico recognized it instantly. It was a celestial sphere—a globelike ball that showed the positions of the moon and stars, used by astrologers to divine the will of the heavens.

The old man's hair was long, as was his beard. Both were pure white. He shook his head slightly, and Ico caught a glimpse of his face. His bushy eyebrows grew so long they threatened to cover his eyes, but still they could not hide his sorrow.

"This is no way to use the knowledge of the ancients," the old man muttered, indicating the cage with the tip of his staff. "Our master has lost the way. There is no destination to our path. It leads only to darkness."

Ico looked around again. It was the same room—but there was no dust on the floor. Nor were the stones in the wall chipped or cracked. The cage shone brightly, like new-forged steel.

"This is a mistake, a dire mistake," the old man said, his voice like a groan. "This castle walks toward destruction."

Ico gasped for breath. It was as though he had been underwater for a very long time and only barely made it to the surface. Like his heart had sunk into a different place for a single, long moment, and only now returned.

His sight came back. The girl was in front of him, their fingers intertwined. He felt the wooden stick gripped firmly in his other hand.

At his feet, a pool of black smoke swirled on the ground. A pair of eyes rose out of the pool, followed by that familiar black shape.

They come from the pools.

Moving quickly, Ico smacked at the head of the newly formed creature with his stick. Still holding the girl's hand, he spun around and struck another of the creatures looming behind them. It dissipated, leaving only its eyes floating in the air. As he watched, the smoke began to coalesce around the eyes again, forming a new creature where the old one had stood. All this had taken place in only a few moments, yet more creatures had already formed out of the pool in the corner.

We have to run. Ico looked up, but the four idols still stood, blocking their exit. The window through which he had first entered the chamber was too high for him to reach, and there was no way to climb up. Neither of the two ladders in the room was tall enough, assuming he could even tear them from their moorings on the wall without breaking them.

In a panic, he swung his stick, letting go of the girl's hand as he did. She lifted her eyes the moment he let her go and began to walk slowly toward the four idols. The creatures advanced.

Ico hurriedly ran to the girl, nearly losing a sandal as he did. The girl looked at Ico only briefly before returning her gaze to the idols. Still moving unsteadily toward the idols, she muttered something in words he could not understand.

Again, Ico took the girl's hand. This time, he could feel *her* pulling *him.* She wanted to go toward the idols. "It's a dead end!" Ico shouted, yanking her back. She shook her head as though annoyed and pulled against him. Her eyes were fixed on the idols, and her expression said *I must go.*

It only took that moment's distraction for the creatures to surround Ico. Ico put his back to the girl and swung his club in wide circles. The girl moved slowly yet smoothly. She avoided the stick when it came too close, and when Ico, breathless from the effort of driving the creatures off, lowered his guard, she extended her long, slender arm and pointed toward the idols. *I know, I know. The idols!* Ico grabbed the girl's hand and began to run. The girl's hair and the shawl over her white dress fluttered in the wind.

They crossed the room, passing by the fallen cage. The girl's pace quickened, and she ran ahead of him—a forest spirit leading a hunter to safety. The four idols loomed before them.

Suddenly, a brilliant flash of white light cut through the air. The girl stopped as though she had collided with an unseen wall and took a step back. Ico flinched and stopped beside her.

The white light was coming from the idols, just as it had when the guard brandished that strange sword. The girl held up one hand as though to shield her face. Ico spotted another of the black creatures, arms outstretched, flanking her. But the moment the creature entered the light, it disappeared like a gust of wind blows away smoke, leaving no trace. Not even a pair of glowing eyes. The light leapt from idol to idol, coming together at a single point where it seemed to draw a quick pattern in the air before disappearing altogether.

With a low rumble, the idols began to move. Like marching soldiers changing formation in mid stride, the outer two idols moved forward, making way for the remaining two to slide to either side, opening the way for Ico and the girl.

Gaping, Ico looked around the room. The boiling pools of smoke on the floor were evaporating, and soon they had vanished entirely. Where they had been, the stone floor looked no different than it had before the creatures appeared.

The girl lowered her hand slowly. She seemed neither surprised nor the least bit frightened. Her shoulders relaxed, and her arms hung loosely at her sides.

They're gone.

With a dry throat, Ico swallowed and put a hand to his chest to still the pounding of his heart. *She got rid of them. She even opened the door.*

The girl stood motionless, looking down at the floor. Ico walked up to her, stepping quietly—though he could not say why he felt the need to do so.

"How did you do that?"

The girl turned, looking at his feet, but she said nothing.

"Oh, that's right. You don't understand me. I mean, you don't speak my language. Er, sorry."

The girl blinked. Her long eyelashes fluttered.

"Look," Ico said, "we need to get out of here before those creatures come back. Come with me, okay? Let's find the way out."

Ico realized he was still holding the stick in his hand. It wasn't exactly what he pictured when he thought of a weapon, but it had done an admirable job of holding the shadows back. He decided he'd better hang on to it. He steadied his grip on the stick and held out his left hand, brushing the girl's sleeve. He tried looking at her face, but she would not meet his gaze. She just looked at his outstretched hand, and for a moment, she did not move.

At last, she made her decision and grabbed Ico's hand tightly.

Her hand was soft in his, with long slender fingers and delicate nails like the newly bloomed petals of a flower. Again, a sensation like a gentle wind passed from her hand to his. Ico recalled diving headfirst into cold pools of water on a hot day in the middle of summer. In an instant, the day's dirt and grime were washed away, making him feel clean down to the bone.

The energy flowing into his body felt so good that for a moment, Ico closed his eyes. He wasn't tired anymore. His hunger melted away. He felt no thirst. Even the pain in his leg from the fall off the top of the cage faded away.

Again, a vision came as his eyes were closed—something that had once been, but was no more.

The four idols—the ones the girl had moved a moment before—were lined up in two rows. Before them knelt a figure in flowing black robes and a long black veil, back turned to them, praying.

The figure was bent over so low that it was hard to make out any details, but Ico decided it was a woman. For a moment, he thought she might be holding something in her hands, but he decided that it was only her intertwined fingers.

Quite suddenly, a brilliant flash like lightning shot from the woman's chest, striking each of the four idols. The idols began to move, lining up to block the entrance to the room, just as they had been when Ico first saw them.

When the idols came to rest, the kneeling figure stood. The veil shifted on her face—or perhaps she had moved it with her hand. Ico glimpsed a white cheek and hair bound up in an elaborate braid. *It is a woman.*

The vision faded. Ico opened his eyes.

Still holding his hand, the girl stood staring ahead of them. *I wonder if she saw it too.*

Ico thought back to the old man he had seen when he first held the girl's hand. He had not prayed quietly like the woman in black; he had been angry. Maybe the celestial sphere on his staff was supposed to suggest that he was some sort of scholar. *Probably a very great scholar,* Ico thought. The elder had books with drawings of the heavens in them, but even he didn't have a device like that.

So who was the woman in black? Had she been praying to breathe life into the idols, or for something else? *Maybe,* Ico thought with a sudden realization, *she was casting a spell ward. Maybe all those idols were meant to seal off the doors and imprison something. No ordinary person could make things move like that. Was she a witch?*

Witches were commonplace in the fairy tales Ico had heard growing up. They were followers of darkness, servants of the evil gods who fought against the Creator. Witches were fallen human women, and while they resembled people in appearance, their hearts were filled with dark curses chanted by evil gods. Wherever they went, darkness followed, even by the light of day.

Was there a being like that in the Castle in the Mist? Was the master of the castle a witch?

Ico shook his head. Thinking about it was getting him nowhere. He didn't even know what these visions were, or why he was seeing them. He only knew that it happened whenever he took the girl's hand.

Ico glanced at her. She did not look sad or even frightened. Nor did she smile or seem engaged with the world around her at all. Though she was right next to him, and he could look directly into her face, he felt like she was standing on the other side of a veil of mist.

Who is she, for that matter?

She could open the doors magicked shut by the woman in black. She carried within her the same power held by that blade.

Ico pulled lightly on her hand. She looked in his direction—or rather, she turned her face toward him, but her eyes did not see him.

I know she's taller than I am, probably a little older...and nothing else. He tried staring into her chestnut eyes, tried to see if some secret might be hiding there beneath her eyelashes, but it was in vain.

His eyes went to the shawl she wore over her shoulders. What if her shawl had the same power against the castle that his Mark seemed to have? She didn't have horns on her head, but she had been kept in a cage. He was sure she was another kind of sacrifice. Just like the elder and Oneh worried for him, someone worried for her, and they had given her the shawl as protection so that she might one day return to them.

"Let's go," Ico said brightly. Whoever the girl was, it was better being two than one.

[5]

THE ROOM BEYOND the idols was smaller and again split into two levels. Ico wondered why the castle had been built in such an inconvenient way. It seemed like there were different levels of floor everywhere, making it impossible to walk straight through.

The rise in this room was very high, but Ico jumped with his arms outstretched and caught the edge. Left behind, the girl wobbled unsteadily on her feet, seeming lost. He had only taken his eyes off her for a moment, but when he looked back he saw that she had turned and was walking back toward the room with the cage.

...and the creatures!

"This way!" Ico shouted. He slid his arms over the edge, reaching down toward her. "Grab my hand, I'll pull you up."

He knew she wouldn't understand his words, so he gestured to get his point across. Finally, she reached out to him and grabbed his hands. Ico braced himself to pull her up—and was astonished.

She's so light!

This was nothing like when he had struggled to pull her out of the swirling black mist. Even though all of her weight was in his arms, she was barely heavier than the basket he used to carry firewood back home. Ico stared at her white skin and the light that seemed to suffuse her.

She is a spirit!

But then he saw the shawl on her shoulders rising and falling.

A spirit that breathes. And has fingers and toes. And hair.

Ico realized he was staring at the girl and blushed. She didn't seem to notice.

"I think we can get outside from here." From this higher level, he could see an arched exit leading from the room through which bright sunlight spilled. "Come on. This way!"

Ico waved his arm, urging her forward. He ran out through the arch, and then stopped and stood in amazement.

They were at the end of a long, straight bridge of stone. The far side was so distant he could barely make it out.

He could hear the sea from here. There was a parapet of stacked stones, and he leaned out over it, feeling dizzy, like he had when he looked down from the tower that held the cage. The blue sea stretched out beneath him. Clouds drifted overhead, and he could hear the cries of seabirds coming from all directions.

The wind whistled in his ears. The Mark fluttered on his chest.

At one corner of the bridge parapet stood a statue. Ico walked closer and looked up at it, entranced, forgetting for a moment the girl behind him. It was a statue of a knight. He wore a breastplate, and his legs were also armored, though most of his body was covered by a long cloak that wrapped around in front. His head was covered by a helmet, shaped just like the ones the guards had worn, complete with horns. His were upturned, and the one on the right had broken off.

The statue of the knight faced toward them, away from the bridge, with his arms hidden beneath his cloak. This was not a statue of someone in battle. He seemed almost too pensive to be a proper knight. The statue was weathered and pitted from long years of exposure to the elements, and though the lines of the face had long since worn away, Ico did not think he looked particularly stern or grand as one might expect a great warrior to look.

Maybe the statue had been made to commemorate someone who served the castle? He had heard that there were many such statues in the capital erected to honor former city guards, or those who had won great battles in defense of their country. Those stony men sat astride horses, brandishing their whips or swords, giving orders to their troops, a perfect picture of the day when their loyalty and bravery had shone most brightly.

But this knight looked like he was just thinking. *Strange.*

Ico stood on the low stone wall behind the statue to get a better look. The wall went up to about Ico's waist, and it was narrow. He tried not to look down at the sea far below him on the other side.

Getting his balance, he turned to face the statue.

Seen in profile, the knight did not lose his thoughtful expression. Ico noticed tiny spots on a part of his cape. Drops of blood? No, maybe they were just stains from the rain.

He guessed that the statue was incredibly old. Maybe even as old as the Castle in the Mist. He wondered when the horn on the knight's helmet had broken. The break was smooth and clean.

Ico's eyes went wide. From his new vantage point it was perfectly clear: the horns weren't *on* his helmet, they were growing out of his head. Though the helmet resembled those of the temple guards, this knight's helmet was a little wider at the nape of his neck, forming a bowl over his head. Small slots had been cut out over the ears for his horns to fit through.

He's a Sacrifice, just like me. But how could a Sacrifice be a knight? What did it mean?

In his distraction, Ico nearly lost his footing and fell from the parapet. The sea filled his vision. With a yelp, he waved his arms and managed to tip himself so that he fell back on the stones at the statue's feet.

He heard the sound of a nearby gasp. It was the girl, standing next to the arched doorway. She had her hands to her mouth, looking frightened.

"Oh, hey, sorry about that! I wasn't going to fall over the edge, really!"

Ico smiled at the girl. Slowly, her hands dropped back to her sides. Then she walked up to him and stood beside him, looking up at the statue. It was the first time he had ever seen her look directly at anything.

A strong sea wind caught her hair, sending it dancing along with her long eyelashes. She blinked a few times, but her gaze never left the statue of the knight.

"I wonder if they put him in a sarcophagus like the one they put me in," Ico said softly. "But he looks so old—maybe a long time ago they didn't do sacrifices, and he was just a knight who served here at the castle."

The girl's lips moved slightly. At first, Ico thought it was the wind, but then he realized she was whispering something. It sounded like—a name. Like something she remembered from a distant past, saying it just to see if it sounded right.

"You know who this was?"

The girl didn't answer. Ico took the girl's hand, half expecting and half fearing the vision he knew would come.

For a moment, Ico thought nothing had changed. Then the statue of the knight moved.

It turned its head, looking in Ico's direction. He felt a thoughtful gaze regarding him from the two holes in the knight's faceplate.

The pieces of the knight's armor clanked against each other as he stepped down from the stone parapet. A gust of wind caught his cape as he stood next to Ico, making it flutter.

Ico could say nothing; he simply stood there looking up at the knight. He felt no fear or danger. Even his surprise faded after a moment, carried away by the wind.

Something rose in his chest, a feeling of intense familiarity, like an old memory from childhood. *Why would the knight look familiar? Is it because of his horns?*

The knight extended an arm and the cloak dropped away, revealing a silken shirt beneath his armor. Small clumps of dirt fell from the sleeve.

Ico suddenly realized that the knight was not a statue. He had not been carved from stone. This was once a man, a man with blood flowing through his veins. Just as some evil power had turned the walled city beyond the Forbidden Mountains to stone, so it had turned this man into a statue.

The statue laid a hand on Ico's right shoulder. His grip was firm, but gentle. Much to Ico's surprise, it even felt warm.

There was a gentle light in the knight's eyes as he looked into Ico's. Although his helmet covered his entire face down to the chin, Ico was sure he smiled. *He looks just like the elder, whenever he was teaching me something. "Listen well, Ico, and you will learn."*

No, it wasn't just that. There was something else. It felt like— it felt like his father was looking at him. *But I don't even know my father*, Ico thought. *How could someone look like him—someone whose face I can't even see?*

Then he heard the knight speak.

My son.

The words sounded in Ico's head. His ears heard nothing.

Forgive my mistake, child—all my children who must endure this trial.

The knight's hand left Ico's shoulder. His head turned, looking up at the tower from which Ico and the girl had escaped, then back at the long stone bridge across the sea, and finally out across the waves.

He spoke again in that soundless voice.

Castle in the Mist!

Resentment this strong.

Sin this deep.

Long years of atonement this cruel.

One thousand years of time did not erase my sentence.

Barren years spent imprisoned here.

Even now it tortures my body, binding me to this place.

But, my son.

The statue looked back at Ico.

I knew love here as well.

Then the knight turned calmly, sweeping his cloak behind him as he walked toward the stone bridge. With each step his steel boots made a heavy sound on the stone, and his cloak whipped in the wind behind him.

The knight crossed the bridge, walking toward the white mist.

Ico found his voice. "Wait!"

He ran, still holding the girl's hand in his own. He ran wildly. His leather sandals scratched noisily against the ancient stones.

He dashed forward with such speed that the barefoot girl nearly fell as he pulled her along.

"Wait! Please, wait! Who are you? Are you my—"

The knight disappeared into the mist.

Suddenly, Ico felt a great rumbling beneath his feet. The bridge swayed, and Ico nearly fell. He flailed his arms, losing hold of both his stick and the girl's hand. Beneath them, the bridge cracked, crumbling away. Ico leapt through the air, only just landing on the far side of the break.

He heard a shout behind him—the girl was teetering over the widening crack in the bridge. She flailed her arms and legs, desperate to catch hold of anything that might support her, but she could not reach the edge. She fell, plummeting downward along with fragments of broken stone, her dress and shawl whipping wildly in the wind.

Ico lunged, barely catching her hand. The girl swayed, her legs tracing an arc through the air that almost reached the underside of the bridge. The momentum of his lunge nearly sent Ico skidding off the bridge himself. He tried to find purchase on the stones with the tips of his sandals and used his free hand to grab hold of the edge, finally stopping just at the point where his shoulder had cleared the edge.

The girl's eyes were wide with terror, and the wind whipped her hair across her face.

"It's okay, don't panic!" Ico began pulling the girl up. "You won't fall, I've got you."

Careful, careful. The girl's left hand reached the edge of the break, and she grabbed on. Now her head cleared the edge. He pulled her until her shoulders were on top of the bridge again, and she was safe.

With a jump, she was standing atop the bridge. Ico led her a safe distance from the edge before he finally relaxed, taking a moment to lie down. The girl collapsed beside him on the bridge. Her thin shoulders were trembling. She had a terrified look in her eyes, and her breath was as ragged as the wind whipping around them.

"That was close." Ico realized he was dripping with sweat. "Sorry. It was my fault. I shouldn't have run like that."

The girl lowered her eyes and shook her head.

"This castle is pretty old, isn't it?" Ico went on. "There might be other parts that aren't safe. We'd better pay more attention."

The girl took a deep breath and sat up, looking back to the other side of the bridge.

Though the air here was thick with mist, they were close enough to the far side to see it now. More idols. Spell wards. There were two of them this time, fit snugly together, blocking their path.

The knight must have come through here, but he was nowhere to be seen.

Rising to his knees, Ico looked back across the gap in the bridge to where they had stood before. There was the knight on the wall, his back turned to them, wrapped in his cloak.

So that was just another vision. Had he imagined the voice he heard in his head?

The girl stood and smoothed out her dress. Ico looked up at her.

"That statue over there," he said, pointing. She turned to look back at the knight. "He used to be a human, you know. He's not a statue, but a man who was turned to stone. I saw him—"

The girl said nothing. Instead, she lifted her hand, brushing back the hair that fell across her eyes.

"The castle cursed that knight too, just like me. It trapped him here. He's a Sacrifice, like I am. What I can't figure out is, why would such a great knight become a Sacrifice? I thought the castle only took kids."

The image of the knight slowly stepping down from the stone parapet and crossing the bridge filled Ico's mind.

Now that he thought of it, when the knight's cloak had blown behind his back, Ico had seen a breastplate and armored skirt, but he had seen no sword—certainly no weapon befitting a knight in armor such as his.

"You said something when you were standing next to the knight, didn't you? To me it sounded like you were saying a name. Did you know him?"

The girl stood with her back to Ico, silent. *Maybe she can't hear me over the wind.*

My son, the knight had called him. It left a bittersweet echo in Ico's chest that would not go away.

My children who must endure this trial.

Ico didn't know the names or faces of his parents. The elder had explained to him that that too was part of the custom. After his mother and father left the village, there was no way to contact them, nor any reason to do so.

Was that my father? But if his father had been a Sacrifice, how had he lived to such an old age? Had he been born with those horns, he would have been taken to the castle like Ico was and placed in a sarcophagus. *He wouldn't have had the chance to become my father.*

Even now it tortures my body, binding me to this place.

Ico stood with a sigh. He brushed the dirt from his knees, much as the girl had, then picked up the wooden stick from where it lay on the stone bridge. By some miracle, it hadn't been lost when the bridge collapsed.

"No going back that way."

The gap in the bridge was too wide for Ico to jump. The bridge was broken, dead. A part of the castle had perished, just like the stone sarcophagus that had held him when he first arrived.

Maybe this was a part of his Mark's effect on the castle. Having power over his prison gave him hope—but it was also a source of danger, as he was fast learning. *We have to be much more careful from here on.*

"Not that I wanted to go back."

The girl turned to him and to his surprise, she smiled faintly. *She's beautiful.* He thought her smile looked like a flower in full bloom, swaying gently in a forest breeze, sending its petals out to drift on the wind. He could almost smell the flower's perfume on her breath.

Holding hands, they crossed the remainder of the ancient bridge. The two stone idols and the mysteries they held behind their expressionless faces awaited them.

[6]

LIGHTNING FLASHED THROUGH the air once more, and the stone idols slid to either side. Ico noticed the girl blinking in the light. She looked almost frightened. *She doesn't know why the idols move any more than I do.*

"Does that hurt?"

A blank stare.

She has no idea what I'm saying.

In this room was a small wooden door and a staircase running around the inside of the room, winding up the walls. They were high enough already. Ico wanted to avoid going any higher if he could. *We have to go down whenever we can if we're ever going to get out.*

Thankfully, the door opened easily.

"You wait here. I'm going to go see if it's safe."

Through the door, Ico found only disappointment. He was standing on a small balcony overlooking a gaping chasm. A similar balcony protruded from the far side. It looked like a bridge had once spanned the gap here, but nothing remained of it now. He looked down and immediately felt dizzy.

Far, far below he could see the green of trees and a bit of white where some dry land was exposed. Maybe a courtyard? From his vantage point on the balcony, it looked like he could go into the tower on the far side, but there was no way to get down there from this height.

Guess we'll be going up the stairs for now. Crestfallen, he turned to go back through the door when he heard the girl scream.

Ico ran, then froze when he returned to the room. The shadow creatures were back, circling the girl like vultures around a kill. A swirling pool had opened in one corner of the small room.

The blood rose to Ico's head and he charged the creatures, swinging his stick. There were several of the larger ones with horns growing out of their heads, just like the ones that had attacked them in the room with the cage. They danced eerily, avoiding his attacks, swarming around the girl with eyes that glowed a dull white. But Ico wasn't afraid of them anymore. *I don't care what they are. I'll send them back where they came from, no matter how many of them rear their ugly horns!*

"Take that, and that, and that!"

It felt good, slashing the air with his stick, dashing them to nothing. But the pool was still seething in the corner. Several pairs of glowing white eyes flitted around the room, shadowy forms slowly coalescing around them.

The girl screamed again, and when Ico looked, he saw another shadow creature, this time with wings like a bird, grabbing the collar of her dress and trying to fly away with her. Ico's hair stood on end. *What, they can fly too?* The girl flailed wildly as the thing carried her toward the top of the staircase.

Ico ran up the stairs, a pair of eyes brushing by his head.

—*Stop, do not do this.*

Ico gripped his stick tightly, his knuckles white. Were the creatures talking?

—*You are one of us. Why do you thwart us? Why do you not show us kindness?*

It was not a single voice, but a chorus, pleading, demanding, admonishing.

He was sure of it now. The creatures were talking to them even as they circled through the room, flying about, spinning around him.

—*You are one of us.*

"You're wrong!" Ico shouted, swinging his stick. One of the creatures in front of him shifted to one side, leaning over him, peering down.

—You are just like us. We are Sacrifices too.

—Your horns, your Mark.

—We gave our lives to the stones. While our bodies decayed, our souls stayed in the cursed castle. We have lived eternal unlives in the cold and the dust.

—We are bound to the Castle in the Mist as we bind the castle together.

—Do not try to stop us.

Chest heaving, Ico steadied his club, but his hands were trembling too much for him to aim properly. The winged creature had disappeared with the girl.

—Little Sacrifice, gifted child protected by the Mark. Do not stop us. Please. Show kindness.

"No way…" Ico whispered, clenching his jaw to stop his teeth from chattering. "You're lying!" he shouted. "I'm not like you!"

Ico shouted until he was out of breath, then ran up the rest of the staircase. At the top, he saw another black pool boiling in the middle of a narrow landing. The girl was sinking into it, already chin-deep in the darkness.

Tossing his stick aside, Ico dove to the ground and thrust his hands up to his elbows into the pool. He grabbed the girl's slender shoulders. The girl's eyes were dark, reflecting the blackness beneath them, and her glowing white body was already merging with the swirling shadow. Even still, when she noticed Ico trying to pull her out, a light of hope came into her eyes, and she glowed slightly, like an ember.

"Hang on, just a little more!"

Ico had managed to free the girl's upper body from the swirling pool when something pushed him from behind, sending him tumbling across the pool. He rolled heels over head and onto his back. He looked around to see one of the creatures hovering directly above the girl. Her mouth was half open in a soundless scream, looking up at the smoke that filled her vision. She stared straight into the creature's dully glowing eyes.

The creature peered back at her.

It shook its head, and the girl's body sank further into the pool. She descended slowly but steadily. The creature spread clawed arms—though it looked less like it was threatening her and more like it was pleading with her, its head lowered almost reverently.

With a start, Ico realized that the creature was talking to her. Calling to her, just as the shadows had called to Ico. And she was listening to it.

The girl's chin disappeared beneath the roiling black smoke. Her hands slowly lost their grip on the edge of the stone beyond the pool. The creature nodded and brought its clawed hands together in a gesture of thanks.

It's praying for her.

By now, the black smoke was halfway up the girl's cheeks. Her wide eyes were no longer chestnut colored but as black as the inky darkness around her. The pool was winning her over.

She's giving up!

NO! A different voice sounded in Ico's head, but before he could think of whose it was, a vision filled his senses.

In the vision, he saw the girl sink. Her head vanished beneath the swirling darkness, leaving a last lock of hair swirling in the air before it too disappeared. Then a bright flash of light—like the light that flared whenever the idols parted—erupted from the middle of the boiling pool. Lightning crackled in the air.

The lightning became a ring flying through the air—it struck the creatures, evaporating them in an instant. The black pool disappeared and the still-expanding ring reached Ico.

Ico shielded his eyes from the light, shouting, mouth wide— and then he turned to stone. Just like the people in that walled city. Like the statue standing at the end of the ancient bridge.

NO!

The voice came to him again, an urgent warning.

Then the vision faded, and as Ico was released, he shivered and screamed, charging toward the pool. All he could see of the girl now was her forehead. *She's going to sink!*

He thrust his hands into the pool, his fingers brushing the soft skin of her cheek. He grasped at her, clawing with his fingers and pulling like his life depended on it. Finally, he managed to grab her shawl. The girl flailed out with her arm and it touched his hand.

"No! I'm not letting you go!"

Now the girl's face was above the swirling darkness. She gasped for breath, half drowned. The fear on her face sent a fresh jolt of energy through Ico. *I've got to save her!*

Ico pulled, losing all sense of time, and when the girl was finally out of the pool, he bared his teeth and growled at the creatures around them. Then he wrapped his arms around the limp body of the girl and, picking her up, leapt from the edge of the upper level.

They landed in a heap on the stone floor below, close to the wall. Ico left the girl there for a moment, retrieved his stick and swung it around with such fury that he struck the wall. His arm tingled with the impact. Still he swung, returning the creatures to smoke. He caught one of the winged ones with a downward stroke, beating it into the floor. Ico roared as he rained down blows on the creatures.

When he finally looked up, the black pool on the floor was evaporating. The light went out of the remaining creatures' eyes and they faded. The attack was over.

Out of breath and shivering, Ico noticed a wetness on his cheek. Tears streamed down his face.

Ico let his hand holding the stick drop. The tip of the stick made a light sound as it hit the floor. He looked around and saw the girl sitting on her knees by the wall, her hands covering her face. She intertwined her fingers, touching them to her forehead—the same gesture that the creature had made by the pool at the top of the stairs. She was praying. *Or maybe she's asking for forgiveness.*

It was hard to resume their search for a way out of the castle. But if they stayed here, the creatures might come back. Of course, there was no way of being sure the creatures wouldn't be lying in wait no matter where they went. This was the home territory of the shadows—they weren't wandering around blindly in the castle like Ico was.

Still, they couldn't sit here forever. Even if Ico couldn't escape while it was still light outside, at least he could lead the girl to a lower level.

Ico called out to the girl, saying they should go, but he didn't dare take her hand. He felt as though his heart had shattered into a thousand pieces and his thoughts were chaos. The mysteries of the castle were deep, and the visions he saw when he took the girl's hand might give him answers—but he was afraid. He had the feeling that once he knew, he would be changed forever. He could never go back.

He tried to remember Oneh's face. Toto's cheerful voice.

Why do you show us no mercy?

You are one of us.

The words of the creatures came back to him, driving off his memories of home. What had they meant about being bound to the castle, and binding the castle?

Do not try to stop us.

Why were they trying to take the girl down with them? Was he getting in their way by trying to save the girl? Who was she, anyway?

In the next room stood a wall that topped out on a large terrace beneath a high ceiling supported by square-edged pillars. Ico was more weary of heart than of body, but it still took a great effort to climb the wall. He had to fight back the feeling that he didn't want to go any farther.

At the top, he turned and called to the girl. She stayed back.

"What's wrong? If you don't come up, we'll be stuck here."

He didn't think she was hesitating. She looked like she didn't want to go.

"Is there something up here you're afraid of?" Ico asked. Then something inside him made him continue. "You know your way around this castle, right?" Ico was surprised by his own words. *Why would I think that?*

The girl stood a short distance from the wall that rose in the middle of the room, looking up at Ico. Her bare feet moved across the stone floor and she turned away from him. She began to walk back the way they had come.

"You don't want to get out of here with me? You want to stay here?"

The girl stopped beside the arch leading to the last room.

"Those creatures will come for you again. They're after you. You know that."

Her head drooped, revealing the nape of her neck, and she placed a hand lightly on the side of the archway. Then she passed beneath the arch.

Ico stood alone on the upper terrace, hugging himself with his arms. The sunlight that spilled between the square pillars lit him from the back, making him look much like the statue of the knight on the bridge.

Now something else spoke within him in a tiny whisper. *Don't go.* That was all it took. Ico cupped his hands to his mouth, took a deep breath and shouted, using the call the hunters used to find each other in the forest. "Hueeeeh!"

The girl lingered on the other side of the arch, her flowing dress making her slender white form seem to float over the stones.

Ico leaned over, careful not to lose his balance, and stuck out his hand as far as he could. "Come on. Come with me."

The girl turned and stepped closer. She began to walk toward him on unsteady legs, uncertain until she took Ico's hand. He squeezed and felt her squeeze back—weakly, but it was enough.

Beyond the columns, the roof gave way to open air. This place was wider than a terrace—it seemed like they were atop a tower. In one corner another staircase rose to a small elevated section of the roof—a watchtower maybe, Ico thought.

The sun was bright, and the blue sky seemed close. This was the first place he had come to in the castle where there weren't any shadows from the sun.

"Looks like some kind of observation deck," Ico said to the girl. She squinted against the sunlight as the wind gently ruffled her hair and shawl. The air up here didn't smell of the sea. It smelled like the woods. Here the seabirds were silent.

They went up the staircase to the highest point of the tower, where Ico could see that it formed a semicircle enclosing a beautiful stand of trees below. Shielding his eyes from the sun, he looked around, then crossed over the deck and went down the stairs he had spotted on the far side, where a narrow walkway ran along the side of the building. There, a narrow ladder descended to a small platform, beside which ran a long set of rails. The tower shaded them from the sun, but they were still far above the ground below.

Ico jumped down onto the rails, following them off to his left where he soon found what it was that rode them. At the end of the line sat a small, flattop trolley with a high railing around the sides. He had seen something like it before in the mine just beyond the outskirts of Toksa.

The wheels of the trolley rested evenly on the rails. Ico clambered on top, and the trolley squeaked but did not move. He found a lever and pushed it, and the trolley began to sway back and forth. *So this is how it moves.* Ico felt revitalized. *I can ride this, and if any of those creatures attack, my club will be moving that much faster!*

[7]

"HUEEEEH!"

Ico called out cheerfully to the girl. He worked the lever on the trolley, jumping to get it going faster, enjoying the feel of the wind on his face. The girl was standing at the edge of the stone platform. She turned at the sound of his voice.

Ico waved. "Come on, get on!"

He reached out and grabbed hold of her hand, lifting her onto the trolley. She looked around the trolley with a bit of wonder in her eyes, then stood beside him and held onto the railing with both hands.

"That's right," Ico said. "Hold on tight. Ready? Let's go!"

The trolley started off with a squeak, but once they got going, the wheels rolled effortlessly, as though the cart had never been abandoned at all. They picked up speed, and the girl knelt, still holding onto the slender railing.

Ico smiled and took her hand, keeping a firm grasp on the lever with the other.

"It's okay, it's safe. Doesn't the wind feel great?"

The rails ran along the edge of the building in a straight line. Ico took a deep breath, feeling the air rush over his body and clear away the lingering darkness of the tower. For a moment, he forgot his questions, his doubts, and his fear over what was to come.

Ahead, the rails curved gently to the right. Ico slowed the trolley. Feeling the wind ripple along the Mark on his chest, he turned to the girl with a smile.

She was gone. In her place stood a little girl of only three or four years. She was wearing a white sleeveless dress that went all the way down to her ankles. Instead of a shawl, the dress had a collar embroidered with a pretty flower pattern. The girl's hair was long, and she wore it tied into a single ponytail at the back. It sparkled a bright yellow, like flax.

The girl grabbed hold of the railing of the trolley with her little hands and laughed out loud. The laughter made her chestnut eyes glow a bright amber.

"Faster! Faster!" she called out. "Isn't this fun, Father?"

The world swam past them. Though the girl's laughter still rang in his ears, Ico saw that she was looking at him, speaking to him. Like she knew him. *Or maybe she sees somebody else here, not me.*

Then she was begging him, still in that bright, childlike voice, wanting to know if he would play with her again on his next visit home. If he would give her a ride on the trolley again, to promise that he would.

The trolley sped like the wind, making Ico's tongue feel dry when he opened his mouth to speak.

"Thank you, Father!" the little girl was saying. "Thank you!"

With a start, Ico realized that the little girl was gone, replaced by the girl he had rescued from the cage—still holding his hand, her other hand gripping the metal bar of the railing. The transition between vision and reality had been so seamless it was hard to tell which was which.

They were approaching the curve. Ico applied more pressure to the lever. The trolley swayed in protest, then began to slow, its inertia carrying it smoothly around the bend.

Who was that little girl? Was she a younger version of the girl at his side? Ico felt like he had been dreaming with his eyes open, like he had plunged into someone else's memory—happy memories of a childhood long past.

Thank you, Father!

The rails ran along the edge of a cliff. Beyond, Ico could see only blue sky and the sea below. *I'd better slow down more.*

When he looked up from the lever, Ico noticed more of the shadowy creatures standing along the wall above them, as though they were seeing the trolley off. They were there only an instant, but Ico sensed their glowing white eyes following their passage.

They're not chasing us.

Something about the way the creatures stood there made them look lonely. Or maybe it was just another vision. It was getting harder for Ico to tell.

Farther ahead, the rails came to an end at another platform. Ico carefully let go of the lever. The trolley slowed, its wheels making a loud rattling noise before the cart settled to a stop.

Ico scrambled up onto the platform, sure that the shadow creatures would be waiting, but there was nothing. He saw a passageway with an arched roof leading from the far end of the sun-drenched platform. *At least it's not a dead end.* He took the girl by the hand and helped her off the trolley.

Through the arch, they passed along a narrow corridor, exiting onto a terrace with square pillars. The terrace led to the balcony of another vast hall with a high, peaked ceiling. A latticework of thick beams crossed overhead, supporting a massive chandelier lit with dozens of candles that hung in the middle of the hall.

A bridge crossed to the far side of the hall. Leaving the girl behind for a moment, he walked to the center of the bridge, testing it carefully with each step. He grasped the handrail and looked down. Below, he saw the decayed remains of furniture. Here was a toppled candelabrum, there a large pedestal where a statue of a woman had once stood, the statue itself now lying broken on the floor. The great hall was nearly round, and he could see a pair of double doors leading outside. Both of the doors were open wide, letting sunlight spill in—perhaps from the courtyard. He could see green grass beyond the threshold.

Ico wondered how far down the cart had taken them. They had been traveling quite fast—they might have come a very far way down in the castle indeed.

The thought put Ico at ease. *Maybe if we can get down to those doors, we can get outside.*

The only problem was, there didn't seem to be any way to get from the top of the bridge on the second floor down to the floor of the great hall. What stairs he could see went up toward the ceiling, not down to the floor below, forming a sort of catwalk that seemed without purpose.

Maybe, he thought, *in the distant past, well-appointed ladies and knights would pass back and forth over the walkways and the bridge, waving down to the guests on the floor below in celebration of some great victory in battle. Cheers would rise up from both levels as they welcomed their hero...*

That is, if anyone ever really lived in the Castle in the Mist.

He went a little farther, each creaking step reminding him of the toll the years had taken on the bridge, leaving it cracked and chipped in many places. The far end where it met the other side of the room was the most precarious. There, a crack as long as the distance from Ico's elbow to his wrist and as wide as the palm of his hand had opened in it. He could see through to the floor of the great hall. He stuck his fingers into the crack, sending fragments of stone down to the floor.

Walking carefully back to the girl, Ico shook his head. "This hall is pretty enough, but what a strange design. There's no way to get down to the lower part. We have to find another way."

To Ico's surprise, the girl shook her head.

Did she understand me?

"Maybe if we had a rope..." He shrugged and offered his hand to the girl. She hesitated before taking it.

"I wonder if we can climb down that wall by the edge," Ico said, looking around. Just then, he saw the little girl with the sleeveless dress and flaxen ponytail running down the right side of the room.

The vision again!

A man wearing loose trousers and a gently flowing tunic appeared behind her, striding slowly along the walkway. Before Ico even had time to call out, the little girl tripped on the hem of her dress and fell. She shrieked and pitched forward, catching herself on the stone floor with her hands. She started to cry.

When the girl tripped, the man quickened his pace, stretching out his arms toward her. "I told you not to run like that." He picked up the little girl, lifting her to his shoulders. "What a tomboy you've become, Yorda."

His voice was gentle. Tucking the girl under his left arm, he rubbed her cheek with the other. Drying her tears. A ring on his finger, deeply engraved, caught the light—

Ico pulled his hand away from the girl, shivering and jumping back. He let go so suddenly that she staggered and nearly fell.

"Who—who are you?" Ico demanded. "Every time I grab your

hand, I see things. It's so real. And they're all right here, in the castle. It's like I can see the past playing out before my eyes. Who are you? Did you used to live here?" He said it all in one breath, growing surer with every word that these visions he was seeing were her memories.

"Yorda…that's your name?" Hands clenched into fists, he walked up to her. "It is, isn't it? Your hair was longer when you were little. You used to run down the corridors here and ride in the trolley. Your father was here too…"

The girl shook her head slowly from side to side.

Does she mean she doesn't understand? Or is she saying I'm wrong?

"I don't know what you mean if you just shake your head like that!" Ico blurted out, unable to contain his irritation. Ico's voice echoed off the ceiling. He imagined that the chandelier even swayed a little.

The girl did not answer. Without a sound, she walked out onto the bridge. When she reached the large crack, she stopped and peered down. Then she returned to stand directly beneath the chandelier, lifted one finger and pointed up.

"What? What are you trying to say?" Ico said, keeping his distance. "What is it?"

The girl kept her finger raised.

"What? The chandelier?" Ico asked angrily.

The girl nodded.

"What am I supposed to do with that?"

Ico put both hands on his waist and glared at the girl. She lowered her hand and her shoulders drooped—a little girl who was scolded.

Ico cursed himself for letting his temper get away from him. There was enough to worry about in this castle without making her afraid. He felt his irritation melt away.

"Look, I'm not sure what you're trying to tell me," he began, taking a deep breath. "But if it will make you happy, I'll go check out that chandelier. You come over here, okay? I don't want you standing underneath that thing."

The girl quickly stepped back to the near side of the bridge. Ico walked up the staircase along the wall. There were rows of small windows set in the far side of the hall—if he used the windowsills as handholds, he might be able to climb up to the rafters.

It wasn't as difficult as he had imagined. Soon he had his hands on one of the thick rafters. Pulling himself up carefully, he stood on top. The rafter was slick with dust, but the wood felt sturdy beneath him and was easily wide enough to walk across. Ico's leather sandals left clear marks in the white dust.

He made his way toward the chandelier, then knelt, inspecting the fastenings holding it to the rafter. Several metal brackets held an iron chain that went down to a central post on the chandelier, though about half of them had rusted and split, and the rest were dangerously warped.

Maybe she was telling me it was dangerous to walk on the bridge because the chandelier might fall on our heads? But then he wondered how she had noticed from the ground. *And if it was likely to fall, why was she standing beneath it?*

Ico craned his neck to look down over the side of the chandelier, careful not to let his feet slip. The girl was doing as Ico had told her, standing far to the side, looking up at him with a worried expression on her face. He tried waving to her. She didn't respond. No other helpful gestures or instructions appeared to be forthcoming.

Ico sat down on the rafter, letting his legs hang down off the side. It was cool and dark up here. Away from the girl, he felt himself relax. The thought made him feel guilty. *Why should being away from her make me relax?* But it was the truth.

He felt like he had been running from the moment he escaped that sarcophagus. He hadn't even had a moment to sit down and think, or even just to breathe. It was a welcome break.

Without even realizing it, Ico had been rubbing the Mark on his chest. It calmed him and gave him strength. *I'm getting out of here. I'm going home. Everyone is waiting for me. The doors outside are right down there. I can see them. I just have to figure out a way to get down there, and we'll be walking on the grass, in the sun.*

There would be plenty of time to wonder who the girl was and what the words of the shadow creatures meant once he was safely outside. Maybe the elder would know something. He could just ask.

There was no point in thinking too hard about it now or worrying about the visions he saw whenever he held the girl's hand. Maybe that was just the castle trying to scare him. Maybe it had nothing to do with the girl at all.

Then why was he so sure that it did?

It was as though something dark had lodged itself in his chest, whispering to him incessantly. *It must be those creatures. When I was fighting them, I took a bit of them inside me. Like breathing in smoke from a fire. Now it's stuck in my lungs, and it's painting them black from inside.*

Suddenly a voice rang in Ico's ears.

—*You cannot escape this place.*

—*You must not leave.*

—*You must not take her away.*

—*Return the girl to the cage. She belongs to the castle.*

—*That is why her memories fill this place. That is why they return when you touch her.*

"Quiet, quiet!" Ico shouted, trying to drown out the voices in his head. Then he saw it—something hanging from the carved railing of the bridge beneath the chandelier. And not just one thing, but many. They had legs, swaying in the air.

They were people, hanging down from the railing. Heads up, feet floating in space.

What are they doing?

Ico strained his eyes. Then he understood, and it felt like a blow to his chest. They weren't just hanging—they had been hanged.

Some were knights still clad in light armor. *Maybe guards,* Ico thought. There were women too, wearing dresses like white clerics' robes. Young girls in petticoats with flowers in their hair. Even a farmer, the cuffs of his trousers and shirtsleeves bound tight, so as not to catch as he swung a scythe in his fields, and a hat on his head to shade his face from the sun.

But there was no sunlight here. Their faces were pale and twisted in agony. Black tongues protruded from their mouths, and their fingers were frozen in place, clawing at the ropes around their necks. Where their arms and legs were exposed, they were drenched with blood. He could see it now, dripping.

Ico was struck by a sudden similarity between the hanging crystals on the chandelier and the bodies hanging from the bridge below—a long, macabre chandelier stretching the length of the room. In place of candles, corpses. In place of light, blood, spilling on the floor of the great hall.

Was this another vision?

The corpses swayed from side to side. Beneath the hanging corpse-candles, Ico saw the knight he had met on the ancient bridge. He walked slowly, heading farther into the castle. His pace was unrushed but steady. He passed through the hall without hesitation, turning not so much as a glance at the gory scene above his head. Knights were familiar with death in all its horror. The blood from the corpses dripped onto his single remaining horn and ran off the curve of his helmet. Some even dripped on his forehead, but he did not raise a hand to wipe it away.

Where are you going? Who are you going to meet?

From his vantage point above the chandelier, Ico could see the knight's gaunt cheeks and ashen lips. His cloak swayed with each stride. As with the statue, the knight wore no sword. Still, Ico sensed tremendous courage and determination in the set of his jaw and the dark gleam of his eyes. He was on his way to battle.

"Who are you?" Ico asked out loud. He had meant it to be a challenge, but it came out as little more than a whimper. Then the room shifted and he returned to reality—or perhaps sanity. His body swayed with the abruptness of his return, causing him to shift on the rafter and lose his balance. The rafters swirled around him, and Ico fell flat on his back on top of the chandelier. His arms and legs smashed into the candles, sending flakes of ancient dried wax drifting down below.

Ico twisted, sitting halfway up, his legs splayed across the top of the chandelier. His left leg had knocked over several candles and was sticking out over the edge. *Good thing I didn't lose my sandals*, Ico thought. He tried not to make any sudden movements, focusing only on breathing steadily.

Creak…

Dust fell in streams from the chandelier. The brackets holding it to the rafter were warping.

His fall onto the top of the chandelier had been the last push they needed. The first broke free with a loud pop, and soon all of them started to snap, one after the other, like panicked soldiers falling out of formation.

The chandelier left the rafter and seemed to pause in midair for the briefest of moments, as though it longed to defy gravity just this once and remain where it had stayed for so long.

Ico sat up a moment too late, his hand missing the rafter by an inch. The chandelier made a whistling sound as it fell, and he could feel the wind in his hair. The chandelier fell away from beneath his feet. He felt himself breaking into pieces, his soul escaping his mouth in a wordless scream. Lighter than his body, his soul remained, suspended in the air, while the rest of him plummeted down.

With nothing else to hang on to, Ico grabbed the central pole of the chandelier, the iron chain that had gone up to the rafter whipping uselessly from its top. With an incredible crash, the chandelier fell onto the bridge. It was just wide enough to extend from side to side, the outermost ring of the chandelier falling directly on top of the railings. Candles flew up from the base of the chandelier, arcing over the railing and falling down into the room below. Ico rolled up into a ball in the middle of the chandelier to avoid the spikes that once held the candles. Dust rose in a great cloud. Ico looked up and jumped off to the side with a shout as the iron chain came chasing after the chandelier. The chain coiled like a snake before falling down through the chandelier, pulling itself after.

Dust stung Ico's eyes. Even his mouth tasted of it. Ico stood, wobbling. He saw the girl, still standing at the end of the bridge, hands over her mouth. Her eyes were wide with surprise.

"It's okay—" he started to call out, when a loud noise reached his ears.

Something was cracking. He felt a lurching vibration, and the bridge buckled beneath him. The chandelier pitched forward, sliding down the railing.

Before Ico could react, the far side of the bridge snapped, falling from its perch at the edge of the second level. Apparently, the bridge was just as worn as the brackets securing the chandelier.

With a sound that shook the very ground beneath them, half of the bridge fell to the floor, forming a slide that started on the second floor where the girl stood and ending all the way down by the double doors that led out to the green grass beyond.

Ico rode the chandelier as it slid down the fallen bridge, coursing on top of the railings like a child at play. It quickly gathered speed, flipping when it hit the bottom and sending Ico flying.

This time he fell facedown and landed on his stomach, knocking the wind out of him. Dust filled the great room like mist, and in the silence, he heard the echoing *plink plink* of candles that flew from the chandelier and struck the ground before rolling to a stop.

Ico lay on the floor a long while, checking to make sure he still had his limbs. *I'm still breathing. Nothing's broken. I'm not bleeding.* He waited until he could hear nothing moving around him before getting up. When he did, he saw that the fallen bridge formed a sturdy-looking pathway from the second floor down to where he sat. The chandelier had flipped over and fallen off to one side.

The girl was still standing where she had through the entire ordeal, hands held over her mouth in shock. Ico stood and walked to the slanting bridge to look up at her.

"Hey!" he called out. "It's not pretty, but I think you can walk down that. Come on. Just watch where you step."

Perhaps she was frightened, but the girl did not move. Ico climbed up the incline of the bridge, using his hands to crawl on all fours.

"If you're scared, you can just slide down on your bottom. It's like a slide."

The girl shook her head. She appeared to be smiling. As if to say, *That's hardly something to suggest to a young lady.*

Something touched Ico's heart—gentle and warm—reminding him of a time long past.

"You can just take it a little bit at a time. You won't fall," he said, smiling and glad that she had smiled at him.

In the end, he had to help her down all the way, one eye always on the railing where the bodies in his vision had hung. He wondered if the ropes had left any marks, and it made his stomach turn.

The railing was coated in dust accumulated over the years, plus a fresh layer from the recent collapse. The stone was rough to the touch and hurt his hand.

When he finally reached the bottom with the girl, Ico brushed the dust off himself and straightened out his Mark. He picked up a candle that had fallen by his feet, thinking it might be useful later. Sticking it in his trousers, he looked around for something that might serve as a weapon to replace the extinguished torch he had left up above. Eventually, he settled on the leg of a chair. He picked it up. It was the perfect weight in his hand.

He looked over at the girl to find she had her back turned to him and was looking across the room in the direction the knight had been walking in Ico's vision atop the chandelier. She was looking intently, concern on her face. Like she could sense something tugging at her memory there.

Quietly, Ico gave the girl's shawl a gentle tug. She looked around and their eyes met.

Ico had many questions, many doubts, but the fresh breeze

blowing in through the open double doors and the shining lawn beyond blew them from his mind and beckoned him outside.

Joining hands, they walked through the doors. Ico could feel the softness of the ground and the grass through the leather of his sandals. It gave him hope and filled him with new energy.

Around the wide lawn under the sun was a terrace and a walkway that led to a large arched bridge awaiting them.

[8]

THOUGH THE INTERIOR of the castle was a maze, out here there was nothing to stop them. Maybe it was the distance between his eyes and the sun and sky above that made him feel free. Here, high walls around the garden blocked the wind that howled incessantly in the corridors of the towers and across the high balconies.

They cut straight through the grassy courtyard, passing under a small walking bridge. There was a drawbridge here too, but it didn't take long for Ico to figure out how to lower it, and they crossed without difficulty. A short while later, they came to a deep waterway, over which the two of them stood, casting their shadows down upon it. The water was a good distance below them and too dark for Ico to clearly make out their reflections. Still, he could see the silhouettes that they formed on the water's surface, which somehow relieved him. If the girl had a reflection, then she wasn't a spirit or a ghost.

A thick copper pipe ran along the wall above the waterway. The pipe climbed up the side of the walls—which were too high for even Ico to scale—twisting and bending before disappearing into the castle. The elder had taught him that they had pipes like these in the capital to carry water to the center of town, so that people wouldn't have to dig wells or go fetch water from the river. He'd seen a number of pipes as the guards rowed him across the inlet when he first arrived at the castle, and so there must have been a number of pipes running along these walls for the convenience of people living here—but what made them all run? However it once functioned, it didn't seem to be working now and probably hadn't for some time.

It frustrated him to know so little about the castle. The wonders he saw here might be commonplace in the temples of the capital, but he had no way of knowing. He wondered if he would ever get the chance to find out. They returned to the center of the courtyard. The sunlight glinted off the grass, and it was hot enough to make Ico sweat. Ahead of them, stairs led to a heavy stone arch.

"Just a little more," he said to the girl, then hurried, pulling her along. He didn't want to get caught in such a large area surrounded by those shadow creatures.

Sweat dripped from his brow, but he reflected on how strange it was that since meeting the girl, he had felt neither hunger nor fatigue. Normally he would never have been able to run so far without stopping.

The two ran to the arch, where Ico saw what he had been hoping to find—the one place in the castle he had seen before entering its walls. They were at the front gate. Its doors were still open wide, pointing out toward the water.

"We made it!" Ico practically whooped for joy. He pointed at the gate. "Now we can get out of here!"

He felt dizzy with relief. Unable to stand still, he held both the girl's hands and jumped for joy.

The only thing between them and the massive gate was a long path, as wide as the gate itself, covered in soft grass. Cobblestones had been laid down its center, and pairs of tall torch stands stood like sentries on either side. The torches were useless under the sun, but even so they seemed to welcome him, beckoning like outstretched arms, showing him the way out.

"Let's go!"

Pulling on the girl's hand, he ran. *Run. Run!* Ico's mind was already ahead of him, floating somewhere near the gate. He wouldn't let anything get in their way now. The gate was so large that even as he ran, he felt like he wasn't getting any closer. It was like chasing after the moon. *No, I'll get there. Each step is taking me closer to escape. Closer to freedom.*

The gate towered in front of them. He wondered what kind of stone had been used to build such a massive structure. From this distance, he couldn't see any of the seams one might expect in something so large.

At the top of each of the gate's hinges stood massive round orbs, sparkling quietly beneath the sun. He remembered catching a glimpse of one of them from the boat on his way in, reflecting the sunlight down onto him.

Just then, the girl gave a terrified scream. Their hands were wrenched apart.

The girl had fallen on the cobblestones, tumbling to the base of one of the torch stands. Ico was moving so fast that he fell forward, tripping over his own feet. When he stood, he froze at what he saw. Still screaming, the girl was clawing at her face and body, her legs writhing in pain.

"What is it? What's wrong?" he asked, crawling toward the girl but unable to bring himself to touch her. She twisted and turned as though her skin was on fire. Something unseen was attacking her, invisible talons raking her body. Ico whirled around, looking for more of the shadow creatures. But there was nothing in the courtyard but the sun and the grass.

They had covered half of the distance to the main gate. If they stood up and ran, they'd be there in no time. There was salt on the wind. Just a little farther and they would be able to hear the waves.

Ico felt the wind on his cheek—not the gentle breeze blowing in from the sea, but a cold, bracing wind rushing down from the Castle in the Mist.

Ico raised his eyes and saw something gathering in the air above the girl. It was the wind—he could *see* it. It came together in threads, slender whips forming in thin air, then entwining.

Countless tongues of lightning flashed without sound in the gathering darkness of the cloud.

Individually, the threads had no shape or color, but when they flowed together, they formed a figure there in the sky—a gathering of dark motes that absorbed the light, waxing stronger as they coalesced, giving off a brilliance that was the opposite of light.

Still on his knees, Ico braced himself. Then his hands fell to the ground and his mouth dropped open when he saw the figure coalescing above the girl. It was not a creature of smoke that appeared there. Though it took form in much the same way, its shape was far more human than any of the creatures he had seen within the castle.

A woman. She wore a wide gown that flowed around her, with elegant embroidery along the sleeves and hem. Her face was small and gaunt, with sunken cheeks and a sharp chin. Her skin was white as bone, her features glowing with the same dull gleam as the eyes of the shadow creatures. But unlike the creatures, this woman's eyes were pools of darkness. Though she had no pupils, Ico could tell she was looking straight at him. She spread her arms like a swooping falcon, her sleeves billowing.

This was the same woman in black Ico had seen praying before the idols in his vision.

The tolling of a bell came from somewhere in the Castle in the Mist. The bell rang slow and deep, and at its signal, the massive doors of the gate behind Ico began to close, cutting off the sea wind. The girl lay still on the ground, unconscious. Ico gasped and tried to grab her. *Stand up! We have to go! The gates are closing—*

Then, floating above them, waves of dark mist lapping at her feet, the woman in black spoke. "Who are you?" she demanded, her voice twisting and bending through the air as though her voice itself were made of smoke. "What are you doing here?" The sound of her voice rose and fell, like a conversation overheard from beyond a wall.

Ico held his arm around the girl's body, sheltering her. He

stared up at the woman in black, his breath ragged through his open mouth. He couldn't look away. He couldn't move.

I shouldn't answer her. The elder, Oneh, and every scary fairy tale he had ever heard had all told him that if you ever met a demon in the woods, even if it called you by name, you were not to answer. Answer, and it would have your soul. Instead, you must close your eyes and tell yourself that what you were seeing didn't exist. Close your heart to it, else the demon would steal its way in.

"I see your filthy horns, boy. You are a Sacrifice. What is a Sacrifice doing leaving his stone coffin, coming all the way out here?" Even when he closed his eyes and pressed his hands over his ears, the woman's voice wouldn't go away.

He opened his eyes again, and they met the woman's black gaze, two pools like fathomless swamps. Ico shivered and scrambled back. His right hand reflexively went to the Mark on his chest.

The woman's eyes, black scars on her white face, narrowed. "What's this?"

The bell rang, its sound echoing through the courtyard. The gates were already halfway closed now. Their shadows stretched all the way to where Ico and the girl lay on the ground.

"I see," the woman said, nodding. "You are a particularly lucky Sacrifice. Thank your luck and leave my castle. I've spared your life once. Begone before I have a change of heart."

My castle—this woman was the master of the castle?

"Wh-who—" Ico stammered, trying to stand. Then he was on his feet before the woman. "Are you the master here?" he asked, forgetting the warnings for the moment.

"Yes. I am master of the Castle in the Mist. I am queen of all who live in its shadow."

The woman moved her right hand, lifting a finger and pointing it directly at Ico's nose. Though what he felt now was so different, somehow the gesture reminded him of the way the girl had pointed at him when she first stepped from the cage.

The queen of the castle was incredibly thin, even down to her fingers. She wasn't just old—she seemed almost a skeleton. The sharp nail on her outstretched finger gleamed like a slice of obsidian.

"Sacrifice. Your life is in my hands. If you do not wish to suffer the same fate as your comrades, leave. Now."

His fear mingled with his determination, and his heart raced. He ran to the girl's side and tried to lift her in his arms.

"Take your hands off the girl!" the queen said, her voice slicing the air. A sharp, cold wind hit Ico's neck like a blade.

"She is not for you to touch, Sacrifice. Do you know who this girl is?"

I want to know.

He shivered and looked up at the queen. He meant to sound defiant, but his voice quavered pitifully. "It doesn't matter who she is! She's trapped here. She's a Sacrifice, like me! I'm taking her with me!"

The queen's pointed chin lifted and her face twisted. Ico's legs turned to jelly beneath him. The queen began to laugh.

The girl moved, getting her arms beneath her and rising halfway to look up at the queen. She looked like she was going to cry.

Ico stepped to the side, kneeling by the girl. He put his hand on her shoulder and could feel her tremble. The girl was transfixed by the sight of the queen.

The queen sensed that she was being watched, and her laughter faded as she looked down at the girl. Even though she was still half lying on the ground, Ico could feel her recoil at the queen's gaze.

The queen spoke more slowly now, weaving her words as she called to the girl. "Yorda," she said, "my dear Yorda."

This time, Ico flinched. His hand tensed on the girl's shoulder and he looked at the queen. She was staring only at the girl now. As she was entranced by the queen, so too could the queen not take her eyes from her. Their eyes met.

"Did you hear what this brazen boy has said? He called you a Sacrifice! How unfathomably rude. Does he not know that you are my beloved daughter?"

Ico felt the strength leave his legs. His arms dropped to the ground.

Yorda did not reply but instead lowered her face to the ground as though she might escape the queen's eyes. She lifted her hand to her mouth. Even her fingers trembled.

"That can't be right," Ico stammered. "There's no way she's your daughter!"

"Oh?" The queen looked at him, smiling. "You doubt my words? You are as foolish as you are headstrong!"

Ico stood quickly and charged at the queen. Laughing, she waved her bony hand at him—her slightest gesture was enough to send him tumbling across the stones.

"You should know your place, Sacrifice—and it is far, far from me." The queen's smile faded and her eyes glowed like black flames in the pale moonscape of her face. "I should kill you just for leading her around the castle!"

Ico stood on unsteady feet. "If she really is your daughter, why did you imprison her in a cage? It doesn't make any sense!"

The queen's pointed chin lifted and she laughed again—a short laugh, like the bark of a dog. "The lowly Sacrifice would admonish me! What I choose to do with my daughter is none of your concern."

Ico made to charge her again. The queen raised a clawlike nail, but Yorda stepped between them. Without a word, Yorda stretched out her arms in front of Ico, holding him back. Ico looked into her eyes and she shook her head, pleading with him.

The queen's eyes narrowed. "Look at that. It seems Yorda pities you." She seemed more bemused than upset. "Your luck is twofold, lowly Sacrifice. I will spare your life a second time, for Yorda's sake. Now leave. Yet I will not suffer you to leave by the front gates through which I once walked in glory, surrounded by the cheers and admiration of my people."

Almost as if they had been waiting for those very words, the giant gates closed fully, shaking the earth with the sound. The light that had come streaming through was cut off, casting the entire courtyard in shadow.

The tolling of the bell ceased.

"I am sure a crawler in the earth such as yourself will have no trouble finding a suitable exit. Wriggle from a crack in the wall if you must, miserable vermin. Or perhaps you would prefer to dig at the earth with your claws and escape through a tunnel of your own making? But you will find a way, and you will leave."

Though there was no wind, Ico's Mark stirred. The queen frowned, her eyes flashing. Ico recalled the queen frowning before when he had touched his Mark—as though she found it distasteful.

He began to walk toward the queen, placing his hand directly over the Mark and focusing all his thoughts on it. Wrapped in robes of swirling darkness, the queen stared him down. Ico glared back.

"If you are truly the master of this castle, then the Sacrifices are being offered to you, right? Why? What is it all for?" Ico asked quickly, his feet firmly planted. "Those black smoke creatures in the castle—they were Sacrifices too, weren't they? You turned them into those things with your magic. You're no queen at all. Queens are good, noble people with kind hearts. They don't make innocent people sacrifice their children. You're a liar. You're a witch!"

The more he talked, the angrier he became, until Ico was practically shouting. The queen waved her hand as though swatting away a fly, and Ico flew backward. This time he went even farther, making an arc through the air before landing on the cobblestones shoulder first. Blood rose on his cheek where it scraped the ground.

Ico felt dizzy, and he ached all over. He was having trouble breathing, and white spots filled his vision.

"That's enough of your mewling, little creature," the queen said in a cold, echoing voice. "Now, Yorda. Back to the castle. Do not waste your time with this Sacrifice. You forget who you are."

Ico blinked, but his vision would not clear. He tried focusing on the queen, still hovering in space, and Yorda beneath her, hunched over on the cobblestones and cowering in fright.

"Don't listen to her, Yorda!"

Ico heard his own voice sounding like it came to him over a great distance. His tongue wasn't moving the way he wanted it to. He thought he saw the queen gesture, and for the third time he flew through the air, hitting the ground hard as he landed beside the girl. *She's toying with me.* Ico felt like his ribs might break. Cuts covered his knees and elbows.

Yorda threw herself over Ico, protecting him with her body. She looked up at the queen, shaking her head, pleading.

"Why do you show mercy to one so low?" the queen asked. "This castle will one day be yours. You are my body. You will reign over the Castle in the Mist with my heart, and wait for the day when we rule in glory once more. Do not tell me you have forgotten?"

In his half-conscious state, Ico was dimly aware that Yorda was crying.

"Or perhaps you have tired of waiting? Still, you may not go against your destiny. Listen well, Yorda. You and I are one. When the time comes, you will realize what a great blessing this is."

The queen's form began to fade. Ico decided it wasn't his vision failing, she really was leaving. "Sacrifice," she addressed him. "Leave at once. You will not get another chance. And do not waste your time with my daughter. She lives in a different world than some boy with horns."

The queen's dark robes of mist began to dissipate. Then, in a reverse performance of her grand entrance, she unraveled into the wind.

Ico lay sprawled across the cobblestones. Yorda was close to his side, hands on the stones, crying. It was the only sound in the courtyard. Ico looked over at Yorda. Her tears fell, making little dark spots on the stones that quickly dried and were gone. It was almost as if the shadow cast by the castle refused to acknowledge her sorrow.

Ico tried lifting his head, and a stabbing pain ran through his neck. He yelped, and Yorda turned to look at him, streaks on her face where the tears had run.

Their eyes met. Seeing Yorda cry made Ico want to cry too.

"Is it true?" he asked in a weak voice.

Yorda wiped away her tears and said nothing.

"Yorda…your name's Yorda, right?"

Yorda's hand stopped, half covering her face. She nodded.

Ico rested his head on the stones. He could feel the strength ebbing out of his body. "So the witch, the queen…is your mother."

Yorda nodded again. Curling up on the stones, she turned her back to Ico.

"So you weren't a Sacrifice after all," he said, more to himself than to her. "You know," Ico continued in a whisper, "when I hold your hand, I see things. Visions. And the queen was in one of them. I saw the knight with a broken horn from the old bridge too. And even you, when you were little."

Yorda did not turn to face him, so Ico talked to her back. "When we were on the trolley, you were there with your father." Gritting his teeth against the pain, he lifted his head and managed to sit up. He hurt in so many different places, he wasn't even sure which places they were. Even his eyes were growing hot with the tears that threatened to come.

"You were riding with him, playing. It seemed like you two were close."

Yorda had stopped crying. She looked up, focusing on something far away.

"Where did your father go?" Ico asked then. "Did he die? Did your mother keep you locked up all the time? Tell me, Yorda. What is going on in this castle? It wasn't always like this, was it? It's different in the visions. What happened to the beautiful Castle in the Mist where you used to play?"

Yorda whispered something, a short word. Though he heard it clearly, Ico couldn't understand.

She moved her legs, coming closer to Ico. She extended a slender arm and touched the scrape on Ico's cheek. He felt warmth. It seemed to flow from Yorda's fingertips into his body, filling him.

The woven Mark on his tunic began to glow from the inside. Ico's eyes went wide.

The pain in his body was disappearing.

Blood stopped flowing from the cuts and scrapes on his skin and began to dry. His bruises faded. His joints, stiff with pain, moved smoothly again.

Ico spread his hands and looked down at his healing body. The Mark was glowing faintly, like a firefly on a summer night, pulsing in pace with the beating of Ico's heart.

When the last scrape had disappeared, the Mark's glow faded. Yorda let her fingers fall from Ico's cheek.

Ico stared at Yorda's face. It was beautiful. He didn't dare breathe for fear of breaking the spell. Her eyes were sparkling.

"Thank you," he said.

Yorda began to smile, but her smile wilted halfway, and her lips turned down at the corners. She lowered her eyes.

"I think you have the same power as my Mark," Ico said. "Or maybe you have the power to make my Mark work better. You know what the elder said? They said as long as I had this Mark, I would never lose to the castle."

Ico took Yorda's hands in his own. "You didn't want to be locked in a cage, did you? You want to leave here, right? I'll take you with me."

Yorda shook her head vigorously, but Ico did not give up.

"You have power, Yorda. More than the castle. And I have the Mark. Didn't you see how the queen looked at it? She said she was sparing my life, but the truth is she couldn't kill me."

It was nothing more than a guess, but when Ico said it he felt sure he was right. If the queen really were that powerful, she wouldn't have stopped at threatening him. She would have snapped him like a twig right there and then.

Filled with hope, Ico looked into Yorda's eyes. He felt like he was looking into an hourglass, trying to pick through the grains of sand for some truth buried there long ago. He hadn't found anything yet, but the warmth of Yorda's hands in his told him that he was getting close.

CHAPTER 3
THE CAGE OF TIME

[1]

YORDA HAD LIVED in loneliness so long and so complete that it had penetrated her being, becoming her flesh and blood.

When she saw herself in the mirror or reflected on the surface of a pool of still water, she saw not a person but a thin skin stretched over a lonely void. *I'm a container, an empty vessel, a collection of nothingness.*

In Yorda's world, time was stopped. Time was her prison. It had held her for so long she could no longer remember when it began, when she had first realized her destiny. Yet finally she had come to an understanding. *Time does not imprison me, I imprison time. Time is my captive. I am the lonely keeper of the key, free to live here so long as I do not relinquish my post. Here I have stayed for so long that time itself is meaningless.*

Why is this so?

Who makes me do this?

By whose command am I here?

She had forgotten. In exchange for the power to hold back time, she had lost the power to mark its passage. Over the long years, this oblivion had been a mercy to her, the only peace she could claim.

A sea of forgetfulness, a barrier from the truth, enveloped her. She became a tiny round pebble, sunken into its depths. Here there was only peace and tranquility. Though the waves of doubt and unease might riffle the surface of the water high above her, they would never reach down to the bottom where she lived.

An eternal sleep, not unlike death.

When will it end?

Who will end it?

On whose command will it cease?

Stopping time meant stopping her heart. Nothing changed, nothing moved. Nothing was born, nothing faded. As it had always been. As it would always be.

At least, that's how it was meant to be—

"Yorda...that's your name?" A voice, calling her. Dark eyes looking up at her. The warmth of another person standing close, the sound of their breathing.

Where there is life and action, time cannot remain still. The doors of the cage must open and let their captive free.

Yorda...yes. That is my name.

Yorda was dreaming. She dreamt in fragments that seemed to come and go as they pleased as she lay in the cage at the top of the tower above the pedestal room. How long had she lain here? Her dreams followed no logical path, nor could she be sure if they were dreams in her sleep or waking dreams in her mind. Often, she'd relive the same dream many times.

As death and oblivion were closely related, so too were death and dreams. *Who can say truly that the dead do not dream? Am I dead dreaming of life? Or am I alive dreaming of death?*

In her dream, someone was climbing the spiral staircase that wound round the tower. In her dream, she heard footsteps, saw a shadow on the stairs. She looked up and saw the figure approach. But after she blinked and looked again, she realized it was just a vision without substance.

That was the way it always was. Always she returned to sleep, in search of the next dream.

In this dream, she saw a dark shadow grow upon the wall

behind the climbing figure, drawing it in, devouring it. The figure said nothing, only cowered in fear as the darkness took it. A great storm raged outside the tower. She could feel the wind on her face and the cool drops of rain. Her dreams were often indistinguishable from reality.

The figure taken by the shadows—it was a little boy. His intense fear bit into her. Her eyes opened in fright. Then, she did see someone climbing up the stairs of her tower. Going round and round, racing up the spiral with a desperate speed.

Is this a dream? Was the figure I saw before the dream? Which is life, and which is death?

Then she heard a voice call to her. "Is anybody there?"

Yorda sat up halfway. It was the boy, leaning up against the railing, looking at her. "What are you doing in there?"

She could see him with her eyes. She could hear his voice in her ears.

Yorda couldn't believe it. *I'm still dreaming. This is a fantasy my heart is showing me. A gentle, soothing lie. That's all.*

The boy was standing on tiptoe now, stretching as high as he could, and calling out loudly. "Hold on. I'll get you down."

He started up the stairs again. Yorda could watch him run with her eyes. He was wearing strange red clothes—a pretty color, though. She wondered at the cloth that fell over his chest and back, decorated with such an intricate pattern. When the boy ran, the fabric flapped and curled like a flag.

Presently, she could no longer see the boy. It looked as though he had crawled out of one of the windows higher up in the tower in her dream. *That's right. I'm still dreaming. I mustn't forget.*

Nothing will happen after this. Nothing will change. I will go back to sleep.

The cage shook around her.

Yorda grabbed hold of the bars, clinging for dear life. The vibrations continued, and then, to her amazement, the cage began to slowly drop. The round pedestal far below her grew larger.

An intricate dream. A dream woven from my wildest hopes.

But the cage did not descend all the way down to the pedestal. Instead, it stopped at the height of the idol gate. There it shook again, and Yorda stood, holding on to the bars.

She could see the heads of the idols just beneath her feet. The four of them stood mute watch over the way out.

She wondered how she knew that. A shiver ran down her spine, and Yorda let go of the bars, retreating to the center of her cage. A fleeting memory bloomed in her mind.

"These idols are our protectors."

"They'll protect us, both of us, during the eternity we must wait here in the castle until the time of the revival is at hand."

"I am you, and you are me. I am what fills you, and you are my vessel."

Yorda shook her head, letting it hang limply from her neck. *I am myself. This is my body. My hands and feet. My hair. My eyes.*

There was a loud clanging sound above her head, and the cage began to rock like a boat at sea. She looked up and saw that the boy from before had landed atop the cage.

The cage rocked, and Yorda was thrown against the bars. Above her, the boy lost his balance and fell from the cage with a yelp. The cage lurched again, more dramatically this time, and the next moment it began to fall. The chain had broken!

There wasn't even enough time for her to blink. The bottom of the cage struck the pedestal with an echoing *clang*, and for a terrifying moment it teetered, threatening to topple, before coming to rest on the ground. A breath later, Yorda heard a sharp metallic whine as the door to the cage swung open, its lock broken.

The boy was sitting a short distance away on the floor. Silence returned to the room, and Yorda heard the crackling of the torches and the wild breathing of the boy.

Am I still dreaming?

Yorda stepped slowly out of the cage.

The boy was still sitting, gaping up at her. He looked young. Small round black eyes. The strange cloth he wore gave off a dim light. And he had horns.

"We will need sacrifices."

Fragments of memories danced in her head.

"The Castle in the Mist will require them."

I am dreaming, Yorda thought. *This isn't some entertainment my mind has woven for me. I am replaying an old memory. It must be, because I know this boy with the horns. I have known him for so long. Together, we walked this castle—*

"It was my mistake to attempt to use your power."

"But do not give up hope. The day will come when a child of my blood will rise to save you."

"And your mother—"

Yorda retrieved her voice from across the span of ages. "Who are you?" she asked the boy. "How did you get in here?"

But the boy just stared at her blankly. She asked him again, and the boy's lips moved.

"Are you…are you a Sacrifice?"

The words had a familiar ring to her ears. They were not her own, but words she knew well all the same. They were the words he had used those many years ago. She knew she recognized them. But that was so long ago. And though she could understand them, it frustrated her that she could not speak them.

The memories washed over her like waves, incessant, present.

This boy is no dream, I know that.

Yorda extended her hand and touched the boy's cheek. *I want to feel his warmth. I want to be sure.* The boy's shoulders lifted and his mouth twisted. *He's afraid. Don't be. But I must be sure you're real.*

That was when *they* appeared.

Yorda called them the shadows-that-walk-alone. They were shades, born of the Sacrifices. The souls of the Sacrifices were removed, steeped in dark magic, and transformed into the misshapen creatures. Yorda's mother, queen of the Castle in the Mist, called them her slaves, and she spoke of them with great disdain.

The shades were looking for Yorda because the queen was looking for Yorda. Yorda held time within her body, the shades held Yorda, and the castle held the shades. Even now, the queen reigned over these three layers of warding.

But the boy protected Yorda from the shadows-that-walk-alone. He took her hand, defended her, swung his thin arm, and fought with his tiny frame, driving them back. If the shades dragged her into their realm, she would once again become a prisoner, and the boy would turn to stone, a sad adornment in the castle. Yorda knew this. But the boy did not—even as he did not know that Yorda was the property of the queen of the castle—and he protected her.

Yes, this must be a dream. A dream woven by my heart, in mourning for my dead soul.

The man had promised that she would be saved one day. But no matter how firm his promise, he was just a man and his strength was limited. After all this time, he would have frozen and eroded, then disappeared without a trace.

But the feeling of the boy's fingers clutching her own and the warmth of his hand were real. He existed without a doubt, burning with anger, trembling with fear, breathing raggedly in the chaos, fighting the shades that sprang up around them.

As she staggered, being led by the boy, she had an idea. She gave his hand a tug. He resisted. He did not disappear. She didn't awake trembling to find herself still inside the cage.

This isn't a dream. Believe this. It's not a dream. The promised time has come.

Yorda pulled on the boy's hand as hard as she could, turning toward the warding idols.

"These idols protect you."

Guardians heed the orders of the one who is guarded. Though Yorda might lack the power to drive off the shadows, she could bring light to open the way out of this place.

"Never move the idols. We must defend the castle against the impurities of the outside world until the revival is nigh."

When Yorda used her own power to move the idols, the shades disappeared from the pedestal room like smoke in a strong wind.

"How did you do that?" the boy asked, glancing between her face, the empty room, and the idols that had parted before them. She saw dark doubts and bright hopes in the innocent eyes looking into hers.

"Come with me, okay?" the boy said. "Let's find the way out."

She looked at the horns growing from his head, then she took his outstretched hand.

[2]

LED BY THE hand as they ran through the castle in search of a way out, Yorda attempted to summon her faded memories. It seemed to her that walking on these stones with her own feet, free of the cage, it shouldn't be too difficult.

The towers of the Castle in the Mist. Landscapes seen from incredible heights. Endless corridors. High spiral staircases. Crumbling furniture and adornments. Everything was as she remembered it. Many times she had run through here, touching, sitting down to rest. She had to be able to remember.

But like a nightmare in which you run and run and never seem to get anywhere, Yorda's memories of the Castle in the Mist hung frustratingly close, but always out of reach. It was as though a dark veil had fallen between *now* and *then*, concealing her past from the present.

Had the castle always been this vast? Always this tangled? Even though each of the rooms seemed familiar to her, the ways between them were strange and convoluted.

The boy was brave—as though he hardly feared anything. Or perhaps that was just a façade. He *should* be afraid. Yet his feet ran and his eyes searched without pause. Except, every once in a while, a thoughtful look would come over him and he would stop. After a moment, he'd shake his head and begin to walk again. Yorda imagined that at these times he grappled with doubts and fears in his mind, but for Yorda, whose own memory was clouded, it was difficult to imagine what these doubts and fears might be. If only she could understand him better.

His words were tangled in her mind. Yorda didn't even know the boy's name. Yet the horns on his head spoke to something asleep in her heart, trying to rouse it. *So familiar, so comforting.* She heard a voice whisper in her head.

"Don't give up hope."

Who had he been? What was he to me? She stretched out her arms in her mind, trying to uncover memories that lay buried in the shadows. How satisfying it would be to pull them out, drag them into the light.

I want to remember. I must remember.

Sometimes, the boy would take her hand and his eyes would go blank, as though his mind had toppled and fallen inside himself. His expression was that of someone peering at something far off in the distance, something that Yorda could not see. *What's wrong?* she wanted to ask. *What are you thinking?*

Then the moment would pass, and the light would return to the boy's eyes. He would tilt his head curiously, looking first at her, and then at their surroundings, as though he had been on some long voyage and only just now returned.

After a while—Yorda realized with some surprise that she could mark the passage of time—they made their way to the old bridge leading to the far tower of the castle, dimly visible through the white mist. The statue of a knight stood on the near side of the bridge.

The boy looked up at it and his eyes grew distant.

Something about the tall statue, one horn protruding from his helmet, made Yorda's heart flutter. Memories swirled inside her, tiny waves breaking against the shores of her mind.

I know this knight. I know him. This is him, the man. But why is he made of stone? Another memory rose, clearer than the others. *This is no statue. The curse turned him to stone, binding him here. I know why. I know…*

But she didn't know. It was so close. She stamped the floor in irritation.

When she looked again at the boy, he was standing beside her, glancing curiously between the statue and the bridge. She followed his gaze, wondering what it was that he could see that she could not.

The boy took Yorda's hand and broke into a run. Yorda ran too, nearly tripping. In a daze, she saw a crack form at their feet across the ancient bridge, and the stones began to fall away from beneath them. Yorda's legs treaded air, and she fell before she even had time to scream.

But the boy caught her, leaving her dangling from the edge of the bridge. She looked down at the calm blue water of the ocean, waiting for her. A breeze ruffled her hair and shawl, and the cries of seabirds rang in her ears.

The boy pulled Yorda back up onto the remnant of the bridge. His face was pale, and he chattered on rapidly. To Yorda, it seemed as though he were apologizing.

It's not your fault, she thought. *The castle is old. It's decaying. That's why the stone bridge collapsed. That's all.*

Or was it? As they ran across the bridge, Yorda found herself wondering why the castle was disintegrating beneath them. *It can't decay. It's alive. The Castle in the Mist is eternal, isn't it?*

For just a moment, the veil separating Yorda from her memories gave way to her pressure. A realization spilled forth. She grabbed hold of it tightly.

It is because I am free. I left my cage, I'm trying to leave. That's why the Castle in the Mist is dying. The castle shares my fate. I am the cage of time, as the castle is my cage.

Though her memories remained dark, after that she knew with each step, with each new room they passed, that she was not to leave this place. The feeling grew stronger and stronger, welling up from inside her, binding her to this place. *What I am doing is forbidden. I cannot escape the castle. That is the one thing I must never do.*

That was what the misshapen creatures told her. They pleaded with her desperately to remember her role. That was why they wanted to bring her back, to quietly end her charade of escape. Just as she had been stopped before once…but that memory too was out of reach.

They ran on through the castle, and again the shades attacked, and again the boy came to her aid, baring his teeth at the dark shapes looming over him, a tiny mouse in a den of lions. The dark creatures vanished, their lamentations left to hang in the air. She realized that the boy could hear them too. As proof, every time he saw them, his fear grew greater…and his hatred, and the tears in his eyes.

Why do I not stop? Yorda wondered. *Why do I follow this boy? And what is this strange warmth that flows within me each time I take his hand? This warmth threatens to fill me, I who have spent so long caged in the castle, my life an empty vessel for time to fill. What if it succeeds? Then I would…I would—*

I would be a girl again.

That's why I have to stay here. The queen wants it. I must follow her wishes.

But—

Is that what I want for myself? Is that what I desire?

Though she uttered not a sound, Yorda's cry of confusion echoed throughout the castle, every corner hearing her question. And so when they finally reached the gates, her answer appeared before them in the form of the master of the castle herself: the queen, destined to rise again, destined to rule the world.

Yet she was wrapped in black, and her once beautiful face was as thin and gaunt as a corpse. Her obsidian eyes flashed with anger, and though Yorda wished it were not so, she had but one name to call this woman: Mother.

The person who bore me into this world.

But I am…I was going to—

The veil dropped away. That which separated Yorda from her memories vanished. Suddenly everything—the whole of the history of the Castle in the Mist—came surging back to her in a great tide.

"Now, Yorda. Back to the castle. You forget who you are."

Yorda looked to the boy at her side. In the shadow of the closing gates, he stood facing off against the queen.

He is the Sacrifice. And I am part of the castle. We can never be together, aligned in one purpose.

Then the queen left, satisfied to see Yorda's memory returned. The gates closed firmly shut. The royal audience was over.

The boy lay on the ground, covered in cuts and bruises. Yorda was crying. It took her some time to realize that the tears falling on the tiles of the courtyard were her own. *I've remembered how to cry.*

The boy was speaking to her. She could understand him now. She even knew what language he spoke. It was the same language of the poor knight turned to stone on the bridge—the swordsman Ozuma. She remembered him now too.

The boy was telling her that when he held her hand, he saw visions. He told her that he had seen her with her father on the trolley.

Father. How long ago had she forgotten him? He'd fallen beyond the reach of her recollection.

"It seemed like you two were close."

Yes, we were. But now I am very far from him indeed. So far that we will never be together again.

Yorda touched the boy's cheek. In that instant, she made a decision. *I will help him escape. I will save this Sacrifice. And I will stay here to play my role, to remain the lock on the cage of time. This will be the last time I take his hand.*

Then the strange pattern on the boy's tunic began to glow. Pulsing. Sending life into the boy, and into Yorda.

As she watched, the boy's wounds healed. It was as though her hand had melted into him. *I can feel it crossing to me. A light of hope. The brilliance of life. The brilliance of wisdom that resists the yoke of darkness.*

"I'll take you with me."

How could he still want to escape with her, knowing she was the daughter of the queen?

"The day will come when a child of my blood will come to save you."

Was this the child? Was he more than a mere Sacrifice? Was he the warrior protected by the light of wisdom?

Yorda took the boy's hand. A new strength flowed from it, washing away her sad determination, cleansing her memories, and beginning to fill the empty vessel that was Yorda.

No. I don't believe it.

But the boy was there, and he was looking at her. That was when Yorda understood what was drawing out her memories of the castle into the boy. It was him. He wanted to know its dark past. He wanted to know everything. No one could stop this. Not even the queen.

The elder sat up in his chair suddenly.

What was that?

He had been dozing, the Book of Light in his hands. Now he found he could not reach down and pick up the book. His hands, knees, even his tongue were numb. It was as though a bolt of lightning had run through his body.

Gradually he loosened his fingers, rubbed down his arms, and finally got out of his chair to pick up the book. The ancient tome was glowing and warm, just as it had been when he had first taken it from Toto's hands. The cover opened of its own accord to a particular page.

There, in the middle of a long line of densely packed ancient letters, he saw the illustration of a single great sword.

The elder looked up, awe rising within him.

"He has found the way. He has found it!"

[3]

TIME LURCHED BACK into motion. It boiled up, whirling in a spiral, arcing like lightning, regaining the pace it once knew in the distant, distant past—

On either side of the castle gate, the celestial sphere in the east and its twin in the west sparkled brightly. A bell rang, signaling with its deep echoing sound the start of the great tournament held only once every three years.

The gates slowly opened, their height such that they appeared to scrape the sky. Knights, soldiers, and mercenaries from every corner of the queen's domain, and beyond, formed two lines that proceeded across the bridge from the gathering place on the other side. The bright sun reflected off of their burnished gear.

More than one hundred men made up the procession. Some wore helmets of bright crimson, others leather armor polished to a glow by years of use, heavy round shields lashed across their backs. Each contestant had his own specialty. Behind one proudly hefting a giant battle-axe walked another dressed in a long black robe out of which poked a segmented whip with a spike on its end. There were youths in the crowd, boys not old enough to shave. There were mercenaries with keen eyes who had seen many battles, and an old man who had seen more, leaving him with but one.

They advanced between ranks of the royal guard lining either side of the high corridor leading through the courtyard. Their ambition was a tangible substance that shimmered above them like heat rising off the desert. The guards stood with their hands at their waists, chests thrust out so that the royal signets upon their breastplates could be seen beneath their surcoats.

Eight days hence, when the victor had been decided by single elimination tournaments held in the arenas, they would look up to one of these warriors as their new master-at-arms. But for now, they simply watched the procession, expressions hidden behind their faceplates. They knew that whatever skill these warriors had with axe and whip, with dagger and trident, it was wasted on a knight. A knight wielded a sword. As to whether they watched with smiles, cold and hard, or with the curiosity of career soldiers, none could say.

Yorda stood on the terrace outside her chambers, looking down at the spectacle in the courtyard. Her tower stood to the west of the central keep where the queen's chambers were located. From this height, the procession of warriors looked like little marionettes in a play. Even still, the crunching of their boots on the stones drifted up through the air, and she could sense their elation in the wind that blew against her cheek.

The castle stood atop sheer cliffs overlooking the sea, the salt wind sweeping it year round. Even now, the breeze played with the ends of Yorda's short-cropped chestnut hair.

Those who were close to Yorda all said that when they returned from a long journey and smelled the sea air, they felt like they were truly home. Not having set foot outside the castle, it was something that Yorda couldn't understand. She had never known a wind that did not carry the scent of the sea.

The queen did not like to expose Yorda to strangers, and so she had forbidden her to leave her tower during the tournament. It was rare for the queen herself to leave the castle, and even within, Yorda saw no one else but the Captain of the Guard who was always by her side, the ministers who managed the castle affairs, the handmaidens who tended to her, and Master Suhal, the great scholar.

"How peaceful your world must seem at a glance," the queen would tell her. "Calm as a windless sea. But peel back a thin layer, and you would find invasions and battles waiting. You could hear the ragged, blood-choked breathing of neighboring kingdoms, eager to expand their domain, biding their time. In such a world, the beauty with which you were born is far too dangerous.

"Beauty is a high, noble thing. Thus are men enchanted by it and seek it out. But those who desire you desire also our lands. I must keep you hidden so that you do not entice them or enchant them—because, my dearest, while your beauty holds the power to command the actions of a few men, it does not bestow the ability to govern.

"It is the same for me. The land I govern is the most wealthy and beautiful of all the lands that divide this vast continent. They crave it, as they crave me. From their slavering jaws and their multifarious schemes have I escaped many times. All to protect myself and my beautiful domain, blessed by the Creator. You, who were born into this world as the lone daughter of the queen, have noble blood and noble beauty, thus must you bear my burdens.

"Beloved child, my daughter. I pity you for your beauty."

The warriors were now lined up in the square before the gate. Mor Gars, Minister of Rites, slowly took his place on the stand that had been erected for the tournament. It was richly decorated with flowers of the season and flags embroidered with the crest of the royal house. The royal guard, in formation around the warriors, lifted their swords as one toward the sky and stood at attention while the contestants dropped respectfully to one knee upon the ground.

The minister began his speech, his voice carrying to every corner of the square with the quiet accompaniment of the leaves rustling in the sea breeze.

A single tear fell on the back of Yorda's hand where it gripped the railing. The tournament had begun. Yorda wondered who would win, and if he had ever imagined in his wildest nightmares what awaited him after his brief moment of glory.

And she had no way of stopping it.

Ten days before, Yorda had gone against her mother's word and attempted to leave the castle. An act born of childish curiosity, nothing more.

Yorda was sixteen, a flower just entering bloom. To her, the outside world was the stuff of dreams and longing, a busy place where people mingled and lived out their lives. She wanted to walk upon the grass beyond the gates, if only just once. She wanted to see towns and villages she had never known. She wanted to look back at the castle looming across the water, to see its grand shape from afar. Her youthful heart wanted to escape the chains of royalty, however briefly.

She had pleaded with one of the handmaidens closest to her, who finally gave in and agreed to help. The handmaiden had a lover who worked as one of the guards.

The two worked out a plan. On the night of the full moon, when the leaders of the merchants' guild gathered and had their meeting with the Minister of Coin, there would be many people of no name or stature on the castle grounds, for one only needed to be a member of the guild to sit in on the gathering and listen. Events such as this meant that there would be many commoners of all ages, both men and women, filling the audience chamber in the central left tower.

If Yorda wore common clothes and mingled with the crowd, she would be able to escape without difficulty. The main gates would open once when the leaders of the merchants' guild arrived and again when they departed. If she left when their meeting began and returned when it ended, no one would be the wiser. As luck would have it, while the guild members were present, things at the castle became too busy, and Master Suhal suspended his lessons. She would not be missed or lectured on the importance of education. And if anyone did happen to visit Yorda's chambers while she was away, her most trusted handmaiden would be there to make excuses.

Yorda thought the plan was splendid. It was fun for her to wear the colorful town-girl clothes her handmaiden had procured. The elaborate tunics and short vests that the merchant guild elders and their companions wore enchanted her with their floral-patterned cloth and matching shoes and toques. How happy it made her to wear things she had never even been able to see up close, let alone touch.

Until then, all the clothes she had been given were simple things of the purest white that wrapped loosely around her, with no variation from day to day save for the embroideries on her sleeves and her shawl. Yet even when they were embroidered with the most intricate patterns and designs, the thread was white, or at best a faded blue or brown pigment made from grasses. The queen would not allow her to wear bright vermilion, yellow, or green, saying they would detract from Yorda's natural beauty.

It was strange when she thought about it. Did the queen not keep her inside the castle, saying that her exceptional beauty was dangerous? Why then did she give Yorda only white to wear, saying that it enhanced her beauty?

The queen herself wore only white. The handmaidens around them dressed in undyed tunics with long sleeves, their hems and sashes of a color that reminded Yorda of the sea. The ministers and other officials working within the castle also wore predominantly white, with perhaps a splash of blue or brown. Though the colors might be fitting for a castle made of brick and copper facing the sea, Yorda found it lacking in gaiety.

At last, the day came when the girls put their plan into action and found it almost disappointingly easy. Yorda ran down the stairs, hid among the bushes in the courtyard, and then made her way from the west tower, careful not to let the guards see her. From there she proceeded from the middle courtyard to the front courtyard and into the crowd. Among the throngs of people, in her full, flowered skirt and apron, with a wide-brimmed hat on her head, no one would recognize the princess. She pretended to ask directions from the handmaiden's lover, who took her to the front gate, and finally she reached the long stone bridge across the water. The handmaiden's mother waited secretly on the far side, having received a letter that explained the plan.

Yet when she had crossed only halfway over the bridge, Yorda heard a voice in her mind.

Enough of this foolishness. Come back.

Yorda jerked to a stop and looked around. The bridge was full of people rushing to get into the gates to hear the minister's speech. There were many going in her direction too, attendants who had seen the guild leaders to the front gate and were now returning to take care of the horses. There was no reason why she should have stood out in the crowd. In fact, when she stopped suddenly, it disturbed the flow of foot traffic around her, and she nearly stepped on the feet of a nearby steward.

Come back, Yorda. You must not leave the castle. Have you forgotten my warning?

But it was no trick of the wind or the crying of seabirds. It was the queen's voice.

I know where you are, my daughter. I know what you plan. All is clear to me. You cannot defy me. Now return.

A hand to her breast, Yorda felt a sudden chill against her cheek.

Please, Mother, she pleaded in silence, *allow me just this once. I want to see what it's like outside the castle. I'll come back as soon as I've seen. Please, Mother. Please.*

Yorda!

The Queen's voice was as cold as a winter's dawn and as unwavering as the rocky crags far below the bridge.

If you do not return this instant, I will destroy the very bridge upon which you walk. I need only lift a finger. You will have no choice but to return. And who knows how many of our people will fall with the crumbling bridge into the waves below. Is that what you want?

Men and women walked past Yorda, chatting busily, smiles on their faces. The stone bridge across the inlet was a part of the scenery, as though it had been there since the beginning of the world. As solid as the ground, a road across the water.

Yet it had been made by human hands. Or perhaps the queen herself had built it with magic. Either way, it could be shattered, and if it was, the life it held would be swallowed by the sea. Even the calm sea on a sunny day was stronger than a mere person, and the sea was very wide and very deep.

Staggering, Yorda turned, heading back toward the main gate. Soon she was running. She thought that if she hesitated even just a moment, her mother would take that as a sign of protest and destroy the bridge.

When she reached the entrance to the west tower to return to her room, the guard in the doorway stepped into her path. Yorda reached up and removed her hat. The guard's eyes open so wide it seemed they might fall out of his head.

"Princess Yorda?"

"My mother has summoned me," Yorda explained in a tiny voice. She ducked past the guard, frozen in place, running toward her own chambers where her handmaiden greeted her in surprise, embracing her as she ran in the door. But before Yorda could explain what had happened, two guards appeared at the entrance to her chambers.

They had come for the handmaiden. At the request of the queen, she was to appear in the audience chamber at once. Their faces were the blank masks of men who carried out orders without question or sympathy.

Yorda stood helpless, watching them lead her handmaiden away. She was sure that the girl's lover was being similarly apprehended at that very moment.

What have I done? Yorda threw herself on her bed, weeping. A short while later, another handmaiden arrived to help Yorda change her clothes. The handmaiden's eyes were clouded, and her lips trembled.

Midday came and went, but by the time the sun had begun to set, Yorda still had not been summoned by the queen. The members of the merchants' guild had left some time ago, and the front gates were closed. Two guards stood by the entrance to her chamber.

Yorda had tried asking them several times already to let her see her mother, but her pleas fell on deaf ears. By orders of the queen, they told her in voices devoid of warmth, the princess was to remain in her chambers.

When Yorda looked in their eyes, she could tell that the guards were frightened.

Dusk fell as Yorda ate her supper alone in her room. This was normal. Of the three rooms that made up her chambers, she had chosen the smallest with the least adornment, the powder room, in which to dine. The room originally appointed for meals was far too large and always felt cold with its thick stone walls and high ceiling.

No matter how warm her food, it chilled the moment it was brought into the chamber. And the table, as large as her canopied bed, could hold any number of dishes and still look empty. She never liked it.

When her father, the king, had been well, the three of them would take their meals in the royal dining hall. The dining hall was vast, with adornments of cold silver and gold on the ceiling and walls, but her father's smile would banish the chill in a moment. Her mother in those days had been far kinder.

Yorda's father had passed away when she was only six—already ten years past. Though the memories were still clear in her mind, they became more distant with each passing day.

Her father's passing had changed her mother. As it changed the castle.

Wracked by sadness and trembling with unease, Yorda found she could not eat. She only nibbled at the food on the trays and platters her handmaidens brought her one after another, then she bade them depart, and sat in a chair next to the window in her powder room, lighting a single candle and looking out to face the deepening night.

From this height, even with the front gate closed, she could see a part of the stone bridge the queen had threatened to destroy under the light of the full moon. The bridge looked pale over the dark sea below, as though it was not truly a bridge, but a phantom created by a trick of the moonlight, and if she blinked, it might disappear altogether.

Yorda strained her eyes, looking for the white spray of the waves where they collided with the columns of the bridge, sighing with relief when she spotted it. It was no phantom. The bridge remained. No one had plummeted into the sea. Yorda had obeyed the queen's wishes, returning to the castle, her tail tucked in behind her.

What would have happened, she wondered, if she had not heeded the queen? What if she had talked back to her?

You can't destroy a bridge that size with just a finger. You lie. You're lying, trying to threaten me! If you can do such a thing, I'd like to see you try!

Yorda planted both elbows on the elegantly carved table, wrapped her hands around her face, and closed her eyes. Behind her eyelids she could see the stone bridge crumbling and hear the screams of the people as they dropped into the waves.

If she had resisted, she knew her mother would have destroyed the bridge without hesitation. It was within her power.

The queen possessed a power that surpassed human comprehension. Yorda had yet to see it with her own eyes, but it was well known. Even Master Suhal attested to it. She had heard the Minister of Coin and the Minister of Rites—even the captain of the knights charged with protecting the queen—say that Her Majesty possessed a power greater than all the knightly order taken together. If any greedy neighboring country thought to take part of their rich land, if they tried to invade, before the knights could even ride, Her Majesty would vanquish the invading force with a single breath.

If one heard only the words, it came across as simple flattery and nothing more. Yet when he spoke of these things, Yorda had seen a chilling fear in the knight captain's eyes. Master Suhal had told her to study that fear and remember it well.

Princess, he told her, lowering his head, *your mother is truly powerful.*

Yorda wondered how old she had been. She had a feeling it was after her father's passing, when unease had begun to spread through the castle. Master Suhal had tried to calm her fears, but Yorda watched the scholar's eyes too, and she saw that they were dark and shadowed.

As the memories stirred Yorda's heart, the candle flame flickered. She wondered if she would sleep that night having not been scolded by her mother. That wouldn't do. She needed to get down on her knees and plead for forgiveness for the kind handmaiden and her lover. She had to beg for them. *It was I who wanted to go outside. They were just following my orders.*

Then came a gentle knocking at the door.

Yorda looked around and saw the thick, ebony wood door of her powder room open. The chief handmaiden stepped soundlessly inside. Her face and her hair were the same shade of gray. It was not merely from age, but from something that seemed to have drained the life from her and the color with it. Yorda did not dislike this emaciated old handmaiden so much as she feared her. It was not that the woman herself was frightening; she was loyalty personified, always obsequious and reverent in her service, and seemed, more than anyone else in the castle, to deeply fear Yorda's mother. That was what frightened Yorda.

Do you know something that I do not? Yorda thought the question every time she looked at the chief handmaiden's face.

"Princess Yorda," the woman said in a whisper. The spring of her voice had dried up long before, when the handmaiden had decided, of her own will, to speak only when absolutely necessary. "Her Majesty requests your presence."

Even though she had been waiting for just those words, Yorda felt her heart seize with fright.

"Very well. I'll go at once."

Yorda stood up from the table. Her hands and her knees

were trembling. Not wishing the chief handmaiden to see, she turned her back.

"You should wear a robe," the handmaiden said. "It is very chilly out at night."

Yorda turned. "We're going outside?"

"By Her Majesty's request," the chief handmaiden said, bowing her head.

Yorda removed a long hooded robe from her wardrobe and put it on. The stars outside her window winked in the sky, watching as she followed the handmaiden, her hooded head hanging low.

[4]

THE CHIEF HANDMAIDEN led her not to the queen's quarters but directly to the courtyard in front of the castle. The guards on night watch stood as still as statues watching them pass soundlessly down the corridor.

Out in the courtyard, their way was lit by torches burning atop pedestals as tall as a building. One here, two there; few were needed in the light of the full moon. When the sun was at its zenith, it seemed as though the torches supported the very vault of heaven, but at night they burned low beneath the dark sky. The darkness surrounding the castle was deep and silent.

Occasionally, she would spot the flame of a torch crossing the courtyard. Patrolmen on their rounds held them aloft. The chief handmaiden led her across the square, taking the stone staircase that led to the central west building and following the long curving arc of the walkway there. Yorda was afraid. The rooms and facilities along this walkway were not familiar to members of the royal house. Even though this castle was Yorda's entire world, she had only infrequently been to the east tower. She possessed only cursory knowledge of its rooms and layout.

The chief handmaiden carried no torch to avoid drawing undue attention. Within the walls of the castle and in the courtyards, the scattered sconces provided ample illumination, but in this place there was nothing of the sort. Even the gentle light of the full moon was blocked by the high walls. The chief handmaiden moved with the quick ease of familiarity, occasionally glancing back to make certain Yorda still followed.

"Where are we going?" Yorda asked. The chief handmaiden did not respond. But when they reached another staircase, she stopped. The hem of her skirts swayed and came to rest.

"Go down these stairs. Her Majesty awaits you below."

The handmaiden withdrew to the side of the passage, bowing stiffly at her waist. Yorda did not move.

"What business did my mother say she had with me here?"

After a short while, the handmaiden replied, her head hanging low. "I'm sorry, but I cannot answer your question. Please go ahead. Her Majesty will tell you herself, I am sure."

Yorda took one step forward. She followed with another, then turned to lean over the handmaiden. "You tremble," she said to the nape of the old woman's neck.

The handmaiden's neatly bound hair seemed to twitch. In the gloom, Yorda could spot countless white lines running through her hair. She was getting very old.

"Are you frightened? I am too."

The handmaiden said nothing and did not move.

"Today," Yorda continued, "I went against my mother's word. I come fully expecting to be punished. But why does that merit such fear?" Yorda leaned closer. "I want you to come with me. I don't want to go alone. I am not frightened of my mother's anger. I'm scared to walk alone at night. I'm scared of the dark."

That was a lie. The chief handmaiden knew it as well as Yorda. Yet she did not move.

"Then I order you," Yorda said, her voice trembling. "Come with me."

Still bent at the waist, the chief handmaiden spoke to the stones of the passageway. "Her Majesty awaits you, Princess Yorda. Please go down the stairs."

Apparently, only her mother could give orders in this castle. Yorda walked toward the staircase, eyes on the floor. She could hear her footsteps echoing quietly. She lifted her hands and pulled on her hood against the cool night air that blew up the staircase.

When Yorda's footfalls had receded into the distance, the chief handmaiden fell to her knees on the spot. Entwining her fingers together, she began to pray. It was not the prayer to the Creator that she knew by rote, it being required of her every day in the castle. It was an old prayer, one she had learned as a child in her homeland far from this place—a prayer to ward off evil.

When she reached the bottom of the stairs and went out into the small courtyard she found there, the full moon—blocked by the walls of the castle until now—appeared in the corner of the sky, looking down on her with concern. Yorda recognized at once where the chief handmaiden had brought her—she was in a graveyard.

Those of royal blood were never buried within the castle walls. In the far distant mountains, a solemn graveyard had been hewn from the rock face of a cliff for the royal graves. Here in this small graveyard rested those few servants whose loyalty was such that they were recognized for giving their lives to the castle. Of course, these were guard captains and high ministers. No handmaiden, not even a chief, would ever be suffered to lie here.

Yorda stood a moment in the moonlight before looking for her mother. The courtyard was surrounded on all four sides by castle buildings and stone walls. Nine gravestones white as bone, washed by the wind and the rain, stood in three rows. The grass was cropped short, and walking on it made her feel like she was gliding across black velvet.

The queen was nowhere to be seen, though under the moonlight her elegant white robes should have been obvious.

Yorda looked up at the night sky and the moon framed by the buildings around her and took deep, quiet breaths. The silvery white robe she wore was woven from priceless silks, and when it caught the slightest amount of light, it sparkled as though coated with silver dust. In this place of death, only Yorda was alive, and the dim glow of her robe only heightened the contrast.

She isn't here. Why has my mother summoned me to this place?

Even as she wondered, she felt herself relax, and when her eyes fell from the full moon back down to the earth, she saw a dark figure standing before her. It was the very absence of light, lacquer black, and it stood directly in the center of the nine gravestones. So complete was the darkness that at first, Yorda had trouble believing there was a person there at all. It was like all the darkness of night had gathered in one place—a stagnating pool of dark mist, so dense it did not even let the light of the full moon inside.

"Yorda," the pool of darkness called to her. *The queen's voice. My mother's voice.*

As it spoke, the pool of darkness took the form of the queen, dressed all in black. Layer upon layer of delicate lace made up the long sleeves of her dress, and when they fluttered in the wind they seemed to melt into the night.

Yorda wondered what had happened to her mother's usual white gown. Struck more by suspicion than surprise, Yorda stepped back. *Am I seeing things? Could that really be my mother? Or has some creature of the night taken her form to trick me?*

"Approach, Yorda."

The queen raised her hand and beckoned Yorda closer. Wrapped in darkness, her face and hand stood out clearly. As the moon shone in the night sky above, so her mother's face shone white in the graveyard.

Yorda walked carefully so as not to trip on the hem of her long robe. Now she was sure the figure was her mother. She could smell a familiar perfume in the air.

"Where is your handmaiden?" the queen asked, looking over Yorda's shoulder.

"She waits beyond the staircase."

The queen smiled. "Very good. The secret I will show you is not meant for one of common blood."

The queen was not angry. In fact, she sounded pleased, as when first trying on an ornate necklace brought to her from a far-off land. Just as when she opened the box, lifted the lid, and took it out.

"You know that only our most loyal servants, those who gave their lives to the castle, are buried here," the queen said, turning slowly as she surveyed the graves. "Their bond to the castle runs deep."

"I know. Master Suhal taught me this," Yorda replied, stiffening against the cold that seemed to creep in through her thick robes. Her breath turned to frost in the air.

"But, Yorda," the queen said, "this is not just a graveyard." She smiled at the suspicion on Yorda's face. "This is a gateway to eternity. I always knew that I must bring you here one day. Tonight has provided the perfect opportunity."

The queen stepped away from her, black gown billowing in the night air, making for a stone in the corner. Yorda hastily followed. Her own footsteps fell loudly on the grass, and she wondered how her mother could walk so quietly.

Stopping in front of the gravestone, the queen entwined the fingers of both hands before her and, with bowed head, began to pray. The prayer was unfamiliar to Yorda, and the queen's words so quiet they seemed to slip down the skirts of her robes to be absorbed directly into the ground.

Stopping her prayer, the queen raised her head and the gray stone at her feet slid to the side with a rumbling noise.

Where the gravestone had stood, Yorda could see a staircase leading down into the ground. She gasped.

"Follow me," the queen said, tossing a smile over her shoulder as she descended the stairs. "What you must see lies below."

The gravestone was not very large, and the entrance to the staircase it had concealed was quite narrow. Yet the queen descended as though being swallowed by the opening where the stone had stood, black gown and all, without even ducking her head. As if she were without substance, able to pass through the earth unimpaired. In the space of a moment, she had disappeared entirely.

"Mother!" Yorda called out.

But no answer emerged from the black maw of the staircase.

Fearfully, she took one step onto the stairs. She felt herself being drawn downward, and to prevent herself from toppling she brought down her other foot. She took another step, then another. Soon her feet were following each other of their own accord. What Yorda wanted had nothing to do with it.

She practically skipped down the staircase, and when her head was underground, darkness enveloped her. It was pitch black, too dark even to see the tip of her nose. Fear clutched at her.

Above, the gravestone returned to its former position, closing off the only exit. Yorda whirled around at the sound and tried to run back. But all she could feel above her now was the cold soil, and it would not yield no matter how hard she pushed. She scratched at it with her nails, and wet dirt crumbled down onto her face and got into her eyes.

In her fright, she stumbled and fell, but what she saw brought her bolting up straight.

Nothing had changed in the darkness. But through it, she could see the steep staircase leading much further down, twisting and turning as it descended. The walls that had seemed to press so close against her were gone. The staircase stood out against the darkness, a jagged white ribbon that shrank into the depths.

Yorda could not believe that a staircase went so deep beneath the castle. It didn't seem possible. The distance between where she stood now and where the staircase disappeared into the darkness—just ahead of the queen—was almost as great as the distance between the high tower of the central keep and the front courtyard. Yorda felt dizzy with the height. She also couldn't understand how she could see beyond the turns of the stair, through what should have been solid ground. *Are these stairs suspended in the middle of some vast chamber? Who could have dug so deep, and when?* Yorda wondered, even as she feared what she might find at the bottom.

The queen was far ahead of her now, past the fifth or sixth turn. The whiteness of the staircase made Yorda think of a bone, and the queen was a black-winged butterfly crawling along it.

"There is nothing to be frightened of." The queen's form appeared tiny in the distance, yet her voice was close, as though she spoke right into Yorda's ear. "Come down," the voice said, "this place is within a realm I have created. It is all a vision, yet through my power it is given form. The stairs may appear steep, but there is no danger of falling."

Yorda carefully began to descend. For the first few steps, she went down like a child does, sitting on each step, holding the edges with her hands. The stairs did not collapse or dissolve beneath her. They were real. The feel of them beneath her fingers was smooth and cold.

By the time she had regained her courage and begun to walk, the queen had disappeared from ahead of her, too far off now to see. The stairs wound around and around, coming to a small landing at each turn before beginning to descend again. As she went down, she stopped being able to tell which way was up. Soon she wasn't even aware that she was descending, and it felt more like she was walking along a single long road. Above her head was only a void—she couldn't even hear herself breathing. Nor did her feet make any sound.

Yorda wondered if this strange space could be the path to the underworld they say the living must walk when they die. *I wonder if the truth of what my mother is going to show me ahead can only be seen by the dead, and that is why I must die. Each step brings me closer to a living death.*

When she realized this, the stairs came to an abrupt end.

Yorda blinked. She had been lost in her own thoughts, unaware of where she was.

She had come into a circular space, no larger than a small gazebo. Above her was darkness. The room was surrounded by round columns and filled with a pale white light, like moonlight, though Yorda could find no obvious source.

The long staircase was behind her now, stretching up from between two of the columns. Now the light was fading, as though a torch had been snuffed out, returning the room gradually to darkness.

The queen stood before her. She wore a smile on her white face, and her hair, bound into a black knot on her head, shone with a wet gleam.

"Come closer," she said. Yorda approached, and the queen took her hand. Her skin was cold, but Yorda clung tightly regardless. She had a sudden sensation like she was floating. The round floor on which they stood had begun to drop. As they went further down, Yorda gaped at what she saw.

They had descended into a large hall. She guessed it to be about the same size as the Eastern Arena. Walls rose at a slant around them, and on their slope stood countless stone statues—a gallery, with the moving platform she rode on at its center.

When the platform stopped its descent, the queen let go of Yorda's hand, and like a singer performing to a crowd, she lifted her face and spread her arms wide.

"This is my secret. Do you not find it beautiful?"

Yorda spun in a slow circle as she looked over the crowd of statues. There were so many it was hard to count—hundreds, she guessed. The platform had settled at the lowest point of the bowl-shaped room, and it felt as though the stone statues were looking back down at her, so lifelike they were.

Spurred by her curiosity, Yorda left the queen's side and walked among the statues, looking at each of them in turn. There were men and women, wearing all manner of clothes. Some were old, others young, all with different expressions. Though the stone of the statues was a uniform gray, they were carved in such detail, she could even tell which way they had been looking by peering into their eyes. Some looked up into the sky, others looked down at their own feet. Some statues' mouths were closed, and others open as though they were about to speak.

She saw warriors with chain-mail vests and knights in full plate armor. *That statue of the old man wielding a scepter must be a priest,* she thought. And there was a scholar, books tucked under his arm and a round hat on his head. There was a girl, smartly dressed, with a woman standing next to her who could have been her mother. There were two women who looked very similar—sisters, maybe—one with a fan half open in her hand, the feathers on its edges so lifelike they seemed like they might blow in the breeze.

"Stunning, aren't they?" the queen asked, obvious satisfaction in her voice. In her observations of the statues, Yorda had wandered quite a distance from her mother. So far, she did not hear the tinge of sharpness in her voice.

"Yes, very," Yorda replied, astonished. "I've never seen such ornate sculpture. Mother, what master craftsmen did you order to make these? I had no idea we had such talent at court."

The queen laughed quietly. There was a coldness in her laugh that made Yorda pause. She turned to look at her mother. The queen stood in the middle of the circular dais, staring directly at her.

"Mother?"

The queen raised her head slightly and pointed with a long finger off to Yorda's right. "Look over there. You'll find my newest works."

Yorda began to walk, her eyes still fixed on her mother. The queen's smile was growing wider.

She's trying to catch me off guard, Yorda thought suddenly, feeling goose bumps rise on her skin. *Why am I trembling?* A dark premonition rose in the back of her mind. Yorda returned her gaze to the statues and found a familiar face standing at the very bottom of the long row.

Though her eyes saw, for a moment she did not comprehend. The statue was of a young woman with a slender figure and oval eyes. Beautiful eyes, frozen in time. Her head was lowered in defeat, yet there was fear and awe in her face as well.

I know that face.

She was wearing a long tunic of a simple design. Her sleeves were embroidered, and her sash had been carefully folded across her waist. Her hair was held in place by a hairpin in the shape of a daisy. Yorda knew it very well. She had seen it practically every day. The pin had been a gift from her lover—

But that's impossible.

For a moment, Yorda's eyes lost focus. At last, she understood. The statue was her handmaiden—the very same girl who had used all of her cleverness to help her attempt to escape the castle for one day of fun.

Next to her stood her lover, the royal guard. He wore his sword in the leather belt that went with his leather armor. Its hilt bore an engraving with his surname and a single star to indicate that he was of the lowest rank of guards.

The boy's eyes were opened wide, and the fingers of his right hand were curved like hooks, gripping at the air, as though he would have drawn his sword, if he had but a second's more time.

"Yes, Yorda," the queen said, her voice incongruously gentle. "I turned them to stone and placed them here to decorate my chamber. Now you see the hideous penalty your foolishness has—"

But before the queen had finished, Yorda fell to the ground unconscious.

[5]

THE MINISTER'S LONG speech was over, and the beginning of the great tournament formally declared. The contestants split, heading off to the eastern and western arenas. Yorda could not bear to watch them go, and so she stepped away from the terrace back into her chambers.

She had awoken later that night to find herself lying in bed, with the queen sitting next to her. It took only one look at her mother's thin smile to realize that what she had seen beneath the graveyard was no nightmare.

"Perhaps that was a little shocking for you," the queen said, her tone no different than if they had been two girls exchanging secrets beneath the blankets. "I had hoped you would be able to spend a little more time observing my handiwork."

The queen told her that she had not created her secret gallery for punishment. Had Yorda looked a little longer, she would have seen that more than a few of the statues were victors from tournaments past.

"When the victors are chosen, they're treated like royalty—true to our word. For a while, they enjoy their post as master-at-arms, and in time they are sent to another keep within my domain, there to serve as captain. While there—say, for a year perhaps—they train the garrison in their techniques. Then, when the conditions are right, I summon them back to the castle."

"Where you turn them to stone? Why? What possible benefit can be had from such cruelty?"

"A stone warrior cannot turn against his master," she replied without hesitation. "War is nothing more than a clash between soldier and soldier. Should one of such quality fall into the hands of my enemies, I would be ruined."

When it became known that the tournament was a shortcut to glory within the queen's lands, confident warriors came from far and wide—even from beyond the borders of the realm. And so she sapped the strength of her neighbors without raising their suspicions.

"And when they go missing? Surely they must have wives and children, brothers and sisters, friends. Have you not thought on how these people must worry, or their sadness?"

"I fear you're mistaken, my child," the queen said. "Not once has anyone demanded to know the whereabouts of one of the victors. That is the sort of people these adventurers are, you know. Nobody cares, no one misses them. If anyone ever should, why, I can simply tell them that the one they search for died a glorious death in battle. That should satisfy all but the most curious."

Yorda couldn't believe what she was hearing. "Did you think of this plan by yourself, Mother? Was this your idea?"

"Why do you ask?"

"I want to know."

The queen put a finger to her chin. "Do you want me to say that it was *not* my idea? That this was some plan dreamed up by my ministers, one of Master Suhal's stratagems? Or perhaps it began at the bequest of your late father."

Yorda knew her father would never do such a thing. Her eyes filled with tears as she looked at the queen.

"My sweet, naive Yorda. You have an innocent soul. Though our land may seem peaceful, look closely and you will find war and strife—even bloodthirsty rivalries for wealth among our own merchants. If it serves to protect our lands from the watchful eyes of our neighbors, no measure is too extreme."

"But, Mother!" Yorda leapt to her feet. She made to clasp her mother's arm, but the queen slid aside and stood. She walked over to the window.

The queen's profile was luminous as it caught the sidelong light of the moon. "You are accustomed to peace and ignorant of the truths in our world. Glory and safety cannot be claimed without a price. This is a lesson which you must learn."

"You have great power, Mother," Yorda said with a trembling voice. "I heard so from the Captain of the Guards and even Master Suhal. They say it exceeds the imagination, though none will tell me how. Then why do you fear our neighbors so? Should they invade, can you not push them back yourself?"

To her surprise, the queen laughed merrily. "Is that respect I hear in your words?"

Yorda gripped the edges of her silken covers tight. "No," she said quietly. "I fear you, Mother."

The queen drew back her dark veil, straightened her hair, and turned to Yorda. "Well said. I am a frightening woman." She sounded pleased. "I was born with great magic, and under the protection of the Dark God it has grown into something even more powerful. Indeed, I could destroy the world if I so wished. Yet I have sworn never to use my power unless absolutely necessary." She lifted a hand, pointing toward the sky. "My power is not the power of the sword, Yorda. That is why I seek only to defend my lands, and never to invade…It is not yet time for that."

Not yet time?

"These people who fear me recall incidents in the distant past when I turned my powers on a barbarian tribe who sought to form a country of their own too near our borders, and then again when one of our neighbors became too greedy for their own good."

"What did you do to them?"

"I turned them to stone and let them fall to dust."

Yorda imagined the scene in her mind's eye. An entire town turned to stone, a howling barbarian horde frozen mid-charge. For years they might stand, until the wind wore their shapes down to sand.

"Among the kings and generals of our neighbors, there are many who have heard of my power. Thus they are cautious and never move directly against us. However, they fear only me, not the strength of my army. Thus the endless skirmishes on our borders, of which I'm sure you're aware."

Indeed, Yorda had heard much from her tutors of the many small conflicts that erupted in the far corners of the realm. "Women are ill-suited to waging war," the queen said, her voice wilting. "And my power is one of destruction, not warfare. So to keep our neighbors frightened of me, I must *be* frightening. I do not wish to face them in open battle. That is why I devise these strategies. Culling the most able of warriors is but the smallest part of my plan—a symbolic gesture, if you will. I have sowed many other schemes that grow in places unseen. Ask Master Suhal and the ministers about them if you wish. They will tell you once I have given them permission to do so."

"Then what is it you want, Mother? Is all this to defend our country?"

"For now, yes," the queen said.

Yorda's vision dimmed. She felt not fear or anger, but to her own surprise, a deep sadness. *What* does *my mother want?* The knowledge was painful, but she had to know. If she did not ask now, there might never be a second chance. "And when the time comes," Yorda said, summoning her courage, "what then?"

The queen nodded slowly. "I made a pact with the Dark God. I will use the power he gave me to wipe this world clean and make a new land with the Dark God as its true Creator."

The Creator Yorda knew was Sol Raveh, the Sun God, who loved and nurtured all from the sky above. So had she been taught since she was a child. The sun's warmth gave life to all living things, even as its light protected them. Not just her own kingdom, but all the lands looked up to this one God of Light.

Was the religion that followed this deity and prayed to him not administered by their own clerics? Had her mother not sworn her marriage vows in a great cathedral to the God of Light?

"You turn against our own religion, Mother?"

The queen turned up her nose at that. "The country needs its religion, that's true. If it will help keep the commoners in line, I will pay lip service to any faith required of me."

Yorda frowned. "I don't believe the Dark God exists. Even if he did, he cannot possibly win against the Light."

"You say that only because you do not know the truth." The queen lowered the curtains, blocking out the moonlight. The light of the single candle in the room flickered, sending shadows dancing across the walls. The queen walked to the foot of Yorda's bed, leaning in close like a sister sharing a secret.

The silken covers sank slightly beneath her weight. *This is my mother,* Yorda told herself. *She's real, not something born from shadow.*

"The gods wage ceaseless war in the heavens, much as men do on the earth below. The God of Light to whom you pray is merely the current victor in this war, thus does he rule. Only under his temporary reign is my god called a demon and made to suffer away from his rightful glory. One day, I will rise victorious, the Dark God's child, and pull the King of Light from his throne."

Yorda fell silent for a moment, considering. "This Dark God," she said at length. "What is he like?"

The queen smiled, pleased at the question. "He is the one who gives true freedom to those who dwell upon the earth. He governs the darkness.

"What light gives birth to, darkness destroys," the queen told her in a chant. "That is why the power of destruction has been granted to me. Darkness, not light, governs life. Why, it can even stop time. Trust me, my daughter, though we may lie in wait now, our day of victory will come."

The queen smiled. "This is written in no history book, and I am sure Master Suhal will not tell you, so I will teach you in his stead. I was born with the blessing of the Dark God, Yorda. The very moment of my birth, the sun in the sky was covered in darkness, unable to shine."

A solar eclipse. Yorda knew the phenomenon occurred only rarely. The priests and the history books said that it happened when the Sun God rested. At these times, all creatures upon the earth were to cease their activity and join in his rest.

"What you have learned is a lie. People interpret the world to suit themselves, even in divine matters," the queen explained, her disdain apparent. "The true meaning of the eclipse is that the God of Darkness is resisting the God of Light, showing him that his power has not been completely extinguished. During that brief time when the God of Light was powerless, the Dark God sent me here. I am his child," she said with evident pride.

"My mother, your grandmother, said it was an ill omen for a royal child to be born without the blessing of the God of Light, and she tried to take my life while I still lay in the birthing bed. But my father stopped her. He said that a child born while the God of Light was at rest would be born with the strength to act in the deity's stead. My father believed that until his dying day and favored me above all of my siblings."

Yorda had never known her grandfather, nor her aunts and uncles. By the time she was born, all of them had long since passed.

"Your siblings died quite young, did they not?" Yorda said quietly. What if her mother, to ensure her father's favor, had done something truly horrible—

"My father was mistaken, of course," the queen said, ignoring the question. "He was a very kind soul." When she spoke, it was without the slightest hint of warmth or affection. "I was not to serve in the stead of the God of Light. Nor was I to serve him. I was born to conquer this world and offer it up to the God of Darkness."

Then Yorda understood. "You're waiting for the next eclipse, aren't you?"

The queen smiled softly. "You are clever, my child. A worthy daughter."

"When will that be?"

"I wonder," the queen said, tilting her head, an elegant curve to her neck.

It was clear that the queen knew. Of course she would know. The many scholars in the castle, Master Suhal among them, could read the unseen calendar of the skies and gain from it knowledge of the heavens. It occurred to her that she had not seen many scholars amongst the statues below the graveyard—her mother wisely divided the world into those she saw as enemies and those whose skills she required.

"Someday I will take my place as queen of this world. Until then, I choose to avoid senseless conflict, to be as gentle as the dove and clever as the snake. Remember this well, for it will serve you too."

With that, she gathered up her skirts and left Yorda's chambers.

Alone again, emotions welled up inside her, and for a while, Yorda could do nothing but curl into a ball, clutching her knees tight to her chest. The strongest of her emotions was fear, but it was her unbridled sadness that made her body tremble unceasingly.

When she had finally settled down, Yorda realized that she still had questions. She wondered if her father had known about her mother's true nature or the atrocities she had committed. She wondered too if her mother worried that Yorda might not live to see the next eclipse.

Both were important questions. The first would solve a lingering mystery about Yorda's late father, and the second would reveal Yorda's own destiny. But the two questions remained inside her without an outlet. They sat by her heart, leeching the life from it and spreading dark branches to block the light from the outside world.

When a contestant in the tournament fell, they were ordered to leave the castle, and so with each passing day the number of warriors remaining dwindled even as the enthusiasm of the spectators grew.

Unless they came from a particularly wealthy merchant family or were artists or scholars of renown, most commoners never had the chance to see the tournament. The noble houses often ran their own swordsmen in the bouts, and there were many highborn ladies who looked forward to the occasion as a chance to don their finest and and present themselves to the world. During these days, the usually austere castle was filled with bustling activity. Its stone corridors came alive with glittering hair and the scent of perfume from ladies vying to outdo each other, while every hall rang with lively conversation.

Tradition held that the queen observe the final rounds on the eighth day from her throne. At the last tournament, three years earlier, when Yorda had been only thirteen, she had worn voluminous robes and a veil over her face to watch the spectacle from her mother's side. Yet she had grown ill at the sight of the men fighting and the blood splattered on the ground, so much so that she had missed seeing the grand ceremony in which the queen herself awarded the victor.

Yorda was glad now that she had missed it. *If I had been there and blessed the champion—*

Now that she knew the true nature of the tournament, she would have been filled with self-loathing, unable even to lift her head from her pillow.

Not knowing her true feelings, those around her assumed that when she said she would not be attending the final round of the tournament nor the ball afterwards, she was still frightened from her experience three years before.

"When you have grown a little more, Princess Yorda, those brave warriors will steal your heart away," the minister said with a laugh. "Wait another three years, and you will feel differently about the tournament."

You're wrong, Yorda thought. *I know the truth now. My feelings will never change.*

The queen did not compel her to attend. For the first three days of the tournament, Yorda wandered the castle halls like a living apparition. Even in her chambers with the windows closed, she could hear the shouts from the arenas and the screams carried on the wind. They revolted her.

The areas of the castle Yorda was allowed to visit were even further restricted during the tournament. Though guests to the tournament came only by invitation to keep out the riffraff, it wouldn't do to expose her to so many, said the queen, even if they were of noble blood. Yorda knew which areas were off-limits by the guards in front of corridors she usually walked and doors she usually opened.

If she wandered out onto the terrace of any room but her own, she would be scolded and sent immediately back to her chambers.

The guards were also excited by the tournament. Their interest was natural, given that they would serve under the victor, but that was not their only stake in the competition. Soldiers were always drawn to the strong and the fiery of spirit. Betting was rampant both within and without the castle walls, with merchants acting as bookmakers, pooling coin from commoners and keeping the bets coming.

Yorda played a little game in which she would walk around the castle waiting to be seen, stopped, and turned back. Even as she walked away, still within hearing distance, the guards would begin talking about their tournament picks, enthusiastic about the performance of this or that combatant. Yorda wanted no part in it. She wanted to walk up to the guards and interrupt their wagering to tell them what the tournament really meant. She wanted to shout it at the top of her lungs. But she knew nothing would come of it. The queen would merely order her locked away, lamenting that her daughter had succumbed to the stress of the event. And that would be the end of it.

There was a kind of intimate fear Yorda felt from the word *confinement* and the understanding that it could happen to her. The feeling was never greater than when she visited the high tower directly behind the central keep of the castle. Officially known as the North Tower, most called it the Tower of Winds.

Atop the island cliffs as it was, the castle was surrounded on all sides by the sea. Yet only from the tower in the north could one see the vast grasslands that covered half the continent. The north was the direction of invasions and barbarians, the source of trouble. This was where the Tower of Winds was located.

Master Suhal had explained it once.

"Our great and glorious castle was constructed by the fifth king of our land, Princess Yorda. By your great-great-grandfather. Yet the Tower of Winds was built some thirty years later, in commemoration of the victory over the nomadic horse tribes to the north, which marked a great expansion of our territory.

"These nomadic horsemen revered a wind god as their guardian deity. The power of the wind must have been hugely symbolic to people who galloped across the fields, climbed the mountains, and kept the great plains as their fortress. When our fifth king defeated them, he took their faith, and the power of the wind god they worshipped, and added them to the defenses of our kingdom. The Tower of Winds was built to worship this god."

In Yorda's imagination, the wind god had been trapped in the foundations of the tower. She had never heard of anyone in the royal house being so confined—be it for political reasons or disease—but if a god of wind could be imprisoned in her own home, what of her?

Now, the Tower of Winds was simply another part of the castle, one she rarely paid mind to. No ceremonies of any kind were held there, nor was it even used for housing. Her mother had decreed it so when she took the throne. Yorda had never thought to wonder why.

But now that she knew by her mother's own admission that she had formed a pact with the Dark God, Yorda had another interpretation for her mother's attitude toward the tower. The queen would not be able to abide the thought of another deity living within her own castle, not even the long-imprisoned god of a vanquished people. It would vex her to have that prison stand on her own grounds, directly behind her main hall. Now that she, daughter of the God of Light in the eyes of her ministers, ruled the kingdom, she had convinced her subjects that there was no need to rely upon the protection of any deity other than their own. Mother would have destroyed the tower if she could. Letting it fall into ruin was the next best thing.

The central keep and the Tower of Winds were divided by a chasm spanned by a long stone bridge. Yorda stood in the middle of the bridge, looking down at the calm blue waters far below. She raised her eyes to the tower. With the lack of upkeep in recent years, the effects of erosion were evident on the tower's walls. It looked decades older than the rest of the castle. Most of the curtains were gone from the square windows lining the circular tower, and a white curtain had been left out on the rooftop to flap mournfully, tattered and dirty, like a ghost caught between this world and the next.

No guards were on patrol here. There was no bright flash of color from the leather armor worn by the patrols that walked the castle gardens and the outer wall. It was quiet, which was exactly what Yorda wanted. She had taken to coming here frequently since the beginning of the tournament.

Not that it was a happy place to visit. Thoughts of a god confined for eternity chilled Yorda's heart. And the only things to look at were the desolate tower and a sky and sea so blue and vast she lost her sense of distance. Standing there on the bridge, she often felt that her soul had lost its moorings and begun to drift toward the sky. Riding on the wind, her soul would go far away. Or perhaps it would be drawn into the tower, to hide in the shadow of the tattered curtain at the top, and from there look down on the queen's domain.

Spurred by such fancies, Yorda began to wonder if she couldn't indeed climb the tower. She tried to find a way up. Yet two strange statues stood barring the doorway, and no matter how much she pushed and pulled at them, they would not budge.

The statues were of a curious shape, vaguely humanoid, but blocky and with the odd proportions of primitive idols. Their bellies had separate carvings on them—idols within idols—a warrior wielding a sword on the right statue, and a mage wielding a staff on the left.

Whatever the idols were, they were the guardians of the tower, barring the entrance. Without an obvious drawbar or lock, she couldn't even begin to imagine how she might get inside. Nor could she ask Master Suhal. He would merely scold her and tell her that the Tower of Winds was no place for the princess to go for an afternoon constitutional.

When she touched the idols with her hand, the sense of confinement she had always associated with the tower struck her more forcefully and more coldly than ever before.

The wind that whipped around the tower blew hard. Perhaps the strength of the wind deity trapped inside had not faded entirely. Or perhaps the god's strength had withered long ago, and this was merely a natural phenomenon, the wind from the sea colliding with gusts from the northern plains.

Yorda left the idols behind, returning to the stone bridge. She had taken no more than a few steps when she noticed a tall, dark figure standing at the far end of the bridge near the castle. Standing and watching.

[6]

YORDA SQUINTED AS she held up her hand against the buffeting wind and the sun. *Who could that be?* Even from a distance, she was sure it was not one of the royal guards.

The figure took a slow step out onto the bridge. He continued walking toward the middle with slow yet steady steps, without so much as a glance at the view to either side. Yorda wasn't even sure whether he had noticed her presence.

Yorda took a step backward. The bridge was long, and the figure still quite distant, but should he mean her harm the bridge was her only means of escape. A few more steps back, and her back would be up against those immovable statues.

The sun had already left its apex and was beginning to fall toward the horizon. The black figure walking with long strides across the bridge cast a short shadow on the stones. Yorda breathed a sigh of relief—if he cast a shadow, he was surely a man of flesh and blood.

As he approached, the silhouette billowed slightly. *He's wearing a cloak. That's what gives him that dark shape.*

Yorda took another deep breath and realized that she had been walking toward the center of the bridge too, matching the other's pace without realizing it.

As the distance closed between them, Yorda realized he was a swordsman—she could see his blade hanging from his belt. He used his right hand to keep his cloak from wrapping around too tightly. A piece of metal armor on the back of his hand caught the sunlight and sparkled.

They were growing nearer each other, but still not close enough for their voices to reach. *What do I do?*

The swordsman arrived at the middle of the bridge before her. As she approached, he moved to one side, his armor rattling with each step. Then he bent one knee, placed the fist of his right hand on the bridge, and lowered his head.

Yorda stopped, surprised by the sudden obeisance. She straightened her posture. There were only five or six paces between them now.

The swordsman addressed her in a voice that was clear and deep. "My apologies for the nature of our encounter. I beg your forgiveness. I had no intention of disturbing the young lady's walk."

Blinking, Yorda put a hand to her chest. "Oh no, I wasn't—" she began, her voice sounding rough in her ears. Perhaps she had spent too much time in silence in the wind.

She marveled at the strangeness of the swordsman's appearance. She guessed his cloak was a traveling cloak. His leggings and armor were clearly leather, reinforced by silver and copper studs in places. The manner in which the leather in his armor had been stitched was unlike that of the castle patrolmen, with larger pieces making for a rougher look. The sword at his waist was wide and double-edged. She guessed it was quite heavy, and the cloth- and leather-wrapped hilt looked well worn.

Yet the strangest thing of all was the swordsman's helmet. It was the color of burnished silver, with holes for the eyes, yet it covered his face from the top of the head down to the jaw. His ears poked out from small holes on the side, and above that animal horns had been attached, apparently made of real bone.

She had never seen anything of the sort. *He is not of our land. A swordsman from another country.* Yorda gathered her wits and cleared her throat, which was, she realized, exactly the sort of sound a noble lady might make in the situation, which in turn made her oddly embarrassed. She was rarely in public, and whenever the opportunity did arise, she was only required to perform a practiced role, nothing more. The only words she needed to say were those she had been taught for the occasion. This had been the nature of her only contact with the outside world until now. In fact, this encounter might very well be her first time ever speaking so freely with a stranger.

"Not at all," she managed to say, feeling her cheeks blush and trying to hide the fact that she was flustered. "I will allow that I was startled, but even still you needn't apologize so."

The swordsman lowered his head again, thanking her for her kind words. There was a sincerity in his manner that made his respect for Yorda clear—but it was also clear that he did not realize she was the queen's daughter and princess of the castle. He probably assumed she was the daughter of some noble family come to visit the castle for the tournament. It did strain the imagination to expect to find the princess walking alone out in a place like this, after all.

Still, she was curious how a clearly foreign swordsman had managed to venture so deep into the castle grounds without an escort or, she assumed, permission.

"You are a participant in the tournament?"

The man looked up, revealing a sturdy chin beneath his faceplate. He nodded. "As you say. I thought to steal a moment of time to look upon Her Majesty's glorious castle—and I'm afraid I've lost my way."

Yorda smiled. "You wandered quite far into the castle."

"Apparently so."

"While we speak here, the time of your next bout might well come and go. Shall I show you the way back to the arena?"

The swordsman thanked her deeply, then added, "And my apologies." He removed his helmet. It was certainly against the custom in any land for a warrior to address a lady with his head covered—though as it turned out, leaving his helmet on might have been the more prudent decision.

Yorda quickly bit the inside of her cheek, trying unsuccessfully to stifle a little yelp. The horns she had thought were a part of his helmet grew *out of the swordsman's head.*

She looked more closely at him. His face and cheeks had been tanned by the sun, making his skin as ruddy as his leather armor. His eyes were a quiet shade of gray, and though he moved with ease, he was not particularly young. His voice flowed like a great river, and from its tone and the serene look upon his face, Yorda guessed his age to be around forty. He was the very picture of a veteran swordsman.

And not just from another country, but another sort of people altogether.

Placing his helmet by his feet, he put his right hand over his breast in a formal manner. "I am the itinerant knight Ozuma. While I wandered the lands far to the east," he told her, "I heard of Her Majesty's grand tournament, and wanting to test my own skills, I traveled far to come here. In the spring I was at last allowed entrance to this country, and it is my honor above all else that I was given leave to participate in the tournament."

He spoke of the lands to the east—Yorda had heard of the city-states beyond their eastern borders. Yet in all of her geography and history lessons, she had never once heard of a land of men with horns.

"Sir Ozuma...tell me, from where do you hail? That is, where were you born?" she asked, uncertain of the proper words to use in this situation. She had just convinced herself that she had made a horrible breach of etiquette, when Ozuma smiled.

"You must be startled at my appearance," he said. "I regret if I have caused you any distress."

"No, there's no need to apologize," Yorda said, coming three steps closer, then taking one step back. "It is I who should apologize. It was not my place to ask."

Yorda clasped her hands together and shook her head, and Ozuma's smile deepened. It seemed strangely familiar, though it was a few moments before she realized it was her father's tender smile it reminded her of.

Why would he remind me of my father? The knight Ozuma's face looked nothing like her father's.

"In the place where I was born, all of us have horns upon our heads," Ozuma explained. "In our people's history, it is written that our ancestor carried in his veins the blood of a fierce wild ox, protector of the earth. He was our guardian deity, rescuing the weak and punishing our enemies, with eternal life granted him directly by Sol Raveh, the Sun God. Thus these horns are a sign of our divine gift and a symbol of our holy contract."

It was the first legend of this sort Yorda had ever heard. "Do all people in your country look the same as you do?"

"We have no country, my lady. As protectors of the earth, we walk among all peoples; it is our destiny to wander from land to land. That is our story, as it is my own."

A wandering protector of the earth—

Just as clouds can suddenly rise to cover the sun, a shadow fell over Yorda's heart.

If this knight Ozuma should win the tournament, he would join her mother's gallery of lifeless adornments carved in stone.

Seeing the sudden dark look come over her, Ozuma's smile faded. In silence, Yorda stepped to the knight's side and knelt. With her knees joining his upon the stone, she had to look up to see him, and his shadow covered her completely.

"Will your next bout be your first in the tournament?" she asked him.

Ozuma blinked before replying, "The next will be my third match. By the good grace of god, I have prevailed in my previous two."

Yorda's shoulders shuddered. It only required six bouts to carry a contestant to the finals. He was already halfway there.

"Is something amiss?" Ozuma asked with genuine concern. "Do you feel ill? Your face has lost its color." Yorda's heart was torn by indecision. Were she to tell him here—but no, she could not. Saving one man would not change the tournament. She was certain he would not believe her in any case.

Yet, she did not think their encounter could be entirely by chance. Perhaps there was some meaning to him wandering the castle and finding her here. Perhaps the Sun God himself had led him here? Was he not a defender of the land?

"The tournament…" Yorda began hesitantly, "the tournament is not what you or the others who participate in it believe it to be. I know the truth. But I do not know how to tell you that you might believe me."

Ozuma's concern only deepened. Yorda took it as evidence of disbelief, and her heart tightened in her chest. "It is a difficult thing to believe, indeed. But I know it for a fact. I've seen it with my eyes. My mother…"

Yorda's fear caused the words to spill out of her in a flood, but Ozuma gently raised his hand. "Wait," he said. Without a sound, cloak billowing around him, he walked past her side so that he stood behind her. Yorda quickly stood and turned.

Ozuma was looking up at the Tower of Winds. His hands were at his sides, but tensed, ready to act should the need arise. Yorda could sense his alertness with her entire body. "What is it?" she asked, her voice barely more than a whisper.

"What is this tower?" Ozuma asked, still facing away from her.

"It is the Tower of Winds. The legend goes that a wind deity from another land is imprisoned there—though it is not used anymore. It's abandoned," she told him, feeling her pulse quicken, though she was not sure why. The wind was as cold as before, whipping up countless tiny waves on the surface of the water below. The sky was blue from horizon to horizon, and the wind whistled around the abandoned tower as it always did.

Yorda joined Ozuma in looking up at it. The square windows in the wall opened like empty mouths, devoid of life, or like eyes looking inward at the gloom within the tower. Then Yorda thought she saw something move in that darkness. Just beyond the window. Like someone had quickly passed by or looked out at them—a splash of dark upon dark. She could make out the silhouette, only the faintest suggestion of movement.

Ozuma squinted, as though looking at something very bright.

"What...was that?" Yorda asked, still doubting she had seen anything.

"Someone is there, though as to who..." Ozuma said, returning his gaze to Yorda. His battle readiness of a moment before was gone. "Sometimes, in abandoned places, there are sad things that live in secret, able to survive there and no place else. I would expect what we saw is something of that nature. Do not let it concern you, Princess. As long as you do not venture inside, there is no cause for worry," he said, his voice gentle, yet his warning clear: *stay away from that tower.*

Yorda's mind, however, was on other matters. "Did you not just call me princess?"

Ozuma smiled. Once again dropping to one knee, he placed his right hand upon his chest and bowed deeply. "So I did. For I have observed that you are Her Glorious Highness the queen's only daughter, the lady Yorda."

The feeling of loneliness rose in Yorda's breast. With her identity known, she felt a distance grow between her and the strange knight, shattering the curious closeness she had felt to him moments before. She realized it had been like speaking with her father again, and the loss felt even more acute.

"You are correct," she said quietly. "But we are outside the castle proper, and I was merely taking a walk. You do not need to bow."

"By your leave," Ozuma said.

The knight stood, his back to the Tower of Winds, standing almost as if he would protect her from the gaze of whatever was inside. "Though it is perhaps not my place as a wanderer to say such things, I would imagine that you sometimes feel inconvenienced by your very position as princess. Walks such as this must be valuable to your heart indeed, and I have disturbed yours. Please forgive me. Also forgive me if I beg that I might accompany you on your way back to the castle. The wind blows stronger than before."

It was clear that Ozuma no longer wanted to remain here. Though he had assured her there was no danger from the tower, he sensed something dangerous about the black form they both had seen within.

Yorda looked around, avoiding the tower. There was no one to be seen. This was likely to be the only part of the castle so deserted. If she were to talk with him further, there would be no better place than this.

"Ozuma?"

"My lady?"

"Before, when I spoke—"

"You spoke of Her Highness, though you called her mother," Ozuma cut in smoothly, "and you said you had something to tell me about the tournament."

Yorda nodded. So he *had* been listening.

"I took it from your words that there is something about the tournament, something unbeknownst to me, that causes you great anguish. Lady Yorda, have you witnessed the tournament before?"

"Only once," Yorda said, telling him about the incident three years before in which she had grown ill and been obliged to retire. "But," she continued, "that is not what I wished to tell you about."

She wondered again belatedly whether telling him the secret was the right choice. It seemed a terribly ominous thing to tell a stranger from another land whom she had only just met. And what if this Ozuma went and told others?

"Do not worry, Lady Yorda," Ozuma said in his gentle way. "For now, allow me to accompany you to a warmer place. It is grown quite chilly here. That, and I have a request."

"What sort of request?"

Ozuma bowed his head deeply. "In my third bout, I will triumph by virtue of my honor at having met you here today. I wager my life on it. My request is this: tomorrow, at the dawn after my victory, I would accompany you here again."

He wants to meet me again? In secret? Perhaps he was asking her to continue her story then.

"You are certain you will win?"

"By my name, I shall."

Finally, Yorda was able to smile. A great feeling of relief spread through her chest. "Then I will honor your request."

"The honor is mine," he said, bowing.

As she looked down at him, Yorda realized that she wasn't sure whether her relief came from the fact that she would not have to tell him her dark secret now, or from the fact that she would be able to tell him all on the following day.

Together they began to walk back toward the castle proper. Ozuma walked slowly, always a pace behind her. They crossed the long stone bridge, and she sent Ozuma on ahead so that they would not be seen together by the guards. Ozuma bowed again, then made his way off down the corridor of brick and stone. Yorda turned to watch him leave, but was astonished when she blinked and found that he was gone—vanished, like a shadow vanishes in the light. As though the noble knight Ozuma and all that had passed between them had been nothing more than a daydream.

Hearing other people around her in the castle, their voices echoing off the walls, Yorda felt as though she were coming to her senses after a long sleep. She wondered anew at how a mere participant in the tournament had managed to make his way to the tower. Who had allowed him to pass so freely through the castle grounds that he had gotten lost?

The more she thought about it, the more she realized how well Ozuma had steered their conversation. For all of his bowing, he had shown very little trepidation. Nor had he seemed particularly surprised when he found out that Yorda was the princess. It was all very suspicious.

It's almost as if he knew I was at the tower and came out to meet me. But who would do such a thing? And why?

If Yorda gave the order, she would be able to watch the third bout that afternoon from the throne. Yet were she to request that of one of the ministers, they would be suspicious, wondering whence came her sudden interest in the tournament. Though their suspicion would not be much of a problem, she was afraid the queen might catch wind of it.

That, and she was not sure whether Ozuma's bout would be in the Eastern or Western Arena. She was sure that if she asked where the warrior with horns would be fighting anyone could tell her, yet that would only raise more questions.

Yorda spent the rest of the long afternoon quietly poring over her history books. At times, the shouts of exultation and the horrified gasps from the arenas would drift upon the wind like leaves and come dancing in through her window. Each time she heard the noise of the crowds, her heart would race, and her eyes would slip from the ancient letters upon the page and lose their place.

It was a peculiar feeling for her that she could have exchanged words so easily with the strange knight and even arranged to meet him again. *Was it because he reminded me of my father?* The thought weighed heavily on Yorda's mind, yet it was not enough to explain her heart, nor the fact that she had almost told him the secret of the tournament.

What did she hope to gain by telling him? Had she wanted Ozuma to abandon the tournament and flee for his life? Alone?

Saving one man and ending the tournament were two different things. Or did she hope he would take her secret and shout it from the parapets, foiling her mother's scheme?

It occurred to Yorda that the chief handmaiden might make a better source of information about the queen than the Captain of the Guard or the ministers. She would certainly be easier to approach—though there was no guarantee that the handmaiden would be her ally. When she came to help Yorda change for supper that night, Yorda inquired, as casually as possible, on the progress of the tournament. The handmaiden's hands paused for a moment while tightening Yorda's sash.

"It's just that the noise coming from the arenas today was quite boisterous," she said, feigning distaste in hopes of sidestepping the handmaiden's suspicions. "I wondered if some strange new type of swordplay had been put on display. Not that it matters how it is done—butchery is still butchery. I know that my mother believes the tournament adds to the glory of the castle, but I do not like it. I wish that it would end."

"I do not know the details of today's melees," the chief handmaiden said while straightening Yorda's skirts. "But as you will be attending the banquet tonight, perhaps you might ask the Captain of the Guard. I am sure he has great interest in the tournament and would be happy to entertain your questions."

"Now I want to go to this banquet even less. That Captain of the Guard is the worst kind of garden—give him but the slightest taste of water and his stories will grow into trees tall enough to block out the sun." Careful not to overdo it, Yorda assumed a look of boredom. "Perhaps I'm just being selfish. I should endeavor to act the part of the princess so as not to disappoint our people."

Yorda smiled and looked down at the chief handmaiden. The handmaiden did not smile back. Her face was the same as it had been the night of the graveyard. Yorda wondered whether it was a mask she wore, concealing some truth beneath it—or whether fear and caution had frozen her face completely.

She would have to be even more cautious at the banquet. There was a strict order in which those attending the banquet were invited, and it changed each day. Of course, all were administrators or higher, but even the highest-ranking people in the castle such as the Ministers of Coin and Rites were not summoned to each and every banquet. During the tournament, only the Captain of the Guard and his deputy attended each banquet without fail so that they could report the day's happenings to the queen.

As the Captain of the Guard began his report that night, Yorda pricked up her ears, trying to pluck the valuable information from his outrageously flowery account. He described each round of combat in such minute detail that the telling took almost as long as the tournament itself.

Yorda waited patiently for mention of Ozuma's name, or anything about a strange knight with horns upon his head. So intent was she on listening that she confused the course with which she was supposed to use her silver fork. At the other end of the long table, the queen noticed the gaffe and lifted an eyebrow at Yorda as she quickly returned the fork to its proper place. The Captain of the Guard stopped his report when he saw the expression on Yorda's face.

"My apologies," Yorda said politely, smiling toward the captain. "Please go on."

"Well," the Minister of Court said with a laugh and a rub of his sizable belly, "it seems Princess Yorda has not overcome her aversion to our triannual entertainment."

"I'm afraid the princess is bored," the queen said, her red lips curling upward into a smile. The deputy captain—newly appointed that spring—peered at the queen, enchanted. "She resembles me at her age," the queen said. "A knight's skill at arms is of no consequence to a frail maiden, is it?" As she spoke, her black eyes stared directly into Yorda's across the table as if to say: *I have told you my secret. If you wish to reveal it here and now, go ahead, my beloved daughter. Ah, but you lack the courage. There is no way forward from here and no way to return. You must bear my secret with me and remain in silence without exit.*

Yorda gritted her teeth, enduring her mother's gaze. The smile on the queen's face widened.

"True enough, Your Majesty," the Minister of Court agreed loudly. "Yet I daresay even Princess Yorda would be interested to learn a bit of the customs of foreign lands. The tournament is many things, not least a gathering of the strongest and mightiest from across the entire continent."

Yorda turned to the minister. "Are there warriors and ladies from faraway lands in attendance?" she asked politely.

"Indeed, there are!" the minister said, leaning forward, his belly pushing the silver plate before him farther onto the table. "In fact, we welcome a most unusual knight to this particular tourney. I've never seen a man of his like. And his skill is remarkable!"

[7]

BY THE TIME Yorda reached the beginning of the stone bridge, Ozuma was already at the base of the Tower of Winds. He stood gazing up at the tower, his back to the bridge.

She quickened her pace, pleased that he had kept his promise. She was past the midway point of the bridge, the sea wind blowing against her cheek and lifting her hair as she ran, when Ozuma turned and saw her. He was dressed the same as he had been the day before. His black cloak billowed in the wind as he began to walk toward her.

When Yorda ran up to him breathlessly, Ozuma once again fell to one knee and bowed. Yorda curtsied in return, but when she spoke, she sounded less like a princess and more like a girl from town.

"I heard you were victorious in the third bout," she said, hand to her breast. "The ministers were enthralled by your skill with the sword. The Minister of Court said your victory was a sure thing, and the Captain of the Guard's eyes gleamed like a little boy, so happy he was at the thought of sparring with you."

Ozuma bowed again. "I am honored I was able to prevail yesterday, and even more so that I meet you here again, Princess," he said in his gentle, resonant voice. "I fear I speak above my station, however…"

Yorda stepped closer to him, putting a hand on his shoulder. "Let us not rest on formalities. I have little time."

Ozuma looked up and met Yorda's gaze, a question on his lips. Today, he was carrying his helmet beneath one arm. His uncovered horns were striking from this close.

"You must not win the tournament," Yorda said in a single breath. She shook her head. "You must not win your next bout. You will lose, and leave. You must escape."

Ozuma was speechless.

"I would not say such an important thing in haste or jest," Yorda continued. "I have good reason, though it is not something I am at liberty to share. Trust me when I say you cannot stay here at the castle. You should never even have participated in the tournament!"

"Yet," Ozuma replied slowly, "even should I leave, the tournament *will* have a champion. I do not see the princess's fears being put to rest by my departure."

Yorda's eyes went wide. "What do you mean?" She stepped closer, grabbing his arm in both hands. "Do you know something? Did you know when you chose to participate in the tournament?"

The wind blowing up from the sea whistled around them. Yorda felt the chill in the air, and she looked up at the Tower of Winds to see, in every empty window, dark shapes staring down at them. In her surprise, she took a step back and would have stumbled had Ozuma not reached out to catch her. He lifted her to her feet and looked around at the tower.

"I believe they can see your heart, Princess. Your presence near the tower agitates them."

Yorda looked up at Ozuma's tanned face, confusion and questions filling her eyes. "Who are they?"

"Those who have been trapped in the tower. See their shapes? They have the form of humans, but they are empty shades, formed of dark mist. Think of them as shadows who have stepped away from their bodies."

Yorda looked again at the windows. They might have been shadows, but they had eyes, glowing with a dull light. She saw several looking down at the bridge—shadows that walk alone.

"I…I had no idea such things were here. Often I have walked this place alone and never seen them before."

"They are sad, cursed things." Ozuma looked at Yorda's face, then put his hand gently on her back as if to push her away from the tower. "When you knew nothing of what happens here in the castle, they had no means by which to notice you. But now that you have knowledge, you know fear because you know the truth. That is why you can see them. And that is why they are drawn to the salvation your heart promises them."

It would be wise, Ozuma warned her, to avoid the tower unaccompanied in the future. "It will only trouble your heart needlessly," he said. "Once they have been turned to shades, there is nothing anyone can do to save them. They are forever imprisoned in the Tower of Winds."

"But…what are they?"

"I must apologize, Princess, for my purpose in meeting you here again today was none other than to test you."

"Test me? How?"

"I wanted to ascertain whether the lady Yorda herself would be able to see those shades in the tower. You can; that means your true eye has opened. Which in turn means that you know the truth, and you have touched the source of fear."

"You mean the truth about my mother."

When she saw Ozuma nod, Yorda's heart split in two—half filled with relief, half with sorrow and shame.

"How much do you know?" she asked. "Why have you come to this castle?"

Leaving the Tower of Winds, Yorda brought Ozuma to the old
trolley on the side of the castle. "When I was young," she explained
to him, "they used this trolley to bring supplies for expanding the
eastern wing of the castle."

The old rails stretched in a long line from the eastern wing up
to the northern side, running perfectly straight save for a single
curve midway. A thin layer of dust coated the rails, and the trolley,
made of sturdy boards fastened together, was chipped and worn
at the edges.

"When the construction was finished, they were supposed to
destroy the trolley and remove the rails, but my father ordered
them to leave everything as it was."

He knew how Yorda loved the view from the rails.

"I was something of a tomboy and always pleaded with him
to let me ride the trolley while they were working. My father let
me. I knew nothing of the world beyond the castle, nor did I have
any friends my own age. I was very lonely as a child. I believe my
father took pity on me. He asked my mother to leave the trolley
there until I grew older and tired of it."

With Yorda already confined to the castle, the queen had no
grounds on which to refuse him.

"My father's duties often took him away from the castle.
Whenever he would return, he would take me for rides."

"Then it is a place of good memories," Ozuma said. He smiled
at the girl.

"Yes," Yorda replied, running her hand along the trolley's handrail.
"Many memories." Whenever she came here, the sound of her father's
voice and the warmth of his hand rose fresh in her mind.

The trolley had been unused for some time, so neither the queen
nor the royal guard ventured here much. It was even possible they
had forgotten it existed.

The doors to the trolley platforms had been locked, but Yorda
kept a secret key. It was the one place she could come when she

needed to be alone. However, as the rails ran along the outer wall, and there were no handrails save on the trolley itself, it was not particularly safe. It was even dangerous to step out on the ledge by the rails on days when the wind from the sea was particularly strong. For these reasons, she had not visited the trolley for some time. That, and sometimes she did not want to remember her father so clearly. It was too painful.

"Here there is no one to watch over us. We can talk in peace."

Yorda had stepped down from the ledge onto the rails where she could take shelter from the wind. Ozuma walked around the platform, looking with amazement at the many interwoven towers of the castle, the strips of sea visible between them, and the blue sky stretching overhead.

"The view from here is incredible."

"Yes, but be careful. The drop at the edge of the platform and the rails is quite steep—like a sheer cliff. One misstep and you could well lose your life."

It was necessary to walk through the castle proper to come here, so though this was a safe place to talk, getting here unnoticed would be next to impossible. Ozuma had said that she need only instruct him which way to go and he would take care of the rest.

She had agreed, and he had taken her under his cloak. Yorda was not quite small enough to fit entirely beneath it, and she thought they would be discovered for sure, but Ozuma assured her it would not be a problem, and curiously enough, they were able to walk directly through the castle without being noticed—even when they passed by others close in the hall.

Perhaps in his training Ozuma had learned how to hide himself in plain sight. That would explain how he was able to make his way past the royal guards and castle patrol to the Tower of Winds, and how he had disappeared so suddenly when they parted the day before.

Or maybe, Yorda thought, *it is a kind of magic. If he truly is the descendant of one blessed by Sol Raveh, he might very well have power befitting a deity. Maybe even power enough to resist a child of the Dark God, the queen herself.*

Hope stirred in Yorda's breast. Yet at the same time, she felt a deep guilt. The queen was her mother. She was not sure that even the Creator, the Sun God who was father to all upon the earth, had forgiveness for children who betrayed their parents.

Ozuma approached and knelt before Yorda, who was sitting on the edge of the trolley.

"I know the secret of the tournament troubles you, Princess, yet you should know that in the outside world, there are already those who know the truth."

Yorda gripped the edge of the trolley tightly. "On this continent? In other lands?"

"Indeed," the knight replied. "Though it may be hard for you to believe, beyond this realm there are many who fear this castle and the power of the queen. In past battles, they have seen her terrifying strength.

"Yet the tournament has long been the only window connecting this land with its neighbors. There are some, like myself, who participate in order to gain information about this land, and others who participate to become a henchman of the queen with all the power that entails. There are many different people in this world, all with different ways of thinking. There are even those who would join your mother precisely because she is so feared."

Yorda thought she could understand that. If it were true that the queen held enough power to destroy not only this continent but the entire world, it was better to be on her side than any other.

And yet it was foolish to imagine one could join her. The queen had no need of anyone else, nor had she any intention of sharing her throne. The only one with whom she joined hands was the Dark God.

"Yet over the many tournaments, the victors have, without exception, vanished. We never hear of their glorious achievements in battle, their rise to power after their victory. No one has seen them on the battlefields, leading the charge."

Yorda slumped, putting a hand to her head as though she could push out her memories of the gallery of statues beneath the graveyard.

"There are those—people who want peace in this world under Sol Raveh's benevolent eyes—who would like to know what became of them. To learn what is going on within the queen's domain and what will happen next. Not from idle curiosity, but from a sense of dire urgency."

Yorda looked up. "And you are one of these people?"

Ozuma's eyes flickered to her face for a moment. "It is as you say," he replied. "Princess Yorda, are you aware of the large country, the Holy Zagrenda-Sol Empire, that stretches from far to the east down to the south?"

She had learned of all their neighboring lands in Master Suhal's lectures. "Yes, but I had never heard it called holy before."

Ozuma smiled faintly. "Its name was changed only three years ago. The founding royal family of the empire consider themselves descendants of Sol Raveh and bear his sign as their family crest."

"Not just priests of Sol Raveh, but actual ancestors?"

"Indeed."

A few days ago, Yorda would have laughed, but now that she knew that her mother was the child of the Dark God, it did not seem quite so preposterous.

"Princess, all men worship the gods and seek connections to them in any number of ways. Royal families and imperial houses desire a close connection to the divine all the more. Creating legends and stories to spread the word of one's own divine heritage is merely another strategy a ruler may employ. What is important is that the people believe, and they are able to display sufficient strength to keep the peace within their domain."

In these respects, Ozuma told her, the Zagrenda-Sol Empire had been successful.

"Not only do they command a powerful army, but they have

developed their lands well to make the country rich. They support merchants in their business and scholars in their endeavors. It is a place not only of material wealth, but spiritual wealth. I do not claim it is a paradise on earth, where all things proceed according to some divine plan. Zagrenda-Sol has her difficulties, as any country does—many, in fact. But these are ultimately inconsequential. No one expects us to be able to create a heavenly paradise during our lives on this earth, and a ruler would be foolish to promise such."

"And yet they call themselves a holy empire?"

Ozuma nodded. "The cathedral of Zagrenda-Sol is impressive indeed. It was constructed over a century ago, yet it boasts a tower high enough to catch the light of the morning star, and the bell tower is wide enough to house an entire village. It takes one hundred strongmen just to sound the vesper bells."

Three years earlier, the knight explained, the fifth emperor of Zagrenda-Sol took his throne at the young age of twenty-five. As dictated by law, his coronation took place in the cathedral, and there, the young emperor had received a revelation.

"In the revelation, the emperor learned that a herald of darkness had appeared upon the land, and that he, as the descendant of Sol Raveh, was to take a great sword of the purest light to destroy it. It was, in essence, a declaration of holy war. After changing the name of his country to the Holy Zagrenda-Sol Empire, he appointed the great cathedral as his headquarters for the coming war. He then created the position of priest-king in the cathedral and declared himself the first. Nothing of the kind had ever happened before in the long history of the empire."

While an emperor has the power to assemble and command an army within his own realm, a priest-king is a servant of the Sun God, the knight said, with the authority to assemble a great army from believers in all lands. In theory, the priest-king could call on anyone living where the Sun God is worshipped.

"After this declaration, the emperor sent out messengers across the continent, putting out a call to arms. I am sure one came here for your mother as well."

"My mother? Is she not feared by the people beyond our borders?"

"Of course. Even in the Holy Zagrenda-Sol Empire, they had concerns about the queen's power. No one knew that she, and the power she wielded, was the very herald of darkness foretold in the emperor's revelation. But as a matter of precaution they sent a messenger to ask her assistance in the coming battle. It was a test."

Yorda knew little of governance. Yet she had an idea of how her mother would have taken such news. She pictured those beautifully sculpted eyebrows lifting at the words *herald of darkness upon the land*, and at the announcement that the children of the Sun God had declared holy war against that darkness.

Against her.

Yorda wondered if she had been frightened—or perhaps she had merely laughed. Either way, she could not take action until the time of the next eclipse, when the Dark God's power obscured the sun. Until that day, the queen would have to quietly gather her strength.

"The queen did not respond to the emperor's request," Ozuma said, his voice sinking. He sounded almost sympathetic. "This, of course, deepened the suspicions of the priest-king. Even as he assembled his forces, the emperor had countless scholars and magi working to answer the question of what exactly these signs of darkness were meant to indicate. The emperor himself spent many days in contemplation and study of the revelation's meaning. And, just recently—"

Yorda shook her head, cutting him off. "They found that the herald was my mother."

Ozuma bowed deeply. "I am truly sorry, Princess."

Yorda sighed and covered her face with her hands. She felt as though she had been wounded deep in her chest and bled sadness from the wound.

Yet in her sorrow she also found solace. *I am not alone. I'm not the only one that knows of my mother's pact with the terrifying lord of the underworld.*

I have friends in the world outside—I hope.

Ozuma put a hand to his chest. "I am but the advance guard," he said, though Yorda detected that there was something he left unsaid.

"In other words, you are one of the warriors of our god summoned to the cause by the priest-king. You're here to find out what happens to the victors of the tournament—not just as the victor, but as the greatest warrior to participate in the history of the tournament."

"It is as you say."

For a time, Yorda was silent, feeling unease and doubt weighing on the scales of her heart. Every time she remembered what her mother had done, it chilled her to the bone, yet she did not think she should be so willing to accept everything that this strange knight told her at face value. The herald of darkness certainly sounded like her mother. Yet that was no proof that the knight's tale was not a false tapestry woven from threads of the truth.

It was certainly possible that a cabal of individuals seeking to oust her mother from the throne was trying to deceive her. The queen's plans were terrifying, yet an invasion was a terrifying prospect too, and not only for Yorda. It was a threat to her entire country.

To place her trust in Ozuma's words was to risk betraying her own country.

"Lady Yorda," Ozuma called to her, his voice like water over stones. "I had another reason for participating in the tournament and coming here to this castle. That was to meet you."

Yorda's eyes went wide. "Why would you want to meet me?"

"Is it not true that you have never left the castle grounds?"

Yorda nodded.

"This is because your mother keeps you confined here."

"Confined? No, she—well, yes, I suppose she does."

"Would it surprise you, Princess, to learn that you are not the only one whose comings and goings are so restricted? All of the people of your realm are barred from visiting other lands. Only a handful of trade routes still cross its borders, and these only by virtue of a treaty signed before the queen took her throne. Stranger still, her people do not find this suspicious or question it in the least."

The reason for this, the knight explained, was that the queen had cast a spell upon the land.

"You mean our citizens are all under an enchantment? That's ridiculous!"

"My sentiments precisely—but no less true for it, I'm afraid," Ozuma said. "This is why none question why someone so important as the princess of the realm is kept here in her castle and shown to no one. They never even think to wonder about you, Princess, not even the ministers in charge of the royal household's affairs."

Yorda felt a chill, and she hugged her arms close about her body.

"I beg you, listen with a still heart. There is more to the emperor's revelation I've not yet told you. Near the herald of darkness there is one who is aware of the darkness and possesses the power to defeat it. This one is already becoming aware of their role—and the darkness cannot be defeated without their strength."

"You mean to say that I am the one."

"I can think of no other. You are the true daughter of the queen, Lady Yorda. You carry her blood in your veins. It is not a stretch to imagine that you wield power yourself, such as might be used against her. That is why she does not let you leave the castle and keeps you within close reach. She bewitches her own people's hearts so that they will not suspect or question her reasons."

"Then why did my mother give birth to me at all?" Yorda suddenly shouted. "If she knew she would have to keep me locked up here all my life, she should never have brought me into this world. And why tell me her secret if she feared it becoming known?"

Yorda put a hand to her mouth. She had not intended to reveal that the queen had confided in her at all.

"It is a mystery, and one which you have encountered already it seems," Ozuma said quietly.

Yorda had no words with which to refute Ozuma's quiet condemnation.

The things she had seen beneath the graveyard tormented her even now, the fear tempered only by her sadness.

Yorda breathed a long, shuddering sigh and began to tell Ozuma everything, beginning with her ill-conceived attempt to venture outside the castle walls. She told him what she had seen beneath the cemetery, of the queen's secret, and her pact with the Dark God.

As she spoke, she felt a weight settle upon her shoulders, and her heart became numb and empty.

For his part, Ozuma did not seem moved to fear or hatred. There was only kindness and sympathy in his face.

When she had finished her story, Ozuma knelt beside her. "Thank you for telling me," he said. "You must've been terribly frightened."

A teardrop slid from Yorda's eye.

"Yet when you heard the truth from your mother's mouth, it opened up the eyes of your heart. That is why you could see the lonely shades trapped in the Tower of Winds. You have awakened, Lady Yorda. And," Ozuma added in a whisper, "the revelation was true."

"But why?" Yorda asked, wiping the tear from her face. "Why did my mother show me those things? Why did she not keep them hidden?"

"That, I do not know for certain," Ozuma said. "But were I to venture a guess, I would say that she was sufficiently afraid of you that she took it upon herself to strike first."

[8]

"NEAR THE HERALD of darkness there is one who is aware of the darkness and possesses the power to defeat it."

Even after a night of restless sleep, Ozuma's words rang in Yorda's ears. It was all real. It was not a nightmare or fever dream.

While she was preparing for the day, Yorda informed the chief handmaiden that she would be attending the fourth round of the tournament that day. She had to see Ozuma's skill for herself.

The handmaiden raised a querying eyebrow as she tied the strings at the waist of Yorda's dress. "The princess will be viewing the tournament?"

"Am I not allowed?"

"No, of course you are. But I thought you disliked the noise."

"It is noisy, granted. But at the banquet last night, I heard that there is a particularly skillful swordsman in this tournament. The Minister of Court and the Captain of the Guard were both flushed with excitement when they spoke of his prowess. I thought this must be an unusual contestant indeed, and I must admit I grew curious to see him."

Yorda smiled, but the handmaiden's frown did not soften. Yorda could see herself reflected in the handmaiden's pale, washed-out eyes.

Terrified as she was of the queen's power, the handmaiden made a convenient pawn for her mother. It was no coincidence that her mother had assigned the woman to her at the same time that she revealed the truth to Yorda. Who better to keep an eye on her daughter?

Yorda's every deed would be conveyed through the handmaiden to the queen. She had to move carefully. Always with a smile, always pleasant.

Yorda knew there was no point in trying to get information from her handmaiden, even though the questions she had were many. She wanted to know what her mother had told the woman, what she had been shown, and why she was the only one to see it. Had her mother revealed to the handmaiden a portion of her secret to ensure her loyalty?

Tell me, Yorda wanted to say, *and I will tell you what I know. I know that it is not only we two who are aware of the truth that lurks behind my mother's beguiling smile. We have allies in the world beyond these walls.*

She would tell her about the spell her mother had cast upon their own people with the power she had gained from the Dark God. How all of the knights and ministers had been enchanted. And how they must be the ones to free them.

But as her mother's only daughter, the thought of what Yorda must do was not only frightening, it was sad. She wanted to ask what the chief handmaiden thought, in all the wisdom of her years, of a daughter who betrayed her own mother.

Could it ever be the right thing to do? If it meant stopping the rise of the Dark God, was it acceptable to ignore ties of blood?

Or perhaps, Yorda thought, *I shouldn't talk to you at all, but to Master Suhal.* Yorda felt certain that her instructor knew more than he had told her about the queen. Perhaps that was the source of those wisps of dark shadow she saw at times in the wise man's eyes.

Who in the castle was awake, and who still slept? She only knew she didn't want to be alone. It was too frightening.

"I will call on the Minister of Rites to prepare a place for you at the throne, that you might observe the tournament," the handmaiden said stiffly, her eyes averted from Yorda's face. "The fourth round is set to begin at noon with the ringing of the bell. Do you know which of the arenas this knight you wish to see will be fighting in?"

"No…" Yorda admitted, "but I'm sure the Minister of Court knows. And I've heard this contestant has a very unusual appearance—horns grow from his head."

"Horns? Like a deer's, or an ox's?"

"That's right—but more like an ox than a deer, I'm told."

The handmaiden furrowed her thin eyebrows. "Strange appearance, indeed. Are you certain he is the one you would watch? I fear the sight of him might trouble you."

"I do not think it appropriate to call one of the men who might soon be master-at-arms of the castle troubling," Yorda said with a bright smile.

The chief handmaiden bowed. Yorda watched her bent, withered frame as she left the room.

Her mother had been there when the men were talking about the strange knight Ozuma, though Yorda had no idea whether such talk interested her mother at all. How would she react when she learned that her daughter wanted to see the tournament? Was the herald of darkness aware that her enemies were approaching? Yorda shivered.

Ozuma's fourth contest was scheduled to take place in the Western Arena. Yorda entered the arena last to the boisterous cheers of a full crowd. She was wearing a midday dress with a veil drawn over her face. At her side, the Minister of Court advised her to raise her hand and greet the crowd, so she did so, giving them a light wave. This simple gesture was met with loud applause. Yorda found herself unexpectedly moved by the warm reception. Respect and love directed toward the princess was also respect and love for her mother, the queen. *Our kingdom is at peace. The people are satisfied in their lives. How could rule by fear produce such happiness?* The people greeted her mother as their true queen— what business did she have disrupting that?

"You may proceed to your seat, Princess," the Minister of Court said, a wide smile across his face. "Until you sit, no one else may," he added in a whisper, then more loudly, "What an ovation!"

Yorda found herself doubting everything. When she looked out on the crowd, she saw only innocent people, ignorant of the true purpose of this spectacle, deceived by the queen. They were livestock bred for the sole purpose of bringing about the revival of the Dark God. *Or is it I who has been deceived by an agent of mayhem and greed, come from another land to take what is ours?*

Yorda's mind reeled, and she nearly lost her balance. Before she drew unwanted attention, she grabbed the arms of the beautifully carved throne and sat, closing her eyes.

From entrances on either side of the arena, two warriors took the floor, led in by royal guardsmen. Ozuma, the taller of the two, walked in easy strides, his helmet tucked beneath his arm. He had taken off his black robe, but other than that, he looked exactly as he had the first time Yorda met him. The longsword at his waist reached nearly to the ground, its tip hanging only a hair's breadth above the arena floor.

The man he faced was also a giant. He wore a wide, leather battle skirt with a thick belt, also of leather, about his waist. Above that he wore only a vest of chain mail on his chest and a battle-axe slung over his back. The man's wide bald head caught the light of the torches set along the walls of the arena. In place of a helmet, he wore a small metal circlet.

Together, the two contestants stood before the throne, then knelt upon their knees. Yorda accepted the gesture with a quiet nod. She had the impression that Ozuma's eyes met hers through her veil for the briefest of moments, but his expression was blank. *Perhaps he expected me to come watch him fight today.*

The knight who presided as judge over the arena introduced the two swordsmen in a voice that rang loudly throughout the arena. First up was the itinerant knight from the far east, Ozuma. Facing him was Judam, renowned throughout the continent for his skill with a battle-axe. While the crowd made their enthusiasm known, Ozuma slowly donned his helmet. Yorda blushed slightly at seeing the crowd's favor for him.

"Princess, are you feeling unwell?" the minister asked, leaning toward her.

"I'm fine. Thank you. I was startled by the crowd's enthusiasm, that's all. I daresay all these people could turn the chilly depths of winter into a summer day."

The Minister of Court smiled approvingly. "That swordsman on the right is the fellow I was telling you about. He's a sure bet for champion."

"The crowd adores him," Yorda agreed.

"Perhaps such talk does not reach your ears, Princess, but there is a great deal of wagering that goes on around the tournament. Ozuma began as a complete unknown, but now he is by far the most popular. I would not be surprised if more than half of the people watching here today have money riding on his victory."

The judge stood between the two men in the center of the arena, one hand on each of the contestants' shoulders. He read off the rules of honorable combat, after which each of the contestants raised his weapon—a sword for one, and an axe for the other—and repeated the rules in unison.

"The fight goes on until one man falls or admits defeat by tossing away his weapon," the Minister of Court explained.

Yorda felt queasy just looking at the two men exchanging glares before their fight.

"They do not kill each other, do they? This is a tournament, not a battlefield."

"Not intentionally, but it does happen on occasion. If one's opponent does not admit defeat, it may come to cutting. Sometimes, there are fatalities," the minister said, seeming far too pleased. "Judam, the one with the battle-axe, lost in the next to last round of the previous tournament, and he's favored to win this year as well. Not only is he a master with that massive axe of his, but he fights like a wild boar and does not know when to yield. In the semifinals three years ago, his opponent, a spearman, wouldn't let go of his spear, so Judam relieved him of both his arms. Ha! If the judge had not intervened, he might well have cut off the man's head." The Minister of Court was lost in the story now, completely forgetting to whom he spoke. "His fight today against Ozuma might well be the deciding bout for the Western

Arena. I doubt any other in the tournament could stand against either—here they go!"

The judge gave the call to begin and withdrew to the edge of the circular arena. Judam gave a wild battle cry, brought his axe to bear with incredible speed for one so massive, and dashed off to one side, putting a little more distance between him and his opponent. Ozuma did not move.

Swinging his axe in a circle as though it weighed no more than a feather, Judam stared down the knight, walking around him in a slow circle. When he reached Ozuma's flank, the knight turned a half step to face him and placed a hand on the sword at his waist. Yorda's eyes went wide. Ozuma drew his sword with such speed, she saw only the flash of metal before the sword was completely out of its sheath.

Ozuma held the sword with its tip pointed toward the ground. Though he followed Judam's every movement with his eyes, his feet were still.

Judam's battle-axe ceased its gyrations. He leapt toward Ozuma. The massive battle-axe cut through the air, while the polished double-edged blade gleamed. A cry went up from the crowd.

When the battle-axe came down, it struck only Ozuma's shadow. The knight had stepped lightly aside, gaining Judam's flank. Ozuma's blade slashed out, stopping only inches from the giant's back as it struck the battle-axe Judam had deftly swung over his head and down across his back to block the blow. Sparks flew and steel clashed. Their blades met three more times before the warriors leapt back, and there was a brief pause in the fighting.

Yorda couldn't believe the speed with which the two men moved. Judam advanced, massive axe held in one hand just off the ground, sweeping it in circles toward his opponent's feet. Ozuma deftly hopped out of the axe's path, and when he landed, his sword was already swinging down toward Judam's exposed shoulder. Judam rolled to the side to avoid the blow and stood, axe already lifted above his head. Though the axe was fully as long as Yorda was tall, in Judam's hands it appeared no more than a twig. It was clear neither its weight nor length gave him any trouble whatsoever. The axe moved like an extension of his own arm.

Ozuma blocked the blow directly to his front with his sword, then lunged forward, pushing his opponent back with his weight. The moment the man's center of gravity shifted back, the longsword drew an arc through the air, grazing Judam's right shoulder before the tip of the sword struck the ground. A roar passed through the arena. Ozuma was off balance; Judam came in for the kill.

Yet Ozuma's defenses were flawless. His sword seemed to dance back up, slashing through one of the leather straps holding the chain mail to Judam's chest. The vest drooped to one side. Judam scrambled to regain his footing. This was the moment Ozuma had been waiting for. Though Judam managed to dodge the next blow, his balance was thrown entirely, and he fell on his side to the ground.

Judam went into a roll to gain distance from Ozuma, and using his bare hand to rip off the remaining leather strap, he took off the chain mail and threw it at Ozuma's face. Ozuma ducked to one side and the vest hit the arena floor with a dull crash, sliding all the way to the foot of the stands.

The sound of the next clash between sword and battle-axe was lost in the roar of the crowd. All Yorda could see were the two men like shadows, first drawing closer, then separating, then engaging once more, lit by the flying of sparks. At one point, the two weapons clashed, but it was Judam who lowered his axe first, and Ozuma's blade bit into the bald man's metal circlet. Blood ran in rivulets down Judam's forehead, and the sweat on his head glinted in the sunlight.

Yorda's hands clenched into fists. Her heart was racing, and her breath was ragged. She could feel her knees shaking on the throne.

Judam gave a howl and toppled over backward. Another cheer rose up from the spectators and Yorda leaned forward to see better.

Despite the fact that he had an easy opening on his opponent, Ozuma did not take it. Instead he took a quick step to the side, putting distance between himself and the battle-axe wielder. It was the right move. Judam jumped up from the ground and used his momentum to swing his weapon around from the side. The shining blade cut an arc through the air.

The missed swing was exactly what Ozuma had been waiting for. The momentum of the axe had carried Judam around until his side was facing his opponent. Ozuma leapt, as agile as a wildcat. This time, not even the swift Judam had time to bring his axe back around to block. Ozuma's double-edged blade swept to the side, cutting the haft of his opponent's weapon in two. The head of the battle-axe dropped by his feet, bouncing off to one side, leaving him holding only the handle. Ozuma's blade slashed out again, and in the next instant the handle, too, was rattling across the arena floor, leaving Judam with a small piece of wood barely larger than the palm of his hand. The massive warrior's mouth hung open.

A deep wrinkle crossed his shiny pate. His right eye was closed against the blood running down from the wound on his head. As Ozuma closed the distance between them, Judam dropped to one knee.

"I yield!"

The bout was decided. Everyone in the stands leapt to their feet. A wave of applause swept across the arena, honoring the victor. Yorda finally let herself exhale and leaned back against her throne. Next to her, the Minister of Court was slapping his ample palms together, doing a little dance in his joy. Yorda had to smile at that. Then she herself stood and applauded the horned knight.

When Ozuma faced the throne and knelt a second time, a smile on his face answered her own.

That night, even wrapped in her silk covers, Yorda had trouble falling asleep. The excitement of the tournament was hard to put out of her mind. Ozuma's skill was plain to see, even to her. He would surely win his next two bouts and emerge the victor. Then he would be welcome to the castle as the master-at-arms—

"I am but the advance guard," he had told her. Finding a place at the castle was his first objective. Next would come spying and gathering information. He would unveil the castle and the queen for what they truly were.

Armed with the knowledge Ozuma had gathered, the Holy Zagrenda-Sol Empire and the fifth emperor in service of the Sun God would come to strike at the herald of darkness.

Should I help them? Yorda wondered. *Is my power truly enough to resist the darkness? Or should I turn my back on the Sun God, the great Creator, and side with my mother?*

When her eyes opened again, the room was steeped in darkness. She wondered if the questions she had asked Ozuma at the trolley were really questions she should ask of her mother. *Why did you tell me your secrets? Why was I given life in this world? For what purpose?*

Yorda stared into the darkness but received no reply.

Yorda saw an unsettling significance in the fact that she had learned the truth about her mother only ten days before the tournament began. She wondered if she would be questioning herself so deeply now. And how would she have greeted Ozuma without that knowledge? Fancy a stranger from another land walking freely through the castle and speaking to her, the princess. No, she would have met him with mistrust, no matter how sincere he was or how kind, or how much he reminded her of her late father. The hunger and greed of their neighbors was one lesson Yorda had learned from her mother, and its roots went deep inside her.

Perhaps, she thought, the curious timing of her discovering the truth was the plan of the Sun God himself. *Believe in me, Yorda,* he was saying. The connection between a person and his god was stronger than the connection between mother and child. Life was to be found only in the light of the Sun God who shared his blessing with all. Therein lay the only prize worth pursuing.

We must not allow the darkness to spread.

Yorda turned over, burying her face in her pillow and squeezing her eyes shut. *Father! Why did you have to leave me like this, alone, enemy to my own mother?* Then she sensed something—a clear feeling that someone was standing in the room, next to her bed.

Yorda threw back her covers and sat up. The sky was cloudy that night—not even the moonlight trickled in through the window. The darkness in the air felt heavy, turning her familiar room into the silence of the deep sea.

I am imagining things. I'm tired. My worries have stepped outside my body and stand there looking over me.

But then, out of the corner of her eye, she saw something move. It shifted in the night and melted into the darkness.

Yorda turned and gasped at what she saw. Just to the left of her bed, her late father's face hung like a pale moon.

"Father!" Yorda called out, though her body was frozen. She saw the face smile—he looked just as he always had. That long straight nose, those eyes. Though his cheeks were sunken and his jaw pointed, there was no mistaking him.

He wore a silver crown on which was engraved his family crest—a divine bird with wings outstretched. The clasp holding his short cloak over his shoulders was in the same shape. Blue peridots had been woven into the sleeves of his long tunic, and the edges were embroidered with flowers. She remembered it all, every detail. He was wearing the same clothes he had worn when they placed him in the coffin, when she had kissed his cold cheek farewell. These were the clothes he had worn for his final journey. Even his haggard face was exactly the same.

"You…are my father, are you not?"

Sliding off the bed, Yorda took a step closer, but her father drew away, holding up his right hand to stop her. She spotted the signet ring bearing her father's royal crest on the middle finger of his right hand. His ring bore only half the seal—the other half was on the ring worn by Yorda's mother.

Memories flitted through Yorda's mind. When her father had been buried, her mother had tried to remove the ring from his finger, but Master Suhal had stopped her, saying it should remain with the king. This had not pleased the queen, and so she sent Master Suhal away and tried once again to remove the ring. Yet even though her father's fingers were thin and bony, the ring would not come free. In the end, the queen had given up and allowed the lid to be placed upon the coffin. In fact, the ring was merely an ornament—the actual royal seal was kept separately. Yorda had imagined that her mother wanted her father's ring as a memento.

The queen had since removed her half of the ring.

Yorda, my beloved daughter.

She heard her father's voice in her mind.

I did not wish to appear before you like this and disturb your heart or give you sadness. Even so, I longed for this time when I might see you again.

Yorda realized she was crying. "I've wanted to see you for so long, Father."

A gentle smile spread across her father's face, no different from the smile in her memory, with a warmth that seemed to embrace her even from across the room.

Yorda, I was always with you. Even when you could not see me, I was by your side. Her father lowered his eyes. *I did not leave because I could not. I am…a captive in the castle. A captive soul.*

"What?" Yorda almost shouted, then she placed a hand over her mouth. "Who did this to you, Father?" she asked more softly.

Her father's gaze wandered, and Yorda saw in his eyes the same worries that lay heavily upon her own heart. The sensation resolved into a bleak understanding. "Did you know of Mother's connection to the Dark God? Is that why you remain here?"

Her father's eyes fixed on hers. Then he nodded, slowly, so that there might be no misunderstanding.

Your true eye has opened. That is why you can see me now. Yorda, my poor, beloved daughter. My wife, your mother, is indeed a herald of darkness, come to bring devastation to this world. I was trying to stop her when my life ended. As my last breath passed my lips, I thought of you whom I was leaving in this world, and my worry was so deep that my heart broke and shattered into a thousand pieces. Yet they did not depart for the land of the dead. Here they stayed, lingering in the shadows—and not to protect you, though I wish it were so.

Yorda stood, eyes open, forgetting to wipe the tears that collected at her chin.

"Is it my mother who holds you here?"

Her father nodded bitterly.

I'm now master of the Tower of Winds. There I am held. Your mother has trapped me and uses my power.

"What do you mean? Do you have anything to do with those dark shapes I saw in the windows of the tower? The ones Ozuma called the shadows-that-walk-alone?"

Yes, her father replied. *That is my true form now.*

Yorda recalled the twisted shades she had seen. That *is my father?*

"Why? What's Mother doing in the Tower of Winds? How does she seek to use your power? How can I help you?"

Yorda spread her arms wide, stepping closer to her father. She wanted to hug him. To ease his suffering. To feel his warmth.

Her father lurched backward. His face, as pale as moonlight, became translucent.

No! She will find me.

"Father?"

Yorda, I am causing you to suffer. Please forgive me. But now, you are my hope. As you are the hope of this castle and of all life upon this earth. You are our light!

Her father began to fade. Yorda ran from her bed. "No, father, don't go!"

Yorda...

His voice grew more distant, trembling as he called out to her.

Look upon the world outside. See it with your eyes. The God of Light will show you the right path.

I love you, he said, in a whisper quieter than the murmuring of the night wind. And then he was gone. Yorda ran, but her arms embraced only darkness.

Quietly as she could, Yorda wept. She wiped away her tears with fingers that would never again feel the warm touch of her father. Then, walking softly, she cut across her bedchamber to the door that led out to the hallway.

She did not need to touch the door or press her ear to it. She could feel the presence on the other side of the door with her entire being.

The queen. A cold crystallization of darkness. Breathing, walking darkness.

She's standing right outside the door.

She must have sensed the appearance of Yorda's father. She stood outside the door right now, extending a slender arm to open it.

"She will find me..."

Her father's frightened voice. Yorda held her breath, staring at the door. *Should it open, you must look into her eyes*, she told herself. *If she stares at you, you must not waver. You must stand and face the truth, for it cannot be denied.*

But the door did not open. After a while, she sensed the queen's presence diminish. Yorda felt a wave of dizziness overcome her, and she knelt on the floor.

Her teeth chattered at the cold that seemed to invade her body. Her slender hands clenched into fists. Something was coming, flowing toward her, and it could not be stopped. The truth that had waited for this moment wanted to be free. It wanted salvation.

I must not run.

[9]

WHEN THEY HAD parted at the trolley, Ozuma had given Yorda a pebble, saying it was magic. It was white, no larger than her thumbnail, and smooth to the touch.

"Should you ever need me, grasp the pebble in your hand and call for me. I will come at once."

Yorda took the magic pebble in her hands now, and after staring at it for a while, she tucked it inside her dress where it would be safe. Walking quickly, she left the room.

When Master Suhal was not tutoring Yorda on history or literature, he was usually to be found in the castle library. The master had been appointed grand chambers of his own, but he spent far more time at the tiny desk in the corner of the library, poring over books and scrolls.

Yorda had never been able to determine Master Suhal's age. She surmised that no one else in the castle knew either. He was thin and shriveled, with a rounded back, and he walked at a snail's pace wherever he went. To Yorda he looked as old as the Creator himself.

Yet a change would come over the old scholar when he opened a book. His eyes would sparkle from the deep wrinkles beneath his bushy eyebrows, and he would flip the pages with all the energy of youth. He was a true scholar who had given his soul to his studies, which he loved more than anything in all the world.

Yorda's arrival in the library caused a momentary stir of commotion among the scholars and students who were there. She had visited the library many times before, but only in the company of Master Suhal, with specialist scholars accompanying them, and only after much preparation had been made.

Yorda tried to smile at the scholars as they frantically scattered, some in an effort to make themselves presentable, others simply to hide. She announced that she was looking for Master Suhal. The old scholar came to the entrance of the library, staff in hand, with a speed she had never seen him before achieve.

"Dear me, Princess! Welcome, welcome!" His voice shook with surprise.

"I'm sorry to come unannounced. But I was reading a book, and I thought to ask you some questions."

The scholar bowed deeply, his robes sweeping across the

floor, and he led Yorda to his desk.

The books and the great library were divided into sections by content. There were no walls. Each section was comprised of a single huge bookcase, and they stretched from the floor all the way to the high ceiling above. Master Suhal's favorite desk was surrounded by the bookcases where the most ancient history books in the library were kept—the perfect place for a quiet, private conversation, which was exactly what Yorda wanted.

"Please don't send everyone away just because I'm here. I wouldn't want to interrupt their studies," Yorda told him. Privacy was well and good, but she didn't want to draw undue attention to their conversation either. "I was thinking," she went on, "how nice it would be if I could just drop in here now and then. It's always such an ordeal, you see, if everyone has to stand from their desks and bow and put on their formal robes and such. I'm afraid it's made me quite reluctant to come here on my own."

"I see. Yes, yes, of course." The old scholar bowed his head deeply. "Very well, I will let everyone know your feelings on the matter. I am sure they will understand. There is no reason why you should feel unwelcome in your own library, Princess!"

He offered Yorda a chair and shuffled off, returning a moment later with a tray on which sat two cups and a teapot. They were not the silver cups Yorda was accustomed to using, but the years had imbued them with a certain warmth.

"As a sign of welcome, I offer you some of the tea we customarily drink here in the library. It is the fragrance of this very tea that refreshes me when I grow weary after long hours with my nose pressed into a book."

While they talked, Yorda could occasionally hear snippets of conversations and laughter from the other students and scholars in the library, though their voices were barely louder than a whisper. To Yorda, it sounded like the rustling of leaves or the burbling of a brook—the easy, calming sounds of regular life. She found herself wishing that she had visited the library earlier, even without a reason such as she had today.

Though wanting to speak about the book she had read had only been a pretext, she was genuinely curious about some things in it—it was a book of myths Master Suhal had recommended to her. He listened to her thoughts on what she had read and commended her deep understanding of the text. He also told her of other books, fictions inspired by the myths she had read, and went so far as to get up and bring her several.

Yorda found herself drawn in by the smell of the ancient paper and the soothing atmosphere of the library. How happy she would be if this truly were her only purpose in coming, to forget time for a while and let her conversation with Master Suhal lead her to new and undiscovered places.

She took another sip of her tea, noting the refreshing chill it left on her lips, then returned her cup to the tray and looked Master Suhal in the face.

"Master. As I was reading the other day, a thought occurred to me," she said. "I wondered if I might not be able to write a book of my own."

The scholar's small black eyes opened wide. "The princess wishes to become a writer?"

"Yes. I know that I have many more studies ahead of me and much more to learn. I know that very well, yet I also feel that I may just have the ability if I tried—do you think it improper?"

"Absolutely not, my dear princess, absolutely not!" The old scholar leaned forward and stood, a wide grin on his face. "Princess, perhaps you have not noticed this yourself, but I have long admired your nimble intellect. I have ever since you were but a child. Your eyes see clearly, your vocabulary is rich, and your mind is always agile. You are more than qualified to scribe your own stories, Princess."

He went on to ask her what sort of thing she would like to write about, and swallowing the sudden quick beating of her heart, she ventured a smile and said, "I thought I would write about my father. My memories of him, that is."

"Oh. Oh dear Creator!" The scholar's hands covered his face like withered branches, and he raised his head toward the ceiling, eyes closed. "I have failed you!" he said, his voice shuddering.

Startled by the scholar's reaction, Yorda sat silently, waiting to see what he would say next.

"Princess," he said in a voice like one who speaks to a grieving child. He took a step around the desk, closer to her. "How sorrowful you must be, and how rightfully angry that I have not provided you any books telling of your late father's reign."

"Angry?" Yorda blinked. "No, Master Suhal, I'm not upset at all, I only—"

The scholar waved his hand. "As your instructor, I believe I recommended to you only two volumes on the subject of our kingdom's history: *The Chronicle of Kings* and *The Golden Gift of God*—is that not correct?"

The Chronicle of Kings he spoke of was a giant tome that told the story of every ruler in the kingdom since the royal house had been established. *The Golden Gift of God* was a more general work, though no less voluminous, that dealt with the geography and customs of the land.

"As I recall," Master Suhal went on, "*The Chronicle of Kings* begins with our first king—the one they call the Conqueror—and continues to the fifth king, the one who constructed this castle which is our home. Perhaps you did not know, but the *Chronicle* is still a work in progress. At the end of this year, the volume treating the achievements of the sixth king will finally be completed. As your father was the seventh king, I'm afraid his story has not yet been put to parchment. Our dedication is to illustrating the achievements of all of our kings with the greatest of historical accuracy and detail, which is to say that our work proceeds at a snail's pace. I must beg you in your generosity to watch over us as we work with grace and patience."

"I know, and I am patient," Yorda said. She rested her hand on the old scholar's sleeve. "Master Suhal, what I want to write is nothing more than the memories of my father I carry in my own heart. I do not think I could do him justice were I to attempt to write about his achievements on the throne."

Master Suhal frowned and stroked his long beard.

"*The Chronicle of Kings* is a wonderful history book," Yorda said, "but it only details its subjects as rulers, correct? What I want to write about is not my father as the seventh king, but about my father as a person. How we played together, what sort of things he liked, the songs he taught me—"

As she listed what she would write, she felt the tears rise in her throat, and she had to stop.

Father. She recalled his sad, pale face from the night before. His lamentations of his cursed fate to wander the darkness beyond the boundaries of the living—

She had to figure out how it had happened. She had to learn how she might save his soul.

Master Suhal rubbed Yorda's shoulder in a kind gesture. "Princess, you are right to grieve. Your father's soul has gone to join the Creator. He has ascended to heaven, led aloft by a golden light."

She wanted to shout, *You're wrong! He hasn't gone to heaven. He's a ghost, a shade, bound in suffering to the earth.* She wanted to grab the old man by his shoulders and shake him, screaming. *It's all my mother's fault! The queen has done this!*

"I'm sorry," she said. "I'm being foolish." Wiping away a tear with her hand, Yorda ventured a smile. "Whenever I think of my father, it fills my heart with light. Yet, I'm afraid, it also brings tears. I love my father, Master Suhal. And before the cruel thief that is time steals away my memories of him, I want to put them down in words that they might last an eternity."

Master Suhal nodded slowly. "I see, yes, of course. Princess, you merely need tell me how I may assist you, and I am at your disposal."

Yorda clasped her hands together and then took the scholar's hands into her own. "Thank you, Master Suhal. Your help will be invaluable to me. For I realized when I started considering this project that there is much I do not know about my father. I know nothing of how he spent his youth, for example. I never heard of his wedding to my mother, nor how the two of them met. And that is just the beginning—"

This next bit was the most important part. Yorda opened her eyes wide and emptied her heart of the truth so it would not show when she looked into the scholar's eyes.

"I don't even know how he died. I was only six at the time. I remember them telling me that Father had fallen ill, that I could not see him or stand by his side. Then, no more than ten days later, I heard that he had passed away. The next time I saw his face was when his body was laid in the coffin, just before they carried him to his resting place at the temple where the funeral was to be held—and then only for the briefest of moments."

The old scholar's face was clouded.

"Now that I think about it," Yorda pressed on, "I am not even sure what disease he died of. No one's told me anything about his final days. You must understand how lonely this makes me feel as his only child. I would like to know all of these things, but who can I ask? Do you know anything, Master?"

In Yorda's slender hands, the master's dry, withered fingers grew cold. Where the wrinkles in his face usually told a tale as detailed as any storybook, now they were blank and lifeless. His eyes had lost their sparkle. The passing years had robbed him of his youth, yet now he even lacked that grounded stoicism that came with age. He might have been a piece of sun-bleached wood, adrift at sea.

"Princess," he said in the stern voice he usually reserved for lectures. Gone was the spring of enthusiasm he had when he spoke of books. "Members of the royal house must at all times strive to keep themselves free of the stain of death—even when it strikes within their own family. It would not be proper for you, as princess, to know the details of your father's passing."

"Do you mean to say, Master, that I may not know and may not ask about it?"

"You may not." The words hit Yorda like a slap. "You should not even think of such things. Lady Yorda, consider your position. Remember that one day you will sit upon the throne. If your rule is to be benevolent, your heart must be pure."

Yorda pleaded, explained—even commanded—but Master Suhal would not budge. Exhausted by the effort, Yorda finally gave up. *It's no use.* She would not have the truth from Master Suhal's lips. *I'll have to think of another way.*

"I'm sorry," she said at last. "Please forgive my imprudence."

Yorda stood, bowed curtly to the scholar, and then left, stepping lightly between the stacks of books. Master Suhal made no attempt to stop her. He seemed to have aged a century over the course of their conversation. When he stood to see her off, he leaned heavily on the back of his chair and nearly staggered several times.

Yorda walked back through the middle of the library, setting off another commotion among the scholars and students in her wake. Yorda smiled to each of them as she passed.

A senior scholar stepped forward to lead her toward the exit. "Will you be retiring, Princess? The shelves here form a bit of a labyrinth, I'm afraid. Please allow me."

The scholar led her down a valley of densely packed bookshelves, their path twisting to the right and left as they walked. They entered a spot where Yorda saw that the books on the shelves had been replaced by boxes for storage. The boxes looked sturdy, with padlocks, but their fronts were fashioned of thick glass so that their contents could be readily identified.

She saw nautical charts and old globes and other intricate devices fashioned of metal whose uses she could not begin to guess at. Then she spotted something like a long, slender tube. Its length was about the same as that from Yorda's elbow to the tips of her fingers, and it widened toward one end in sections.

A spyglass, she thought, recalling an illustration she had seen in a book many years before.

"Excuse me," she called out to her guide. "This tube—is it not used for looking across great distances?"

The scholar nodded, smiling. "I'm impressed you know of such things, Lady Yorda. Master Suhal has not been negligent in his duties!"

"I was wondering," she asked him, "why is it here? Wouldn't it be useful for keeping watch in the castle?"

As soon as she asked the question, it occurred to her that she had never seen anyone in the castle, be it the guards or even the court astronomers, using a spyglass. The reason was obvious. *My mother's enchantment.*

They weren't allowed to look out upon the world outside.

It wouldn't even occur to them to try.

Fingers intertwined, the scholar smiled at her cheerfully. "Such contrivances are unnecessary. By Her Majesty's glory, our land has been ensured of eternal prosperity. Its rivers, mountains, and even the seas surrounding us are always at peace. Why, that spyglass there broke some time ago, and no one has even thought to repair it."

"It doesn't work at all?"

"I'm afraid not. Look through it, you will see nothing. Yet, as its design and features may yet be useful as a subject of study, we keep it here. Just in case."

Yorda's heart stirred. *It's not broken. My mother's enchantments made it dark. She thought of everything.*

But then Yorda wondered what would happen if she were to look through it now that her true eye had opened. The words of her father came back to her. *"Look at the world outside,"* he had told her. See it with your eyes. The Creator will light your path.

The beating of her heart grew faster. She tensed her stomach so that she would not begin to tremble. Then, with the most innocent smile she could muster, she said, "It is a beautiful instrument, even though it's broken. I've never touched such a device before. Would it be all right if I picked it up?"

"By all means," the scholar said. "Allow me to—" his hand went to his pocket. "Now where is that key for the storage boxes? A moment, please, Princess."

The scholar dashed off between the bookcases and promptly returned bearing a small copper key in his hand.

He opened the door to the storage box and gingerly pulled out the spyglass, proffering it to her. Yorda took it in both hands. It was heavier than it looked.

"It's beautiful!" Yorda held the telescope to her chest. "Might you lend this to me, just for a little while? I would love to examine it at my leisure."

"Of course, Princess, but I'm afraid it won't be of much use."

"That's all right. I don't intend to look through it. I intend to look at it. The craftsmanship is simply masterful."

Yorda lifted a single finger to her lips and leaned closer to the scholar. "Don't tell Master Suhal that I've borrowed this. I want to surprise him later with my intimate knowledge of it!"

The scholar's face blushed bright red with approval. He looked like he might melt on the spot. Yorda slipped the spyglass between the soft pleats of her dress and, walking even more quietly than before, left the library with her heart pounding in her ears.

Back in her own chambers, she quickly transferred the spyglass to a hiding spot beneath her pillow and ran back to the door. She didn't want her handmaiden walking in and seeing her using it. If she was going to do this with any degree of privacy, she had to take precautions.

There was no way to lock her chamber door from the inside. Looking around, she spotted a poker by her fireplace and propped it against the door at a precarious angle. When it fell, she would know someone was at the door.

Yorda shook her head, thinking ruefully how feeble her attempts at subterfuge were.

Retrieving the spyglass, she took a few deep breaths to calm herself. Her terrace would be the best spot for viewing, but if she wasn't careful, one of the guards might spot her. She would have to settle for her next best option: a window.

Fortunately, Yorda's chambers had windows on three sides, looking out to the south, north, and east. To the south was the central courtyard of the castle, which she deemed too dangerous. She would start with the east. There were no towers to block her view in that direction.

Yorda lifted the spyglass in both hands, as though praying, and then, holding her breath, she quickly brought the small end up to her right eye.

She could see the blue ocean, but the light was so bright it made her eye water. She quickly lowered the telescope, realizing that she must have caught the sun reflecting off the waves.

Even still, Yorda's heart leapt for joy. *It works!*

She began experimenting. Adjusting the dial she found on its neck, she tried different angles for holding it. When Yorda finally had it working, she looked through and saw the white feathers of a seabird skimming the surface of the water. It appeared so close it seemed to fly right by her nose, and she gave a little yelp of excitement.

Whitecaps crested the blue water. She saw small rocks amongst the waves, sending up white spray where the water collided with them.

She was used to looking out at the sea, even though she had never touched it in her life. Now, looking at it through the telescope, it seemed near enough for her to reach from her own chambers. After a while, her initial excitement faded, and disappointment reared its head.

This is the world outside.

It wasn't as exciting as she had hoped. She wasn't even sure if the spyglass was powerful enough to see what lay beyond the castle. Perhaps she would be able to see nothing more than what she already could from the walls.

Still, it was better than doing nothing. The spyglass, cast off as junk by the others in the castle, was useful to her. That must mean something.

She focused the spyglass to its maximum distance, trying to see as far away from the castle as possible. It was then she noticed a strangely shaped rock jutting from the waves near the shore. When she lowered the spyglass, she found it was too far away to discern with the naked eye.

She took another look through the spyglass. The rock was triangular, growing wider nearer the bottom. It looked almost like a ship sunk at sea, with only its sail remaining above the waters.

Yorda gasped and almost dropped the spyglass.

It didn't just look like a sail. It *was* a sail. A sail of stone.

She looked closer and spotted people on the deck of the boat. Their arms were spread wide, as though they were surprised by something, and their faces were turned upward toward the sky.

The stone looked weathered, battered by waves and the relentless wind. Below the sail, the ship itself was almost entirely worn away. The people on the deck, too, were weathered, making it impossible to discern their clothing or features.

Part of the sail had fallen away, though whether it was ripped before turning to stone or crumbled afterward, she couldn't say. Though the boat retained no identifying markings, it had most likely sailed from another kingdom. A merchant ship perhaps, one that had earned her mother's wrath and paid dearly for it.

Spyglass clasped in her hands, Yorda ran across the room to the north window. Here, much of her view was obscured by the Tower of Winds. Yet she found that though the tower itself was a familiar sight, with the spyglass she could see the windows on the upper stories far more clearly than she could from the base of the tower.

As she observed the tower windows, she thought she saw something in one of those square, dark holes glimmer with a dull light. She looked again but saw nothing. Perhaps something near the top of the tower was set to reflect the light of the sun?

Looking at it this closely, she could clearly see the effects of weather on the tower, how parts of the wall had crumbled away and the bricks themselves had begun to sag. In places, the window frames were cracked or broken, leaving torn and soiled curtains to whip dolefully in the wind.

My father is a captive in there. What did he mean when he called himself the master of the tower?

Yorda shook her head, trying to will away the sadness and doubts rising in her mind. She turned the spyglass toward the grasslands. The grass was green, and it sparkled under the sun as it swayed in the wind. She looked far, as far away as she could, wanting to see, wanting to expand her world.

Suddenly her hand stopped. She lowered the spyglass and rubbed her eyes, thinking what she had seen was some trick of the light. But when she raised the glass again, they were still there: an endless line of marching figures.

Figures of stone.

Around them, the grass shimmered from pale green to almost blue as it caught the sunlight, but the statues stayed the same, gray and unmoving. She was shocked both by their number and their condition. These people had been turned to stone long before the boat near the shore. So weathered and worn they were that they resembled people only in their silhouettes. Their equipment and clothing had worn away years ago. Were she able to walk closer, to touch them with her hand, Yorda wondered what she would see then.

Yet the longer she looked, the more she could make out. Here there was something like a sword, and there, the lingering shape of a helmet on one of the statue's heads. There were horses too, and something that looked like a palanquin supported on long poles and hoisted by several porters. She guessed that someone important had once ridden in it. Now they were frozen in place for all eternity.

At any rate, it did not appear to be an invading army, nor a merchant caravan. They looked more like emissaries. If only the flag had frozen at a different angle, she might even have been able to see its design.

She wondered when it had happened and why. All she knew was who was responsible.

Mother, why?

Real fear washed over her, and Yorda staggered back, falling to her knees on the floor.

She had seen the world outside—if only a slice provided her by the spyglass. To think that such horror lay so close, and she had never seen it.

I knew nothing. The people of our country, even those who work at the castle, spend their days in ignorance, under an enchantment. This was what her father wanted her to see.

Yorda withdrew the magic pebble from her pocket and gripped it tightly. She had to see Ozuma, before it was too late.

[10]

OZUMA STOOD LOOKING off into the distance beyond the old trolley.

"What I believe you saw," he said without looking around, "was an emissary caravan sent from the Holy Zagrenda-Sol Empire some twenty-five years ago."

The ocean winds were unusually calm that day. The warmth of the sun on the stones by the trolley made it the kind of afternoon that inspires catnaps.

Yorda shivered. "She turned them to stone without even speaking with them," she said. "A miracle it did not lead to war on the spot," she added in a whisper.

"Sadly, it is never that simple," Ozuma admitted. "Those emissaries may well have had an ulterior motive your mother was right to suspect. The rich land and hardworking people of your country are an enticement to your neighbors. Regardless of what documents the emissaries bore in their satchels, or what niceties they poised on their lips, their intentions were not entirely pure." He smiled at Yorda. "It is possible that your mother turned them to stone so that worse might be avoided—to protect her country."

Yorda considered that. What if, for argument's sake, her mother were not a child of the Dark God but had obtained her powers through some other means? Would Yorda then praise her mother's leadership? War is war. What was the difference between turning an entire caravan to stone by magic and sending out a banner of knights to put them to the sword?

Even without the threat of a "herald of darkness" to spur them to action, Zagrenda-Sol was an empire, and all empires waged war to expand their borders. It was only natural for those with land and power to desire more. How, then, were the Dark God's designs to rule the world through her mother any different from those of an emperor? How were his desires any different from those of a mortal man?

"As one who must protect her people," Yorda said in a quiet voice, "it shames me to admit this. But what troubles me more than any other thing is the fate of my own father."

Ozuma watched her in silence.

"My mother took my father's life, and even now that he is dead, she has bound him to the Tower of Winds. I would free him."

"That is nothing of which to be ashamed."

Yorda shook her head. "Why did she do it? I want to know—no. I *must* know. My father will not appear before me again unless I take action. His fear of discovery is too great now. I must go to the Tower of Winds and find a way to open the doors."

"I will join you," Ozuma announced. "Yet, though your true eye may be open, Lady Yorda, I do not think you able to break the enchantment that bars the doors to the Tower of Winds."

"Then what must I do?"

"That is something which you must ask your father. I believe he, and none other, holds the key. Pray at the Tower of Winds, speak to him. I will protect you while you do this."

Yorda raised an eyebrow. "Sir Ozuma, do the shades in the tower pose a threat to me? My father told me that he is master in the tower. If the shades heed their master, why would he not protect me?"

With a practiced movement, Ozuma swept the longsword at his waist to one side and knelt closer to her. "It is as you say, however—" His voice faltered.

"Please speak," Yorda urged. "I told you, I'm not afraid."

Ozuma cast his eyes down for a moment and spoke slowly, carefully choosing his words. "Lady Yorda. The shades who dwell within the tower are, like your father, souls trapped there by the queen's power. Those pitiful creatures fear your mother greatly, almost as much as they resent her. Lady Yorda, you carry the queen's blood in your veins."

"You mean to say the shades would hate me for what she has done. Of course. How could they not?"

"That is why your father is the key," Ozuma said. "In order for you to enter the Tower of Winds, you must have some mark, some proof of your connection to him. His permission, you might say. I believe that is the key that will open the doors."

"But what could that be?"

"That, I cannot say. You must call upon him, Lady Yorda. Only then may we find what it is we require."

Yorda stood. "Then let us go at once."

Even on a quiet day like this one, the wind around the northern-most tower howled so fiercely not even the seabirds dared approach.

Yorda knelt before the sealed doors, hands intertwined in prayer. She pictured her father in her mind and called out to him. *Please, Father, appear before me once more. Guide me. How might I meet you? How may I open the doors to this tower? Please tell me.*

As she prayed, Yorda felt a strange presence envelop her body. When she opened her eyes, she saw the shades spilling from the tower windows, spreading darkness down its walls, descending toward her. Even when she closed her eyes she could feel their gaze upon her, cold needles on her skin.

Ozuma stood by her, hidden from view in that way he had of being in a place, yet not *being* there. She could feel him pushing back the shades through sheer force of will, preventing them from attacking Yorda, driving them back into their sadness, their anger; back into the darkness.

Kind Father, Yorda called to him. *Lend me your strength. With your help, I can do this.*

Then she heard his voice, coming to her like thunder far in the distance.

...Yorda. Come tonight to the place where your memories of me are strongest.

Yorda tensed and looked up. The shades covered the walls of the tower like ancient moss, too numerous to count, their glowing eyes fixed on her.

"Do not worry," Ozuma whispered. "Shadows cannot long stand before the light." Ozuma brandished his longsword, and the sun reflecting off the steel sent the shades writhing away.

"I'm sorry," Yorda whispered, eyes closed and head hung low. "Please forgive me. I will free you from this prison if I can. All I require is time."

Yorda...Let the moon's light guide you. Come to the place of memories...

The voice grew more distant until it faded altogether. Yorda stood slowly and began to walk away from the tower.

That night the moon was full.

When the sun set, the positions of the royal guard and the routes they patrolled changed, but Yorda was intimately familiar with their schedule. Slipping from her chambers quietly, she sped quickly toward her destination, weaving along corridors and skirting the edges of chambers where she knew the guards would not come upon her.

The place of memories her father spoke of had to be the trolley. As a child, she had loved to ride upon the trolley, feeling the wind in her hair. Tonight she wore a black robe, her face hidden in the deep hood. Her soft footfalls echoed down the stone corridors as she ran.

She recalled what Ozuma had said to her earlier that day when she told him of her plans, and the strange question he had asked her.

"Was your late father born in this kingdom?"

"My father is the descendant of a family of ministers who have been close to the royal family since antiquity," she told him. "That is why, though he is not related to the royal house, he was given a title and a crest of his own."

Ozuma nodded. "I thought, perhaps, that he might have come from a lineage of priests."

"Actually," Yorda said then, remembering, "my father's family was in the clergy, on his mother's side. As I recall, one of my ancestors rose to be high priest of the kingdom. Perhaps that's why my father was so devout, even though he himself was a man of the sword." Yorda shuddered, imagining her mother married to a man her own father had chosen for her, pretending to follow her husband's faith—then killing him to make herself a widow queen and advance the Dark God's plans.

Ozuma said, "I believe it is clear then why the queen killed your father, and why she trapped his soul in the Tower of Winds. No matter what truth you learn from your father tonight, you must not waver in your resolve, Lady Yorda. Never forget that whatever else you may be, the blood of a priest of Sol Raveh runs in your veins as well."

The silence that hung over the trolley at night was so deep that Yorda might have been walking along the bottom of the sea, yet the cold light of the moon illuminated the rails as though it were day. The wind picked up around midnight. Yorda held her robes closed with a shivering hand as she looked for any sign of her father.

She heard a creaking coming from the wooden platform of the trolley. Yorda looked and saw the rusted lever rocking slightly back and forth. Almost as if someone were testing it to see if it still worked.

Father!

Without a moment's hesitation, Yorda jumped onto the trolley, grabbed the handle and began to push, her memories of her childhood filling her. Though the rails were red with rust, under the moonlight they gleamed bright silver. It was as though time had slipped back to when the trolley ran every day, bringing Yorda back with it. This was another kind of magic. Yorda was elated.

With a loud creaking, the handle slid forward and the trolley lurched into motion. At first it tilted a bit to one side, then to the other, but soon it was running straight, the wheels turning smoothly.

Yorda lifted her head and held on to the railing, giving it a light rap with her knuckles to urge the trolley on. "That's it, that's a girl. Go fast, just like you used to."

The trolley seemingly heard her request and soon began to pick up speed. Riding on the wind, Yorda's memories raced ahead of her. She could see her father standing there beside her, hear her own laughter in her ears.

I still love you, Father.

The trolley raced on, the wind whipping through Yorda's hair. It seemed like the silvery rails stretched off into the night sky, that they would race on and on, carrying Yorda from the castle into freedom.

As she raced along, Yorda soon came to the place where the rails turned to the right, following the outer wall of the castle. Here was another place where one could get on and off the trolley.

She pulled the lever back, dropping her speed, and looked up to the side of the rails.

Yorda held her breath. On the narrow stone ledge by the rails, she saw three dark figures standing, shadows without people.

The one in the middle turned toward her, raising a hand. Yorda desperately grabbed the handle, summoning all her strength to slow the trolley. The wheels screeched and sparks flew. The trolley wobbled, leaning to the outside of the rails, but it did not slow immediately. Yorda watched as she sped by the standing shadows.

The tallest was most certainly her father—but who were the other two standing next to him?

She had glimpsed them for only a moment, but the merciful moon lit their features clearly. The faces were familiar, stirring distant memories within her. The two men were her father's most trusted advisers, one a scholar, the other a soldier. They had accompanied her father from his birth home when he came to the castle, and he had always valued their counsel in matters of state.

Whenever the young Yorda would visit her father's offices, she would see them there. When her father was too busy to play, they would be the ones to console her. Now that she thought of it, she realized that they had often been there when her father took her for trolley rides. They would smile and wave, remaining out of the way until it was time to return inside, when they would help Yorda as she stepped off the trolley.

They were kind gentlemen, with clever minds and a sense of loyalty as deep as the sea. Only now did she realize that they had disappeared from the castle after her father's death. Yorda had been too young at the time to even wonder where they had gone, and no one bothered to explain to a child what became of advisors when they were no longer needed. Even had she realized, the shock of losing her father was so great, she would have had no tears left for them.

But now she saw they were reunited with her father. Her mother's curse had bound them to the Tower of Winds too.

Eventually, the trolley came to a stop. Yorda leapt out and

ran back along the tracks, toward the platform she had passed. She tripped once but didn't feel the pain. The platform seemed impossibly far behind.

"Father, Father!" she called out, crawling up onto the stones.

But the shades were gone.

Panting to catch her breath, Yorda looked around. Abandoned materials sat in piles, and a marker of some kind stood at an angle, casting a curious shadow across the stones.

When she lowered her eyes again, despondent, she caught a glimmer of light a short distance away. Something that sparkled like gold. She approached and slowly knelt, reaching out her hands.

The golden glimmer did not fade. The object felt hard to Yorda's fingertips. She picked it up and placed it in her palm.

It was her father's signet ring.

Yorda.

Her father's voice filled her mind.

That is a token of love once sworn in sincerity, even as it is proof of a broken promise, a gravestone for a sacrificed soul. The ring will open the way into the tower.

Yorda gripped the ring tightly.

Beloved daughter. This will be the last time I can venture forth from the tower to appear before you. The queen has sensed my presence outside of the prison she built for me. The closer I come to you, the more danger I place you in. I'm sorry I cannot guide you myself or lend you further aid. Please forgive your father.

"Father!"

Yorda shouted into the empty night. She caught her father's voice again, receding on the wind.

You will face many unpleasant truths within the tower. The most difficult of these will be the truth that your father is no longer the man he was.

As master of the tower, I possess none of my former nobility and little of my reason. Barred from entering the underworld and cut off from the joys of life while still tied to this world, as a captive, a shade,

I live in eternal suffering. To me in the tower, you would not be a beloved daughter, but prey to be possessed and devoured. That is what your mother, my wife who swore her undying love, has made of me.

That ring you now hold is the only weapon by which you may stave off the shades that serve me within. It will open the way for you and protect you. Keep it close to your person and never let it go.

Yorda clutched her father's gold signet ring tightly to her chest. Fighting back the tears, she stood straight and spoke, her voice piercing the moonlit silence. "I understand, Father. I will go to the Tower of Winds. And I will free you!"

How cruel a father I am to ask this trial of you. You must do more than free me, you must free this entire kingdom from the clutches of the Dark God. My brave daughter, you must climb the Tower of Winds and there claim the true light.

"The true light?"

It was her first time hearing the words. "What is that? Is it something in the Tower of Winds? Does it wield some power over the Dark God—over my mother?"

In the silence that followed, Yorda's conviction grew. *It must be true.* That was why her father's suffering was so deep. He wanted her to destroy her own mother.

The light searches for you, her father's voice said at length. *Be careful, Yorda. The queen is wary. She must not be watching when you go to the tower.*

…How many times my heart told me that you were better off not knowing, your true eye closed, spending your days in peace.

"No father, that's not true. I'm glad I know the truth."

Then I pray the Creator will protect you and give you courage. And, her father added in a voice grown thin and weak, *though it is not how I would have wished to see you again, I am glad we could meet once more, Yorda. I love you.*

Then Yorda felt his presence leave, receding swiftly into the distance.

This was goodbye.

[11]

THE FOLLOWING DAY was the final day of the tournament. Yorda used the magic pebble before dawn had broken, and by the time she had finished her morning routine and come out to the trolley, Ozuma was already waiting for her.

That morning, Ozuma was wearing a fresh chain-mail vest and new gauntlets on his hands. While it was normal for a swordsman to replace worn equipment, to don new and untried gear the morning of such an important bout was a bold move. Yorda took it as a sign of confidence.

Yorda had placed her father's signet ring on a silver chain, which she wore around her neck. She pulled it out now, showing it to Ozuma, and told him of the events of the previous night. Ozuma appeared genuinely startled when she produced the ring. He was clearly pleased. But not as pleased as he was to hear Yorda tell of the true light her father had mentioned.

Ozuma's eyes opened wide. Yorda did not think the stoic knight capable of such surprise. "Sir Ozuma, do you know what the true light is?"

"The priest-king of the Holy Zagrenda-Sol Empire gathered many scholars together over the last few years," Ozuma said. "Their purpose was none other than to define exactly what would be required to prevent the Dark God's revival and destroy his child."

"Did they discover anything?"

"Yes." Ozuma nodded. "The Book of Light."

"A book?" Yorda asked, somewhat taken aback. Demons were supposed to be banished with great swords or strokes of lightning—not books.

"It is a magical tome. In it are inscribed the spells that were used to stop the Dark God from rising in ancient times. Were a sword to be engraved with those spells and imbued with magical power, it could drive back the Dark God—or so they say."

Suddenly, all became clear to Yorda. "That's it!" she said, feeling her heart grow lighter. "The Book of Light is in the Tower of Winds, I'm sure of it! Why else would my mother hide it and surround it with guardians?"

"It would make sense," Ozuma agreed. His face was stern, but his eyes sparkled the same as Yorda's. "Because this book was created so long ago, no one knows where it rests—or if it has survived at all. If it is here, in the Tower of Winds, that would be a tremendous boon."

Yorda clenched her hands into fists. "Then I will find it and retrieve it! I will drive back the Dark God!"

Ozuma's lips drew together, and he stared at her. In silence, he shook his head. Yorda saw in his face the same emotion she had sensed in her father's hesitation the night before.

"It is I who should go to the Tower of Winds," he said at length.

"No," Yorda cut him off. "This is something that I must do. That is why my father risked alerting the queen by appearing before me. That is why he came to me with this task."

After saying her farewells to her father the night before, Yorda had lain in bed sleepless, consumed by her thoughts. She struggled with her father's suffering and the love that still remained in her heart toward her mother. Now there was no doubt in her mind. "I am the heir to the throne of my kingdom. I must protect this land and its people from the Dark God. That is my duty as its future ruler." Yorda stood straight and tall, her voice ringing clear. "You requested my help because of the revelation, and my help you will receive. But do not be mistaken. I do not act at your behest. Nor do I ally myself with the Holy Zagrenda-Sol Empire or take orders from your priest-king. I am merely carrying out my duties as sovereign-in-waiting."

Ozuma blinked, as though looking at the sun as it emerged from behind a cloud.

"If I'm able to defeat the Dark God and ruin his plans of revival, then perhaps I will be able to save my mother as well."

"Save the queen? How?"

"My mother is the child of the Dark God, she has said so herself. Yet she did love my father, and she did bear a child of her own. She is as much a woman of this world as a servant of the other. When the Dark God has been driven back, I pray that the darkness will release her. Like this country, a curse lies upon my mother. That is what I must try to break. That is my battle."

Yorda smiled, feeling more in control of her own destiny than ever before. "That is why, Sir Ozuma, I would beg your assistance. Your skill as a swordsman is of great use to me." Yorda extended her hand toward Ozuma, as a queen does to her loyal servant.

The wind whipped at Yorda's hair as she stood staring up at the aging, desolate tower.

She could feel the weight of her father's ring on her breast. When she picked it up in her fingers and lifted it, it sparkled in the sunlight.

The sky above was deep blue and free of clouds, and the sea below reflected its light. Tiny waves sparkled across the water as white flocks of seabirds wheeled in the sky, flecks of paint against the sky's azure canvas.

She walked across the stone bridge, stopping halfway to look over her shoulder. She had heard a snatch of cheering mingled in with the howling of the wind.

The Eastern Arena was beyond the castle proper. That she could hear the roar of the crowd from this distance meant that their excitement had reached new heights on this final day of the tournament.

Just then, Ozuma and his final opponent would be entering the ring. The spectators standing in the packed gallery around the arena floor would stand as one and applaud. She wondered for whom they would cheer, which contestant had inspired more of them to wager their hard-earned coin. The outcome of this match could make a significant difference in the weight of their money pouches.

She closed her eyes, steadied her breathing, and began walking again. Though she had walked here a hundred times before, today the distance to the tower seemed much greater.

As she approached, she spotted the shadows-that-walked-alone gathering by the windows. She wondered if they had come because they sensed her, or if they always stood there to look out on the world beyond the tower, much as she looked out of her chambers at the land and sea beyond the castle walls.

Now she faced the stone idols before the door to the tower. Yorda brought her feet together and raised her father's ring. Pointing the mark on the ring toward the idols, she spoke in a high, clear voice.

"As I bear the signet of the master of this tower, I command you. Stand aside!"

A bright light shone from the ring. The flash was so brilliant, Yorda staggered, taking two or three steps backward before she regained her footing. As one, the idols' heads glowed in response. Unbound energy ran along the lines of their misshapen forms, and a bridge of lightning spanned the air between statues and ring.

With a heavy grinding sound, the two idols parted to either side, revealing a dark rectangular space behind them. At the same time, the light faded, leaving Yorda's hands numb and tingling. The spell ward was broken.

Yorda stepped forward. A chill wind blew out from the tower, brushing past her cheek. She was alone in darkness and silence.

Yorda had given Ozuma his orders that morning: he was to fight his best in the final round of the tournament and emerge victorious. Yet it must not seem an easy win. Even if his opponent was no match for him, Ozuma was to drag the fight out, driving the spectators to a frenzy. She wanted everyone in that arena to forget, if only for a while, the passage of time. She wanted them to lose themselves in a fight so spectacular they could not tear their eyes away, not even for a moment.

She needed time.

The queen would be watching the final match with cruel curiosity, her eye on Ozuma as he worked his craft on the arena floor. She alone knew that he would one day be a statue in her gallery, and she would want to see just how good he was so she would know what she would be taking from this world.

All that Yorda required was that the queen's interest be held long enough to distract her attention from other things.

She remembered her father's quaking voice when he visited her chambers. *She'll find me,* he said.

The queen knew everything. Even the slightest disturbance, the merest presence within the borders of the enchantment she had laid upon the castle could alert her, as it had when Yorda made her attempt to leave the castle that day. And yet the queen was only human. She might be the child of the Dark God, but she was no god herself. If something captured her mind and heart so forcefully that for a moment she had no attention to pay to stirrings within her enchantment, then it might just be possible for Yorda to enter the tower unseen. It was, in essence, Yorda's only hope: a wager more desperate than any taking place in the arena that day.

Ozuma had promised to carry out his end of the bargain. "I will make it a match such as they have never seen, and steal the queen's eyes with my sword," he told her. "When her attention is captured, that will be your chance to run into the tower and do what you must do."

There was no time for dawdling. She took a step, then another, toward the entrance to the Tower of Winds. She passed by the idols sitting silently at the sides of the doorway. She could now see inside the first floor of the tower. She was inside its walls.

The tower had few windows for a structure of its size. The darkness seemed to pool here at the bottom, thick and still. For a tower, the space was vast. The bottommost floor was shaped like a round courtyard and paved with square stones packed tightly together. The construction was very similar to the corridors within the castle proper, save for the occasional stone jutting out from the floor, its edges cracked or smashed altogether.

There was nothing here resembling decoration or furniture at all. There were no sconces or pedestals for torches; the walls were bare. Above her head was only space. The Tower of Winds was as empty as it could be.

Not the best place for hiding something, Yorda thought. *Is the Book of Light truly in this place? Is my father's soul kept here somewhere?*

She spotted a spiral staircase winding up the inside wall of the high tower. A railing went along its length, adorned with sharp spikes. The bottom step was off to her right, beckoning her.

Yorda looked around in a circle. The shades she had spotted by the windows were nowhere to be seen. Had they disappeared, or were they watching, hidden in the gloom? She looked up for so long, her neck began to hurt, but she could not see all the way to the top of the tower. Yet now she sensed that the darkness above her was not entirely empty. Something was there, mingling with the natural shadows of the place. Silhouettes against a black backdrop.

Yorda stared for a while longer before finally giving up. It would be quicker to walk up the stairs to the top. *My time here is fleeting.*

Stepping briskly toward the stairs, she noticed something on the floor of the tower. It was a large circular design, wider than she was tall. She ran up to it and found that it had not been carved into the floor, nor painted there. Instead, it rose from the floor in relief, forming a sort of dais with its edge raised a full inch off the stones of the surrounding floor.

In the back of her mind, she dimly recollected seeing a design like this one in history books she had read years before. Suspicion grew inside her, and she found she could not take her eyes off the dais on the floor. Eventually, she had to force her feet to carry her back to the stairs. Her earlier confidence had fled, and unease was only too eager to take its place.

As she began to climb, pools of blackness emerged from the floor below her. The pools boiled and seemed to writhe across the stones as though living things. Yorda grabbed the handrail in terror and watched as pairs of glowing eyes began to emerge from the dark pools. Pair after pair spilled out into the tower, followed by inky black arms that grew out of the pools like swiftly sprouting weeds.

They were the shades of the tower, the shadows-that-walked-alone. As she watched, one after the other emerged onto the floor, their legs twisted and their backs bent horribly. They staggered more than walked, their movements an eerie dance that would have been almost humorous had the creatures not been unmistakably evil. They advanced up the stairs, leaping from step to step as they rose toward her.

Her voice fled her and Yorda put her hands to her cheeks, realizing now where the shades had gone. Quickly, she dashed up the stairs, only to see another black pool boiling on the landing just ahead of her. A creature emerged from the pool with white eyes like those behind her, but with the shadowy shape of a bird. Its wings grazed Yorda's head as it shot across the empty center of the tower to the other side of the spiral staircase.

In that brief moment, Yorda saw that the bird-monster had a human face, its mouth open in a silent scream. Three more of the bird-shaped creatures flew up from the landing. One of them spotted Yorda as she cowered against the wall and dove straight at her. Yorda was unable to do anything but throw her hands in front of her face—but as she did so, the ring at her chest flared with a bright light.

With a whistle of wind, the creature's wing struck Yorda's shoulder before it careened into the wall behind her to disappear in a puff of smoke. The smoke drifted past Yorda's face, leaving a lingering chill in the air before vanishing altogether.

Yorda looked down the stairs and saw that the creatures coming up from the floor of the tower had stopped. They recoiled in horror. The figures closest to Yorda were beginning to lose their shape, their limbs melting away and drifting off into the air.

It's as my father said. The shadows-that-walk-alone are powerless before the ring, the symbol of this kingdom's former glory and his love for his people.

Yorda held the ring up in front of her face. As she watched, the threads of darkness spilling from the pool on the landing ahead of her dissipated. Soon the pool evaporated entirely. Yorda quickly ran up the stairs, going so fast she stumbled once or twice. Each time, she caught herself with her hands on the stairs and continued to climb. Once, she nearly lost her balance and made the mistake of grabbing the handrail to her left. Her hand caught on one of the sharp spikes and began to bleed, yet still she climbed, legs in constant motion. Finally, when she was breathing so hard she felt her chest would burst, she stopped for a moment to catch her breath. She looked around and saw that she had climbed more than halfway up the tower.

Looking down over the railing, she spotted more than a dozen shadowy things on the floor of the tower, aimlessly drifting. Some of them were crouched on the dais in the center. The birds clung to the walls, slowly beating their wings.

Yorda looked up. At this height, she could finally see the top of the tower. There, hanging from the roof, was something like a giant metal birdcage. There was no other way to describe it. It was cylindrical in shape, the gleam of the iron darkened with age. Yet when the wind that whipped around the tower blew in through the windows, past the ragged shreds of curtains, the dim light of the sun glinted off the thick-looking bars. Yorda realized that this was what she had seen when she peered at the top floor of the tower through her spyglass.

She was amazed by its size. Though its design mirrored a birdcage, it was large enough to contain a grown person. There were sharp spikes all around the bottom and top edges—a strange, deadly looking adornment. *Perhaps to keep people from coming too close,* Yorda guessed.

A chilling sensation ran up Yorda's spine. Maybe it *was* built to hold a person. *Maybe there's someone in it right now.*

She heard a voice shouting but could not make out any words. Then she realized it was her own voice, and the sound brought her back to reality. Once again, Yorda dashed up the stairs. She had to go higher. She had to learn what was inside.

Pressed by desperation and fear, Yorda ran, taking two steps at a time. Finally, she approached the base of the cage. A little farther, and her head was level with the bottom. She clung to the railing and leaned out as far as she could.

"Father?" she heard herself call out.

An old, faded robe lay in tatters on the bottom of the cage. She could faintly make out the remnants of gold embroidery around the sleeves. It was her father's tunic—woven of wool, a deep navy color, softer than silk to the touch. This was the same tunic he often wore for public occasions; the clothes he had worn as he lay in his coffin at the funeral.

She looked closer and saw a tuft of white hair protruding from one end of the robe. *My father's body is here too. Confined even in death.* He was the master of the Tower of Winds.

Yorda fell to her knees and wept out loud.

[12]

YORDA LOOKED AROUND desperately, trying to find some way to release her father's remains from the cage.

The cage hung from the ceiling of the tower by a chain thicker than Yorda's arm. The chain was old, its luster long gone, and it was covered with rust. From what she knew of similar devices in the castle, Yorda expected there to be a winch somewhere to raise and lower the chain, but she saw nothing. Tears still streaming down her face, she continued to climb the spiral staircase.

Unused to such exertion, her legs were beginning to give out on her. Her calves were painfully cramped, and her knees and ankles ached. But sorrow and indignation kept her moving, even when she had to crawl up the last ten steps on her hands and knees.

At the top of the stairs was a square landing surrounded by pointed spikes. At the edge, she spotted a metallic lever. She followed the chain from the cage up to the ceiling where it connected with a winch, then ran back down to the lever by the landing.

That's it!

The lever was set firmly in the stone floor, and when she touched it, the device wouldn't budge. Whatever oil had been applied to it was long gone, and the lever was stiff with rust. She took it in both hands and brought all her weight to bear on it, forcing the lever very slightly back with a horrendous creaking noise. She saw the chain holding the cage shudder, and the cage dropped a few inches, its base tilting.

Yorda pulled with all her might. She blinked against the sweat and tears that mingled in her eyes. Again she pulled. The skin on her hands was raw and bleeding. One of her fingernails cracked. Once, the sweat on her hands made her lose her grip, sending her sprawling onto the ground and biting her lip. Her entire body screamed in protest at the effort—it was more physical work than she had ever attempted. But Yorda did not give up.

The cage continued to descend at an obstinate pace. She stopped only once to check on its progress and found it was halfway down the tower. This gave Yorda hope, and she turned back around and continued her battle with the lever.

At last, there came a *thud* she felt in her hands. The lever was all the way down. She heard a heavy, reverberating clang drift up from the floor of the tower far below. Yorda looked over the railing once to check that the cage had, indeed, reached the bottom, then she began climbing down the stairs. She had to fight her legs to make them do as she bade. For a moment she paused, hands on her knees, steadying her breath and wiping the sweat from her brow with the back of a hand.

Suddenly, she felt dizzy, as though her legs were swaying beneath her. *No, I can't fall now,* she told herself, but the swaying sensation continued. She realized it wasn't dizziness—she really *was* swaying.

Spurred to action by animal reflexes Yorda never knew she possessed, she leapt just as a part of the landing beside her feet crumbled and gave way. The stone of the stairs dissipated in the dust, tumbling toward the base of the tower.

There was no time for fear. The staircase was continuing to collapse beneath her, cracks running through the stones directly toward her feet. She fled down the spiral staircase, the sound of crumbling stone close behind her. Ahead of her, too, there was a gap where several stairs had fallen away. She cleared it with a jump, landing with the tips of her toes on the far edge. She lost her balance and slammed into the wall but was back on her feet immediately and resumed her mad dash.

She felt like she was playing a game of chase where the stakes were her life. She wondered that the stairs in the tower should suddenly grow too weak to support her weight, but then she understood the darker truth. Her mother was trying to smash her against the stones of the tower floor. Had the tournament ended? Had Ozuma emerged victorious?

Now she was practically sliding down the stairs. When she finally reached the bottom, her legs collapsed beneath her, completely numb, and she sprawled across the floor. For a while, she just lay there, gasping for breath. No matter how much she breathed, her chest ached, and her vision grew dim, the floor on which she lay shifting nearer and farther in turns.

Finally she was able to get her arms beneath her and pick herself up. *I did it. Just a little farther.*

She looked up to see the spiral staircase hanging above her in the tower, as though nothing had happened. It was so quiet, it seemed almost like she had dreamed the collapsing stairs around her, though she could spot the gaps where she had had to jump, and there were piles of rubble around the edges of the tower.

Yorda hugged her arms across her chest. The giant cage holding her father's remains sat directly atop the round platform in the middle of the floor. The shades were nowhere to be seen.

Careful not to catch herself on the metallic thorns, Yorda approached the door of the cage. With a trembling hand, she reached out and touched the door, grabbing hold of one of the bars.

With a screech that made her teeth ache, the door swung outward.

I guess you don't need to lock the door that holds a dead man, she thought with relief, though it made her father's imprisonment seem that much more contemptuous. A fresh tear rolled down Yorda's cheek.

"Father…"

She stepped inside and tried to pick up the faded tunic. The fabric disintegrated like cobwebs in her hand, sending up a plume of dust. Yorda spotted her father's bones beneath the tattered cloth. With her eyes she marked the curve of a rib. There was a shoulder. She brushed away more of the tunic and found the bone of an arm. She guessed the bones protruding from the bottom of the tunic were his legs.

Judging by the arrangement of the bones, she guessed her father had been lying stretched out on his right side. But something was missing—she couldn't find the skull.

Crouching low, Yorda moved around the remains to the other side of the cage. From this vantage point she could clearly see the skull, tucked in beside the ribs, beneath the protruding ridges of one of his arms—as though he had been holding his own head under one arm.

Yorda had seen her father's body lying in the coffin in the castle. And not just Yorda—a ceremony was held for the entire kingdom. Ministers and noblemen great and small had gathered to pay their respects. After the ceremony, a great procession carried the coffin throughout the kingdom for two weeks, so that the commoners could say their farewells before his remains were laid to rest in the royal graveyard in the mountains. The line of mourners behind his carriage had snaked for miles.

But his bones were lying right here, back at the castle. Was the coffin they took out on the procession empty? Mother must have removed the remains in secret before they left the castle, and then...

Yorda's tears had dried. She sat down in shock, staring at her beloved father's bones, when she noticed something curious. The bones were discolored in places. Here and there light purple splotches, like bruises left after a fight, marred the dry parchment color of the bone. Yorda could not bring herself to disturb the bones by lifting them up or moving them, so she poked and prodded, shifting them only slightly, making sure the discoloration was not a trick of the light.

Convinced the bones were discolored, Yorda wracked her brain trying to come up with some explanation. *Perhaps*, she thought, *this was a mark left by the disease that took him.* But she knew her father had appeared healthy when he died. It made no sense that a disease could do such damage internally without showing some outward signs. Poison, however...

Yorda did not think her mother would have been capable of both poisoning and disposing of the body all by herself. She must have ordered someone to help her—someone helpless to resist her. And then, when the grisly work was done, her mother had made her helpers disappear—either by killing them or turning them to stone along with the other statues in her underground gallery. It was unthinkable. "I will get you out of here, Father, I promise," Yorda said, her voice quiet but firm. She reached out for the skull.

The skull was facing away from her, down into the ribs, so nothing seemed out of the ordinary until it was in her hands. Then she saw that something had been placed between the skull's teeth. She lifted the skull gingerly, as one raises a crown, and gasped with surprise. It was a book. The long teeth, exposed without lips to cover them, were clenched on a single book.

The Book of Light!

Her theory had proven correct. The queen had used the Tower of Winds to imprison the book, much as it had been used ages before to imprison the Wind God from which it took its name. But in order to be sure the book would never be uncovered, simply locking it in the tower wasn't enough. So her mother had chosen to sacrifice her father, murdering him and binding him to this world with a curse, changing him into one of the shadows-that-walk-alone, and placing him here as the book's final guardian. Then she killed her father's advisors and a host of others to serve him in the tower, before sealing its doors with the idols.

As her anger flared, Yorda grabbed the edge of the book and pulled. In her hands, the skull began to move. She had the curious sensation that its empty sockets were looking, no, glaring at her, their sightless gaze boring a hole into her.

Before she could react, the skull leapt from her hands like a living thing, dancing up into the air. She heard a low moan, filled with rage and resentment.

"Father!" she called out, screaming. The skull sped toward her.

Yorda scrambled to dodge out of the way. She caught the skull with the back of one hand, dashing it against the bars of the cage. It bounced, falling onto the floor before shooting back up into the air. In midair it turned, facing Yorda to come at her again, howling like a wounded animal.

She watched as the jaws opened, spitting the book out onto the floor like a carnivore spits out tattered skin and cartilage from a kill. The discarded book fell with a whoosh of dust onto the tattered robe.

"Father, stop! It's me! Your daughter!"

The skull flew at her. Yorda dodged to the side, but not quickly enough—teeth bit into her right shoulder, gnawing at her skin like a starving animal. She knocked it away again and again, but it kept attacking, lunging erratically like a rabid dog. Yorda ran in circles around the inside of the cage, sobbing with fear and sadness, horror and pity.

Then she remembered the book. If it truly was as powerful as Ozuma had said, perhaps it could break her mother's enchantment.

But first she had to reach it, and the skull wouldn't give her the chance. The moment she took her eyes off the skull, it would come for her, dancing, teeth chattering. After several attempts, she realized what the skull was aiming for. It wanted her neck—to chew through her veins and bathe in her blood.

She lunged for the book, and the skull swooped down and bit her hand. Blinded by the pain, Yorda flung the skull against the bars. *This is my father no longer—it's nothing but a monster!* She wondered if she had made it this far only to die with this twisted abomination gnawing at her neck.

"Somebody, help!" she shouted, her voice echoing in the empty tower. She ran, and the skull continued its dogged pursuit.

The next time it came at her, she blocked it inches from her neck and it bit down into the flesh of her palm. Reflexively, she swung her hand, and the skull ricocheted off the bars of the cage, spinning in the air and howling with its teeth bared like a hungry animal. The cry pierced to her bones.

At that moment, the silver chain around her neck broke with an audible snap, as though it had a will of its own. Her father's signet ring fell down her chest, past her waist, and down her leg, before rolling out onto the ground where it glimmered in the dust.

Yorda bent down quickly, scooping up the ring. Blood gushed from the wound in her wrist, splattering her white dress.

The skull was coming directly at her. Reflexively, she thrust out the hand holding the ring, trying to knock it away. A clear light shone from the ring, disorienting the skull, and it brushed past her head and fell behind her. She turned to see its empty sockets glaring at her, and its long, sharp teeth chattering.

The jaws opened, making a sound like howling laughter as it flew toward her. Yorda focused her mind, forcing all her attention on the skull, her eyes spear points. Time seemed to slow. Aiming for the gap between the teeth, she flung the ring with all her strength. The ring flew through the air, directly into the mouth of the skull as it sped toward her throat.

Time stopped. Her father's skull screamed.

The light of the ring blazed from the skull's eye sockets, from its nose, and from its mouth, growing more brilliant, until it seemed to shine through the bone itself. The skull howled a final, bitter howl of rage and pain. Yorda clapped her hands over her ears, knowing that if she listened to it, her heart would break.

The skull exploded. Fragments ricocheted around the cage, trailing particles of golden light, before becoming a rain of sparks that trickled down to the floor, glimmering as they fell.

Quiet returned to the tower. Yorda felt her body sway, and she clutched the bars of the cage. The strength left her legs. At her feet, her father's remains lay wrapped in his tunic, still once more. Atop the tunic lay the Book of Light. Yorda moved in slow half steps toward the book. She leaned over, bent her knees, and finally reached out her hand.

The book was warm to the touch, like a living thing. The cover was ancient and dry, and it bore five words written in a script Yorda could not read. Yet the spirit of those words hit her like a wave, engulfing her, bringing her back to her feet. Yorda closed her eyes and clutched the book to her chest.

As she did, she felt something flowing into her, a divine power, making her entire body glow so that even when she closed her eyes it was bright.

The power healed her, closing the wounds and cuts she had endured during her descent from the crumbling stairs and the fight with the skull. When she opened her eyes, the bite marks on her wrist had vanished entirely.

She still glowed from the inside, the book filling her with light. When she looked around again, she saw a crowd of the shades surrounding the cage in series of concentric circles. There were too many to count. Nearer still, she saw her father, appearing as he had when he visited her chambers as a ghost. His advisers were there too, standing at his side.

Yorda stared at the apparition of her father. Her father looked back, his eyes filled with warmth and gratitude. He raised one hand, his skin the color of shadow. He was waving farewell. The shades in a circle around the cage began to drift upward. They climbed in silence toward the top of the tower, fading as they rose, evaporating like mist in the light of dawn.

Her father's shade lingered the longest. There were no more words. Yorda watched her father's form as he lifted into the air, free at last. When all of the shadows were gone, the Tower of Winds was filled with light.

For a moment, Yorda stood praying to the Creator, the book clasped in her arms. The words of the prayer she had known since childhood flowed from her lips, leaving her filled with joy such as a child knows tasting a sweet, fresh fruit.

The enchantment was broken. The tower had been purified.

Yorda walked back outside between the idols at the door, heading toward the long stone bridge. At its far end stood the queen.

She was not dressed in the long, flowing white dress she wore that morning on her way to the final match. In its place she wore a black gown, dark as night—the same gown she had worn when she summoned Yorda to the graveyard.

This is my mother's true form. I have torn away her mask and revealed her for what she is.

The queen was walking across the bridge, coming closer. No, not walking. She was floating.

They faced one another—the queen wrapped in shadow, the castle looming behind her, the daughter clutching the book to her chest, radiant with light.

"What have you done?" The queen's voice pierced Yorda's heart like a knife. "Do you even understand?"

Yorda did not reply. She stared at her mother's face, framed by her flowing black hair. Her skin was whiter than her poor father's bones. Not the pure white of new-fallen snow, but of nothingness—an absolute white that permits no other color to exist in its presence.

It was this evil darkness and absolute whiteness with which her mother sought to conquer the world. There was no room here for the color of a man's flesh or the red of his blood, the rich brown of the soil and blue of the sea, or even the deep green of the trees and grasses. She knew then without seeing that the Dark God, too, must resemble his child: black clothes, black hair, and a bloodless white face.

"I did not expect my own daughter to betray me," the queen said, stepping close enough that they might reach out and touch one another. "It is not too late, Yorda. Return that odious book to the Tower of Winds."

Yorda shook her head, clutching the book tight. "It isn't *odious*. It is a book of freedom. I've used it to release your enchantment upon the tower, while you were busy watching men try to kill each other. Men you value little more than the stones upon which you walk."

"Naive child," the queen breathed, her face twisting into a scowl.

Yorda blanched but stood her ground. "Do you enjoy watching men squabble over swords and wagers? Do you like to see them inflict pain on each other, Mother?"

Yorda was sure now that Ozuma had fulfilled his promise to her by distracting the queen. As her cruel lust for bloodshed had risen, she had lowered her guard.

"What do you want?" the queen asked, her voice crackling, echoing.

"I don't know yet. But I do know what I *do not* want. I do not want a world where the Dark God reigns. I do not want the kind of world you scheme to bring about. I will stop you!"

"You are a fool!" the queen said. With a flourish she spread her arms wide, her long dark sleeves becoming giant wings, blocking Yorda's sight.

"As child of the Dark God, I will be queen of his world. And you are my daughter. What is mine will one day become yours. Why do you not understand?"

"I don't want a world of darkness!" Yorda shouted. "I want a world of people. I want a world of love, love like my father showed me. That is what I want!" Yorda took a step forward, closing the distance. "Did you not love my father? Did you never feel any guilt at what you did to him? What was my father to you? A tool? A warm body to fill a throne while it suited you? Did you hesitate at all before killing him, before cursing him to a suffering worse than death?"

"Love?" The queen tossed back her head and laughed. "Where do you get such precious ideas? Do you even know what love is?"

"I do!" Yorda said, the queen's words like knives in her chest.

"Then," the queen said with a smile, "you know that love between two people is worth nothing more than dust! Your trifling sentiments reveal how little you comprehend, my child. I am one with a *god*, and a god is something far greater than any man!"

"You're wrong!" Yorda shouted breathlessly, looking like a sparrow defying a hawk.

The queen clucked under her breath. "I see now that it was a mistake to bring you into this world. Why did I think to share my life with you? How did I ever imagine something worthwhile could come of an alliance with a mortal? With one misstep I have earned a lifetime of lament!"

Yorda knew she could not cry—that she had no tears left to cry—yet the sadness rose in her all the same. She felt a tear run down her cheek, and she bit back a sob.

The queen beamed. "Foolish human child. See what has befallen your home, all because you had to free your miserable father!"

The queen flitted up into the air and disappeared from Yorda's sight. In her place, Yorda found herself looking out on the castle. The place of her birth, a homestead from which she had never left. The castle was her entire world. Now that world was shifting, its outline bending in ways it should not, like a scene viewed through warped glass. The sky was frozen, and the very wind had stopped.

Yorda ran across the bridge, looking for someone, anyone. She listened for voices and heard nothing. When she reached the castle proper, she saw guards, all frozen in place like living statues. One man had been stopped in mid-step, one foot hanging in space. Another was about to speak to a comrade, his lips slightly parted.

She looked around more and found a handmaiden, frozen holding a tray of silver goblets. Her other hand was behind her head, frozen in the act of fixing her hair, fingers outstretched. Even the air inside the castle seemed frozen in stasis.

She heard the queen's voice, seeming to come from nowhere and everywhere all at once. "This is your doing."

So dependent was the castle upon her mother's enchantment that it could not live in its absence. All who lived within its walls, cut off from the outside world, living in false peace, were frozen in time.

"In preparation for the Dark God's arrival, there had to be people upon the land, for the Dark God takes sustenance from the evil in men's hearts. Human greed and wickedness are my offerings to him."

Her mother had not struck sooner, wielding her powers to lay her enemies low, so that she might have a greater population to offer up to her god when the time came. Sacrifices were always fed handsomely until they were brought to the altar.

"Destroy me, and you destroy them," the queen's voice said in a low growl by her ear. Yorda felt a cold finger stroke the back of her neck. "But, should you repent and help me imprison that cursed book once again, I will replace the enchantment, and all will be as it was before. What wrong have these people done? Think on it, Yorda. To the ignorant, it does not matter what form their Creator takes. They care not whether they serve a god of light or of darkness, as long as their prosperity is ensured. One god is easily exchanged for another."

At some point she had appeared directly behind Yorda, and now she stepped in close, enveloping her in an embrace—no different than when Yorda had been a child, sitting on her mother's knee.

"Why must we argue over such things? Are we not mother and daughter?" Her voice was soothing now, tickling at Yorda's ear.

Yorda looked down at the graceful curves of her mother's arm, wrapped in delicate, near transparent black lace that only accented the whiteness of her skin. In that embrace, Yorda felt powerless and immature, her bones slender and fragile, her chest flat like a child's. And yet, Yorda's body still glowed with light. The energy that had flowed to her from the book coursed through her veins, illuminating her skin from within.

Yorda gripped the book more tightly, lowering her head and shutting her eyes tight. *My mother was chosen by the Dark God, and I was chosen by the God of Light. If I do not stand down, we will fight as the avatars of our chosen deities. The queen says it is a meaningless battle—but I am my father's daughter. His blood flows in me. And what did she do to him?*

She pictured her father's skull burning with rage and chagrin, locked in the tower for an eternity, the book clenched between his teeth. "You would deceive me, Mother," Yorda said, opening her eyes. "Did you not tell me, just a moment ago, that I should never have been born? Have you forgotten how you shamed my father? Forgotten the horrible treatment you showed him?"

After a brief moment, the queen replied in a gravelly voice, full of power. "You find my actions unforgivable? You would deny your own mother's love?"

Though her cheek was still wet with tears, Yorda had to laugh. "I thought love between people is no better than dust." She took a deep breath and wrenched herself away, turning to face the queen. "I'm tired of your lies!"

Yorda held the shining book up high and thrust it toward her mother's face. A horrifying scream rent the air around them, echoing off the walls of the castle. The queen covered her face with both hands and flew up into the air like a grim, ungainly bird.

Writhing and screaming, the queen ascended halfway up the Tower of Winds, throwing her body against the stone wall. Her robes spread out wildly in the wind like a black flower blooming in the sky.

"What have you done?"

The queen's soft, soothing voice was gone. Now she screamed, glaring down at Yorda from high above her.

"You were wrong, Mother!" Yorda shouted up to her. "You tried to deceive me!" She caught her breath, then continued. "Why? Of what worth is it, being the child of a god? Where is the meaning in ruling the world? You did not love your husband as you do not love me! Where's the glory in butchery and lies? So many lies!"

The book held high over her head gave more power to Yorda. She watched as it grew brighter, filling her with strength, sweeping away the last wisps of doubt as she strode forward to stand beneath where the queen floated in the sky.

Yorda's hands moved of their own accord, flipping through the pages of the Book of Light. There she found a new power, and it flowed forth in a blinding holy radiance directed squarely at the queen. The light caught the queen in midair, flinging her against the tower.

"Have you forgotten what I said?" the queen screamed. "Kill me and you kill everyone in the castle!"

Suddenly time returned to the castle around Yorda. Everyone who was frozen lurched back into motion. Within moments, screams of terror rose up from every hall and courtyard in the castle. The long enchantment over them was gone entirely now, and as one, every minister and handmaiden, guard and patrolman were returned to their senses, and the reality of what they saw drove them mad.

Yorda did not flinch. Her eyes fixed on the queen, she chose to believe in the power of the book and held it still higher over her head. The Book of Light knew its enemy well. It would not let the queen escape. Again and again, she was dashed against the tower, the white light burning her body, and she howled, unable to escape the reach of the light.

Yorda watched, weeping, as the queen lost her shape and began to unravel into threads of dark mist. Yorda wept more and louder, yet her hands remained firm, pressing the book toward the queen. She was quickly dissolving into the stuff of the black pools Yorda had seen in the tower.

She's becoming like one of the shadows she created.

Perhaps this was, in fact, her mother's true shape. Perhaps she was nothing but an apparition, a gathering of motes of black mist. *This gave birth to me? My father took* this *as his loving wife?*

The mist dissipated into the sky, winding into the wind, almost entirely gone now. Yorda stood with her legs firmly planted, forcing her weary arms higher. The mist was very thin now, hardly more than the last wisp of smoke from a cold fireplace. The wind picked up, blowing it away.

But a single thread remained, twisting with rage, and from it the queen's voice sounded in Yorda's ears, saying, "I will not be destroyed! Look well, for you have failed!"

A powerful unseen force slammed into Yorda, sending her sprawling across the stones of the bridge. The shock of the impact was enough to knock the Book of Light from her hands.

Yorda scratched with her fingers on the bridge, trying to stand. Finally on her feet, she picked up the book and clasped it to her chest. The sounds of disquiet from the castle were growing louder. She heard the clashing of metal on metal, women screaming, men shouting.

The noise washed out over the bridge like a rumbling earthquake. Yorda stood as still as stone, not believing what she saw. On the far side of the bridge, a great throng of people were pushing their way out of the castle, running toward her in a wave. She saw guards, patrolmen, handmaidens, and scholars. The soldiers wielded swords and spears, while the handmaidens bared teeth and nails. She spotted the Minister of Court, his fists clenched above his head as he charged out onto the bridge—at Yorda.

Though they could not have been a more varied crowd, they all had one thing in common—their eyes were clouded with a dark mist. With a deepening sense of despair, Yorda realized what had happened. Her mother, the queen, had turned to mist and possessed them all, driving them mad. She was wielding them like puppets, sending them to kill.

Kill, kill, kill! Kill the one with the book! Kill Yorda!

Yorda had few options. She still held the Book of Light in her arms, yet she lacked the will to lift it again.

This is my mother's strength. In the end, I could not defeat her. I merely forced her hand and brought ruin to us all.

The shouts grew louder, and the rumble of feet swept closer. Yorda closed her eyes.

"Lady Yorda!" A powerful voice shouted over the noise. "Lady Yorda!"

She lifted her face and saw that the crowd had stopped just a few paces away from her. They were turning, looking back toward the castle. Then their ranks began to dissolve, as new screams of rage and fear rose from the mob.

It was Ozuma. He was brandishing his longsword, cutting down people in his way, charging toward Yorda.

"Ozuma!"

Ozuma swung his sword in all directions, driving back the possessed throng around him, shouting out to Yorda. "The book, Princess! The book!"

Buoyed by his voice, Yorda once again lifted the book in her hands. When she raised it over her head, the crowd on the bridge shrank back, some fleeing altogether. Ozuma pushed them aside, making a path to the front. When he was finally free of them, he ran up and took Yorda's arm. "Now!"

Grabbing Yorda, he pushed her toward the edge of the bridge.

"What are you doing?"

"We have to run!"

Run? Run where? The Tower of Winds was a dead end. If they ran inside the tower, they would only be trapped.

She hesitated and the crowd regained their fury, advancing, a dark light in their eyes.

"Come with me!" Ozuma shouted. Not waiting for an answer, he picked Yorda up lightly in one arm. He returned his sword to its scabbard, tossed his helmet aside, and ripped off his chain-mail vest to lighten his load. Holding Yorda in both arms now, he leapt from the top of the bridge. Yorda pressed her eyes shut a moment before they touched the foaming waves. Icy water wrapped around her, but her heart was filled with a song both triumphant and sorrowful. *The book is safe.*

With the Book of Light still clutched in her hands, she slipped into unconsciousness.

How much time had passed since then?

Yorda looked up at the boy staring into her eyes, clasping her hands tightly. *I know you,* she thought.

And he knew her as well. The memories of the castle—how it had become enveloped in mist until the mist became its name, and fear and awe its reputation—she had shared these with him, through his hand in her own.

That was why doubt now clouded the boy's eyes. That was how he knew she was the queen's daughter, the only one who could hope to defeat her.

He knew she had left the castle, bearing the Book of Light, and so escaped the queen's dark grasp. He knew that when she and Ozuma had plunged into the sea, the waves acted as a veil, blinding the queen to their whereabouts until the currents carried them safely ashore.

But why did you come back? the boy wondered. *Why were you imprisoned here? The steel cage that held you in the top of the tower was the cage that once held your father. The cage you fought so hard to free him from. Yet it was you I found lying in that cage. Without hope, sadness your only companion.*

And the gallant knight Ozuma was turned to stone by the edge of the old bridge, as lonely as you. Why does he stand there, the knight from a foreign land come to save you, now stripped of his life and the sword he wielded for you? With the passing months the weather wears away at him. He is mindless and cold.

So too do the shadows-that-walk-alone fill the castle once more. The pools from which they spawn form freely on the stones, trying to take you back into their embrace.

What happened after you escaped the castle? the boy wondered. *Why, though you held the book, could you not defeat the queen? What terrible misstep did you make that sealed your fate?*

Though Yorda could now understand the boy's tongue, he could not understand her. Still she whispered in her heart:

In the end, I could not defeat my mother.

It had all been in vain. In the end, the child of the Dark God was still master of the Castle in the Mist, and the Dark God still awaited the day of his revival. The threat to their world had not been defeated, merely delayed.

And it is all my fault. I could have defeated her, yet in the end I betrayed myself.

Yorda knew that, though the boy's language would not rise to her lips, her memories would tell the tale of the great battle that ensued after her escape from the castle, of the tragedy and deceit that followed. If she just held on to his hand, he would learn it all.

But what good would that knowledge bring him? What meaning was there in showing him the defeat her own hands had wrought? The deceit that dragged Ozuma down, cursing his blood, the curse that spanned generations, down to the boy himself.

No, even if there was meaning in showing him, Yorda did not

want the boy to know. Not now, when she was powerless, able only to offer apology after apology.

I should release his hand. I will return to the tower, and he may leave here on his own.

But the boy only gripped Yorda's fingers tighter. His eyes flashed. "The knight Ozuma was my ancestor. The blood of the knight who defended you runs in my veins." He stood. "This time the blood will not fail."

CHAPTER 4
THE FINAL BATTLE

[1]

THE GIANT FRONT gates of the Castle in the Mist were closed once more. Ico and Yorda stood together in the sunlit courtyard. The memories of the castle and its history now returned to Yorda formed a link between her and the boy, a link firmer than his grip upon her hand.

Ico squinted in the breeze, looking up at the gates that blocked their escape.

"We'll get out, I promise," he said. On her knees, Yorda whispered something weakly. Ico looked down at her, still not understanding her words. "It'll be okay this time," he said.

How can you say that? she thought, her eyes widening. *How can you know?*

Ico smiled. "I just know. I can see it now."

He understands my thoughts, even though he cannot understand my words, Yorda realized.

"There was a battle, wasn't there?" Ico whispered. Yorda trembled, recoiling from her own memories.

"You broke the queen's enchantment. Then you and Ozuma escaped and took the Book of Light to the outside world. That's why the armies of Zagrenda-Sol finally launched their attack."

Yes, Yorda thought, *they came—*

At once, a new vision spread before Yorda's eyes. She saw a massive host of armed men, battle-worn and brave. An armada of warships covered the sea. Atop the deck of the lead galleon flew the flag of the Holy Zagrenda-Sol Empire, and on its bow stood the priest-king himself. She saw him closely now, in profile, his face filled with determination and battle lust. The sun lit his face and made the imperial emblem on his shoulder glitter like gold. Ozuma stood at his side, the longsword at his waist imbued with the power of the Book of Light.

Yes, they came to destroy the queen. With her enchantment gone, the seas around the castle were as easy for ships to enter as a grassy field is to a brigade of footmen. There was nothing to stop them. They crossed the narrow sea, made landing by the castle, and the sound of their boots upon the stones drowned out even the howling of the sea wind.

They arrived to find nothing waiting for them—not a single soldier stood in their way.

Yorda jerked her hand from Ico, wrenching him from the vision of the past. The phantasmal armada upon the waters vanished into the sunlight.

A seabird passed overhead, its cry plaintive. For a while the boy stood there, looking down at Yorda, whose hands covered her face. Then he knelt close beside her and rested a hand on her shoulder. "You don't want to remember, do you?"

Yorda's head drooped lower.

"There was a battle, but the castle still stands," the boy said, thinking aloud. "In the end, Zagrenda-Sol and Ozuma couldn't defeat the queen."

Yorda was silent. Again, the seabird cried out, high above them in the clear sky.

"It's all right," Ico said. He knew the castle would tell him what Yorda would not. He would learn soon enough of what had come next. Now that the path to her memories had been reopened, the visions would continue whether Ico wanted to see them or not.

"Well, I'm not worried," Ico said.

Yorda looked up at him, her reddened eyes full of pity. *How can you know?*

"Because of this," he said, patting the Mark on his chest. It rippled slightly at his touch. "Remember, I told you the queen doesn't like it? Well, I think I figured out why my Mark is so special. The pattern on this must be the pattern from the Book of Light! When the elder said I was their light of hope, that's what he was talking about!"

Ico was young and his body, though small, was full of courage and strength. But it was the Mark that distinguished him from the many Sacrifices who had come to the castle before, and that had bade the phantasm of Ozuma to appear to Ico. The elder was right. Ozuma was right. There was nothing to fear.

Now the boy was talking about another friend, a boy named Toto. He must've found the book, Ico was saying. Yet the more he spoke, the deeper Yorda's sadness became. His efforts to encourage her were valiant, but Ico was still too young to understand the dark tangle in Yorda's heart, much as he was still too young to wonder why the elder had told him not to speak of his Mark to the priest from the capital. Too young to let the little doubts build up inside him and shake his confidence.

There was much he could still ask her: Why had the priest-king of the Holy Zagrenda-Sol Empire been unable to destroy the castle? Why had Ozuma failed? Why did the queen remain here? How did the castle become enshrouded in mist, why was it insatiably hungry for Sacrifices made in the image of the knight Ozuma? Why had his bloodline been chosen for this dark destiny?

But Ico was more concerned with the future than the past. Mistakes were mistakes, and failures were failures. Why torment someone with memories of their past?

He would accomplish what his ancestor had not. That was what Ozuma wanted. He would free the Sacrifices as Yorda had freed her mother's victims so long ago. He would bring peace to the world.

He would defeat the queen.

Ico put a fist to his Mark, feeling his own heart beat through the fabric. Ico did not know that there were limits to the power of the Book of Light. He did not know that the priests in the capital—the new seat of the Holy Zagrenda-Sol Empire on this continent—knew of the book's failings all too well. That was why they maintained their silence and proffered up the descendants of Ozuma to the castle. Not all history is told in stories and chronicles. The parts untold, the dark passages of time, were those that swallowed men's hopes and made the distinctions between good and evil as nebulous as mist.

Ico stood, taking Yorda's hand, secure in the belief that their path and the answers to his questions would be revealed.

Ico thought back, recalling the pier at the bottom level of the castle where he had first arrived with the priest and his guards. The guard had gone to a room on that same level to retrieve the longsword that opened the idol gates—which was almost certainly the longsword that had once belonged to Ozuma. *That's why it was able to move the idols. It's imbued with the power of the Book of Light. Just like Yorda.*

It made sense now that they had found Ozuma without his sword. For some reason, he had let go of it, and that had led to his defeat.

I have to find Ozuma's sword. I'll just retrace my steps back to the underground pier.

With Yorda by his side, he would be able to pass any idols they came across on his way back.

Ico decided that he would first take Yorda to safety when they reached the pier. With the double protection of Ozuma's sword and the Mark, Ico would be more than ready to face the Queen. There was no sense putting Yorda in any more danger—and it would be too cruel to force her to face her mother again.

Ico nodded to himself and then turned to the girl. While he

had been lost in thought, she had wandered some distance away. She was standing near the gates by the foot of one of the stone torch pedestals that lined the courtyard like two rows of soldiers, her head hung low.

"Hueeeh!" he called out to her. When she didn't come, he ran to join her. Grabbing her hand, he took her to the stone archway that led back to the drawbridge.

But now the stone archway doors were closed, and the arch was much too high for him to climb. Ico pushed and pulled at the doors, but they wouldn't budge. He gave them a swift kick and immediately regretted it. *Ouch.*

It was as though the queen had foreseen everything he would do and gone ahead to foil his plans. The castle was like a labyrinth that changed to suit her needs.

Ico growled and, hands on his hips, glared at the arch. Yorda had begun to wander away again. She was off to the right, drifting like a shadow, looking up at a high point on the walls.

Yorda stood at a dead end too. It looked like the way here had been hastily barricaded. Large boards had been nailed to the door jambs. They overlapped one another, leaving gaps large enough for him to peek through.

Ico thought he might be able to pull off the boards if he got his fingers through the gaps, but even though he tugged till his face turned red, the barricade remained firmly in place.

He had all but given up when he looked to see Yorda pointing to a corner of the wall near the barricade where some round objects lay in a pile.

"What are those?"

Ico walked over and examined the black objects. They were each about the size of his head and too heavy for him to lift with one hand. He leaned down and sniffed one. It smelled like dirt and—

Firepowder!

He had seen hunters smear tar mixed with firepowder on arrows to take down particularly large or dangerous animals. Because of the risk, he had never been allowed to handle the tar himself, but he recognized the smell at once.

"There's gotta be a ton of firepowder in each of these!" He looked at Yorda, his eyes wide. "They must've used these during the battle!"

"Find the queen!"

The voice in Ico's head, heavier and more fierce than any he had heard before, made him pause for a moment. *Is that the priest-king?* He realized he was experiencing another memory of the past. *"Destroy the barricades! She can't hide forever!"*

The voice faded. Ico blinked his eyes, coming out of the vision. Yorda was standing next to him, so quiet he couldn't even hear her breathing. The round, dirt-encrusted balls filled with firepowder sat at his feet, looking as harmless as lumps of mud.

"I wonder if they still work?"

Ico ran back to the front gates and lit his stick on one of the torches he found there. Returning, he lit the fuse on one the balls with his newly fashioned torch, and it began to spark and sputter. After pushing the ball up against the barricade, he took Yorda's hand and moved away as quickly as he could.

The ball didn't explode with quite as much force as he had expected—he didn't even have to cover his ears. Even still, it blasted the wooden barricade to smithereens, sending a thousand pieces of wood scattering in every direction. The wind from the blast even extinguished the torch.

Ico grinned. Beyond where the barricade had stood was a narrow passageway with stone walls on either side, a strip of blue sky visible high above.

He would have to move more carefully from here on out. The queen was watching. Ico took the lead, holding up his extinguished torch and walking down the stone-lined corridor.

At the end of the corridor, the walls opened out. To his left was a stone staircase going down to a patch of grassy lawn—another inner courtyard of the castle.

Behind him, Yorda gasped.

"What's wrong?"

Ico looked back, then followed the girl's eyes. He looked down at the lustrous green grass below and saw a line of square stones. *It's a graveyard.*

Ico took Yorda's hand. "Is this where the queen took you that night? The underground gallery?"

Yorda nodded and took a step in front of him, looking down at the gravestones lined up in the sun.

"That means we should be able to get back into the castle from here," Ico said, thinking out loud. He went down the stone stairs. The grass felt good beneath his feet. He walked through the graveyard, trying to read the inscriptions on the stones, but the weather had worn them all away. He touched one. Even the corners of the stones were now rounded. Maybe they were already old when Yorda was here before—the night the queen summoned her below.

Despite what must have been years without care, the grass was uniformly short and not a single blade was out of place. The turf was soft, its bright green contrasting with the darker moss growing on the stones.

It was like time had stopped, preserving the stones, keeping the grass fresh—

Something pricked at the back of Ico's mind, and then the realization came. The visions of Yorda's past were all from long ago. *Of course! Why didn't I think of that sooner?* The emperor that came here with Ozuma to fight the queen had been the fifth emperor of Zagrenda-Sol. He was pretty sure that the emperor in the capital now was the eighteenth.

For that much time to pass, Yorda must have spent ten or even twenty lifetimes trapped here in the castle—and she was still a girl.

Had the queen placed another enchantment on the castle? The Castle in the Mist was separated from the world he knew, and not just by geography. This was a different world entirely.

Ico rubbed his own arms to stop himself from shivering. Yorda was crouching by one of the gravestones, just as Ico had moments before, trying to read the markings. Or maybe that was the grave that had slid to the side, revealing the stairs? If Yorda touched it, would the gravestone move? For a moment, Ico held his breath, but the stone showed no inclination toward motion. Apparently, it took a queen to open that door.

Ico explored, eventually discovering the stairs and corridor that the chief handmaiden had taken when she brought Yorda here. At the top of the stairs, the wall had collapsed, preventing him from going any farther. The great mountain of gray rubble here didn't look like something he could blast away, either.

He returned to the graveyard. The walls of the castle rose on all four sides here. The windows were all too high for him to reach. Then he noticed double doors standing in a shadowed corner of the graveyard. The doors, with an arched façade that made Ico think of a cathedral, seemed to lead to a different section of the castle.

Wherever the doors led, he hadn't been through there before, which meant it wasn't part of the castle Yorda had shown him in the visions. He called out to her, waving toward the doors. "Looks like some kind of hall. Does that go back into the main castle?"

Yorda only stared at him with a sad look in her eyes.

Ico shrugged. "Well, let's explore it anyway. It's not like we have many other choices."

He took Yorda's hand and began to walk, when suddenly he felt his hair stand on end. The air around him had grown suddenly colder and darker, even though the sun was shining above.

Then he saw them: dark swirling pools opening, one on the grass, one between the gravestones, one on the landing atop the stairs. They boiled and seethed, and a horned shadow-creature with long, sharp claws emerged before them. He spotted another with wings flying over the stones.

"Run!" Ico shouted. He pulled on Yorda's hand and made for the doors leading to the hall. He beat back one of the creatures that rose up in their way with his stick. It dissolved instantly, leaving two eyes floating in space. Ico knew it would be back soon.

"Don't stop!" he shouted. "We have to get through those doors!"

The creatures were on all sides of them now. Yorda swung her free arm, batting at the winged creatures thronging around her head.

Even more creatures emerged from the black pool on the landing behind her. They came down the stairs, jerking strangely, as if walking on tiptoe, one after another.

Yorda pulled away from Ico and ran in a crazed circle to evade the creatures, then her knee connected with a gravestone and she fell sprawling across the grass. The creatures swarmed on top of her, circling as though they were performing a macabre celebratory dance.

"Get away!" Ico growled through clenched teeth. "Don't touch her!" He swung his stick and roared wildly, and when that didn't seem like enough, he swung his arms and kicked with his legs, trying to push the monsters away. "Back!" he shouted. "Back to the shadows!"

Ico knocked away another of the creatures trying to seize Yorda, then picked her up by the sleeve of her dress. "Run!"

A single large creature slid in front of them as they made for the doors. Its clawed arms hung down by its side, and it leaned forward, peering at Ico. Its eyes flared.

Why do you protect the girl? It was her mistake that made us what we are.

The creature's shoulders heaved, as though it were gasping in pain, and its eyes shone with the cold light of winter stars.

From this close, Ico could see what looked like an expression in the swirling dark mists—he saw pain, misery, and anger. But anger toward whom?

You are of our blood.

The creature gestured with its horns toward Ico, as if to prove his point.

Our lives were given to the castle so that the girl could live. Now, we will take her as payment for what we have surrendered.

Ico blinked, not comprehending.

"What?" he said out loud.

His grip on Yorda's sleeve loosened. She fell to her knees, slumping down on the grass. The creatures advanced, tightening in a ring around them.

Ico took a half step backward, and the shadow-creature in front of him slowly shook its head.

Flee, young Sacrifice. Leave this castle while you still enjoy the book's protection. We are bound to this girl by a curse that can never be broken. The queen tortures us as we wander her castle, so we will take the girl she wants and keep her to ourselves. It is justice, and justice is eternal. This is not something you can change, young Sacrifice.

Ico took another step backward, eyes still fixed on the creature. He tripped and fell to the grass. Another creature picked Yorda up and lifted her across its shoulder.

The creature turned and walked off, making for the black pool that had formed between the gravestones. Yorda's arms hung limply down the creature's back, swaying as it walked.

Young Sacrifice. Enjoy your own fortune, and pity us.

As the creature before him spoke into Ico's mind, the one carrying Yorda had begun to sink into the pool. It was already down to its waist.

Ico sat helpless, watching her go. He didn't know why he wasn't jumping up to save her. He felt almost…sleepy.

The creature nodded to him. *There. That's right. Now leave.*

At that moment, the Mark on Ico's chest began to glow, a silvery light coursing along the complex pattern. It was a jolt of energy, snapping Ico out of the creature's spell. "I'm not leaving!"

Ico rolled to the side and sprang to his feet, dashing toward the pool. He reached in, getting his arms around Yorda's waist, feeling her weight in his hands. Summoning all his strength, he yanked her out of the pool so hard he nearly fell over on his back. Yorda seemed dazed, asleep with eyes open and unfocused. Ico shook her shoulders, and her wispy hair swirled in the air.

"We have to run! Through those doors!"

He gave Yorda a push on the back, then retrieved his stick and took a swing at the creatures writhing around them.

Fool!

The creature's voice echoed in his mind as the dark shapes behind him gave chase. Now he heard other voices shouting, weeping.

—*You can change nothing. The curse will never be lifted!*

—*The girl is the cause of our misfortune.*

—*You cannot save us.*

—*You cannot defeat the queen.*

Ico's hair stood on end. His legs threatened to buckle under him. But he managed to make it to the doors and broke them open with his shoulder, then pulled Yorda along behind him.

Suddenly, all was dark and quiet. Ico couldn't see a thing. His breath felt stifled. For a moment he feared he might pass out, until he realized that the darkness in which he swam was simply a matter of his eyes having yet to adjust to the gloom within this wing of the castle.

His breathing grew steadier. Soon the floor came into view, and Ico could even make out the mortar in the seams between stones.

They were in a vast, empty hall. High up along the wall, a small shelf ran down either side, with windows that let in a trickle of light above it. The doors had slammed shut behind them, and the creatures seemed to have given up for now.

Someone was crying. For a moment he thought it was the creatures again, but then he realized that it was Yorda. She was lying on the floor, hands over her face, weeping uncontrollably.

Ico sat down beside her, his own legs shaking, his elation at their narrow escape fading rapidly.

Why are you crying? Was it true what those creatures said? That you—what did you do?

Ico hadn't intended to say anything out loud, but Yorda looked up at him as though she had heard. She put a hand on his arm and gently pushed.

"What?" Ico asked, his voice hoarse. "You want me to run away by myself too?"

Yorda nodded.

"Why? Why would you say that? I don't understand." Ico's voice grew louder, his hands clenching into fists. Yorda simply shook her head, tears rolling down her face.

"Don't tell me you want to stay here. That you want to crawl back into that big birdcage!"

Ico sat for a moment, catching his breath. He realized that he was close to crying too.

"They were talking to me," he said to Yorda, more quietly now. "Those creatures out there were talking to me. They said that you were the cause of their misfortune."

The girl's shoulders tensed; she hung her head.

"They said I wouldn't be able to defeat the queen." Ico sat up on his knees beside her. "Okay, so what do I know: You and Ozuma escape here with the book, right, then Ozuma comes back with the book's power in his sword to kill the queen—at least he tries. He fails, gets turned to stone, and I guess loses one of his horns along the way, and now the queen's master of the castle again." As he spoke, Ico could feel himself gradually calming. The shaking in his arms and legs had stopped. "The shadow-creatures, they used to be Sacrifices—the queen used her power to make them that way, so she could have them as guards for her castle.

"And the Sacrifices are the descendants of Ozuma—I'm guessing that happened at the queen's request. Some deal she worked out with Zagrenda-Sol in exchange for not destroying them, right?"

Yorda blinked slowly, looking up at him.

"Because they failed to remove her from the castle, that's all Zagrenda-Sol could do. They had to protect their people."

Yorda said nothing.

"That's what the custom of my village is all about," Ico whispered, looking down at his own fists. He opened his hands to look at them. They were covered with scratches where he had scraped against the wall and the floor while swinging his stick around. There was dried blood on his skin.

Ozuma's blood.

"It has to end," he said. He wasn't saying it for Yorda. He wasn't saying it for himself. It was a declaration of war. "I have to end it. That's what the elder wants me to do." Ico's voice grew louder, and his confidence grew with it.

"If we just sit around here and do nothing, then one day, the next eclipse is going to come and the Dark God will rise up and blow this entire continent away. There's no stalling for time anymore, if there ever was. This castle has to be destroyed, along with the queen."

Ico grabbed Yorda's slender arm with more intensity than ever before. "That's why I need you to tell me why Ozuma failed. I have to know why he couldn't defeat the queen!" *So I don't make the same mistake,* he added to himself.

Yorda took her free hand and placed it against her chest, directly above her heart.

"What?"

She was saying something, but Ico still couldn't understand. He growled in frustration.

It's my fault, she said. *I let my mother escape. I took pity on her and so fell into her trap. At the last moment, our victory turned to defeat.*

Yorda struck herself on the chest two, three times.

"You mean…you did it?"

Yorda nodded swiftly, without hesitation.

"You let the queen win? That's why you want me to leave by myself? Is that what you're saying?"

Yorda nodded, flooding with relief that he understood.

Ico was staring at her now. "The queen used you, didn't she?"

Yorda lowered her eyes, and Ico knew he had hit the mark.

"I knew there was something more going on inside you when I found you in that cage—more than just sadness. It was regret."

Ico noticed new tears welling in Yorda's eyes and shook his head. "No, we can fix that. We can win this time. Then there'll be nothing to regret. Think about it. The queen locked you up because she was afraid you'd run away and be out of her control. If you're free of the castle, you'll be free of her."

Ico put his hands on Yorda's shoulders. "We have to do this, one last time. Don't let everything Ozuma fought for be in vain. You're still alive. This isn't over. Don't give up!"

But Yorda merely shook her head, like a tiny blossom trembling in a strong wind. *No, no, no.*

She had already paid too great a price for her last mistake, and now she could see it happening all over. *I cannot defeat my mother. I will never be able to defeat her. And we both know it now.*

Please, she thought to Ico, *let me go back to sleep. Put me back where you found me. Nothing good will come of this.*

If her heart fell asleep once more, if she were locked inside the cage, Yorda would feel nothing. She would never see the Sacrifices sent to the castle, never see their faces or hear their voices. If she didn't know their names, she could pretend they never existed.

As long as she could free this one, the boy looking into her eyes, the Sacrifice named Ico. That would be enough.

I have no right to want more than this. Ignorance is my penalty and my salvation. My final rest. This must be, because I…

Ico let go of Yorda's shoulders. She looked up, thinking perhaps he had understood her again, but the boy's face looked even more determined than before.

"Fine," he said, standing. Though his legs and his arms were covered with scratches and bruises, he showed no signs of pain. "If you can't fight—if you think you're what brought Ozuma's plan down the first time—then we can't risk you being here. I'll fight the queen alone." The smile returned to Ico's face. "I'll be fine. See? I'm not scared a bit. After all, I'm fighting to free my family."

Ico looked down the hall at a door that appeared to lead back into the castle. "We need to find some way to open the main gates or find a way down to the underground pier. Either works for me. Except, I'm going to need your help getting past any idols along the way."

Ico offered his hand. Yorda stared at it for a moment and then stood on her own. Ico glanced at his hand, hanging lonely in the air, before letting it drop to his side. Either he had caught a whiff of the fear welling inside her, or he no longer cared.

The Castle in the Mist seemed to change the layout of its corridors every time Ico walked them, so that he could go down a hallway into a room where he was sure he had been before and find it looking like it belonged to an entirely different building. Ico grew more frustrated with each mistaken turn, though he knew his anger was wasted on the castle's stone walls.

Ico wondered if all castles were designed so confusingly. He suspected the queen's twisted sense of humor was the real culprit here.

He climbed up wide shelves in the middle of chambers, clambered up chains hanging where staircases had crumbled, then called for Yorda once he had found a way for her to join him. After making his way through three or four rooms in this fashion, Ico had entirely lost track of where in the castle he was. *Which way was it to the stone bridge where Ozuma stood? Which direction am I facing?* He stuck his head out of the window to check the sun and found it to be straight overhead. *So much for that idea.* He knew that he had to go down to reach the water, but how to go down when he couldn't find any stairs or ladders leading in the right direction?

As Ico wandered, he found himself outside again in a corridor with grass growing in tufts on the dry ground. There were some trees resembling willows with long slender branches that shook in the wind.

Ico had seen these same trees near Toksa Village. They kept their leaves even in winter and sprouted new green buds in spring. They were highly sensitive to changes in the wind and given to rustling, so much so that they often alerted hunters to the whereabouts of prey or gave early warning of approaching danger.

Ico stopped beneath the trees, feeling the sun on his skin. For a moment, he felt like he was back home. Whoever had planted these trees here must have loved the forest—something told him it wasn't the queen. He closed his eyes and took a deep breath, when he noticed the sound of running water.

Yorda was standing behind him a distance away. Ico ran quickly down the corridor. It extended straight for a while, then turned sharply to the right.

He ran down to the end, finding a clearing with a large pool of water in it, like a cistern. A rusted pipe ran left to right across the wall on the other side of the cistern at about Ico's height. From there, a thinner pipe extended straight down into the water. It was another dead end. But Ico could hear water flowing beneath his feet. He went to the edge of the cistern and leaned over, looking down to see that part of the underwater wall on the near side had a grate set into the stone, its bottom half submerged in the water. The water was flowing through the grate, back toward the corner Ico had just turned.

The cistern looked deep. Before he could change his mind, Ico jumped straight out, away from the edge, landing in the cool water with a little splash.

His feet couldn't reach the bottom, so he treaded water, scooping up some onto his face to wash off the dirt and sweat. It felt incredibly refreshing.

Unfortunately, the grate on the near wall was strong, and no matter how much he kicked or pulled at it, bracing his feet on the edge for support, it wouldn't budge. He looked around for a lever or some other device that might open the grate, but there was nothing.

When he looked through the bars, the water on the other side was dim, but he could see patches of light falling on square pedestals that protruded from the water at regular intervals.

He wasn't sure why there would be a room as part of an underground waterway, but the light he saw had to be coming from some sort of ventilation shaft—possibly big enough for him to get through. If the water was flowing through the grate, then it must be going down somewhere ahead, which meant that the underground room might be a way down to the lower levels of the castle.

Now we're getting somewhere!

Climbing up the pipe on the far side of the water, Ico made his way back to the top of the cistern. Heading back down the way he had come, he found, just as he had expected, several square openings hidden in the tall tufts of grass. The openings ran in a line down the corridor. Each was covered with a thin grate, but he was able to pry one free with a little work from his fingers.

Crouching by the hole he called out to Yorda, who came running from around the corner.

"I'm going down—you wait here," he told her, then he slid down through the hole so fast he didn't see Yorda waving her hands, trying to stop him.

Ico landed back in water, but at least here it was much shallower than out in the cistern. It only came up to around his knees. The air smelled of mold, and the walls were damp.

He quickly found one of the square pedestals and climbed up onto it—and immediately fell into the past.

[2]

FOR A MOMENT, Ico didn't realize he was seeing another vision. He blinked and saw people—many people—crowding around him in the dimly lit underground waterway.

What made it so different from his previous visions was that, this time, Ico wasn't just an observer—he was part of the scene. Right next to him, a skinny boy raised one bony arm, trying to touch Ico's Mark with trembling fingers.

"Wh-who are you?" Ico asked, and the boy disappeared, only to reappear an instant later a short distance away, standing alone up to his knees in the water. He looked cold.

Ico turned his attention back to the other people. There were men, women, young and old, about thirty in all, he guessed. They all looked terribly cold and exhausted, their backs bent with despair. Their pale faces, drained of life, hovered eerily in the light that spilled down through the opening above Ico's head.

"What are you doing down here?" he asked, turning around. No one replied. "What's going on? Is there a way out of this place?"

In silence, a few of the people broke away from the crowd and began walking slowly down the waterway, making dull, metallic noises with each step.

Beside him, a boy lent his hand to a slender girl to help her step up onto one of the pedestals. Ico gaped at her legs, so skinny they looked like skin stretched over bone. Wooden manacles went around both of her ankles, the heavy chain connecting them coiled at her feet like a snake.

"This is a prison," Ico breathed. "Who put you in here?" he asked the crowd.

He felt someone tapping him on his shoulder from behind—a vision of the past, actually touching him.

Ico whirled around and saw a stocky man standing on the pedestal behind him. He looked like a soldier, possibly a guard. Though he wore no sword or chain-mail vest, the shoulder of his tunic was woven with some kind of emblem, and he wore a metal helmet with a short visor over his eyes.

He held his right hand over his right eye, peering out at Ico with the left. His eye was clouded, like a deep pool, far underground where the light does not reach.

"Who are you?"

The soldier shook his head, and Ico heard a voice in his mind.

What happened when the enchantment was broken? the voice asked.

Eyes opening wider, Ico took a step back into the water with a splash.

We were prisoners here, but the enchantment was our protection. What happened when it broke?

"How should I know?" Ico said with a shake of his head. While the voice had been talking in his mind, the others gathered in the underground prison had formed a circle around him and the soldier.

Madness took us all. People trying to run, others trying to stop them. Fear and a mindless rage gripped the castle.

Ico stood gripping the Mark on his chest and listened to the soldier's story. "I thought someone had invaded, or the queen had put everyone to death—but no, you were killing one another."

The soldier, a former member of the castle patrol, looked down at the water running past his legs, his right hand still firmly over his eye.

There were arrests, executions, massacres, and melees. Who caused this madness? Who broke the enchantment?

Ico remembered the bridge across the grand hall in the castle where he had seen the hanged people. Was that one of the executions the soldier spoke of? Had the people of the castle gone to war against each other?

It had to be the queen's plan. This was her doing.

It explained why the armies of Zagrenda-Sol had found no one upon their invasion of the castle. Everyone was already dead—executed or simply killed in open combat.

"Was there no one who resisted, no one who kept their sanity?" The guard slowly shook his helmeted head.

"And you? Who put you in here? Did they survive?"

The soldier lifted his face and finally removed his hand, showing Ico the empty socket from which his eye had been gouged out.

Everyone died.

The words rang in Ico's mind. When they had faded, Ico was alone again. Nothing remained to indicate what he had seen, save that his shoulder was cold and slightly damp where the soldier had touched him.

For a while Ico just stood there, unable to move. His limbs felt heavy, while sadness and anger whirled inside him. He gripped his Mark so tightly he thought the fabric might rip, and when at last he released his hand and looked back up, he felt tears forming in the corners of his eyes. Ico blinked and wiped them away. *Now is no time for crying.*

If this place had been a prison, there would be no exit, which meant no way down toward the ground floor of the castle. He jumped and managed to climb back up through the ventilation shaft where he had first entered, back out onto the surface. The sun beat down on him, warming his waterlogged skin. Ico stood, letting the life flow back into his limbs, before calling out for Yorda.

She had gone quite a distance. He had to backtrack a significant way, stopping to call out every few paces. When at last he found Yorda, the sight of her slender frame sent a stab of pain through Ico's chest as he remembered the girl he had seen in the water.

He reached his hand out to her.

"Did you know there was a prison down there?"

Yorda took his hand, flinching at the question.

"I saw it. The ghost told me that when the enchantment over the castle was broken, they started killing each other. No one survived." He wasn't trying to blame Yorda, but he couldn't help the sharpness in his voice. "I saw a vision back in the tower after I lowered your cage. It was an old man, a scholar, wearing a long robe. He was angry about something—that must've been from after the enchantment was broken, otherwise how would he have gotten into the tower?"

Yorda nodded quietly.

"Was that Master Suhal?"

Yorda nodded again. Her eyes were dry, but the pale glow that seemed to emanate from inside her had dimmed. *Maybe,* Ico thought, *when Yorda is weak, the power of the Book of Light within her grows weaker too.*

"So when the enchantment was broken," Ico said, "Master Suhal learned what the queen had been up to in the Tower of Winds. That's why he was angry. It was probably the first time he learned the true cause of the king's death. Or maybe, it was less like learning and more like remembering."

"But what I don't get," Ico continued, "is why Master Suhal was still sane. Why didn't he go crazy like everyone else in the castle? What happened to him when everyone was killing each other?"

Even as his lips asked the question, the answer rose in Ico's heart. Master Suhal *had* been killed in the ensuing chaos. No matter how rational he might have remained, a single old man would not have been able to stand up to a garrison full of bloodthirsty soldiers.

"What was it the queen said—something about the Dark God feeding off people's greed and malice?" Ico looked up at Yorda. "I bet the queen works the same way. That's why when you got hold of the Book of Light, she had to release everyone under her enchantment. She made them kill each other to increase her power!" The more Ico thought about it, the more it made sense. "She used up the sacrifices she had been saving for the Dark God's revival—she consumed them herself."

And then the queen had fled from the searching eyes of Zagrenda-Sol, hiding somewhere in the castle.

The mystery was what had happened next. If the queen had gone into hiding, how did the Castle in the Mist become what it was today? Something even more terrible must have happened to place the queen back on her throne as master of the castle, in a position where she could demand the Holy Zagrenda-Sol Empire to provide her with new sacrifices from Ozuma's descendants.

Yorda knew what had happened, as did the shades in the tower. Only Ico was still in the dark.

Back in the outside corridor, Ico found a way to climb up to a higher level and spent the next several minutes helping Yorda up. They were inside again. He knew he was back in the castle proper, yet this place was completely unfamiliar to him. He found he preferred the outside corridor. Even if he knew it was a dead end, being out in the sun was better than wandering through these labyrinthine passages. They walked along, stone walls on either side, passing through several rooms where the air hung chilly and still. Despite his best intentions, Ico discovered that they were going up again. Every room seemed to have a rise in it up to a higher platform, and all the stairs went up. They were getting ever farther away from the underground pier.

Every time they came to a terrace, he made a point of stopping to look at the view and take in a deep breath—but he was still no clearer as to where in the castle he was. Everywhere he looked seemed unfamiliar.

He continued on. Fatigue had begun to gnaw at him, and then he came to a large window and spotted one of the giant celestial spheres that stood beside the main gate. He could only see the very top of its orb from where he stood, but still his heart leapt.

The sun was already beginning to slant in the sky, by which Ico could tell that the sphere he was looking at was the one on the eastern side of the gate.

Images from half-remembered visions flooded Ico's mind.

"Yorda!" he called out. The girl was several paces away, having stayed behind when he ran up to the window. "If we can make it over there, we'll reach the Eastern Arena—the celestial sphere's right next to it!" Ico stopped. *Why was the celestial sphere important again?*

Another image flitted through his consciousness: curved dishes rotating, the brilliant sun, and a great groaning of wood and stone.

Of course! Ico clapped his hands with excitement. *When the light from the mirror-dishes hits the spheres on the east and west sides, the gates open!*

Pleased at even this hint of progress, and that his many visions of the castle seemed to be making more sense to him now, Ico grabbed Yorda's hand and resumed walking briskly, checking out every window they passed to make sure he was still heading toward the eastern sphere.

Soon, more of the sphere came into view—then they hit another dead end.

It was a terrace, wide and grassy, that extended from the side of the castle with no corridors or stairs, save some leading up to what looked like a viewing platform on the right-hand side. Ico's attention, however, was entirely captured by a separate building standing at the edge of the terrace, facing away from them.

It was a windmill. Ico had heard of these being used near the capital. Mechanically, they were similar to the waterwheel that ran on the river outside Toksa Village. The water, or in this case, the wind, turned a shaft that was used to do something else, like rotate a grindstone to grind wheat. He couldn't imagine what this mill was used for. Its position high up in the corner of the castle, far from a granary or field, did not seem like an ideal placement. He went up to the edge of the terrace and looked down, seeing the tops of trees far below. Behind him, the Castle in the Mist rose, its walls stretching even higher than the top of the windmill.

Though the white sails on the mill were tattered and dirty, they still rotated, creaking gently in the wind.

"I wonder if we can go any higher here?"

Ico turned to Yorda just in time to see a person standing directly behind her topple from the edge of the terrace and plummet to the ground below.

[3]

ICO YELPED, CAUSING Yorda to jump back in alarm. She landed with one heel hanging over the edge of the terrace. Ico grabbed her arm at the last moment, pulling her back to safety.

"Someone just fell! Right there, behind you!"

He had seen it happen with his own eyes. *Another vision?*

Ico stepped carefully to the edge of the terrace, looking down over the precipice to the treetops far below. He could see no bodies lying on the canopy, no obvious places where branches had broken. No bodies lay sprawled out across the small patches of grass he could see between the boughs.

Though he had only caught a glimpse, he got that the fallen person was a woman. Chewing his lip, Ico walked the same path he had seen the vision walk, trying to figure out what she might have been doing. The long hem of her robes had dragged on the grass behind her as she walked, and her black hair had been tied up into a bun on her head.

"A handmaiden…maybe?"

Yorda had been following Ico with her eyes, but when she heard him say that word, her expression changed.

"Do you know who it was?" he asked. Yorda looked away in silence. Her eyes were dark, the way they had been ever since Ico learned about her name, her parentage, and her past.

"Well," Ico said as he paced, "maybe she threw herself from the wall when the castle descended into chaos. It would fit with everything else that was going on." He looked up at Yorda for some acknowledgment, but she did not appear to be listening.

Ico left Yorda with instructions not to get too close to the edge of the terrace and began climbing the foundation at the base of the windmill. The stones were worn and cracked, so it was easy for him to find handholds. While he toiled, climbing, the windmill blades creaked merrily on above him.

When he had reached the top of the foundation, he picked his moment and jumped onto one of the spinning blades. The sail flapped, snapping in the wind as the blades turned to carry Ico all the way to the top. He held on tight and enjoyed the view.

From here, he could see the eastern celestial sphere as well as a view of the winding path along the top of the castle wall he would have to take to get there. To the left of the sphere was a separate structure connected to the wall, which his borrowed memories indicated was the Eastern Arena. Beyond the wall stretched the blue sea. He jumped off the blade onto one of the roofs of the castle. Up here, the stones were even more weathered, with large cracks and tufts of weeds growing up from the gaps.

He looked out toward the arena. Something like a giant circular window dominated one of its walls. The window was closed with gray shutters made of the same material as the walls around them, but when he squinted his eyes, he could make out a thin line running down the middle where the shutters opened. He could draw a line between the circular window and the celestial sphere that led directly to the main gates. If he could open up the window on this side and the west and get the light through there to the spheres on either side of the gates, the gates would open.

He would start with the east, then would just have to run through the castle to the opposite side. Ico checked the route several times to make sure he wouldn't forget. It would take a while, but actually knowing where he was going was a huge boost to his morale.

He walked along the wall from the place where the windmill had brought him and found an idol gate—a pair of squat statues— waiting at the end of the passage to block his path.

It would be impossible to bring Yorda up by the route he had taken. She could manage clambering up small rises and the like, but he couldn't imagine her clinging to spinning windmill blades.

In the end, he was able to find some old wooden crates that he stacked to create steps at a place further down the wall. It was a long way around, but it was better than nothing. Ico ran back to the windmill, growing increasingly nervous with each moment Yorda was out of his sight. He didn't want to think what would happen if the shadow-creatures attacked while they were apart.

He spotted her, standing on the terrace, lost in a reverie. For a moment, he wondered what exactly was going through her mind, then he shook the thought from his head and called out to her.

"You have to go around! I made a place for you to climb up! Around that way!" He jabbed with his finger back toward his makeshift stairs. "Understand?"

After a long pause, she started walking. From his high vantage point, he could watch her every move and call out to her whenever she was walking in the wrong direction.

Once she had climbed up to a higher landing, there was another problem. In order to get to the idol gate, she would have to cross a gap in the walkway. It had been easy enough for Ico to jump, but for Yorda, it would require quite an effort, and if she missed, she would plummet to the ground far below. The thought made Ico's knees go wobbly. "No looking down, okay?" he called out to her from across the gap. Yorda immediately looked down and took three steps backward.

"It's really not that far across. You can make it if you jump." He reached out his arm to her. "I'll reach out and catch you, all right? Don't worry, just give yourself a running start and jump when you reach the edge. Just like jumping over a creek," he said, realizing that Princess Yorda had probably never jumped over a creek. She might never have even seen a creek.

"See that?" He indicated the idol gate behind him. "If we go through there, we can get to the Eastern Arena. I figured out a way. We just have to get through here, and I need your help to do it."

Yorda shook her head and took another step back.

"Well, I can't do this alone," Ico retorted. "Look, if we waste any more time—"

As soon as the words left his mouth, a black pool of shadow began to boil on the ground behind the girl.

"Yorda! The shades are coming! Behind you! You have to jump!"

Yorda took a quick look around, then back at Ico's outstretched hand. She hesitated.

"You know if they get you I won't be able to get out of here either!" Ico shouted, wondering if it were even really true. If the shades grabbed her, wouldn't they be satisfied and leave? They had asked him not to interfere, that was all. Maybe if he gave them what they wanted, they would leave him alone. He could find another way out of the castle.

The first dark shape began to emerge from the pool, wobbling eerily as it stuck a misshapen foot out onto the stone. Its glowing white eyes found Yorda and glowed brighter.

Yorda turned back to face the creature, even as it spread its clawed arms to envelop her in an embrace.

Leave me. Run. Save yourself.

The words seemed to ring in Ico's mind, though his ears heard nothing. A wave of weariness crashed over him. If she wanted to stay here in the Castle in the Mist, who was he to stop her? *I should just leave—*

Suddenly, Ico's head began to ache as though someone had set fire to the base of his horns.

With a start, he realized it was Ozuma. Somehow, the spirit of his ancestor had crept inside his mind, driving back the shadows that threatened to cloud his thinking.

"Jump!" Ico shouted, swinging his fists. "Jump now!"

Yorda turned away from the shadow-creature just as its claws were about to close on her shoulders. Her eyes met Ico's, then fell to his outstretched hand.

Finally, fear spurred her to action. She ran and jumped. Then she was falling forward, the wind blowing up from the chasm beneath her feet making her hair and dress flutter.

Ico grabbed her hand in midair, then her weight began to pull both of them down. He fought against it with all his strength.

The two collapsed onto the near edge of the gap, arms and legs tangled together. One of Yorda's feet was still hanging over the edge.

"This way!"

Helping Yorda to her feet, Ico ran toward the idol gate. On the other side of the gap, the horned shades stamped their feet in soundless frustration. As Ico watched, two of the flying creatures swooped over the heads of their comrades to pursue Yorda.

The idol gate flared with light at Yorda's approach as the power of the Book of Light within her shot forth and pushed the statues off to the sides. The two dashed through the opening. Ico looked back; the flying creatures made keening sounds like wind through bare branches. Then they dissipated into formless plumes of smoke.

Ico caught his breath. "That was close."

A smile returned to Ico's face, but Yorda remained glum. She spread her hands and looked down at them as though she were having trouble believing what she saw. *Why am I still here?* she seemed to be asking herself. *Why did the creatures not catch me? Why did I not let them?*

"You can't let them get you," Ico said. "Ozuma said so. I heard him."

He brushed his fingertips over the base of his horns. The burning pain had subsided, but he still felt its message loud and clear.

When they arrived at last in the Eastern Arena, they found it standing silent and cold. Ico crossed the arena slowly, one step at a time. On the round platform in the center of the arena he spotted dark stains that were almost certainly blood. They were the last remnant of the battles waged here—and of Ozuma's performance that had distracted the queen for those few vital moments. Not even the many years since the last tournament had been able to erase it. Though the life that had drained here onto the floor had become nothing more than a dark smudge, it still held its meaning.

When he found the device for opening the large circular window in the wall, Ico felt like he might jump all the way to the arena's high ceiling with joy. He pulled down on the lever, and the shutters on the window opened with a heavy creaking noise.

A band of light shot across the arena floor, gradually widening to envelop Ico and Yorda in its brilliance. Ico climbed up the outer frame of the window. From here he could clearly see the light hitting the sphere. It sparkled, creating a glow that seemed to fill the stones all around the eastern door of the gate. Soon, what had been nothing more than a solid stone obstruction to Ico's escape was glowing with a white, pure light, becoming almost transparent.

"Yes!" Ico shouted.

A fresh sea breeze blew in through the window and teased at the edges of Yorda's hair. She too was looking off into the distance at the sparkling sphere by the gate. Then Ico spotted something long and thin lying on the floor by her feet. He jumped down from the edge of the window and picked it up.

It was a sword—a knight's sword. It was covered with rust, and the blade was pitted and marked in places.

What was a sword doing here?

Ico looked up at the open window and thought. He recalled the thin gap he had seen between the shutters on the window from the windmill. Could this sword have been wedged in between a pair of shutters to hold them open, then fallen down when he opened them all the way?

He grabbed on to the handle and gave it a swing. Though the blade had lost its luster, its weight felt good in his hands. This would be a weapon far superior to his makeshift club for driving off the shades.

Ico's imagination traveled back to that dark day when the enchantment on the castle lifted, plunging its occupants into madness. Maybe someone had come here in their desperation to escape but had forgotten or been unable to work the mechanism to open the window. In a last attempt to spill the light onto the celestial sphere, one might have thrust his sword into the gap between shutters in the hope of prying the window open, and there the sword had remained.

They wanted to bring light back to the castle—to free the trapped souls.

Then it seemed to Ico that the band of light stretching from the Eastern Arena looked like a sword had cut a blazing path across the sky on which not even the mist that enveloped the castle dared tread.

[4]

REACHING THE EASTERN Arena had lifted an incredible weight from Ico's mind. He could picture the ruins of the castle now, and the route he would need to take to cross over to the western side. The ease in his mind had lightened his step as well.

Yet, next to him, Yorda seemed even more burdened by sadness. The light of the book within her had not faded, but her face had. She was expressionless, wearing an unfeeling mask.

Though they had never been able to speak normally to each other, Yorda's face had always been a clear signal of her feelings. When danger was near, she shook her head and looked reluctant. At times she was scared, and at other times she wept, or showed surprise, or tried to console Ico.

Now she looked like a being molded from wax. When she stopped to look around, she was like a statue—a priceless object of art left behind in that abandoned castle. Still possessing its beauty, but robbed of its life.

Ico pressed onward, dragging her along by the hand. Through a long corridor, they entered a room where the shades once again attacked, but Ico handily drove them off with the sword. The weapon served him as well as he had imagined it would. All it took was one swipe to send the shades back to smoke.

The sun was beginning to redden in the sky and had dropped to a level with Ico's shoulder. He picked up the pace. He would have to open up the window in the Western Arena and throw light on the western sphere before the sun set. *No way am I spending another night in this castle!*

He climbed up three stories, passing through rooms and corridors with familiar shapes, reaffirming his newfound confidence in the layout of the castle. From the windows he passed, Ico occasionally caught glimpses of the Tower of Winds. It seemed to beckon to him, standing apart from the rest of the castle as it did, but he resisted the urge to stray from his chosen course.

After a particularly long climb up a staircase, Ico entered an unfamiliar room. He caught his breath. The room was almost perfectly square and not particularly large. The walls were straight and entirely unadorned save for eight sconces in which torches crackled and sputtered, casting their light across the room. Only the very top of the arched ceiling remained in shadow, as though some dark creature lurked there, devouring all light that strayed too close.

The only prominent feature of the room was a raised dais about twice as high as Ico was tall, with a solid-looking chair set in the middle. Both the dais and chair were made of stone and looked as though they had been carved from the living rock of the room itself. Behind the dais, the rear wall of the chamber had crumbled, leaving a pile of gray rubble upon the floor.

It's a throne, Ico realized. *Which would make this the queen's room—the place where she sat, hands on the wide armrests, staring down at her ministers*. A shiver went through Ico and he raised the sword. *If the queen should appear again...*

Ico steadied his breath, senses alert, but the only thing he noticed was a white mist drifting through the room. Ico breathed a quick sigh of relief and turned to see Yorda standing at the entrance by the strangely adorned archway, slowly shaking her head.

"What is it?"

Ico walked closer to her and noticed she was crying.

"This is the queen's chamber, isn't it?"

Yorda nodded, her head hanging.

"Was this her only chamber? Is this where she managed the affairs of the castle? Where else might she be hiding?"

In response to the barrage of questions, Yorda lifted her face and walked briskly past Ico's side to the throne. She was almost running as she clambered up onto the dais, straining with the effort.

What's she doing? "Is something there?"

The rubble behind the throne seemed like an easier route to the top of the dais, but by the time Ico announced he was coming, Yorda had already finished the climb and was standing next to the throne. A teardrop sparkled on her chin.

Gingerly, Yorda touched one of the armrests. To Ico, she looked like a hunter maiden, reaching out to touch the fur of a sleeping savage beast, not wanting to wake it and yet overcome with curiosity. *Stop*, he thought instinctively. *Let sleeping dogs lie.*

Holding her breath like a swimmer about to plunge into the water, Yorda slid onto the throne. She brought her slender legs together and rested her arms at her sides.

"Wait," Ico said through the thickening mist. "Was this your throne?"

He looked around. The mist was streaming into the room now, making it a sea of white fog so thick it was hard for him to see as far as the throne.

Ico walked quickly up to the dais, waving his hand to sweep away the mist. He felt like he was swimming. *Is this the queen's doing?*

"Yorda!" he called out, but there was no reply.

The figure on the throne was no longer Yorda.

In his surprise, Ico jumped back and let the point of the sword drop down to the stones with a loud clang.

On the throne was seated a female corpse wrapped in black robes, a black veil over her face. Her slender body was tilted, leaning up against one of the armrests, one arm dangling over the edge so far the withered fingertips almost touched the floor.

He could see the corpse's face through the flowing veil, the strong line of the nose, and the tightly closed, bloodless lips.

Ico blinked. *It's the queen*, he realized.

Next to the throne, he saw two tall figures standing side by side, facing away from him—one with horns clearly visible through the flowing mist.

Ozuma!

He held a sword that glowed with the blessing of the Book of Light.

"Behold, the queen of the castle," a low voice echoed in Ico's mind. He listened, his feet rooted to the floor. "She is our greatest enemy, herald of darkness, child of the Dark God himself."

Is that Ozuma's voice? Ico wondered. *Who is he talking to?*

Now the other figure stepped off to the side, showing his face in profile. He wore a slender golden crown upon his head, an elegant doublet, and a battle cloak trimmed with leather. In his hand, he gripped a crystal scepter of the sort that priests from the capital used during ceremonies.

It was the priest-king of the Holy Zagrenda-Sol Empire.

"It is she," said the trembling voice of a young girl from somewhere in the mist. "These are my mother's remains. This is the queen of the castle."

The priest-king hung his head and closed his eyes for a moment before looking up again. "The body is cold. She must have taken her own life and the lives of her ministers when she realized she could not stand against the power of the Book of Light." The priest-king lifted his crystal staff and turned toward Ozuma. "Hers was a foolish, pitiful life. Now, Ozuma, end it. The battle has been won."

"As you say, Your Excellency," Ozuma said quietly, his eyes fixed on the queen's remains.

The two men took a step away from the throne, and Ozuma raised his sword, his chain-mail vest creaking with the movement.

"The queen is finished!" the priest-king declared as Ozuma's sword swung down through the air. There was a flash of brilliant light, and a moment later, the head of the corpse sitting upon the throne separated from the neck and fell to the floor, trailing the long black veil behind it.

"This castle has been purified in the name of Sol Raveh."

The priest-king made a gesture in praise of the Sun God, lifted his scepter high, and looked up toward the heavens. The white mist swirled upward, concealing his form. Thick and deep, it swallowed Ico whole—

Yorda had witnessed it all. The head dropping from the queen's body. The corpse upon the throne. Ozuma and the priest-king returning to the castle to declare the end of her mother's reign.

There was a loud thud, and Ico jumped back as though he had been slapped across the cheek. He blinked. The white mist was gone, vanished, or perhaps it had never been there at all.

Yorda had slipped from the throne and was lying on her side at its foot. Ico ran up to the dais, leaping to the top in a single bound. "Yorda!" Reaching down, he lifted her shoulders off the floor.

Yorda's eyes were closed tightly. Even still, tears ran from beneath her eyelids, streaking down her cheek. Ico tapped the side of her face, stroked her hair, and gently shook her. "Wake up. Wake up!"

Yorda's eyes opened. They were swimming with tears.

"I'm so sorry," Ico said. "I didn't know she was dead. I didn't know Ozuma killed the queen."

Yorda's face was blank, her eyes unfocused. Ico was not even sure if she knew he was there.

"It's all right, it's all right," he whispered.

Gradually, strength returned to Yorda's body and she gripped his hand. Ico gripped back. Yorda sat up on the floor, but her eyes were still distant.

Suddenly, Ico felt cold. A chill emanated from Yorda's body as he held her in his arms, as though she were a pitcher that had just been filled with ice water. He had the sensation that something else was inside the girl, pushing aside the Yorda he knew.

Her head turned, and she looked at him, her eyes sharp like a hawk focusing on its prey.

"If the queen has died, then how can she be here now?" Yorda asked, her lips like flower petals in spring, the space between them forming an ugly scar.

The voice was wrong. *This isn't Yorda.*

"How is it that I still rule this castle, when the sword took off my head?"

Ico recoiled, but Yorda moved quicker, arms wrapping around his head and chest, holding him tight. Their faces came close, until he could feel her breath against his cheek. Their eyes met. Not Yorda's eyes, but the queen's. Bottomless pools of darkness, black as the abyss.

"Tell me, young Sacrifice. How am I here?"

The queen's cruel smile spread across Yorda's face, but Ico saw nothing but those dark eyes staring into his.

[5]

ICO TRIED TO think, but his mind had lost its moorings, and he couldn't seem to hold on to any thought for long.

"No answer, Sacrifice?" Yorda's delicate lips spat out the cold words. "Then I'll tell you: I am everywhere. I can do anything. The Castle in the Mist is me, and I am the castle."

Even while Yorda's body spoke with the voice of the queen, he could still see the true Yorda deep within the pools of her eyes. But her back was turned to him, and she was drawing away, sinking deeper inside.

"You're the castle?" Ico asked, struggling for breath. The queen tightened her grip on him, squeezing out the air. He felt his ribs about to crack.

That meant that all of the madness, all of the killing that had come when the enchantment fell had been happening inside the queen. She had enveloped the slaughter within herself, absorbing the screams and the bloodshed—all of it.

She loosened one arm from around Ico's shoulders, grabbed him by the scruff of the neck and raised his head up till they were eye to eye. The true Yorda was nowhere to be seen. There was nothing but void, dark emptiness swirling with madness and the sparks of wild laughter.

"Tell me, Sacrifice," the queen said in a voice like honey, "did you really think that the child of the Dark God could be defeated by a mere inconvenience to her mortal body?"

"But you couldn't face the power of the Book of Light!" Ico said through clenched teeth. "Yorda drove you back with the book! She broke your enchantment!"

"Indeed she did," the queen said, a smile spreading across her face. "But I was not defeated. The only thing I lost when my enchantment was broken was my human form. Just a mask. By destroying my enchantment, Yorda freed me to become what I was destined to be! And the Book of Light? Why should I fear that? No paltry scrap of ancient spell can hope to defy me!"

The book didn't rob her of her strength. Her strength grew!

If the queen was the castle, then no matter how great an army marched through her gates, they would be nothing more than ants in the palm of her hand.

"But wait," Ico said, "if you weren't here anymore…then who was beheaded on the throne?"

The queen laughed low, until Yorda's body shook with her deep, rolling mirth. "Men are weak and easily deceived. They see only what they want to see. And if the phantasm before them takes the shape of their hearts' desire, they believe it all the more. Not even a priest-king is immune."

Ico's mouth opened. "The chief handmaiden…"

The queen raised an eyebrow—Yorda's eyebrow—and drew Ico's face closer, so that their noses were practically touching. Her breath frosted on his skin. "Very clever, Sacrifice. But what difference?"

But the difference was everything. It meant that there was one person who would have realized the truth. When she stood there, looking down at the woman draped in black on the throne, one person would have known: *That is not my mother. That is not the queen. That is my pitiful handmaiden, now just a corpse who still trembles in fear of my mother's power.*

Yorda.

Ico knew from the vision he had seen by the throne that Yorda had been there when they found the body. She had seen everything.

She lied to them.

Ozuma and the priest-king had believed her, of course. Everyone else in the castle was dead. The queen's fell presence had dissipated. There was no reason to doubt Yorda's words. Had she not previously betrayed her mother, helping Ozuma steal the Book of Light in order to drive her away?

No one could have imagined that, even as the sword bit into a woman's neck, Yorda was protecting her mother.

The queen laughed merrily, and it seemed to Ico that Yorda's body was no longer hers at all, but the queen's possession entirely. Ico trembled in the queen's arms.

She laughed one last time, a high, derisive laugh, and then flung Ico away like a child throws away a toy. Ico flew through the air, landing on his back on the stones near the throne. His head smacked against the floor, sending sparks dancing behind his eyelids. He couldn't move.

Yorda stood slowly and walked over to Ico's side. Ico looked up at her, his eyes watering with tears. They were not for the pain, they were for Yorda.

Ico moaned. He could taste blood in his mouth. "You're horrible. How could you make Yorda do that? She's your daughter!"

"You poor thing. It is precisely because she is my daughter and I her mother that the bonds of affection between us are so strong. We protect each other, she and I."

"Liar!"

The queen leaned down and grabbed Ico by the collar. She tossed him across the room again. This time he landed below the throne. Despite the pain, Ico looked up. "What lies did you tell Yorda?" he shouted. "How did you deceive her?"

"I've already told you," the queen said. "There was no deception. Do you not recognize the love between mother and daughter when you see it? Why should it be strange for a daughter to want to save her mother's life? Why would she need another reason?"

Yorda slid down the side of the throne platform and walked again toward Ico. She moved differently now. This was not the Yorda he had led through the castle by the hand, the Yorda who would wander aimlessly if he did not call out to her. This was the queen's double, her puppet.

The realization led to another. *What if Yorda hadn't deceived Ozuma and the priest-king of her own will?* The queen could have been controlling her the very moment she stood by the throne, looking down at the body of the handmaiden. Her own self could have been locked away inside her body, held in thrall to her mother's wishes, just as it was now.

Fresh tears ran down Ico's face. His back ached, his arms were numb. He couldn't even reach up to wipe his eyes. Ico lay facedown, crying.

Yorda had been weak, an easy target for her mother's spell—because she was the queen's daughter, and she loved her mother.

At last Ico realized why Yorda had struck her own chest and insisted that everything had been her fault. Even though she could have had no way of knowing what suffering her actions would cause over the years in the dark castle, where shadows walked alone, she blamed herself for it all. The shades blamed her too.

"Why the tears?" the queen asked. "For whom do you cry?"

Ico shook his head for an answer. Getting his arms beneath him, he managed to lift himself off the floor. Sitting up now, he turned his tear-streaked face to look at the queen. "I don't know my real mother," he said. "My parents were taken from me after I was born. It's part of the custom when you're the Sacrifice."

The queen stared at him. The glow given Yorda's body by the

Book of Light still shone, dim and low like a sickly firefly, as waves of darkness flowed from the queen's heart into her veins.

"But I was never lonely. My foster parents took care of me. They were always there for me. They looked after me."

An image of his mother rose in his mind. With a gentle hand, she reached out to rub his cheek, comb his hair, and put him to bed at night. She may not have given birth to him, but she nurtured his life. And she loved him.

"Did you ever love Yorda?" he asked the queen. "You tell me she had feelings for you, but did you love her like my foster parents loved me?"

The queen's lips twitched, then the right side of her mouth curled upward, as though caught by a fisherman's hook.

"I am Yorda's mother. I gave birth to her, I gave *life* to her. That is the greatest thing a mother can do for her child, the only thing! Love is meaningless!"

The rage that had been boiling in Ico's heart burst forth, and he shouted, "But Yorda loved you! That's why she was deceived! That's why she saved you! Can't you see that? Is she only a tool to you—is that all she's ever been to you?"

The queen turned her back—Yorda's back, as supple as a spring leaf—to Ico and ascended to the throne. Ico watched her go.

She sat on the throne, the queen inhabiting Yorda's body. She was lost against its tall back, the broad armrests. The light of the book was lost as well. There, on that throne, she was nothing but darkness in human form.

"They saw what they desired, my death, and believing that they had defeated me they left this place," the queen said quietly, her voice barely more than a whisper. "They left that nasty sword in a cave by the sea—a symbol of the castle's pacification, I suppose. There they held an empty, meaningless ceremony, bowing their heads to that ungainly hunk of metal.

"All while I became one with the castle. At the same time, Yorda became mine. She was my eyes and my hands. The bonds of blood are great. She was my most faithful servant. I was there, you know, at the ceremony. I watched it through her eyes. The cheeks of the men were flushed with their so-called victory over me—men who are little more than lumps of dirt, pretenders to their weak god's glory. I watched them board their boats and leave—and Yorda with them," the queen said, her voice like a song.

"Through Yorda I knew this, and I decided to wait until they had returned home to their capital. I am unshaken now, as I was then. I feel this castle, every inch of her stone is mine. The loss of my inhabitants, my sustenance, was a setback—but only a minor one. I had time on my side. And my task remained the same: to lie in wait until the next eclipse."

So long as the queen remained the world was still endangered, and the people of the Holy Zagrenda-Sol Empire were too busy celebrating the defeat of the "herald of evil" to notice.

"They took Yorda to their walled capital beyond the mountain. There they rested their armies and gave Yorda time to rest as well. She was happy. They even let her stand atop the city walls and wave down at all the fools, together with that greatest of fools, the man they call their priest-king. Yorda acted the part they wanted her to play to perfection."

The queen shook her head slowly, like Ico's mother used to do when scolding him.

"Yorda thought that by deposing me she had saved me. She thought that she had driven back the Dark God, released me from his spell, and saved my human soul by taking me within her body."

"You tricked her into thinking that!" Ico shouted back.

He didn't want to imagine how Yorda must've felt, the happiness at being together with her mother at last. And yet he could hear the lies the queen's soul had whispered to Yorda's heart as though she were reciting them aloud to him now.

I am free at last. Free of the Dark God's control. Though I have lost my human form, I am finally myself again. It is as if all that happened until now was but a long, dark nightmare. Beloved daughter, I will be inside you always. Your joy is my joy. Your life is my life. We will share these together. Bless your heart and your gentle nature for forgiving me!

It had all ended in betrayal. The anguish weighed on Ico's heart so heavily he felt he might sink into the stone floor. It seemed like no matter how many tears he cried for Yorda, his eyes would never dry.

The queen sat in her borrowed body, watching him. White mist drifted through the room, wrapping around Ico as he lay trembling on the stones. When at last he looked up and wiped his eyes, the queen was staring down at him.

"They still had the Book of Light," she said through her teeth, the alluring smile on her face contrasting with the venom in her voice. "That is why I moved, thinking to destroy the walled city, the priest-king's army, and that cursed book with one blow."

"The city of stone…" Ico groaned.

The queen turned her eyes upward toward the dark ceiling high above. "Yes, beautiful stone. Its lifeless forms are a joy to behold. Art as a sign of ultimate power."

When the queen lashed out at the city, the empire realized for the first time that its struggle with the darkness was not yet over, and their ignorance of the ongoing conflict meant that they had utterly lost the initiative.

"Part of their army simply fled, including the priest-king and that knight with bestial horns like yours. However, the Book of Light was lost, and the stone city became part of my domain, its statuesque citizenry my new subjects."

The queen leaned forward, arms draped elegantly across the armrests of her throne. "Imagine my surprise," she said, her tone growing more familiar, "when I discovered the power of that same book woven into the cloth you wear on your chest. It can only mean that the people who sent you to me as a Sacrifice somehow retrieved the Book of Light from my city."

Ico felt his heart sink. The elder believed in the power of his Mark. They believed in the absolute power of the Book of Light—

that he was their light of hope. And yet it seemed now that the book was not as powerful as they had thought. The Book of Light could not defeat the queen. It had failed once already. It was less a poison and more a nuisance to the queen.

Was the elder wrong?

"As it happens, I do remember a particularly mischievous insect slipping into the city quite recently. A little boy, just about your age. He must have found the book and carried it to the place where you lived."

Ico tensed. *She's talking about Toto!*

"What's wrong, Sacrifice? You look pale." The queen smiled at Ico. "Don't worry. That little insect feels no pain anymore."

For a moment, Ico felt like he couldn't breathe. "W-what do you mean he can't feel pain?"

The queen's smile widened.

"Toto's dead? You killed him!" Ico felt the strength leave his body. The elder had told him Toto was fine. *Why would he lie?*

"Poor little Sacrifice," said the queen on her throne. "In truth, I pity you."

"Why should you pity me?"

"Because you are mistaken, so terribly mistaken. You have all these misconceptions in your head, and you've never been given a chance to set them straight. That is why I pity you." Though she still spoke with the authority of the queen, a gentleness crept into her voice that reminded Ico of Yorda, and that made him tremble all over.

"You're trying to trick me, but it's not going to work!" he shouted, but half of him wanted to believe. *Don't listen to her lies!* he told himself, but the other Ico within him wanted to hear more. *This could be important,* he heard himself thinking. *This could be the key to discovering the truth of what happened.*

Truth? What's "truth"?

"What did they tell you back in your village?" the queen asked. "What did you learn of your role, of the custom? What great purpose did they claim you were fulfilling?"

"Quiet!" Ico shouted. "Quiet! I don't want to hear any more!"

"Did they tell you to resign yourself to your fate?" she asked, ignoring him. "Did they say you were a hero for giving yourself up to this noble cause? Did you picture yourself as a great person for what you did, drunk on the draught of their lies? Yes," she said, nodding, "there's nothing sweeter than false glory."

"Quiet, quiet, quiet!" Ico shouted, covering his ears with both hands. He could hear his pulse pounding in his head, and his breath was ragged—and all this time, his Mark did not glow, nor did he feel its strength flow into him. It was just a thin piece of cloth pressed against the floor beneath his body.

"I don't believe anything you say!"

"Whether you believe or not is entirely up to you."

Ico looked at the queen's face as she brushed aside Ico's protests and could find there neither the queen's pale visage, nor even Yorda's, whose face it truly was. She looked like his foster mother, the gentle woman who had raised him and taught him all he knew.

Beware, a voice said inside him. *You're being tricked.* He wanted to look away, but the effort was like trying to grab water in his fists.

"You know, Sacrifice, I think I'm growing to like you. You have a simple, uncomplicated soul. It glitters like gold among the meaner examples of your kind. Truly you must be loved by all the gods," the queen said. "So I will tell you the truth you seek."

The queen slid from the throne and walked to the edge of the platform as she brought her hands together in front of her chest and looked down at him. "Know that I never once asked them to sacrifice to this castle. Not a single one of you was offered up at my request. It was the rulers of the empire who came up with the custom, chose the sacrifices, placed fetters on their arms and legs and pressed them into the enchanted stone sarcophagi. Your people did this."

The words reached his ears, but Ico couldn't grasp them.

"It is not I who devours the Sacrifices," the queen continued, "nor is it the castle. I am here as the castle is here. We require no sustenance."

"Liar!" Ico yelled at her, though his voice did not seem like his own. He wasn't even sure he had shouted.

Silence fell on the room. Even the mist stopped its drifting.

"You lie…" Ico said again, much more quietly this time. "Why would they do that to one of their own?"

"They don't think of you as one of their own. You are a horned child, a Sacrifice. Nothing more."

The mist brushed Ico's cheek like a gently consoling hand.

"When I destroyed their city, the priest-king and his men realized that I was not yet defeated, and they were afraid. Yorda's treachery also stood revealed. They blamed her, and struck her."

Ico shook his head, feeling like one of the little wooden dolls with springs for necks that Toto's father used to make for them.

"They realized that even with the power of the Book of Light they were too weak to ever stand against me. More so now that I had lost my human form! I was indestructible. Even if they managed to cross the waters again and march through my gates, I would merely turn them to stone and wait for the wind to reduce them to dust."

The queen fell silent. Ico looked up. "So?"

"So…"

"What did the priest-king do?"

The queen leaned very slightly toward him. "He stopped time."

"They cast an enchantment over the entire castle so that time would stop and I would be trapped within these walls," the queen explained. "That is why the torches still burn, and the grass still grows green, and the gravestones stand in a neat little line. But in order to do this they needed the power of the Book of Light that was within Yorda. It was through her body that they worked their spell."

The elder had once told Ico that the Sun God was the source

of light, and as the sun wheeled overhead, so did time flow on. What better device than a Book of Light to control the passage of the days?

"They brought her back to the castle to be the cage of time. You see, the glow within Yorda was not just that of the book. She glowed with the time she held captive. It was she over whom the Sacrifices stood guard, not me," the queen said. "They watched her, making sure she did not gain back her human awareness. The fools who rule your people sent Sacrifice after Sacrifice, encased them in stone, and let the magic of the sarcophagi transform them into monsters. One by one, the shades grew in number while time outside the castle flowed on. They continued sending the Sacrifices so that Yorda might not escape. But the more time she held within her, the greater their unease became. So they sent still more."

That explains why the creatures wanted to take Yorda back with them so badly. That has to be the answer. That has to be the truth!

The more time accumulated, the deeper their sin. And the hotter their rage and resentment burned. They couldn't stop the sacrifices, they couldn't change the custom. The leaders of the empire kept converting people into shadows to keep their lock on the castle safe. It was exactly what the queen had done in the Tower of Winds. Ico understood it with such clarity that it nauseated him.

The queen nodded slowly. "You see it now, Sacrifice. They blamed me for my evil deeds, yet while their words still sang on their lips, they committed the same acts over and over, for many long years."

The duty of the Sacrifice was never-ending. They would never return to their former selves. *Pity us*, they had begged him. And he had understood nothing.

"It was Ozuma's idea that horned children be offered to the castle," the queen said. Ico listened, forgetting even to breathe.

"When Yorda was chosen for the cage, he offered himself and his descendants as her protectors. 'If Yorda is to suffer for this, then I deserve the same fate. I will go with her to the Castle in the Mist,' he said."

So Ozuma had returned once more to the castle, this time with Yorda. He came without his sword, one horn removed as a sign of his penitence—to show that he had lost his right to be a defender of the land, beloved of the Sun God.

"I greeted them," the queen was saying, her voice becoming part of the mist that flowed around Ico. "Do you understand why? Why would I let them freeze time around me? Why would I admit Yorda and Ozuma to the castle?"

Ico himself was frozen, as though he had become stone.

"Because I was satisfied, Sacrifice. They were doing my god's work for me! Picture, if you will, the beloved creations of the Sun God here on the land, the very ones he told to go forth and prosper, sacrificing one of their own kind, twisting them into horrible shapes and locking them away across the sea, and then accepting the resultant peace as their rightful reward. Did they really think they could sin and just wash their hands of it, pretending that nothing was wrong? Is that the proper way for men to behave?"

Another derisive smile spread across the queen's face. She lifted her hands toward the sky beyond the darkened ceiling of the throne room. Then her hands moved, tracing the shape of a globe in the air.

"When men do such things of their own accord, then the entire land is an offering to the Dark God. My master takes as his power man's fear, man's hatred, and man's anger. How pleased he must be! I had won. The darkness had won. Now you see why I was content."

Now Ico saw the truth. When the custom of the Sacrifices had been established, the battle between light and darkness had already been decided. The long line of Sacrifices throughout the years had been nothing less than the procession of the defeated army. If men were reduced to sacrificing other men to appease the darkness, the Dark God's reign had already begun.

The queen had only to sit back and watch the foolish humans do her work for her. Once they had decided to kill not just one person, but an entire race, the way was set. They had come up with their own reasons for the sacrifices, and their own method for carrying them out. There was nothing to stop them. People were always good at justifying their actions if there was a need, or even the appearance of one, and were quick to turn to violence when necessary. They washed away blood with blood, kindled hatred with more hatred, killed, plundered, always claiming that they were in the right as they built their mountain of corpses—an altar to the Dark God.

The Dark God's revival was imminent, with or without the queen's help. The Castle in the Mist would rule the world, and the queen would regain her former glory.

Ico sat limply, head hanging down, unable to stand up from the stone floor. He lacked the strength even to cry. He wanted to shout at her again, to tell her she lied, but he couldn't summon the words.

This is the truth, a voice said inside him. "That's why…that's why you didn't kill me," he said, eyes on the floor. "There was no need to."

The queen said nothing, nor did Ico need her to. "You said that I was lucky. You meant I was lucky because my Mark freed me from the sarcophagus, saved me from an eternity as a shade. That's why you didn't need me, why you said I could leave."

Only now did the elder's parting words make sense. He would be able to return to Toksa Village thanks to the Mark. A Sacrifice who could not become a shade was useless. That was why they didn't want him to tell the priests about the Mark. If they had learned of its power, they would have ripped it from his chest on the spot.

"How will you live?" the queen asked abruptly. "Now that you bear the truth upon your back, where will you go? Do you have hope, little Sacrifice?"

Ico had no words with which to answer.

"Do you still want to take Yorda from the castle?" she asked gently.

Ico felt fresh tears well in his eyes.

"You might as well try. I won't stop you."

"What?"

"I believe you're actually capable now. You have clearly been chosen by someone or something. Take her by the hand and cross back to the land, if you so wish."

"But if I do that—"

The queen nodded deeply. "Indeed, the rulers of your empire would not forgive you. Do you fear their wrath? Why? You're strong. And you're right to be angry."

Ico looked up at the queen—a little boy standing at the feet of a maiden.

"If you really wanted to change things, if you really wanted to lift the cruel burden that has been placed upon the Sacrifices— if you are ready to rise up in anger against those who told you false histories and sent you to your death, then I will serve as your master and your protector. I will give you sword and shield and an army to lead!"

Ico blinked, not understanding at first. *Me, under the queen's protection? She wants me to follow the master of the Castle in the Mist?*

"I am not your enemy," the queen said. "Nor is the castle. No, your enemy sits in the capital, reveling in the prosperity they have gained through the sacrifice of your kin."

And they must be punished—the thought rose in Ico's mind of its own accord. He took a hesitant breath.

"Sacrifice!" the queen called to him. Her voice was stronger, and her appearance more noble than ever before. Her tone was that of a sovereign addressing her subject.

Ico felt his posture straighten.

"There is no time within this castle. Consider your choice for as long as you like. And, if it so happens that you collapse before the sadness, and you fall into despair, and you choose to hold your anger deep inside you, then I will turn you to stone and place you among the others here. As I did Ozuma so long ago.

"But do not misunderstand—I turned him to stone from compassion. Stone men have stone hearts, and stone hearts cannot be wounded or broken. I would show you the same compassion, if you wish it."

The queen vanished, along with Yorda's body.

Ico was alone, the dark truth his only companion.

[6]

ICO SAT CURLED into a ball, his arms around his legs and his chin resting on his knees. He sat like that for a long time, fading in and out of awareness. He might even have slept. When he finally opened his eyes, his body was cold, and he ached all over from the punishment he had received.

He was tired, and his limbs felt heavy.

Ico closed his eyes again. *I'll just go to sleep. I'll keep sleeping. I don't want to think, I don't want to do anything. I don't want to move. I don't want to have to make any decisions. If I sit here long enough, maybe the queen will make good on her promise and turn me to stone.*

Ico didn't really care if she did. He felt as though he was made of stone already. He liked what she had said, about stone hearts being impervious to harm. It made perfect sense. A lot of things she said had made perfect sense.

But I'm not stone. My heart does hurt. A lot. That's why I can't stand.

He wondered where Yorda had disappeared to. Ico looked up at the queen's throne. It was empty. Everything was quiet. Sunlight shone in through a window along the corridor ahead. Everything was perfectly normal, as if nothing had happened here at all.

The queen had offered to let him escape with Yorda, but then she had gone and hidden her somewhere. *Does she want me to look for her again? Or was she hoping that I would just give up after all?*

Another possibility occurred to him: *Yorda might have left on her own. So I could leave the Castle in the Mist by myself. Maybe that's what I should've done in the first place. I'm the lucky Sacrifice, right? Why throw that luck away?*

If he went back home, he could see his foster parents again. Wouldn't they be happy to see their prophecy fulfilled, their little Sacrifice returned to them to live in peace?

Then the voice of doubt rose in his mind. *Peace? Really? Even with Toto gone? Even though he's probably turned to stone?* Toto had traded his life for the Book of Light. He had purchased Ico's life with his own.

Ico sensed another presence in the room, and he turned, almost expecting to see Toto there.

It was the shadow creatures—several of them stood in a semicircle behind him. Their eyes glowed, fixed on him. For a while, Ico stared back at them as though beguiled, his breathing slow and labored. Save for the slow rippling of their silhouettes caused by the faint motion of the air around them, the shades were stock-still. But to Ico, it looked as though they were trembling, weeping.

"I'm sorry," he said at last in a breathless whisper. He swallowed, then said again, louder, "I'm sorry. Forgive me. I didn't know—you're the same as me, but I didn't try to understand."

The shades made no response. Ico sat up on his knees, then swayed as a sudden wave of dizziness came over him. His hands hit the floor, and he sat hunched over for a while, fighting back nausea. When he looked up again, the shades were gone.

Ico stood slowly and walked over to where the shades had stood. No trace of them, no sign of their presence, remained.

He left the queen's audience chamber and walked out into the sunlit corridor. The light hurt his eyes. Ozuma was standing at the end of the corridor, his back to a single, high stone step leading to another passageway. His figure cut a dark silhouette against the pool of light at the corner.

Ico stopped and faced him.

"This was your fault," he said. The words came to him quickly.

With the light at Ozuma's back, it was impossible to see his expression. Unlike the shades, his eyes were covered in darkness and gave off no light at all.

"It's all your fault!" Ico screamed as he raised his fists and charged the knight. A moment before he reached him, Ozuma slid to one side, his cloak billowing behind him.

Ico's fist came down on empty air, and his momentum carried him sprawling onto the ground. His knees, legs, and fists smarted.

"Your...fault."

Ico struggled back to his feet to see Ozuma vault to the top of the step. The knight moved smoothly, betraying neither hesitation nor any acknowledgment of Ico's presence.

"You did this to me! To everyone!" Ico shouted as he ran after him, trembling with rage. Clambering up the stairs, he found himself at the beginning of a passageway that curved gently to the right. Ozuma was walking down it, away from him. Ico paused, catching his breath with one hand on the wall. "Turn and face me, coward!"

Ico felt the strength come back to his limbs. He ran, determined to catch Ozuma, to make him face his descendants—Ico and the other shadowy Sacrifices. This time he would answer for what he had done.

Ico ran through several rooms, clambering up large steps and dropping down over ledges. He climbed, vaulted, and used chains to swing across otherwise impassable crevices. The more he ran, the faster he went, until he felt his body become as light as the wind. Even still, he couldn't catch Ozuma. The black knight was ahead of him, always visible, yet always out of reach.

It's almost like he's leading me somewhere.

After running for what seemed like an impossibly long distance, Ico had to stop, out of breath, hands on his knees. He looked up. *I recognize this place.*

It was the small room he and Yorda had come to after they first crossed the old stone bridge. He recognized the walls and the columns, the hanging chains, and the positions of the sputtering torches on the walls. There were the idols, and beyond them, the bridge.

Will I find him standing out there again? The stone watcher on the parapet?

Ico could hear the sound of the sea. A briny smell reached his nose. He could feel the wind on his skin. He stopped, hand resting on one of the idols by the door. *He led me here...he wanted me to follow him. But why?*

Ico passed between the idols, hearing a seagull cry close by. He was standing at the end of the long stone bridge now. On both sides, the sea reflected the color of the sky. Waves leapt, sending up a spray where they hit the stone columns supporting the bridge. Ico felt like he had emerged into the vast space between heaven and earth after months in a tiny box.

The bridge was collapsed, no, severed, in the middle. The statue of Ozuma stood on the far side, back turned to Ico. From here, he was so distant, he looked barely larger than Ico's upraised finger.

My child, a voice said in Ico's mind. *You and your brothers have borne the great burden of my sin these many years. Yet after all this time, nothing changes, and I remain bound here to the Castle in the Mist.*

For the first time, Ico had the strong sense that he was Ozuma's child, his descendant, the bearer of his blood. He felt like running to him, up to that motionless figure, and screaming, *Why did this happen? Why?*

But what he said was, "What do you want me to do about it?" Ico felt the rage rise inside him and just as quickly slip away, as though his body were too weary to hold on to it. He sobbed quietly. "What am I supposed to do?"

There was love here, the voice said.

Ico blinked. The seagull was hovering, flying against the wind only a few arm spans away from him, its beady black eyes watching him for a moment before it angled its wings and sped off into the distance.

Ico walked up to where the bridge had crumbled. He looked down over the ragged edge at the rolling waves far below, the deep greens and light blues swirling beneath white foam. The castle might be frozen in time, but all around it the sea was alive, in motion.

The sound of crashing waves rose up from beneath his feet, wrapping around him. Ico squinted, looking toward the statue of Ozuma. *He couldn't leave Yorda here alone,* Ico thought. *Even after she became the cage of time, he returned here to be her protector. He chose this.*

Why? Because he regretted his powerlessness, his inability to defeat the darkness?

Was he just trying to live up to the expectations of the empire?

Or maybe he had realized that there was no place for him in the world outside.

No, Ico thought. *That's not it.* It was because he couldn't save Yorda. He couldn't leave her to bear the burden of his failure alone. He, who reminded her so much of her own father when she was a little girl.

That's why Ozuma returned and remained.

Ico's heart ached as though he had been stabbed. He gave a cry and fell forward onto his knees, hands to his chest where his Mark was glowing brightly.

There was love here, the voice said again.

But whose love, Ico wondered. He had assumed Ozuma was talking about the queen and her daughter—but maybe…

From the very first time he had seen her, Ico had wanted to save Yorda. There had been no thought, no reason—when he saw her in the cage, he knew he had to set her free.

Ico shook his head. *I didn't know anything then. I could just do what my heart told me to do. But not anymore. Right?*

With his newfound knowledge, why should he care about Yorda? Why should he worry about saving her if she wasn't to be saved?

I could leave her and escape this place.

Or I could take her with me and become a fugitive of the empire. The thief who stole the lock holding time in place over the castle. He wondered what the rulers would do if he took her and escaped, and kept running, and running.

They would probably find another cage to trap time. But would that save Yorda? Would it save me?

There was another alternative. He could choose to serve the queen, fight against the empire that made his people sacrifices. With the queen's strength behind him, victory was certain. Then he would serve the queen, and they would rule the world.

But what of Yorda? What would she think, she who had wept even as she aided her mother's enemies in an attempt to destroy her?

And Toto? Could he be brought back to life by the queen's power? Would he even be my friend if he did come back? Would he forgive me?

Ico grabbed the intricate woven lines of the Mark tighter, trying to catch the rainbow brilliance that ran along its curves. Then it felt as though the world had brightened around him.

Toto's courage, Yorda's pleas—how could he turn his back on their tears?

My child, Ozuma said to him. Ico looked up, smoothing the rumpled cloth of his tunic with his hands.

Go find the sword. The sword calls to you. Take it in your hands and you will know the way.

Ico looked down at his empty palms. The sea breeze whipped through his hair. "Will the sword let me defeat the queen? Will I be able to save Yorda then? I don't think so. I don't—" without realizing it, Ico had begun to shout. "Why couldn't you wield the sword again yourself? Why couldn't you defeat the queen?"

The sword rested in a cave beneath the castle, still imbued with the power of the Book of Light—why hadn't Ozuma tried using it again? Was he prevented somehow? Was no one in the empire able to do it?

Now that Ico thought about it, it struck him as extremely curious. There must have been many people in the empire that knew about the sword—the priest and the temple guards who led him here were just a few of them. They had even used it. Had no one thought to raise that sword against the queen? Did they think it was enough to cage her? Had they denied the truth of the situation for so long?

Why didn't they do what had to be done?

Because our minds were closed. Ozuma's voice rose and fell with the sound of the waves. *Because all that we saw was within her hands, we saw only what the queen wished us to see.*

"That's no different than me," Ico muttered, shoulders drooping. "I've been wandering through the castle forever, not even sure where I'm going. I've just been running in circles in the palm of her hand."

Ozuma spoke again, a smile in his voice. His words were gentle, reminding Ico of the first time he had seen the knight's face up close.

My child. You already know the truth—you are the only one not caught in the queen's embrace.

"How do I know that? How can I be sure?"

Remember the queen's words. Remember the elder's words. The knowledge and courage once separated have come together again in you.

The wind picked up, and Ico staggered several steps backward. He could feel Ozuma's presence slipping away. The warmth he had felt coming from the distant statue had faded.

Maybe that was all the strength he had. Or maybe he left.

I'm alone.

He touched the Mark again. Its glow had faded. And with it the understanding that had been so close—

What did he mean I already know? Know what?

Maybe getting the sword would solve that mystery.

Unfortunately, that presented another problem. Ico didn't relish the idea of another aimless trip through the castle in search of a way down.

Ico looked up at the sky. The sun was still shining. The world still moved outside the castle.

Then it hit him. Ico's eyes went wide. *The castle is the queen's domain. No wonder I can't get anywhere running around in here.*

I have to leave the castle.

It felt like a ray of sunlight had penetrated the clouds of his mind.

This was the answer he had been looking for. The sword was calling to him, beckoning him. If he could escape the queen's clutches, the sword would draw him to it. *That's what Ozuma was saying.*

Ico stepped forward again, looking down at the sea. The water swirled around the foot of the pillars. White froth sprayed into the air. He licked his lips and tasted salt. The sea was moving beneath him.

Ico looked back up at the sky, at the seabirds wheeling above him. He wondered if they ever knew fear. Whether they ever collided with walls they could not see and broke their wings. Whether they ever faltered in their trust of the open sky.

The sky was limitless and vast, as the sea was deep and wide. These things were beyond the reach of human designs. Not even the iron will of the queen could hope to rule them.

Trust the sea.

Ico closed his eyes and took a deep breath. Holding his arms by his sides, he clenched his fists tightly for a moment, then let go.

He stepped forward with his right foot and then brought his left foot even with it. His toes were looking out onto empty space.

Ico pushed with both legs.

The very moment his body hit the wind blowing up from the sea, his Mark began to shine with a brilliant, pure light, like a shooting star. Then he fell, plummeting downward like an arrow trailing a tail of light.

In the back of Ico's mind he saw himself and Toto back in that cave, shouting, jumping into the pool of water they had found without any fear.

The blue sea opened its arms and welcomed him.

[7]

ICO'S EYES OPENED to the pleasant rush of running water. The light was dim around him. He was by an inlet, at the edge of a rocky crag jutting out into the water. Beneath him were pebbles and sand, a half-washed-away beach. *The waves must've carried me here.* He was lying on his stomach, halfway up on the sand. His legs were still in the water.

Ico got his arms beneath him and crawled on his elbows away from the water's edge. He was drenched. Sitting up, he began wringing the water out of his shirt and trousers and the Mark on his chest. He sneezed loudly, hearing the muted sound of water caught inside his ear.

I'm alive, he thought. *The sea swallowed me, carried me, then spat me back out. But where am I?*

The warped wooden planks of the pier were nowhere in sight. Dark rock wet with sea spray rose around him in a tall cliff. That was what was blocking the light.

Across from the narrow triangle of sand where he sat, he saw a cave with an entrance like two hands steepled together, the fingers touching.

The sword is in there. It must be.

He looked around and saw the source of the running water he had heard over the gentle wash of the waves—a tiny waterfall that ran like a beautiful silver thread down the side of the cliff.

No matter how high up he looked, he couldn't see the castle anywhere. *It must be over the top of the cliff.* This place was hidden from its view, a narrow strip of beach between the sea and the rock.

Thank you, he thought, looking over his shoulder out at the water. Then he began walking toward the cave. Even though the waves must have tossed him quite some distance, he had not lost the sandals on his feet, and the sand was packed firm under them.

It was dark in the cave, despite Ico's eyes having long grown accustomed to the gloom. He could only just make out his hand if he moved it in front of his nose. When he extended his arm, everything past his elbow was lost in the darkness. Ico groped for the rock walls with his fingers, feeling his way forward, testing the ground beneath his toes as he advanced deeper into the cave.

Even still, he felt no hesitation. The cave would take him to the sword, of that he was sure. It was as though he had been here many times before.

Maybe the sword really is calling to me, he thought, *setting a path before me I can only see with my heart.*

He continued on, feeling his way deeper into the cave. When he reached a curve in the wall, he pressed up against it and walked sideways, and eventually the sound of the waterfall at the entrance receded into the distance until he could hear it no longer. It was replaced by the whispering sound of water flowing somewhere down by his feet.

For the first time, he realized that the water was a living thing. It spoke with many voices. Ico listened to them and understood that none spoke of danger. There were deep voices and high trilling voices, loud voices and soft ones, all telling him that this path was true. *Walk on and you will reach your destination,* the water seemed to say to him.

He walked until he could not remember how long he had been walking. Water dripped down from the roof above him, splashing off the top of his head. He looked ahead and realized that there was a light coming from higher up, a place where the rock bulged out from the walls and ceiling like the fists of two stone giants.

He put his hands to his waist and caught his breath while he looked around in surprise. He realized that he had been climbing up a rather steep slope to get here, clambering over folding layers of rock, jutting boulders, jagged walls, and narrow passages.

No wonder I'm out of breath.

Ahead, the rocky slope continued upward for some distance, leading up to the place where the giants' fists met and a narrow sliver of light shone through. He thought the gap might even be wide enough for him to pass through.

At the top of the slope, he wedged his way through the gap between the rocks and heard the sound of a greater body of water echoing beyond. This new noise was almost like rain, and it came with a deeper tone that seemed to come up from the ground. He crawled on his elbows across the gravelly floor, coming out into a wider space where he could raise his head again—and caught a blast of water directly in his face.

I'm behind a waterfall. The watery veil spread out in front of him. Water splashed up in a fine mist, wetting his arms and legs.

Thankfully, it was brighter here. Ico peeked around the edge of the waterfall to get a better look, like a child peering around his mother's skirts, and he realized that the opening he had reached was looking out over the sea. He was midway up a cliff that curved forward on either side, like a horseshoe with him roughly at its center. From here there was no apparent way to climb farther up, and when he looked down, the sea seemed impossibly far below. Several waterfalls coursed gracefully down the inside of the horseshoe cliff, and the sound of the rushing water was enough to make his ears go numb.

He also noticed something else—two thick pipes crossing from the cliffs to his right over to the cliffs on his left. They seemed to be made of copper, darkened by the spray of the water, with green rust clinging to the seams where lengths of pipe were joined together.

Several chains—he counted eight in total—hung down from the pipes, each with something like a giant ring suspended from its end. Ico looked closer and saw that they resembled giant spinning wheels, easily as wide across as a man was tall. While he looked in amazement, he could feel his heart racing. The sword was calling to him. *Come, come. This way.*

As though pulled by a thread, Ico's eyes looked in the direction of the soundless voice. It was coming from above the cliff to his left. Trees grew thickly along the top, and he thought he saw something among them sparkling, catching the sunlight.

Great, now I know where to go—but how do I get there?

Fear rose in Ico's chest. *What if all this running around, all of this fear, all of the sadness has made me lose my mind? What if the sword calling to me is just an illusion? What if madness brought me to this cliff?*

He saw another light shine in the trees atop the cliff, a sparkle like a star guiding a lost hunter.

He wondered again how he would get there, when the answer rose in his mind: he would have to jump down to the wheels hanging from the bottom of the pipe, going from wheel to wheel until he reached the one furthest to the left. Then he would climb up the chain, and if he could get back on top of the pipe, he would be able to reach the forest at the cliff top.

Each of the chains hanging from the pipe was a slightly different length. Unfortunately, the one closest to him was also the longest, which meant he would have to fall a great distance before he reached the wheel suspended at its bottom.

He considered just jumping down into the water, when he remembered the warnings he had often received as a child not to swim near the base of the waterfalls that fell near Toksa Village. The water there swirled in such a way that if you went too far down, it would trap you there and never let you back to the surface.

He would have to make a jump for it, and if he missed the wheel at the bottom of the chain, he would just have to brave the waterfalls.

Come, the sword beckoned.

This is another test, Ico thought. *If I don't pass this one, it just means I wasn't worthy of the sword.*

Come to me.

The sword's voice had a sweet ring to it that reminded Ico of his mother—or maybe it was just that he chose to ascribe a familiar sound to those clear, beckoning vibrations that seemed to beat against his very soul.

Then the adventuresome child inside him perked up. Grabbing the Mark firmly in one hand, he leapt. Wheeling his hands through the air, he worked his legs as though he might gallop on the wind, trying to keep his balance.

With a surprisingly light sound, Ico landed directly on top of the wheel. His legs swayed beneath him and he quickly grabbed hold of the chain. When he looked around, he saw rainbows in the air all around him, so close it seemed he might be able to grab them with his hands.

Drenched to the skin, Ico grinned, letting his eyes follow the rainbows through the air. They winked in and out of existence, their sparkling light looking like applause for his courageous jump off the cliff.

He looked up at the blue sky, rimmed by the curve of the top of the cliffs. The sky seemed less blue than it had before he jumped from the old bridge, and it was veiled by a thin white mist. Evening was approaching.

I have to hurry. He looked across at the other wheels hanging from the chains, plotting his course, and it seemed like the rainbows twisted to guide him, showing him the way.

"Here goes!" he shouted and jumped out into the air. Ico's arms and legs moved smoothly, no trace of the fear that had sent shivers up his spine moments before. The more he moved, the less he feared. He made the last jump easily and began climbing up the chain toward the pipe, a smile spreading across his face.

He walked along the top of the pipe, nearing the forest, when he stopped and turned to look behind him, wondering what the strange wheels had been placed there for. *Why were they hanging from the pipe? What was their purpose?*

Looking down at them from this new angle he realized

suddenly that they looked like cages. *That's what they are, round cages.*

People were kept here, hanging high above the waves—

He trembled with the horror of the thought.

But those cages had led him here. Maybe the rainbows were the traces of the souls of the people who had died in those cages, come back to lead his way. All of them wanted release from the Castle in the Mist.

"I have to hurry," he said aloud, quickening his pace, leaving the thundering sound of the waterfalls, the dancing rainbows, and the eight silent cages behind.

Ico made his way through the thick foliage, over a rocky crag, and along the stone face of the wall. He found he could hear the voice of the sword best when his mind was cleared of thoughts.

He headed down along the cliff, descending until he figured he was about halfway back down the slope he had climbed inside in the darkness. The path here was narrow, and he had to cling to the cliff to avoid slipping and falling into the ceaselessly pounding waves far below him.

His memories returned to him as he moved carefully along the side of the cliff, grabbing at protrusions with his hands and finding indentations for his feet, jumping when he could not reach the next handhold. The look of the sea, the shape of the rocks, and the flow of the water all reminded him of his first visit. When he had descended even further, a scant three body lengths above the waves, he jumped off the cliff into the sea. This time he fought against the current, swimming with strong strokes into the cave that held the underground pier.

Ico arrived at the lowered portcullis and found that there was enough of a gap at the bottom for him to swim through. He broke through the surface of the water on the other side with a splash. He was about to continue on when he had a change of heart and decided it was a better idea to investigate and raise the portcullis before continuing further.

The rope was easy to find, and though the wheel above creaked noisily when he pulled on it, it was easy for him to raise the portcullis. He brought the rope down as far as it would go, watching water stream off the portcullis back down into the channel as it lifted.

Even as he watched, he wondered why he had bothered to raise the portcullis at all—when he realized the answer. *I'm coming back through here. And I won't be alone. I'll be with Yorda. I'll bring her back.* It was likely she wouldn't be able to swim as well as he could, so raising the portcullis was a good idea.

I will save Yorda. That's what I'm doing. I haven't given up.

He dove back into the water and swam swiftly onward. Within moments, he could see the leaning piles of the underground pier.

It was quiet. The sound of the waves did not reach this far inside the cave. He swam until his feet could reach the bottom. Then he stood and walked toward the pier, scrambling up on top of it.

Here I am, back at the beginning.

He wasn't going to take the queen up on her offer. *I'm making my own way now. With my own hands—and the sword.*

The cave seemed different than when he had passed this way before. It was dimly lit and warm. A gentle breeze wafted through, feeling like the morning wind that blew down through the village at dawn, when the hunters gathered to check the gear and choose the path they would take that day. The armor clinked, laughter echoed down the street, and their voices turned to white steam that drifted in the air. *We are off. All is ready for the hunt.* It was an energy in the air here that did not exist before. Ico realized with a start that it was coming from himself. And there was another source—

He would have been able to find it even with his eyes closed. He walked along the path that led from the pier, turning right at the intersection. White light shone up ahead. He could almost hear a noise each time the light winked, its outline so sharp he felt he could trace it with his fingers. If he had, he felt like its shape would be the same as the morning star that shone at dawn and the evening star that stood watch over the twilight.

Ico walked toward the white light.

The path ended in a stone wall, and there he found it.

The sword was on a surprisingly small altar, and at first it was hard to make out, so glorious and blinding was the light that shone from it. As he drew closer, he saw that the altar resembled the shape of the Tower of Winds, except instead of the walls that covered the tower, there were four pillars.

Ico's sandals made wet sounds that echoed off the walls seemingly in time with the singing in Ico's breast and the light flowing from the altar. The sword sat at the height of Ico's waist, in the center of the four pillars. It had no scabbard, and its hilt faced toward him.

Come, take me.

I am yours.

The sword spoke to him in his bones and blood, not words.

Ico reached out, taking the handle in first his right, then in both hands, slowly lifting the sword.

It was a long blade but light as a feather. He gave it two or three swings and then shifted it to his right hand, lunging forward then back, then in a circle, raising the sword to eye level. It felt like an extension of his arm, a part of his body.

I am you.

The Mark on his chest pulsed with light in answer to the sword's vibrations. Mystical power and purifying light crisscrossed the patterns woven there by his mother's hand.

We meet again, and again come here together to form a single light!

Ico held up the blade, looking at his own reflection in its broad surface. He felt like the sword wanted him to do it. Warmth spread in his chest.

He saw his own eyes, the straight brows. When he was still young enough to sit on his mother's knee, she would stroke his eyebrows with her finger and say, "You are a strong-willed boy.

Look how straight your eyebrows are."

He had never heard what his foster mother said next, what she muttered under her breath—but now he knew.

"What a fine man you would have become—"

But he was fated to go to the Castle in the Mist.

I have to give him up to the castle.

The memories became more real inside him until he was feeling them anew, and Ico closed his eyes. When he opened them again, he saw a face in the blade of the sword—but it was not his own.

It was a boy with horns like his. His eyes had a bluish tint to them and were lighter than Ico's. A long scratch ran down his right cheek.

The horned boy was looking out at him, blinking his eyes. Ico almost called out to him. He felt the boy would hear him if he did. But before he could, the boy in the blade turned and vanished. As though someone behind him, someone unseen, had called him away.

Ico followed after him, into the world the sword was showing him. His soul left his body and chased like the wind after the running boy.

Ico's senses were sharp, and he felt his awareness spread as fast as the sky and deep as the sea. Past and future seemed like one moment. He could hear it. He could feel it. One second was an eternity, one thing was everything, he himself was limitless, and at the same time, everything was becoming one.

The boy he had seen in the blade was riding on a large bearded man's shoulders. He was laughing out loud. They were walking through tall reeds. No, wheat. This was a field. The boy was singing, and the man whistled cheerfully, accompanying him. Then they laughed together, the sound of their laughter sweeping across the field rows.

Then he came upon another scene. This time there was a girl with horns. She was sitting in front of a loom, holding thread and spindle in her hands. An old woman with a stern face stood next to the loom, and whenever the girl made a mistake in her weaving, she would slap her with the broad flat of her hand. The girl would pout, but then she would go right back to her work.

What are these things that I'm seeing?

Ico stood, entranced by the shining sword. The scene in front of him changed again and again, but in each a horned child was jumping, studying, running, laughing, crying, playing with friends, or sleeping—living their lives just as Ico had in Toksa, each with a different face.

These children are the Sacrifices.

They had all been brought here to the castle and placed within the stone sarcophagi. He was seeing their lives before they became creatures of darkness and shadow. He could hear their voices, see their smiles, listen to their words. He watched them working under the sun, harvesting grain, scythes in hand and baskets upon their backs. They walked down the field rows, swinging tree branches and singing songs to drive off the birds. They sat in front of plain wooden desks and practiced their letters. They fished in the shallows and splashed water on each other, squealing with delight.

A gentle breeze blew through the village, carrying with it the scent of new leaves and fresh blossoms. They went to sleep tired from the day's work, thin quilts to keep them warm on the chilly spring nights. They listened to stories told in tender voices by the men and women who raised them as their own. On summer days, their skin was brown from the sun and mud and dirt. On autumn evenings, the moon rose full above them and the sky was filled with stars. Then came the brightness of dawn. The taste of freshly picked fruit. Teeth biting through the skin, smiles brightening as the juice hit their lips. They hunched their heads low in the cold winter, huddled around fires for warmth. They looked up with pride at the village hunters returning from the hunt, taking off their gear, the faint smell of the blood of their catch still lingering around them.

Always shining, always warm, always alive. He saw their lives in an endless series of scenes, like paintings of everyday moments. And faces, so many faces—too many to count.

All the Sacrifices, in every age—they were alive.

And the people who had sent them to the castle were alive. Toksa was the sorrowful farewell port for the Sacrifices. But it was also the place blessed with the task of raising them.

The sword had lain here in the Castle in the Mist as a symbol, an object of worship—but had they ever known that all of the days lived by all of the Sacrifices were still here, kept safe within its blade? The blessing of the Book of Light was nothing other than the joy of life itself.

Ico returned to his body, feeling as though he had come arcing across the sky, through shining clouds, back down into the cave. He was still holding the sword in his hands. Only his face was reflected in its shining blade.

And now the blade was asking him a question. It wanted to know if he was ready. If he was, it would show him the way.

Ico understood. He knew what he had to do. The clarity of the task before him was like the light of the midday sun, shining high in the sky inside his heart.

[8]

HAD IT BEEN yesterday or the day before? Or had an entire month already passed? In this sequestered world, a world without time, it was impossible for Ico to say how long ago the priest and the two guards who wore horns on their helmets had led him through this place.

He lifted the sword before the idol gate, and the stone idols, bathed in the sword's light, slid to either side. Ico stepped onto the platform he knew would take him into the castle above—alone, this time, without the pride or the fear he had known upon his first arrival. He worked the lever, and the floor began to slowly rise, lifting him into the hall of the stone sarcophagi. He brandished his sword, yet still he hesitated.

This was the path. Ahead lay the queen. Through the hall of the stone sarcophagi he would find her true throne. The sword had told him that.

What slowed his pace? Was it the fear that he lacked the resolve it would take to fight those he would soon face? Or was it that he lacked the strength to cut them down?

No, that's not it. Ico looked in vain for the words he needed to express his turmoil.

Pale light shone between the idols framing the passage into the hall. He knew exactly what that eerie, ill-omened color represented now.

He stepped out into the hall, shining sword in his right hand, left hand clenched into a fist by his side, and looked upon the source of the pale light.

Every one of the many sarcophagi lining the walls was glowing. Or rather, the designs upon their surfaces, the enchanted patterns, were undulating with living light.

Several torches burned along the walls. Yet their light did not reach the sarcophagi. The designs on the sarcophagi were slithering snakes. One snake per stone. They slithered across the surface of the sarcophagi, weaving patterns that had no head or tail—engraved chaos.

In harmony with the movements of the pale-glowing serpentine patterns, the sarcophagi were humming. It was as though the sarcophagi were in ecstasy, growling like animals lacking mouths. It was a horrifying sight, and yet it possessed an otherworldly beauty. For a moment, Ico stood entranced, his heart held by the strange light of the sarcophagi. He felt the strength leave his arm gripping the sword. The point dropped down toward his feet.

What's going on?

A wind blew through the hall, making the Mark on his chest

flutter. His hair got in his eyes. Ico blinked, forcing them to focus.

Someone was crouched amongst the sarcophagi on the landing halfway up the wall in front of him. He took a step closer to see who it was, then realized he was looking at a statue. The figure was bent over as though in lamentation, forehead pressed to the ground. Its arms might have been part of the stone landing, they were pressed so low, and the slender arch of the back made Ico realize who it was.

It's Yorda! She's been turned to stone!

The enchantment woven around him by the sarcophagi and their light broke in an instant. Ico launched into motion, running toward her when he saw shadowy shapes rise around her, drifting up like shimmering waves of heat, like shadows forming in a sudden flash of light.

Ico went a few steps farther and then stopped, looking up at the landing. The shades did not move. They merely looked down at him with their dully glowing eyes.

Ico was breathing hard. The shades held their ground. Ico's heart threatened to burst from his chest. Still, the shades did not move.

Ico steadied his grip on the sword.

"What's happened to her?" he whispered, his voice hoarse. "I know who she is now. I know what she means to you."

The shades continued to stare.

"B-but Yorda didn't want what happened to you. She never wanted you to suffer…"

Ico's knees buckled beneath him.

Have I come this far only to lose my nerve? No. It's these sarcophagi that are doing this to me. It's those eerie glowing enchantments. They're happy. They enjoy my pain, enjoy the grief of my fellow Sacrifices. That's the source of those vibrations I'm feeling.

The visions Ico had seen when he looked into the blade came back to him in a rush of memory. It was as though the sword were cutting through his confusion. He saw the eyes of the Sacrifices shining with happiness. The joy of their lives in the village. The brilliance of their existence.

These creatures I'm facing aren't shapeless things of smoke. They're not dark souls come boiling out of whirling pools of black. These are the Sacrifices. These are children. The descendants of Ozuma. My brothers and sisters.

They are me.

Suddenly, a howl of rage escaped Ico's lips. His throat trembled and his voice echoed off the walls of the vast hall.

Ico lifted his sword and charged. He ran up the steps. He wasn't charging at the dark creatures, he was charging at the sarcophagi. He was going to destroy their pale glowing curses.

He split the first stone sarcophagus he reached in two with a single swing of the sword. On the backswing he destroyed the one beside it. *Look how fragile they are, look how weak!*

Ico screamed as he ran from sarcophagus to sarcophagus, swinging his sword. As they broke under the sword, their shattered pieces shone brightly, and when Ico cut the lines of their enchantments, they howled like steam escaping a kettle. The coffins crumbled, lost their lives, and fell to cold fragments of stone.

The shadow creatures began to move. Large ones with horns were gathering around Ico, bobbing up and down as they trailed him. They advanced and retreated, formed a line and pulled away. Winged creatures flew in circles over his head. The moment he thought they might land on his shoulders they would peel away or swoop low by his face and flap their wings at him.

Yet they did not hinder his progress. They were just trying to be as close as possible to the sarcophagi when they were destroyed, to be as close as possible to the light of the sword. They wanted to relish the dying screams of the stones.

Up at the highest level, with the chaos of destruction all around him, Ico slipped from the ladder. Yet he did not fall. One of the shades grabbed his collar with its long claws, and he hung in midair, kicking his legs.

Then he was back on the landing. The creature with long crooked horns, much taller than Ico, was standing next to him, looking at him with its white eyes.

He helped me.

Ico steadied his grip on the sword, thinking. The shades thronged around him in a circle. They were swinging their hands, stomping their feet, their eyes burning with the same rage that filled his.

Joy filled Ico's heart.

More strength filled his arms. The brilliance of the blade drowned out the light of the glyphs on the remaining sarcophagi. Ico gave another shout and brought his sword down on the sarcophagus in front of him. Then with one stroke, the stone sarcophagus split in two. Its keening fell silent, and it crumbled to lifeless stone.

He was a cyclone, a thunderbolt, the power of the maelstrom. Incredible energy moved through Ico's limbs. Each time the sword crushed another sarcophagus, each time its enchantment lifted, he grew stronger. Ico ran through the hall, bounding up stairs and ladders, then leapt to the next to begin again. He ran across narrow landings, the cacophony of the destruction erasing the whispers of the enchantments.

Ico destroyed the last sarcophagus. Shoulders heaving, he stood. His eyes flashed, watching each of the cursed fragments fly to its final rest. Until his prey was motionless, he would not remove his gaze, like a hunter who would not lower his bloodied sword.

Silence filled the hall. Ico's breathing gradually quieted. Like a child laid down to sleep, his inhalations grew farther and farther apart until he breathed so quietly he could hardly hear them at all.

The shadowy creatures had moved around Yorda once again. Ico stood at the bottom of the stairs below, looking up at them.

"Let's finish this."

Ico held the sword high above his head, and from behind the shades, part of the wall forming the hall began to rumble. Fine dust accumulated over the years drifted slowly from between the stones. The next moment, the wall collapsed with a great cloud of dust and rubble. The way was open through it—a stone staircase.

Ico's eyes traveled up the staircase, past the shadowy creatures, past the shape of Yorda frozen in grief, all the way to the true throne room of the queen.

The ceiling of the throne room was shrouded in darkness, making it impossible to judge its height. A wall covered with carvings stood in the center, coming to a peak at its top, where two swords hung over a graven crest. This was the seal of the royal house. He wondered why such a thing would be here—what did the royal bloodline mean to the queen? Was this perhaps some lingering trace of pride or attachment?

Directly beneath the crest in the center of a raised platform sat the queen's throne.

No one was here. Ico could sense no presence. The throne was empty.

Out in the room, four of the stone idols stood, two to each side and slightly in front of the throne. These were slightly taller than the ones that guarded the doors, and their patterns were different. Ico walked between them quietly, holding his sword ready.

He walked up to the throne. Its design was similar to the one that had sat in the room where he had been separated from Yorda, but it was carved from a different stone. That throne had been made of the same gray stone as the walls around him, but this one—the true seat of the master of the Castle in the Mist—was carved from a block of smooth obsidian.

The back of the throne was like a slab of stone, covered with carvings. He saw dragons, two-headed creatures spewing flame, ringing the edge of the throne. *No—that's not flame they're spewing. It's jet black mist.*

A faint carving stood out in relief at the center of the throne's back. Ico took another step closer, and its lines came into focus: a perfect circle, surrounded by swaying flames, set in a sky of countless stars.

The scene of an eclipse.

The sun was a mirror reflecting the power of the Dark God, instead of the light that was the source of all life. Light consumed by darkness.

Ico gingerly set his hand on the throne. *Cold.* He lifted his fingers and saw the silhouette of his own horned head cast across the seat.

Readying himself, Ico stepped back from the throne. He looked up at the crest above his head and turned to step down off the platform when a voice called out to him from behind.

"Is this your decision, then?"

Ico spun around.

The queen was sitting, leaning back in her throne, lustrous black hair and long black sleeves spread wide. Her arms perched upon the armrests. The many folds of black lace covering her held the shape of her body, but at the same time they seemed empty. If it were not for her pale white face and the tips of her fingers extending from her sleeves, it would have looked as though her gown sat the throne alone.

"Foolish boy," the queen said, her voice strangely gentle, coaxing. "In the end we find that a Sacrifice child has no more wit than his forebears. I offered you my protection, I offered you my strength, and you turned your back on me. As I assume you have turned your eyes away from the true enemy you were meant to fight."

Ico stared at the queen's pale face. For the first time he realized that nowhere could he see any resemblance to Yorda.

Because her face is just a mask, Ico thought. *Those fingers I can see are not real. All that is here is a dark void.* Hadn't the queen said so herself many times? She had already lost her true female form. Destroying this thing on the throne would only be destroying a mask.

"You lied to me," Ico said, his shrill voice echoing in the darkness of the throne room. "You said you would let me go free if I wanted to take Yorda with me. But I saw Yorda turned to stone. You lied."

"Ah," the queen muttered, her fingers twitching. "But I have not lied. The Yorda you saw in the room of the sarcophagi is the way you wanted her. Were you to take her hand and separate her from her loving mother, that is what she would become. I've merely prepared her for you."

The queen's black veil trembled with mirth.

"I have not done anything so foolish as to lie—though perhaps there was more of the truth I could have told you, Sacrifice."

Ico felt the blood rush to his face and his body grew hot. The sword in his hand began to glow with a brilliant light. In response, the Mark on his chest began to swirl with white energy.

"Regardless, the time for us to share words has long since passed," the queen said, slowly rising from her throne. "Turn that sword on me and I will destroy you!"

The queen quickly spread her hands. Ico jumped back, opening the distance between them, readying his sword.

"So pitiful, so foolish. How could a wretched little creature such as yourself hope to defeat me? How could such lofty dreams have found root in your heart and spread their branches through you? Sacrifice, it is clear that my duty here is to right the terrible mistake your shallow heart has made."

"You can't trick me again!"

As Ico charged with his sword, the queen's hands moved gracefully, tracing the shape of a glyph in the air. Fingers of bone thrust forward, and wind spilled forth with a howl.

Ico was blown back. The wind was freezing cold, enough to take his breath away, and it robbed the sword from his hands and sent it flying.

He fell on his back hard, but was again on his feet in a moment. Just as he regained his footing, the sword landed by one of the idols standing to the right—a considerable distance away from Ico.

He launched himself into the air, diving headfirst for the sword. A second blast of wind billowed out from the throne, striking him at the very moment he grabbed the sword. Once again, the sword was ripped from his hand. It flew end over end, then clanged against the stone wall at the side of the room and fell point first to the floor like a twig tossed by a winter gale.

The queen was playing with the sword as though it were a child's toy, the purifying strength radiating from it seemingly powerless.

The queen was now standing on the throne. Her hands were raised to summon another gale. Without even time to find where the sword had fallen, Ico quickly ducked behind one of the idols. The wind would have blinded him. It was an icy blast, carrying a thousand poison needles, ten thousand sharp, bared fangs, and limitless hatred.

When the idol caught the brunt of the queen's cursed wind, the patterns on it glowed and sparked like lightning. It was the same as the effect Ico had seen when he used the sword to part the idols by the door. When the wind had passed, the idol's light faded once again. Only the sword and the mark on Ico's chest remained bright.

I have to retrieve the sword. Where is it? Where did she send it flying to this time? He found it almost directly across the room. Ico waited for the queen to raise her hands again and darted behind the idols on the left-hand side.

One of his leather sandals, faithful companions this entire time, finally gave out, splitting as he ran. His left foot felt suddenly lighter, and the sandal shot off, lying with its sole facing toward the throne, directly between the two pairs of statues.

The queen's wind picked it up, and Ico held his hand up over his face to protect himself from the cold. When he pulled his hand aside, he almost yelped.

His leather sandal had been turned to stone, the severed thong that had held it to his leg crumbling at the end where it had broken.

I have to stay out of that wind!

But what had happened before? The wind had hit him and he was fine. *Maybe that was the power of the sword. If I can get the sword, then I can face her.*

"Are you running, Sacrifice?"

The queen's black robes trembled with derision and laughter. "Run. Run until you are exhausted. Run until your legs grow weak. In my castle we have all the time in the world!"

Ico kicked off his remaining sandal.

I have to get that sword back. It's my only chance.

The queen was moving her hands almost as though she were dancing. She drew glyphs in the air, fingers leaving black trails that lingered in his eyes. *I have to wait for my chance. When she's ready to send out her next blast, I have to pick my moment and run to the sword.*

Ico grabbed the Mark firmly in one hand. It crumpled between his fingers, but its light remained steady. *Now go!*

Waiting for the queen's shoulders to bend back, Ico ran toward the sword. His extended fingers touched its hilt and scraped at it, getting it into his hand when the queen's next blast of wind came over him. Ico clutched the sword. Its light wrapped around him, shielding him from the blast.

Ico stood and ran over to the wall, tracing a wide circle back to where he had begun.

Another blast of wind. Ico lowered his head and met it, sword raised. He took one step toward the throne. Then another. And another. But when he raised his sword again and looked up, another blast hit him, knocking away the sword. Ico was flung into the air. He tumbled to the ground, defenseless. The impact of the hit made his body scream. His right horn struck the floor and blood flowed.

Ico's head spun with pain and rising nausea. He got an elbow under himself and sat up, looking down at the blood that flowed from his head pooling on the ground. His right horn hung loosely from its base.

A broken horn—the sign of defeat and shame.

"This is your end, Sacrifice!"

The queen's arms lifted again.

An icy gray wind blew forth. It erupted like a living thing from the lines the queen's fingers traced in the air. Ico saw it coming for him, he saw it tremble with a cruel appetite.

A black shadow fell across his legs.

Ico curled up into a ball and shut his eyes tight, but the moment passed and he realized he was still breathing. His eyelids trembled open. His head felt like it would split.

Can stone feel pain?

He looked up to see a large shadow looming over him, broad shoulders on stunted legs, with the same horns that he had. Strangely curved arms spread out, protecting him.

It was one of the shades—turned to stone. As Ico watched in shock, it crumbled to dust before his eyes.

—*Be brave, Brother.*

—*Stand. Fight.*

Ico heard disembodied voices coming from every direction, near and far.

He looked around to see that the queen's throne room had filled with the shadowy creatures. They were hovering around Ico as they had once surrounded Yorda. Winged shades flew over his head, and those that resembled men stood around him, supporting him.

—*We will be your shield!*

The shades advanced step by step, forming a rank around the throne with Ico behind. The cursed creatures the queen had created had broken the chains that once bound them.

Ico looked at their shadowy features and gasped as he saw the living faces that the sword had shown him.

—*Take the sword, Brother.*

—*You can destroy her.*

The words wrapped around Ico, and he felt strength welling from the core of his being.

The queen remained on the throne. The pale mask of her face did not move or betray any expression, yet her voice was filled with rage, and her mounting anger ruffled the hem of her black robes.

"Wretched things, you would turn on me?"

Another blast. A row of the slowly advancing creatures turned to stone, preserving their misshapen forms for a moment before exploding into dust. Yet still the mob continued their advance toward the throne.

It was a moving wall, defending Ico.

Flying shades turned to stone and fell as dust from the air. The feel of powdered stone on Ico's face brought him back to the present. He got to his knees and stood, looking around for the light of the sword. When he found it, he ran directly to it, picking it up in both hands just as one of the creatures next to him turned to stone.

—*Use the sword.*

—*Use its strength.*

—*Defeat the queen.*

Suddenly, the sword's power increased. The blade extended until it was longer than Ico was tall, longer even than the shades in front of them, and it shone with the brilliance of the noonday sun, sending forth waves of power that made the stones on the floor of the throne room ripple.

—*You can see the queen.*

—*It is the power of your Mark.*

—*You can see the queen who has lost her mortal form and become the castle.*

—*You can see her true shape.*

The shades' words brought Ico a deeper understanding. The final key he needed for his battle.

Of course—what had Ozuma said? *Remember the queen's words. Remember the elder's words.*

The Mark would help him see the queen's true form—this was

the knowledge.

The sword would help him defeat her—this was the courage.

That which was once split had come together again.

"If I can see it, I can fight it!" Ico shouted, and the shades echoed his cry. The ring tightened on the throne. Even as their brothers turned to stone and fell to dust, they surged forward. An army of Sacrifices.

"Hateful things!" the queen roared, and her hand faltered as she traced another glyph in the air.

Ico lifted the sword above his head. He charged up onto the platform, making directly for the throne. The sword traced a beautiful arc in the air, trailing white light as it cut straight for the queen's chest.

There was an explosion of light centered on the tip of the sword. It grew, enveloping the throne, and Ico saw the ring of dark creatures around him evaporate in it.

It felt as though the sword had struck nothing as it pierced cleanly through the queen's black robes. Ico followed its momentum until he was practically leaning over the throne, seeing its black obsidian reflected in the blade.

The queen doubled over, her chest collapsing onto the seat of the throne. Her arms, stretched over her head, stopped abruptly, grasping the air. Then her fingers lost their strength, her elbows bent, and her head fell backward, revealing her white throat.

The strength left her shoulders, and her arms fell down on the armrests together.

Ico looked at the queen's white face, so close to his own. He was looking at a white mask. Where her eyes should have been were two dark holes. Then the darkness faded.

"I…" the mouth of the mask moved. Ico kept his grip firm on the sword. "I cannot be…"

Ico shut his eyes tight. Then with his remaining strength he thrust the sword forward again.

The white mask crumpled. Like white paper burned by an

unseen fire, it fell inside itself, wasting away to nothing. Her black robes lost their shape and color, turning to a drab gray, their embroideries fading, until the cloth itself began to thin and disappear.

No one was left sitting upon the obsidian throne.

The last ring of light emitted by the sword reached the corners of the throne and evaporated to mist.

The sword dropped from Ico's hand.

With a clang, it fell upon the throne. It was no longer shining. Now it was dull, aged. Rust showed on the hilt, and the notches in its blade told the tale of its many years.

For a moment it hung balanced, half off the throne, before falling onto the floor next to Ico's feet.

Ico lowered his arms and stood a while just looking at it.

The glow of his Mark had faded as well, as had the shades from around the room.

Ico staggered back, almost toppling off of the platform. He found it hard to control his own body.

Fresh blood flowed from the base of his right horn. It ran down his neck and trickled onto his shoulder. New blood flowed with every beat of his heart. His knees bent and he sat, face dropping. He raised his right hand to hold down his horn, but couldn't lift it all the way before he lost what strength remained in him and collapsed on the spot. His face was calm, peaceful, like that of a sleeping boy.

The Castle in the Mist realized something was different—its core, its soul, was gone.

In countless rooms, walls of stacked stones sighed. Cobblestones in the floor began to rattle.

We are cages. We are empty.

The strength that held us in place is gone. The darkness that bound us together has faded.

The vibrations were so faint at first that not even the most wary bird would have noticed them. Yet the entire castle had begun to tremble. Every stone, wall, and floor began to shake. Tiny particles of rock fell from the cracks where the ornamented walls met the ceilings. As one, every torch in the castle was extinguished. Water in the copper pipes ceased to flow. The wind that whistled through the towers and across the terraces and along the outer walls grew still.

We have held this false shape for so long.

All of this should have faded years ago.

Minute vibrations became a noticeable trembling that came with a keening noise. The birds sitting on the Tower of Winds or flying around the old bridge sped away from the castle.

It is ending. I am ending.

On two slender legs she climbed the stone stair to the queen's chambers, the tattered hem of a dress falling around them.

Yorda was free of the stone, and her body had begun to glow again as she walked.

She saw the boy lying on the stone floor, his back to her. He was exhausted and covered with wounds.

Yorda approached. She knelt by his body. She extended her fingers and touched his cheek as she had when they first met.

The boy's face was dirty with blood and dust. His eyes were closed.

All around them the Castle in the Mist shook with a low rumbling noise Yorda felt in her body. The sound of the deep, vital foundations collapsing. Yorda looked up at the royal crest over the throne. The vibrations increased until Yorda could see the stones shaking.

The carving of the crest split in two. Along with the pair of carved swords, it fell to the floor behind the throne with a loud crash.

Yorda put one hand on the floor to support herself as the castle shook anew. She could hear the castle screaming through her hand.

There isn't much time.

Yorda reached out and picked up the boy in both her arms.

Pillars crumbled, floor tiles buckled. Yorda continued on, ignoring the swirling dust and the collapsing walls. She advanced with steady feet through the groaning, screeching, lamenting castle. She passed through a corridor and it collapsed behind her. As she crossed a hall, she saw its floor give way, crumbling down into the earth. A chunk of rock grazed Yorda's heel. She did not stop. Through the next room and the next, destruction and collapse followed close behind her. But Yorda did not look back. Over swaying steps and collapsing bridges, down secret stairs that only Yorda knew, they reached the underground pier. Yorda stepped across the wet sand, making for the water. The ground rumbled under her feet. The shock waves were growing more violent. When she stepped on the pier, one of the rotting pilings gave way and the pier collapsed, leaving nothing but a few scattered boards floating on the water.

Yorda smiled.

Still carrying the boy, she stepped into the water. The vibrations in the castle above sent ripples across the surface of the water. Yorda lifted her arms, keeping the boy's face above the lapping waves.

Pushing her way forward, she reached one of the planks from the shattered pier. She laid the boy atop it. He was still asleep. Blood oozed from where his right horn attached to his scalp. The blood dripped down onto the board, staining it red.

Yorda kept moving forward, pushing the boy along on the board. The water rose until it was just below her chin, and then higher until she could go no farther.

Summoning all her strength, Yorda pushed the board forward as hard as she could. As though it heard her unspoken plea, the current shifted, carrying the plank out through the grotto toward the open sea. Yorda watched it go.

The final dying cries of the castle reverberated through the grotto. Yorda whispered something as the boy drifted away, though even had he been awake it would have been impossible to hear her over the clamor of the collapsing castle. He had never been able to understand her language, in any case.

"Goodbye," she said.

Then, pushing back through the water, she quietly turned back toward the castle.

One of the pillars gave way. When it fell, the one next to it cracked and buckled, as though victim of a fast-spreading plague, followed by the next and the next.

In the Western Arena, the viewing stands crumbled first. Rubble buried the platform where knights had once fought for their lives and for honor. Finally the arena itself collapsed under the weight of the rubble, dragging the walls down with it and burying the queen's observing throne.

The large reflectors to the east and west shone brilliantly, standing through the quakes. As their bases shook and the earth split, they fell to the ground, facing up toward the sky. At the same time, the two spheres above the main gate collapsed into dust.

The branches of the willow trees in the courtyard swayed like a maiden's hair, brushing against the inner walls of the castle as they began to crumble. Gravestones toppled and split or were swallowed into the ground as coffins were spat out onto the grass.

Waves passed along the water filling the underground jail, and the copper pipes running through the castle boomed with echoing noise, sounding like bells tolling the doom of the castle. Water sprayed from cracks in the pipes, flowing down into the earth.

Gray dust rose up, mingling with the white mist that floated around the castle grounds. Wrapped in its veil, the towers of the castle leaned and toppled. They fell to the inside and to the outside, new rubble falling upon old.

By the giant waterfall, the chains of the eight hanging cages split one by one, and the cages plunged into the water far below.

The water increased in volume, sending up a terrific spray notable for its absence of rainbows. Their purpose voided, the cages sank below the water.

Towers in the east, west, and main keep collapsed, as though the castle had been nothing more than a painting upon a folding screen that was now being put away by giant hands.

The last thing remaining was the main gate, the only path to the outside world, and the Tower of Winds that had stood so long and seen so much darkness.

We are ending. Ashes to ashes, dust to dust.

Then the main gate and the Tower of Winds leaned and began to topple beneath the scarlet sky of evening, above the indigo blue of the waves. When the Tower of Winds fell, the statue of Ozuma still stood at the end of the old stone bridge, looking up at it. As the outer wall of the tower came crumbling down, the half of the stone bridge closest to it gave way under the weight of the rubble. The anchorage of the other side crumbled, and the rest of the bridge was pulled down by the collapsing castle, bowing down into the waves far below.

Yet the stone Ozuma did not shatter, did not crumble, did not break. The only thing he'd lost in his long years of penitence had been a single horn. When the bridge collapsed behind him, and the stone parapet began to topple, the statue faced up toward the top of the tower, and stone from its walls fell down on his face.

Legs still attached to a piece of the stone, the statue of Ozuma plummeted toward the sea, the Tower of Winds and the Castle in the Mist following behind him. Ozuma, the wandering knight, the horned challenger, protector of the land. Once again, his black cloak fluttered in the wind, as he led the castle's charge toward oblivion. The charge from which no one would return. A charge toward freedom.

The sky and sea watched all. Between them, the castle gently crumbled away to stone and grass, and the mist rose from the land.

At the same moment, far off in the capital, an unseen surge of energy stirred through the hall where the priests had gathered for their vespers, blowing the hoods from their heads. The nobles lost their crowns to a sudden gale, while the soldiers' helmets flew from their heads and rolled across the ground.

In the center of the capital, in the great temple to the Sun God, every bell began to ring though there was no one there to sound them. The people of the capital looked fearfully at one another and up toward the sky, listening to the sound of the bells. Though no command was given, nor any decree issued, one by one, the people dropped to their knees and began to pray.

In the forgotten walled city to the north of the Forbidden Mountains the long curse was at an end, and time began to move once again. The stone bodies of the people began to crumble, and the wind whipped up their dust into the sky. After enduring an eternity of silence, their souls were finally free.

As the stones of the city returned to the flow of time, they withered to dust in an instant.

Yet among them, there was a single breath of life. A sheen returned to the hair of Arrow Wind's coat. His mane rippled, and he snorted. Freed from his stone prison, the horse stomped his hooves and looked around for the little hunter who had ridden him into this place.

Turning his nose into the wind, he searched for the scent of home. The sun was low in the sky. He needed to find his young but brave rider and make sure he was all right.

Arrow Wind kicked with his hooves and broke into a gallop straight across the empty plains where the walled city had once stood.

The elder was tired. His body couldn't keep up with his eager mind—a common lament of old age. He dreamt at his desk, the Book of Light beside his head.

In his dream, he saw an unknown place far in the distance.

There, a great light blazed and within it, a dark form was toppling, though its shape was beyond his ability to comprehend.

"Are you in there?" Oneh called from outside. The elder sat upright in his chair. The window by his desk was lit by the evening sun. His eyes fell on the Book of Light on the desk, with his hand resting next to it.

"Are you there? It's Toto!"

The elder ran from his home and clasped Oneh in his arms. Her weathered, beautiful face was filled with joy, and tears wet her cheeks. "Toto's awake!"

Hand in hand, they ran to the house where Toto lay. Villagers were running down the street, asking if the news was true. The elder pushed through them, keeping hold of his wife's hand.

Beyond the simple wooden door, someone was crying out loud—Toto's mother. He could hear Toto's brothers and sisters calling his name.

Legs trembling, the elder stepped inside.

Toto, no longer stone, was lying on the bed his father had crafted out of wood for him. His mother was hugging him. Toto clutched her shawl, eyes wide.

"Toto!" the elder called out.

The boy's cheeks were sunken and his lips dry and cracked. The air coming out of his nose was thin, and far too weak. But his eyes sparkled with life. "Elder, I...I—" Toto's eyebrows sank, and his mouth curled into a frown. His cheek twitched. "I'm sorry I didn't listen to you."

The elder and the boy's mother hugged him tight as he cried.

"Elder?" Toto asked through his tears. "Where's Ico? Did he go to the castle? Did he leave me? I didn't want him to be alone."

Tears filled the elder's eyes. Hugging the boy, he looked up at Oneh beside them and found the same conviction in her eyes that he felt in his own heart.

"It's all right," the elder said, hand on Toto's head. "Ico's done it. He'll be back soon. Back home."

EPILOGUE

Who could be singing a lullaby so gently with a voice so sweet? Whose fingers stroke my hair? Why does the soft pillow beneath my cheek smell of the familiar hay of Toksa Village?

Where am I?

Ico had been dreaming a very long time. Now it was time to awaken. He could see the light against his closed eyelids. It was morning. Soon he would hear his foster mother's voice. *Wake up, Ico. The sun's going to leave you behind if you don't get out of bed.*

He opened his eyes, though his senses were still asleep. Facedown against his pillow, he stretched his arms and legs. Whatever he was lying on, it felt great. Soft with the warmth of sunshine.

The lullaby continued, rising higher then lower, tickling his ears.

It was the sound of the waves. The song the waves make as they sweep up and down the shore.

Ico opened his eyes.

Still lying on the ground, he tried moving his arms. His fingertips touched something granular. He brought them up to his face and saw flecks of white sand clinging to the skin.

He could smell the sea now.

Ico sat up and saw he was lying on a white beach that seemed to stretch on for an eternity. The sun shone bright down the long curve of sand.

Ico's mind and memory were as white and unblemished as the sand. A gentle wind blew over him.

Maybe I'm dead. Maybe this is Heaven.

He looked around and saw a rocky outcropping in the distance. Trees grew from the tops of the rocks, their branches gently swaying.

Birds wheeled through the blue sky overhead. He wondered how they could stand flying so close to the brilliant sun. He wondered if they ever got lonely, flying so high above the ground.

Maybe I'm still alive after all.

He looked down at his disheveled clothes. They were only half dry, with salt crusted on the seams.

Ico rubbed his chest with his hand. He felt like he had been wearing something else on top of his shirt, but there was nothing there now.

He saw blood caked beneath his fingernails. When he turned his head, his neck ached too, and his head throbbed, especially the right side. He reached up and touched his right horn and felt it wobble like it was about to fall off. Ico gaped with surprise, realizing that the stickiness he felt on the right side of his face was dried blood.

Suddenly, he was very lonely. He moved his arms and shoulders. He tested an elbow. Nothing seemed broken. He tried standing, but his legs wouldn't cooperate. The sound held him down, telling him to stay sitting, that he shouldn't move yet.

Sea stretched all the way out to the horizon, and the beaches stretched on for what seemed like forever.

How did I get here?

Next to him, where the waves lapped against the shore, rested a single wooden plank. It was sticking halfway out of the water, gently bobbing up and down with the waves. A small crab had worked its way up on top of the board and began skittering across it while he watched.

Ico's belly rumbled.

He laughed. *I'm starving! I should get something to eat—I should go home. Mother will be worried.*

Where have I been, anyway? What am I doing out here?

Ico had the sense that he had been on a journey to someplace very far away. But the memory remained lodged somewhere in the back of his mind, and he couldn't pry it out no matter how hard he tried. It was like even though he was awake, his memory slept on.

He tried again and managed to stand. He was covered with scrapes and bruises. Brushing off the sand, he bent his knees and stretched a little. Ico looked down the beach, sure that it must end somewhere. *Maybe there's a way up onto that outcropping?* He started off in that direction.

His feet slapped across the sand and Ico noticed he was barefoot. *What happened to my sandals?* At least the sand was soft.

Far off to the right, the rocks extended out over the beach into the water. Birds had gathered on top of the rocks. He headed toward them.

After his first step he wobbled, and after three steps he rested. That was how he began. But as he walked, it grew easier. His feet found their pace and he fell into a rhythm.

Closer to the rocks, he could hear the cries of the birds overhead. They flew up, making little circles in the air, flapping their wings busily.

Ico stopped and looked at the rocks beneath where they had been sitting—there was something at the edge of the water in the shadow of the rocks.

Someone else is lying on the beach!

Ico broke into a run. The white sand grabbed at his feet, and he swung his arms into the air, trying to go faster. He could make out the person as he got closer.

Ico ran, holding his arms out for balance, and the seagulls flew up even higher. He ran in among the rocks, and the slender form of the person lying there, her long wet hair, tickled the edges of his memory and made his pulse quicken.

It was a girl in a white dress.

She was sleeping just as Ico had been a moment before. She

looked exhausted. But her chest was rising with her breath—she was alive.

The waves washed her legs and the sun reflected off her smooth skin.

Ico knelt and reached out, touching her cheek. Her skin was so white and unblemished at first he thought she might be a doll, but her skin was soft beneath his touch.

I know this girl.

He had a feeling that when he first met her, she had been light itself, a drifting fairy.

Now she was just a girl, her warmth a human warmth.

His memory struggled to awaken in the back of his head—dim images of cold, timeless stone rising like a wall in his mind's eye. The vision passed, driven off by the warm sun beating down on the beach, the rise and fall of the waves.

The girl's eyelids fluttered open. Ico saw his face reflected in her dark eyes.

He smiled at her.

The girl sat up, wind teasing the hair that fell down over her forehead.

Ico took the girl's hand in his own, the gesture feeling intensely familiar, as the sun shone brightly over the end of their long story.

ABOUT THE AUTHOR

Miyuki Miyabe's first novel was published in 1987, and since that time she has become one of Japan's most popular and best-selling authors. Miyabe's 2007 novel *Brave Story* won The Batchelder Award for best children's book in translation from the American Library Association. *ICO: Castle in the Mist* is Miyabe's seventh book to be translated into English. Her Haikasoru novels include *Brave Story* and *The Book of Heroes*.

HAIKASORU
THE FUTURE IS JAPANESE

GOOD LUCK, YUKIKAZE BY CHŌHEI KAMBAYASHI

The alien JAM have been at war with humanity for over thirty years...or have they? Rei Fukai of the FAF's Special Air Force and his intelligent plane Yukikaze have seen endless battles, but after declaring "Humans are unnecessary now," and forcibly ejecting Fukai, Yukikaze is on her own. Is the target of the JAM's hostility really Earth's machines? And have the artificial intelligences of Earth been acting in concert with the JAM to manipulate Yukikaze? As Rei tries to ascertain the truth behind the intentions of both sides, he realizes that his own humanity may be at risk, and that the JAM are about to make themselves known to the world at large.

THE CAGE OF ZEUS BY SAYURI UEDA

The Rounds are humans with the sex organs of both genders. Artificially created to test the limits of the human body in space, they are now a minority, despised and hunted by the terrorist group the Vessel of Life. Aboard Jupiter-I, a space station orbiting the gas giant that shares its name, the Rounds have created their own society with a radically different view of gender, and of life itself. Security chief Shirosaki keeps the peace between the Rounds and the typically gendered "Monaurals," but when a terrorist strike hits the station, the balance of power and tolerance is at risk...and an entire people is targeted for genocide.

TEN BILLION DAYS AND ONE HUNDRED BILLION NIGHTS BY RYU MITSUSE

Ten billion days—that is how long it will take the philosopher Plato to determine the true systems of the world. One hundred billion nights—that is how far into the future he and Christ and Siddhartha Gautama will travel into the future to witness the end of the world and also its fiery birth. Named the greatest Japanese science fiction novel of all time, *Ten Billion Days and One Hundred Billion Nights* is an epic eons in the making. Originally published in 1973, the novel was revised by the author in later years and republished in 2001.

VISIT US AT WWW.HAIKASORU.COM